VOICES
LOUDER THAN WORDS

Edited and with an Introduction by

W I L L I A M S H O R E

Vintage Books

A Division of Random House, Inc. / *New York*

VOICES LOUDER THAN WORDS

A SECOND COLLECTION

●

23 New Works
Donated by their Authors
to Share Our Strength
to Help the Hungry
and Homeless

A VINTAGE ORIGINAL, NOVEMBER 1991
FIRST EDITION

Library of Congress Cataloging-in-Publication Data
Voices louder than words : a second collection / edited and with an introduction by William Shore.
p. cm.
"Twenty-three new works donated by their authors to benefit the hungry and homeless."
ISBN 0-679-73429-5
1. Short stories, American.   2. American fiction—20th century. I. Shore, William.
PS648.S5L69   1991
813'.0108—dc20   91-15344
CIP

Manufactured in the United States of America
10 9 8 7 6 5 4 3 2 1

CONTENTS

Acknowledgments • *ix*

Introduction • *xi*

ROBERT BOSWELL
The Products of Love • *1*

TERRY McMILLAN
Quilting on the Rebound • *29*

ANDRE DUBUS
The Lover • *46*

BOBBIE ANN MASON
Weeds • *59*

ROBERT LOVE TAYLOR
The Bride of His Life • *74*

JANE SMILEY
Turnpike • *97*

JOHN EDGAR WIDEMAN
A Voice Foretold • *114*

SUSAN MINOT
While It Lasts • *123*

RON CARLSON
On the U.S.S. Fortitude • *130*

BRET LOTT
Two Stories • *136*

ROBERTA SILMAN
Tightrope • *158*

MICHAEL MARTONE
It's Time • *171*

HELEN EISENBACH
Twenty • *176*

NORMAN LAVERS
The Wrecker • *190*

ANTONYA NELSON
The Facts of Air • *208*

SCOTT RUSSELL SANDERS
Harm's Reach • *233*

PATRICIA HENLEY
Same Old Big Magic • *243*

JONATHAN BAUMBACH
The Two Most Beautiful Women • *248*

MELANIE THERNSTROM
Broken Glass • *269*

DAVID HUDDLE
Night • *279*

JILLA YOUNGBLOOD SMITH
Easy • *287*

DAVID LONG
Perfection • *297*

TESS GALLAGHER
*Seven Poems: Northwest by Northwest; Glimpse Inside an Arrow
After Flight; Wake; Fan-Shaped Valentine; Moon Crossing
Bridge; At The-Place-of-Sadness; So Beautiful* • *313*

ACKNOWLEDGMENTS

Twenty-three excellent writers donated their work to this volume. Their role, of course, was the most difficult and most indispensable: putting pen to paper and creating something of value and beauty where once there was nothing at all. I am deeply grateful for their generosity. They have given us a fine book, and set an inspiring example.

Rarely has one person had so much support putting together a book. Much of that came from Robin Desser, who is my editor at Vintage Books, and Flip Brophy, my agent at Sterling Lord Literistic. Even if the need did not exist I would want to do a book like this just so I could work with, and learn from, each of them. I value their advice, experience, and especially their friendship.

The hardest work of all is not the work that goes into a single project like this, but the persevering, committed, day in and day out work that builds an organization such as Share Our Strength to make efforts like *Louder Than Words* possible. That work is done by a dedicated staff, which includes Brigit Dermott, who provided crucial assistance in organizing this anthology, Jennifer Hadley, Steven Kessel, Nathan Kreie, Karen Napoli, Marisa Nightingale, Harriet Robinson, and Joann Shepherd. Their work is inspired, organized, and overseen by two others: Debbie Shore, who has been at Share Our Strength from the very beginning, and Cathy Townsend, who followed not far behind. While I've done a pretty good job of keeping it a secret so far, I am in awe of both of them—their talent, energy, and commitment.

The most important names associated with this book are not included here. Indeed, they are unknown. But they belong to the people—poor, disadvantaged, left behind—that the contributors to this book intend to help. In that way this entire book is an acknowledgment of their plight.

INTRODUCTION

Charities have a bad habit of asking for money.

This is not a facetious complaint but rather an observation about the relatively narrow manner by which many worthy causes seek support for their efforts. Those who raise money—whether for the arts, the environment, or the poor—usually solicit the same people over and over again. They grow weary of asking for money and the contributors grow weary of being asked. Checks are written and all too frequently forgotten. Whether the hook is a fancy ballroom dinner or a slick direct-mail piece, there is sadly often little or no personal connection between the donor and the cause. There must be—and there are—other ways. *Voices Louder Than Words* is one of them.

The nonprofit organization with which I work, Share Our Strength (SOS), raises funds to fight hunger, homelessness, and illiteracy. First established in late 1984 as a vehicle for mobilizing chefs, restaurateurs, and food industry executives on behalf of hunger relief, SOS steadily expanded and is now the largest national private hunger relief foundation in the United States. Over the past twenty-four months more than $3 million has been distributed to hundreds of food banks, homeless shelters, and training programs in virtually every city and town in America, and to relief and development projects in thirteen countries around the world. These funds are used for everything from buying refrigerated food transport vans in Charleston, South Carolina, to digging wells critical for agriculture in West African villages. Our goal in all of these diverse activities, however, is the same: making nutritious food available to people, many of whom are homeless, who would otherwise have none at all.

Hunger continues to be a problem of epidemic proportions in the United States. It is estimated that as many as two to five million American children are now going hungry. According to a report issued by the mayors of America's largest cities, demand for emergency food assistance increased 22 percent just last year. The worst of the classic nutritional diseases—scurvy, pellegra, and beriberi—are now rare. But damaging nutritional deficiencies, particularly anemia due to iron depletion, have a substantial impact on growth, weight, attention span, concentration, and susceptibility to disease and infant mortality. Because the problem of hunger is a symptom of and closely connected to other issues that make up the web of poverty in America today, Share Our Strength also commits a portion of its funds to literacy and job training programs, as well as educational and advocacy activities. These dollars make a difference, and more are needed.

In 1987 unsolicited financial contributions from several best-selling writers encouraged us to try to raise funds through America's literary community. What we asked for, though, was not money, but literature, a previously unpublished work of theirs they would be willing to donate. The quick and generous response from both established writers and new voices suggested that writers were willing to do more than write checks for a cause they believed in—rather they were eager to contribute through their craft. The result was twenty-two short stories that composed the first volume of *Louder Than Words*.

We wanted *Louder Than Words* to sell so that it would raise money for our hunger relief efforts, and it did. The book went into a second printing, magazines and literary journals purchased first serial rights, and foreign rights were also sold. Equally important was the attention the project brought to the issues of hunger and homelessness. "Words That Nourish" headlined the *Washington Post* article that set the tone for coverage of the book's publication. Authors participated in special readings held in bookstores from Los Angeles and Chicago to Albuquerque and Columbus. At the 1990 convention of the American Booksellers Association, seventeen independent booksellers who had been involved in promoting *Louder Than Words* met and decided to launch an organization called Booksellers for Social Responsibility so that they could continue— as an organized network—to give special treatment to publishing projects related to a social purpose. Looking back, it was as if our own small experience with this one book had affirmed Goethe's wise observation: "The moment one definitely commits oneself, then Providence moves too. All sorts of things occur to help one that would never have otherwise occurred. A whole stream of events issues from the decision—raising in one's favor all manner of unforeseen incidents and meetings and material assistance which no man could have dreamed would have come his way."

Looking ahead, *Voices Louder Than Words* creates a model for new ways of thinking about how one can contribute to one's community. This may turn out to be its most important contribution. In addition to this second volume of fiction we will soon be publishing other anthologies made up of donated original work from contributors as diverse as scientists, children's book authors and illustrators, and sportswriters.

Each of the contributors to *Voices Louder Than Words* has chosen to spend weeks if not months creating work that is ultimately far more valuable than any check he or she could write in a few short moments. As a result of this act of generosity they will be able to feel a personal connection to the cause they are supporting. This, of course, is the whole point, and is the underlying philosophy of SOS activities in many communities around the world.

In thinking about how these writers have connected their fiction to the moral imperatives of the real world in which they live, I'm reminded of the words of Dr. Robert Coles, the Pulitzer Prize–winning author and child psychiatrist, who described the struggle to match one's conduct to one's intellect this way:

> Dr. William Carlos Williams taught me that if we are going to be saved, in a sense, religiously and spiritually, it has to be by our conduct, not by the amount of reading we've done. In that sense he was struggling with what Tolstoy struggled with in the last half of his intellectual and personal life, mainly the question of not only an intellectual life and its nature but what we do with that intellectual life, namely the question of conduct, moral conduct. It's a great thing to have all kinds of ideas including moral thinking and moral ideas but what do we do once we put the book down? Does the book, for instance, the novel, the literature, does it inspire us some way in our everyday life? And if it doesn't, Dr. Williams said, then the response is aesthetic, which is fine, intellectual, which is fine, but there is no connection between that and the lived life, and that, of course, that lack of connection, can be very sad.

Voices Louder Than Words is just one way for both writers and readers to connect to the "lived life" that William Carlos Williams and Bob Coles are talking about. Like the volume that came before it, this book stands as a tribute to the idea that sharing one's strength can be one of the truest forms of self-expression.

—William H. Shore
Executive Director,
Share Our Strength

THE PRODUCTS

OF LOVE

O

Robert Boswell

W H E N I W A S nineteen and first married, my wife
said something I still think about today, twenty years later.
"You believe love is beautiful like sunlight," she told me,
"but it's more like the wind—you see only its consequences."
On a grassy lawn at the center of the university, we sat with
our legs intertwined, speaking seriously. We had married a
month after meeting and treated our romance with solemn
reverence. "You confuse love with the effects it produces,"
she said.

My marriage broke up a long time ago. I begin here because I'm convinced this story is as much about the products
of love as it is about love.

Paula and Eugene Loroun moved into my neighborhood
three years ago, a childless couple in their thirties. They rented
a broken-down adobe house and avoided paying rent by doing
repairs. I met them through a blunder. I asked their yardman

what he got paid for cutting the grass. "He" turned out to be Paula.

Wide-shouldered and small-breasted—superficially manly in appearance—Paula maneuvered the mower with the ease of long practice. Her hands were callused, nails bitten short. Hers is not the kind of beauty you recognize just by looking. You have to hold her in your arms and feel the muscles moving beneath her skin. Don't misunderstand, we were never lovers, but there were times when I held her and understood her beauty.

She shut the mower's engine in order to hear me. I saw my mistake then, but I pretended not to be surprised and calmly asked what she was paid.

"I get to sleep with the fella' who lives here," she told me—an old joke, but we both laughed. By way of apology, I asked her and Eugene to dinner, and we quickly became friends.

Paula and I were both chronic early risers. She fell into the habit of dropping by while Eugene slept. I couldn't explain to friends what it was about her that made me look forward to those mornings. I hesitate to describe it now. She was an intelligent woman who thought and acted in a manner unlike anyone else I'd known. Despite that, I felt, almost from the beginning, as if I'd spent my whole life with her—although her life was as different from mine as dust is from coffee.

Our first important talk came late that summer, a brilliant morning after a night of rain. She propped her bare feet against my drop-leaf table and rocked back in her chair, a cup of coffee held with both hands, balanced in her lap. Sunlight from the slatted window over the kitchen sink fell across her hair. I stood at the kitchen counter, filling my cup. The smell of coffee permeated the room.

"You're the same height as my father," she said abruptly. Saying this embarrassed her, and she continued, as if to justify having begun. "My father raised me by himself. We moved around a lot. He kept us moving."

I sat across from her and listened as a story emerged,

staring all the while at her feet rising above the oak plane of the table, the feminine curve of her soles. I recall wondering why I hadn't noticed before the incredible beauty of her naked feet. How was that possible?

Paula's father, an itinerant salesman, once managed a trailer court in Apache Junction, Arizona, and set traps for the women who lived there. He and Paula kept up the miniature yards and accepted midday ice teas or lemonades from women home alone. Often, as they were about to leave a trailer, Paula's father would drop his wallet on a chair or beneath the kitchen table. When a woman sought him out and returned the wallet without taking the crumpled twenty he'd left inside, his immense gratitude would somehow make her beholden to him and he would seduce her. The others, the thieves, he also courted, making use of their guilt.

"He thought the trap was a good test of character," Paula said. "Though I don't know whether he preferred the women who took the money or those who returned it."

"He seduced them all?" I asked her.

"It seemed that way," she said with a mixture of both shame and pride. "There was one who mailed the wallet to him in a Manila envelope. And another who had her husband return it. He didn't mess with them."

The intimacy of the story seemed to demand a reply. I shifted in my chair to avoid staring at her feet, reminding myself that Eugene slept just three houses away—the thick and dulling sleep of the unemployed. Thinking of him made me feel guilty. "Have I ever mentioned my ex-wife?" I asked her.

Paula said I hadn't.

I told her about how we'd met and what she'd said about love. "Sometimes I think she wanted children," I said, "although she always denied it. She was older than I was and a philosophy major, so I wanted to give her credit for deep thoughts. But all that about the products of love—kids are the obvious products of love, aren't they?"

Paula frowned at this. "Children are the product of

screwing." She shook her head derisively. "And careless screwing, at that."

"I guess I never did figure out what she meant," I admitted. "It seemed like a test I was constantly failing. Until finally our marriage failed. Your father's trap—his test—reminded me."

Paula let her chair settle against the floor and crossed her muscular arms. "Marriages are strange. Mine's strange. Can you tell? Does it show?"

"No," I said. "You and Eugene seem happy."

"I didn't say we weren't happy." She paused, as if wondering whether to continue. I put on another pot of coffee. She leaned back in the chair once more and began the story of her romance with Eugene.

They met in Colorado, a town north of Denver. Eugene taught mathematics at the high school where Paula cut the grass and raked litter. During his first month at the school, he called her into his classroom to complain that she had neither cleaned the blackboards nor swept the floor. She didn't tell him that she stood outside his window in order to trim the hedge that grew beneath it. Instead she retrieved a bucket, mop, and cloth from the storage room she shared with the custodian. While Eugene graded papers at his desk, Paula silently washed the blackboards and mopped the floor. She cleaned the room as a means of testing him.

A week later, he called her in again. "You manipulated me," he said to her flatly. "You let me behave badly."

Paula smiled at this, admiring him for turning the tables. "You're right," she said. "I apologize for mopping your floor."

Each afternoon that week, she made a point of stopping by. He made a point of waiting.

Wearing a white dress but carrying a bucket and sponge, she appeared one evening at the front door of his apartment.

"I'm here to manipulate you again," she told him. She had to be persistent. A year passed before they became lovers, another five before he proposed. She had never worked so long and hard for anything, and success left her mildly deflated.

As long as she had remained the yardwoman at the high school, Eugene wouldn't marry her. He never said this openly, but circled job descriptions in the classifieds and offered to borrow money from his parents to help her start a business.

Paula found work with a construction company, but her employment was erratic. She tried selling clothing for a few days. She considered managing a 7-Eleven. Finally, she landed a good job with the state on a road crew. The wedding quickly followed.

Mildly deflated: at times she thought of other men. Unable to sleep, sitting in her nightgown at the kitchen table, she recalled an artist in Santa Fe who had asked to photograph her, then dressed her in secondhand clothes and had her pose in a filthy alley. Afterward, he had shown such kindness to her body, a sort of tenderness she could have only guessed existed. She thought of him, then woke her husband, her fingertips at his ribs, hips. Was this a vicarious form of adultery?

Even when it was solely Eugene who aroused her, how could she know it wasn't due to the way he carried his shoulders or lifted his chin, reminding her of some man she'd loved as a girl? She knew men had loved her for the woman they imagined. Later, when they saw her clearly, they would either leave her or continue to love her anyway. Paula had long ago separated the real Eugene from the man she imagined, but now she wondered whether she could separate real desire from imagined desire, separate real love from the tricks of memory.

Of course, Paula didn't tell me all of this that first morning. It came out in pieces, like a child's elaborate toy. It's taken concentration—and some guesswork—to assemble the parts.

.   .   .

The road crew was widening a canyon two-lane into a freeway. The job required blasting. An enormous drill, held by two men, skewered rust-colored rock. Traffic in both directions was halted while engineers placed dynamite in the holes. The percussion echoed through the canyon. Boulders tumbled across the road and into the swift water. Bulldozers scooped up the mass of collapsed stone. Men and women like Paula shoveled and swept behind it, clearing the way for traffic, backed a mile in either direction.

While she worked in the canyon, Paula had disturbing dreams, which she related in great detail to Eugene—and later to me. An example: engineers place too many sticks of dynamite into the routed holes. Paula begins running. The whole of the canyon shudders with the explosion. She gallops past miles of stalled cars while the canyon collapses behind her in a rush of dust and mayhem.

"Dream of me," Eugene told her when she recounted the nightmares in the bedroom of their little house in Colorado. He pressed his body against her, kissed her cheek. "You're so hot." He rocked his forehead, back and forth, against her neck. "My sweaty baby," he whispered, running his hand over her chest. "My working woman."

"Working woman work now," she said, opening her nightgown, crawling on top of him. "Working woman earn her keep."

Early June—ten months into their marriage—the weather abruptly turned. Two days before, there had been an inch of snow, but all at once the narrow canyon grew hot. Melting snow made the river rise and turn muddy brown. Paula's lungs suddenly shrank, making her pant, denying her breath. Minutes before the first blast, she found her supervisor and quit. A good state job, decent pay and benefits—Eugene called it a job with a future—but she'd had enough. Her supervisor, a kind man, gray sideburns showing beneath his fluorescent hard hat, nodded sadly at Paula, his lips pursed to indicate compassion.

Seeing no point in going home, Paula lit out in her truck, heading west across Colorado.

When she reached this point in her story, I remember saying, "You left Eugene?"

Paula nodded. "Without a word."

I'd invited them both to dinner, but Paula was called in to work at the last minute. She waitressed at a nearby steakhouse. Eugene came alone and brought Mexican beer. He had East Coast looks, if there is such a thing—dark hair but a light complexion, the rumpled, sinewy type. He'd gone to private schools in Connecticut, and the way he slouched handsomely in a chair seemed practiced.

I made enchiladas and green chile. I enjoy cooking, and most of my friends are vegetarians. That's one of the reasons I first liked Paula and Eugene—they were unapologetic meat eaters.

"Paula's told you about us, right?" Eugene said.

"A little," I admitted. We'd finished eating but remained at the table to drink. "She said the two of you were separated for a while."

"Separated?"

"That's my word, really."

"She left me is what happened. She ran away. I still don't know what went on, exactly, during that time." He hesitated, glancing at me as if I might fill in the missing parts. When I said nothing, he finished his beer and helped himself to another.

"Women are mysterious," he said. "Not men. Men are simple, you know? Men are like cars: once you understand the mechanics of them, they're simple. But women . . . women are like the ocean. You following me?"

"We're Chevys," I said. "They're the Mediterranean."

"You think you understand her, but there's no end to her. Do you know the Pacific is deeper than Everest is high?"

Eventually, I coaxed him into telling his side of the story.

· · ·

When Paula didn't return from work, Eugene called her supervisor and heard that she'd quit and driven her truck west—the opposite direction of their home. Eugene immediately blamed himself, thinking she must have heard about Willa Abrams. He fetched the road atlas from the kitchen pantry and traced his finger along the route Paula had taken. He drank gin in the big reclining chair his mother had given them as a wedding gift, the phone on the table beside him.

Eugene had long loved Willa Abrams. A married woman. Two daughters, a Labrador, a ninety-thousand-dollar mortgage, a swimming pool. Willa and Phillip Abrams had married in the early sixties on Eugene's tenth birthday, a coincidence that caused him considerable pain. He'd slept with Willa during the years he dated Paula, cutting it off only after he and Paula became engaged. During their ten months of marriage, he'd seen Willa secretly, although—Eugene was adamant about this—they no longer made love.

He related an episode with Willa that took place early on, before he and Paula were lovers. To Willa, he'd said, "I'm testing you." Paula had told him about her father's trap.

Willa laughed contemptuously. "The teacher must give all his girls tests," she said. She pointed at him with her wine glass, which was filled with Scotch and ice—they'd both had a lot to drink—and said, "Let me have it. What is my test?"

"*This* is your test. Right now," he explained. "How you behave."

She nodded in mock seriousness. A sleek and handsome woman with arching brows and nostrils, she'd recently turned forty and wore a new hairstyle, dying all but a few strands of the gray. "How I behave," she muttered. She set her drink on the coffee table, then leapt onto the couch and began running in place on the cushions. She lifted her skirt and made animal noises, naming them.

"The donkey," she yelled. "Hee-haw! Hee-haw! The rooster. Cockadoodle-doo!" She worked her legs so feverishly that Eugene could not resist and began laughing.

When she finally fell to her knees beside him, she said, "Now you may tell the janitor that I behaved like an animal— several animals." She was panting and lay her head against his leg. "Did I pass the test?" she asked him.

"Maybe," he told her. "If I grade on a curve."

She lifted her head and moved close to his face. "The janitor"—she always referred to Paula as "the janitor" and Eugene no longer corrected her—"is another symbol in your dreamily self-destructive motif—"

"Of which you were the first element," he quickly added.

"Screw you," Willa said calmly. "Don't interrupt me."

"Paula doesn't mind when I interrupt."

"Then screw the both of you."

She finished her drink and spat ice cubes into his lap. "Marry the janitor for all I care. Let her have your idiot children. That'll be the result of your love—tiny drooling idiots."

All of Eugene's stories about Willa included this sort of nastiness, but they were told with real longing. He didn't realize they cast her in a bad light.

The night that Paula left him, Eugene slept in the chair beside the phone and woke there the following morning, groggy but not as badly hung over as he would have guessed. However, he had wet his pants. Seeing this, he burst into tears.

"I cried like a child," he told me. "I was miserable."

I couldn't think of a way to respond, which added to the embarrassment of his confession. Finally, I said, "When my wife left, I drank and acted like a moron. We had an old refrigerator that wasn't keeping my beer cold. I hacked at the ice around the freezer so the door would seal. I used an ice pick and it had the predictable result. Freon sprayed across the room. The floor became slick with it."

We laughed, a masculine sort of chortle. "What'd you do then?" Eugene wanted to know.

"I took off my shoes and slid across the room in my socks, sloshing my beer everywhere." We roared at this. "I turned the stereo up as high as it would go and skated on my kitchen floor."

It had been the most pathetic night of my life. Eugene and I became nearly hysterical, laughing at our manly displays of weakness.

A young Mexican family lives in the house directly behind mine. They own a late-model Corvette, which they rescued from a wrecking yard and repaired on their own—although it doesn't yet run. For years the car has had its gray primer paint, but they have never gotten around to (or can't afford) the final coat of color. Nevertheless, the car is a source of pride. They wash it every Saturday afternoon. Their children eat cantaloupe and watch. Friends drop by to help.

I'd been a regular washer of the Corvette for months and convinced Eugene and Paula to join. Eugene knew a little about mechanics and tried to help with the repair. "It needs a whole new engine," he told me confidentially. "It'll never run otherwise." This news discouraged him, but Paula and I continued to scrub the car weekly.

Several months passed before Paula confided what happened after she ran away. During that time she never once mentioned Willa Abrams. I came to understand that she knew nothing about Eugene's love for another woman. She didn't consider it possible. Even now, I'm the only one who knows the whole story.

As you've already guessed, I fell in love with Paula. That was my part of the story, and I tried to keep it secret. I never had an affair while I was married, and I never slept with a married woman after my divorce. The desire I felt for Paula contradicted the way I wanted to live.

I suppose I should have stopped seeing her altogether, but all we did was talk. Besides, the story was not finished, and

I wanted to have all of the pieces. This may sound strange, but I'd begun taking notes, filling in what was left unsaid. My job permitted me to work at home—illustrating and editing computer manuals. Every day I'd alternate between computer jargon and the story of Paula and Eugene. Paula's voice, low and feminine, would return to me throughout the day. I carried her with me the way her hair carried the scent of the sun.

One day after washing the Corvette, she and I went to my kitchen to make sandwiches for everyone. While we fried bacon and sliced tomatoes, I persuaded her to resume the story.

As soon as her pickup began moving down the canyon road, Paula was able to breathe again. She flew past the waiting line of eastbound cars. When the explosion came, she was miles away, the sound nothing more than hands clapping. Hours later she pulled her truck into a gas station, now in Colorado flatland, the temperature reading ninety-two degrees. Paula had grown up in the desert. Hot weather could be as oppressive to her as certain old songs. The gas attendant suggested Telluride—nine thousand feet and a pretty place. People were going there that weekend to hear bluegrass, a kind of music Paula didn't like, but she headed in that direction.

Her arrival in Telluride corresponded with the breakdown of the dishwashing machine in The Nugget Bar and Grill. She found herself working before she had a place to stay. "Keep your butt moving," the owner told her. "There's always something that needs to be done."

"The guy's a jerk," the cook said to Paula after the owner left. "A ski-head. Born into money, then married more money. All he knows is skiing and money." The cook's name was Cyrano Cook. He went by Cook. "I ought to do *anything* else," he said, "but cooking's all I'm good at." Under his white apron, he wore a spaghetti strap T-shirt, which revealed big shoulders and muscled arms tattooed with several navy insignias.

"Were you a cook in the navy?" Paula asked him.

"Hell no," he said. "I was Joe Swabby—you know 'Swab them decks.' Try to get a job around here doing *that*."

The lone waitress, Stevie, was in her twenties and barked her orders at Cook, then thanked him when she picked up the prepared plates.

"I force her to say thanks," Cook confessed. "Makes my job nicer that way." Then he added, "She's Kirk's girl."

Kirk was the bartender. He stayed out of the kitchen. Paula saw him only when she carried a tray of glasses to the front—a conventionally handsome man who had a bartender's ingratiating smile. "The machine never did this," he said, smiling, referring to Paula's delivery of the glasses. The second time she brought him a tray, he said it again, which made Paula think he was nervous around her. She found this endearing.

After closing, Paula stayed to help Kirk and Stevie clean. Kirk made a pitcher of margaritas and put reggae on the stereo. When Paula revealed she didn't have a place to stay, they offered to rent her a room. They owned a condominium by the river and leased the room to skiers during the season. "You'd have to move out after summer," Stevie told her. "We charge skiers a lot more." Paula assured them she wouldn't be in the same straits by then.

"This is a great place to live," Kirk told her. They had left by the back door, passed through the alley, and out onto the sloping mountain street. The condo was within walking distance, and Paula trailed them home. "Movie stars come here on vacation," Kirk said. "We saw Jane Fonda last month."

"We think it was Jane Fonda," Stevie said.

"I used to live in Malibu," Kirk continued, "and I'd see Mary Tyler Moore in the grocery store all the time. Once I was in line with Linda Ronstadt."

"I guess everybody has to eat," Paula offered.

Her room was small with a view of the San Miguel River. She fell quickly to sleep, but woke with a start an hour before dawn, realizing she had left her truck on the street near the

Nugget. She dressed quickly in the same clothes she'd worn to work that morning—the only clothes she had with her—and tiptoed outside.

Cold and wet, the night air pressed against her face as she trotted up the sidewalk. She wondered whether Eugene had called the police to report her missing. This was the first time she'd permitted herself to think of him, and it caused a deep pain in her chest. The peaks of the San Juans loomed over Telluride. Above the mountains floated a half moon. In storefront windows, her skin shone blue.

The truck rested peacefully against the curb. Paula considered driving across the state and returning home. Instead, she pushed in the clutch and let the truck coast down the asphalt to the condominium.

"In one day, I quit my job, left home, moved across the state, got a new job, new friends, and a new place to live," Paula said. "It was the busiest day of my life."

"You're an amazing woman," I told her.

She shook her head. "My father once had and quit four jobs in three different towns within twenty-four hours. To top it off, he stole something from each place."

"Where was your mother when all of this went on?"

"Dead. Pneumonia. My father claims she was always frail." As if to prove her own heartiness, Paula lifted my ficus tree and moved it next to the window. "Needs all the light it can get," she explained. "I've been meaning to do that for months."

I thanked her. She looked at me expectantly, as if I might offer more. She said, "In some ways, leaving Eugene was easy. It's the kind of thing I'm capable of doing."

That was the first moment I had the courage to think she might love me, too.

The nights Paula did not work, the three of us went to movies. Then Eugene started graduate school, and Paula and I went out alone. We pretended otherwise, but we were relieved to be without him. More and more, I grew confident that she loved me. This became the only subject matter that was taboo. We made our time together safe by including Eugene even when he was absent, discussing whether he would have enjoyed the film, the meal, the wash of stars across the heavens.

I know this sounds corny, but our love had become a source of light, a glow that illuminated the world around us. Walking together one night, I actually saw it—light circled our bodies and fell to the sidewalk at our feet, light that emanated from our hearts and shone through our flimsy skin.

However, we didn't hold hands while we walked. Once we acknowledged it, our love would cast a shadow over Paula's marriage, over my friendship with Eugene. It would spoil the reconciliation whose story I was still attempting to construct. We protected the light by letting our love go unrecognized. We lived our lie happily.

One night Eugene revealed that Paula had decided to set me up with a waitress at the restaurant. "Beautiful woman," Eugene said. "I told her to do it, but she changed her mind. Seems she can't locate anybody good enough for you."

I smiled along with Eugene and quickly changed the subject, overjoyed Paula could not find it in herself to introduce me to another woman.

Until he started graduate school, Eugene and I watched a lot of television. Baseball, especially, but other sports, too. We talked while we watched, conversations interrupted by cheers for good plays. Once he asked me if he was in the way, wondering whether I was seeing a woman. I told him no. It wasn't until I lay in bed that night that I realized he was trying to feel jealous. But Eugene was no more capable of believing Paula might love me than she was able to imagine his loving Willa.

He told me Willa could not understand why, once Paula was out of the way, he would not sleep with her. The exchange

I'm about to relate took place in the living room of Eugene and Paula's rented house two days after Paula disappeared. Afternoon sun shone through the windows, which were large and square. The furniture, unmatched pieces Paula had purchased at yard sales, were made of laminated wood and foam rubber cushions. Eugene preferred the big chair his mother had given them. I picture him in that chair as the conversation began.

"I just can't," Eugene told her, his head falling back against the soft headrest. "That's what got me into all this trouble in the first place." They were talking about making love, but he was referring more generally to their love.

"What trouble?" Willa insisted. From what I know of her, I would guess the uncomfortable couch offended her sensibility as well as her body, embodying her vision of Paula—trashy, second rate, cheap.

"My wife has left me," Eugene went on. "You may see that as a wonderful thing, but I don't."

"Did she ever go to school for any purpose but to mow the grass?" Willa asked, stretching out now on the offensive couch.

"She's smarter than you think." Eugene jumped from his chair and began pacing about the room. "She may even be smarter than I am. She just doesn't have much education."

"A magpie is smarter than you. Magpies at least seek out entertainment and take it without feeling guilty."

"Say what you want." He leaned against the wall with his arm and elbow. "You happen to be intelligent *and* well educated. Paula is every bit as smart as you, but she never finished high school. She ran away."

"It's a habit then, this running off?" Seeing that he would not respond, she said, "Oh, that poor, poor, poor child. The waif. The darling. If only I could find the poor thing and wrench her neck."

"She'd knock you silly." He turned and faced her, a bit of drama in his eyes. "Don't kid yourself. She's worked all her life. I've seen her carry—"

"Thank you, thank you for this informative aside. I'll take care to shoot the bitch from long distance. Please shut up about her."

"My wife is missing, Willa. What would you like me to talk about?"

"Missing?" She laughed at him. "She's not missing. You think someone kidnapped her?"

"All right, all right."

"The janitor dumped you like yesterday's garbage," she said.

"She was never a janitor. Don't call her that." He began pacing again, his hands shoved deep inside his pockets. His mind's peculiar logic frightened him: the more he defended Paula, the more aware he became of his abiding desire for Willa. "I think you should go. I want you to go now."

"I don't feel like going."

Eugene walked into the bathroom and locked the door. Paula had left a paperback by the toilet and he began reading. Willa cursed him loudly. She hurled record albums against the walls. The crashes lent to his act a feeling of righteousness. He read Louis L'Amour and waited for Willa to tire and go home.

Near closing time, Paula's third night on the job, a stranger appeared, a short man with curly blond hair, rapping gently at the rear of the Nugget. Paula removed her hands from the soapy water and stepped to the screen door.

In the harsh light of the back alley, the man's milk-white face shone as clear as a child's. When he spoke, his voice was soft and friendly. "Girl named Stevie Welsh work here?"

"Yeah," Paula said. "You need to go around front."

The man squinted and shook his head. "Could you ask her to come back here for a moment?"

Before Paula could reply, Cook yelled, "No! We're working."

Paula shrugged, as if in apology, and stepped away. Later she saw him at the bar. "He found you," Paula said. Stevie had stepped into the kitchen for an order. She nodded, but offered nothing.

Cleaning up that night was an especially drunken affair. Paula wanted to ask Stevie about the mysterious man but thought she shouldn't in front of Kirk. She drank so many piña coladas she became emotional. "I *have* to do something with my life," she exclaimed suddenly.

"You are doing something," Kirk told her. "You're living here. Who wouldn't want to live here?" He pinched her bottom and forced her to dance with him, which eventually cheered her.

"You're my family now," she said, insisting on dancing with Stevie after Kirk. "We're sisters, me and you."

"We're loaded," Stevie corrected her.

Stevie declined a second dance. She spent a lot of time in the bathroom. When Paula looked in on her, she was standing in front of the mirror touching her face. "Wrinkles," she explained.

The cold night air sobered them. They had taken only a few steps into the alley when Stevie said, "I was afraid you'd still be here."

Only then did Paula see the man, the strange man. He wasn't all that big, and his face was gentle, pale. He said to Stevie, "It's a matter of integrity."

Paula could tell he'd had nothing to drink, which made her worry. Who spent all evening in a bar without drinking?

But Stevie threw her arms around him, twisting back and forth in his embrace. When she told Kirk and Paula to go on home, she was smiling. She even teased them about warming up the bed for her.

Kirk should have been upset, but when Stevie winked at him, he returned it and took Paula's arm. He grabbed playfully at her as they headed toward the river.

Drunk as Paula was, they might even have gotten into

bed together, but Kirk had forgotten his keys. No one had made a copy for Paula yet. They had to hurry back and catch Stevie.

When they got back, not more than twenty minutes from the time they left, they found Stevie dead.

Paula screamed. They happened upon her in the alley, her body draped over the concrete stoop of the Nugget.

Kirk said, "How do you figure?" More than a minute passed before he began to cry and slumped to his knees, falling against the greasy screen door.

Stevie's throat had a long, ragged tear. Blood covered her face and drenched her hair, as if she'd been lifted by the feet to drain like a butchered animal. The police noted that Stevie still had her wallet and keys. She had not been raped. One said, "A shame the kind of people these concerts drag in." Paula told him music didn't have anything to do with it, but Kirk got most of the attention. He didn't say much about the stranger who had murdered his girlfriend, but he took a good photograph and it ran in the local papers.

Paula never missed an hour of work, which Cook found cold-blooded. "What could I have done?" she asked me. "I didn't know a soul outside the Nugget." The owner filled in as waiter the first night, then traded jobs with Paula. Before another week passed, the dishwasher had been repaired and Paula had Stevie's old job. Cook remained distant with Paula the remainder of her time in Telluride.

"Had he been in love with Stevie?" I asked.

"I don't think so."

"Where you in love with him?"

"With Cook? Are you joking?"

"Well?"

"I can't explain his behavior. Or mine," she said. Then she added, "It's lousy when someone you like thinks you're a bad person."

This conversation, I recall now, took place on my patio one cloudy morning. The air was charged with the coming heat but wasn't yet hot. Paula, barefoot as always, rested her feet on my picnic table, heel and sole facing me, blackened with dirt, her chair rocking back and forth on its rear legs.

During the second year I knew Paula and Eugene, we had an adventure together. We spent the day in Mexico, a border town not far from here, shopping and eating.

Eugene tried out his college Spanish in an increasingly aggressive manner. By evening, he was bartering for trinkets he had no intention of buying. "I've been too shy with the neighbors," he said expansively. "I figured they'd know more English than I would Spanish, but it's all come back."

We'd begun drinking at lunch and stopped various times to snack and have another beer. Paula bought a leather jacket—Eugene bickering for twenty minutes in order to save two dollars. After dark, she slipped it on. It was November and the night was cool. I purchased a large wooden mask. I have a collection of primitive masks, and this was a find—the head of a coyote in whose open mouth is a fierce-looking crow, and in the bird's mouth is a snake, whose open mouth reveals the mouth of the wearer.

I wanted to sober up before the drive home. We found a bar near the border where Eugene and Paula continued to drink. A woman at another table began staring at me. She was roughly my age, a bit heavy through the middle, but attractive and familiar, though I couldn't place her. Eventually, she left her friends and came to our table. She put her hand on my shoulder. "Don't you remember me?" she said.

"Please join us," I said.

Paula introduced herself, saving me the embarrassment of asking the woman's name. "I was his wife's best friend way back when," Julia Mills said. "We were all close." She took my hand from the table and patted it, then pressed it between her palms.

We reminisced for a while. Julia had married twice and

was twice divorced. She had not heard from my wife in a long time. I told her what I knew.

"You took it hard," she said to me.

"I suppose I did," I said, "but that was a million years ago." By the time I felt sober enough to drive, she had told her friends she'd catch a ride with us.

The sky was cloudless, cold and dark. I switched on the heater and we hunched together, all four of us in the front seat as the rear was filled with computer manuals and the mask. Pressed against the passenger window, Eugene fell asleep and began to snore.

Paula said, "When I first met him, he didn't snore."

Julia commiserated. "Both my husbands snored." Then she slapped my knee. "You don't snore, though. You're the only grown man I know who doesn't snore."

"What makes you so sure?" I asked her.

She answered by speaking to Paula. "His wife and I used to tiptoe in while he was asleep and trim his hair. He had long, long hair back then. The worst split ends you've ever seen. And he never snored a bit."

"I wasn't asleep," I told her.

"Sometimes you were," she insisted.

Julia and Paula talked for the remainder of the drive, but an ache had begun in my chest and I kept quiet. I had forgotten that dark bedroom, the flannel sheets that had been a wedding gift, the sounds of young women trying to be silent as they approached me, their fingers in my hair, the scissors opening and closing so close to my ear, the music of restrained female laughter.

Eugene revived himself at the trip's end. We decided to have another drink in my kitchen. Although they lived just three houses away, Paula and Eugene spent the night in the guest bedroom. Julia slept with me. "I always had a crush on you," she confessed.

That morning, Paula entered the bathroom and found me on my knees before the toilet. She wore only a T-shirt but stretched it with her hand to cover herself. I was naked, my elbows on the porcelain, waiting for the upheaval that was not to come.

"Can I do anything?" she said, then knelt beside me and rested her hand on my back.

"I don't like being seen like this," I said and turned my head, as if not seeing her were the same as not being seen.

While I stared into the bowl, her hair touched my shoulders and her lips—unmistakably her lips—brushed across my back. Then she rose and left the room.

That was the only time Paula kissed me.

As it turned out, Julia was just in town for the weekend. She hadn't lived in the desert in fifteen years. Sometimes she calls, but we haven't seen each other since that night.

A month after Stevie's death, Kirk still hadn't returned to the bar. All he seemed capable of doing was cooking. Paula came home at two in the morning to veal in wine sauce or chicken cooked in cognac. The meals were excessive and badly done—the meat overcooked, the sauces too sweet. But Paula supposed it was something like therapy for him. She ate whatever he prepared.

One night after burnt lamb chops and a viscous Greek salad, Kirk appeared at her bedroom door wearing pajamas, a plaid long-sleeved shirt and matching pants. "Would you mind?" he said. "I'm not getting any rest. I need to sleep." Then he added, "You've been so good to me."

He wanted Paula to talk while he lay with his eyes closed and drifted. The first night, Paula told him the plot of a sitcom she'd seen. Talking and sleeping was all they did for several nights, but Paula knew it was the kind of situation where one thing would lead to another.

She let it happen. Soon Kirk began acting toward her as he had toward Stevie, whom, Paula found out later, he'd known only three weeks before they pooled their money to buy the condo.

Paula moved into Stevie's bed, shared it with Stevie's

boyfriend, and paid for it by working at Stevie's job. She even wore Stevie's old uniform and some of her clothes. She had hardly known Stevie before she was killed, but she was getting to know her better all the time.

One of the first things she realized was that Kirk was a lot more attractive when he was someone else's boyfriend. He had trouble following conversations. At times he smiled or winked or pinched her butt, which had a certain boyish charm, but she discovered it meant he hadn't understood her, didn't have a clue as to what she was talking about. All the flirting things—the way he licked his lips or pinched her or lifted her blouse and wiggled a finger in her belly button—were repeated so often she started seeing them as his own little short list of personality.

Stevie's job fared better than her boyfriend. When winter came, skiers filled the bar nightly. A second waitress was hired. Kirk went back to bartending, and Paula's former room was rented for the whole season to a kid from New Jersey whose father owned a tool company.

Cook became especially disdainful of Paula when he heard she and Kirk were lovers. "You landed on your feet," he said to her.

"I'm not the one who was thrown," she replied. "Kirk was thrown. I just stumbled into the middle of it."

"And you sure made the most of it."

"You don't know the first thing about me." She sounded angry but was more hurt than mad. For whatever reason, Cook had become her touchstone in this new place. Impulsively, she told him about Eugene, how she had left her husband without a word. "You are now the only person I've told."

"I guess that explains something," Cook said. "I don't see how, but I guess it does."

"Why are you so mad at me?"

"Who said I was? If I was, I won't be, all right?"

That was the end of the conversation. That night at home, Cook phoned information for the number of Eugene Loroun.

He never told Paula this, and he didn't dial the number that night. Eugene said the call came in March. They talked for a long time before Cook revealed the whereabouts of Eugene's wife.

I sometimes find myself thinking about the months that passed between the point Cook discovered Eugene's number and the day he called. What a treasure he had, valuable only as long as he refused to spend it.

"It was a peculiar life, living with a man I didn't love or have any kind of feelings for, not having friends except Cook, who would still be a bastard half the time, but it had become my life anyway. I wasn't thinking 'This is what I'm doing until my real life starts up again.' It was my real life." Paula had come to my house in a brand-new bathing suit. I have no pool and she made no mention of swimming or even sitting in the yard and sunning. She carried a small purse with a long strap looped around her bare shoulder.

I made eggs. This was near the end, shortly before she and Eugene moved away. Outside, beyond my yard, the neighbors hauled out buckets of soapy water to wash their stationary car, but on this day neither of us considered helping. Paula, in her pink one-piece, rocked on the back legs of a kitchen chair—she never sat still—and talked about the night Eugene appeared at the bar.

He was alone at a table watching her. When she approached, he said, "I'll have a gin and tonic." Then he added, "It's good to see you." He claimed he had tracked her all over the state.

Paula was moved by the story of his search. She felt the familiar combination of tenderness and fear that comes with love. But the fear was darker. Not the apprehension that usually accompanies strong feeling, but some larger fear.

Eugene drank his gin and talked about the high school and their neighbors, all that had happened while she'd been away. He did not ask about her motives for leaving. She understood he was giving her the opportunity to come back.

But her anxiety grew despite the friendly talk. Much later she would figure out the nature of the fear. At the time, all she could do was act on it.

She went into the back and took off her apron. "See you," she said to Cook and skipped out the back door. In another hour she was on the highway, following the Dolores River west. She angled across New Mexico and then hurtled through the White Mountains of Arizona. As it was March and still cold in the high altitudes, she decided to return to the desert. Which is how she wound up here.

"I didn't figure it out for a long time," Paula told me. She scooted her chair away from the table, close to mine, and crossed her legs. Her bathing suit was the pink of my roses. "I was happy to see Eugene, but this fear . . ." She looked at my face several moments, not into my eyes but all around my face. Through the open windows, phrases of Spanish drifted in. "There aren't many things I'm afraid of," she said.

"What was it?" I asked.

She shook her head and stood, suddenly angry with me. "There I was in Stevie's old life and damned if someone from my past hadn't tracked me down. Don't you see?" She became exasperated. "Aren't you going to say anything?"

"How did the two of you finally get back together?" It was the wrong thing to say. She charged out of my house, leaving her purse.

The one lie—if you do not count silence as a lie—that Eugene told Paula was that he had tracked her down. Cook had called him. But there had been someone tracking her.

"Willa hired a detective," Eugene explained. "She thought once I saw Paula again I'd become enraged. She thought I was making Paula out to be larger than life."

The detective failed to locate Paula, but months later he

did manage to find Eugene. "Willa called me this morning, out of the blue," Eugene told me. "Same old Willa. Says as soon as her daughters are in college, she'll leave Phil. I hate that name, Phil. I hate proper names that are verbs."

"What did you say to her?" I asked.

"I told her we were through." He threw his hands up, as if in resignation. "There's no percentage in the past," he said sadly.

I asked him then how he'd caught up with Paula after she left the Nugget. He didn't respond directly. "Willa used to say awful things about Phil. She did impersonations."

"I've never mentioned Willa to your wife," I said.

"I know that," Eugene snapped. "No one's accusing you of anything."

I left the room to pour myself a drink and let him cool off. He caught up with me. "Make me one, too," he said. I gave him my bourbon and he downed it. "When I was a school-teacher I knew who I was. I had Paula, I had a job I liked, I more or less had Willa." He held the glass over his mouth to let the last drops fall on his tongue. "Does Paula make fun of me? Is that what you two do?"

"No," I said. "She thinks the world of you."

His smile was ironic. "The world's gone to hell lately, hasn't it?"

After another drink, he resumed the story.

When Paula didn't return from the back of the bar, Eugene guessed what had happened. Telluride is a box canyon. There is only one road out. He drove to the edge of town, thinking he'd have a while to wait, believing Paula would pack some clothes, but she had merely run to her truck and taken off. If she hadn't gotten into the habit of leaving the pickup at the condominium and walking to work, he would have missed her altogether.

He followed her for hours, keeping his distance. When

she finally pulled into the Desert Aire Motel, he waited in his idling car, trying to decide what to do. The car's engine sputtered and died—he'd run the tank completely dry. He took this to be a sign.

He left his car by the side of the road and walked to the room he'd seen Paula enter. He knocked gently.

Telling me about this moment, Eugene became shy. "She didn't seem surprised," he said. "She put her arms around me and took me inside."

Paula was more generous with details. "For the last hour of the drive, I'd regretted leaving him. But it was done, and I didn't see any way to undo it. I had just taken off my shoes when I heard the knocking. I thought, 'That would be Eugene. He's tracked me down again.' And there he was."

He had stood in the doorway with his hands clasped together on top of his head, eyes red from the long drive, hair stiff from the wind. The first thing she did was touch his flannel shirt. One of the buttons had come undone and she buttoned it.

"I'm tired," he told her.

She nodded and said, "It was a long drive." They embraced.

This embrace should end the story. They found a house on my street. Paula got a job. Eugene eventually received a graduate degree in high school administration. But it's the embrace that shows the lovers together again, the embrace that provides the story with a happy ending.

However, Eugene left Paula after finishing his degree. His leave-taking was not dramatic. He consulted a lawyer, an agreement was reached.

The day he drove away, I broke the silence. "I love you," I told her. We were on the telephone. She hadn't come to my house in weeks, wouldn't open her door to me. "This clears the way for us, don't you see? Before, it would have been so . . ."

"Inconvenient," she said.

"Come live with me."

"Not now," she told me. "Not like this."

"Why won't you?"

She said, "It's a matter of integrity."

A pain rocked my chest, as if I had been struck by a hammer. "I should have . . ."

"You should have moved. You should have made a move." The phone went dead.

I've come to understand the light that had engulfed us was not love. Love permits the light, creates the light, but is not the light. We concealed our love to protect the light, much like throwing a blanket over a fire to conserve heat.

But there was more to it than that. Something Paula doesn't understand—I alone knew the whole story. The little misunderstandings they each clung to, the aberrations of logic, the lies, the failings of faith, the odd course their love had taken. I knew it all, and knowing paralyzed me.

Eugene lives in California and says Paula is somewhere in New Mexico. She's asked him not to tell me where. This is the ultimate product of our love: we're each alone, spread across the southwest.

Maybe I should include Willa, too. She's still in Colorado with her husband and children and swimming pool, longing for Eugene. And I suppose my ex-wife should get her due. She's remained single all these years. At Christmas she sends me a card. The last one was from Moab, Utah. "I have a nice yard here," the card read, "room for tomato plants and a few stalks of corn. I refinished our old chairs. You remember those chairs?"

Love advances mysteriously. The wind remains invisible. We shudder in its wake. I understand now, finally, that love is more important than happiness.

The last time I spoke face-to-face with Paula was when she came by in her bathing suit. That evening, after supper, while Eugene readied himself to leave, I retrieved his wife's purse, which still rested on the kitchen chair.

"Must be new." Eugene had entered the room and took

the little bag that dangled from my finger. He immediately opened it and thrust his hand inside. His expression quickly changed. "Oh, Paula," he said softly, as if she were standing beside him.

"What is it?" I asked, but he had already walked away. "Hold on," I said. "Have another beer."

He didn't reply but stopped at the door and revealed the contents of the purse: a single twenty-dollar bill.

He turned and stepped out into the dark. The pace he set was not fast but steady. His shoulders cut the night squarely. Before entering his house, he raised his arm as if to wave, but it was only to show me the purse a final time.

QUILTING ON THE

REBOUND

O

Terry McMillan

F IVE YEARS AGO, I did something I swore I'd
never do—went out with someone I worked with. We worked
for a large insurance company in L.A. Richard was a senior
examiner and I was a chief underwriter. The first year, we
kept it a secret, and not because we were afraid of jeopardizing
our jobs. Richard was twenty-six and I was thirty-four. By
the second year, everybody knew it anyway and nobody seemed
to care. We'd been going out for three years when I realized
that this relationship was going nowhere. I probably could've
dated him for the rest of my life and he'd have been satisfied.
Richard had had a long reputation for being a Don Juan of
sorts, until he met me. I cooled his heels. His name was also
rather ironic, because he looked like a black Richard Gere. The
fact that I was older than he was made him feel powerful in a
sense, and he believed that he could do for me what men my
own age apparently couldn't. But that wasn't true. He was a

challenge. I wanted to see if I could make his head and heart turn 360 degrees, and I did. I blew his young mind in bed, but he also charmed me into loving him until I didn't care how old he was.

Richard thought I was exotic because I have slanted eyes, high cheekbones, and full lips. Even though my mother is Japanese and my dad is black, I inherited most of his traits. My complexion is dark, my hair is nappy, and I'm five six. I explained to Richard that I was proud of both of my heritages, but he has insisted on thinking of me as being mostly Japanese. Why, I don't know. I grew up in a black neighborhood in L.A., went to Dorsey High School—which was predominantly black, Asian, and Hispanic—and most of my friends are black. I've never even considered going out with anyone other than black men.

My mother, I'm glad to say, is not the stereotypical passive Japanese wife either. She's been the head nurse in Kaiser's cardiovascular unit for over twenty years, and my dad has his own landscaping business, even though he should've retired years ago. My mother liked Richard and his age didn't bother her, but she believed that if a man loved you he should marry you. Simple as that. On the other hand, my dad didn't care who I married just as long as it was soon. I'll be the first to admit that I was a spoiled-rotten brat because my mother had had three miscarriages before she finally had me and I was used to getting everything I wanted. Richard was no exception. "Give him the ultimatum," my mother had said, if he didn't propose by my thirty-eighth birthday.

But I didn't have to. I got pregnant.

We were having dinner at an Italian restaurant when I told him. "You want to get married, don't you?" he'd said.

"Do you?" I asked.

He was picking through his salad and then he jabbed his fork into a tomato. "Why not, we were headed in that direction anyway, weren't we?" He did not eat his tomato but laid his fork down on the side of the plate.

I swallowed a spoonful of my clam chowder, then asked, "Were we?"

"You know the answer to that. But hell, now's as good a time as any. We're both making good money, and sometimes all a man needs is a little incentive." He didn't look at me when he said this, and his voice was strained. "Look," he said, "I've had a pretty shitty day, haggling with one of the adjusters, so forgive me if I don't appear to be boiling over with excitement. I am happy about this. Believe me, I am," he said, and picked up a single piece of lettuce with a different fork and put it into his mouth.

My parents were thrilled when I told them, but my mother was nevertheless suspicious. "Funny how this baby pop up, isn't it?" she'd said.

"What do you mean?"

"You know exactly what I mean. I hope baby doesn't backfire."

I ignored what she'd just said. "Will you help me make my dress?" I asked.

"Yes," she said. "But we must hurry."

My parents—who are far from well off—went all out for this wedding. My mother didn't want anyone to know I was pregnant, and to be honest, I didn't either. The age difference was enough to handle as it was. Close to three hundred people had been invited, and my parents had spent an astronomical amount of money to rent a country club in Marina Del Rey. "At your age," my dad had said, "I hope you'll only be doing this once." Richard's parents insisted on taking care of the caterer and the liquor, and my parents didn't object. I paid for the cake.

About a month before the Big Day, I was meeting Richard at the jeweler because he'd picked out my ring and wanted to make sure I liked it. He was so excited, he sounded like a little boy. It was beautiful, but I told him he didn't have to spend four thousand dollars on my wedding ring. "You're worth it," he'd said and kissed me on the cheek. When we got to the parking lot, he opened my door, and stood there staring at me. "Four more weeks," he said, "and you'll be my wife." He didn't smile when he said it, but closed the door and walked around to the driver's side and got in. He'd driven four whole blocks without saying a word and his knuckles were almost white because of how tight he was holding the steering wheel.

"Is something wrong, Richard?" I asked him.

"What would make you think that?" he said. Then he laid on the horn because someone in front of us hadn't moved and the light had just barely turned green.

"Richard, we don't have to go through with this, you know."

"I know we don't *have* to, but it's the right thing to do, and I'm going to do it. So don't worry, we'll be happy."

But I *was* worried.

I'd been doing some shopping at the Beverly Center when I started getting these stomach cramps while I was going up the escalator, so I decided to sit down. I walked over to one of the little outside cafés and I felt something lock inside my stomach, so I pulled out a chair. Moments later my skirt felt like it was wet. I got up and looked at the chair and saw a small red puddle. I sat back down and started crying. I didn't know what to do. Then a punkish-looking girl came over and asked if I was okay. "I'm pregnant, and I've just bled all over this chair," I said.

"Can I do something for you? Do you want me to call an ambulance?" She was popping chewing gum and I wanted to snatch it out of her mouth.

By this time at least four other women had gathered around me. The punkish-looking girl told them about my condition. One of the women said, "Look, let's get her to the rest room. She's probably having a miscarriage."

Two of the women helped me up and all four of them formed a circle around me, then slowly led me to the ladies' room. I told them that I wasn't in any pain, but they were still worried. I closed the stall door, pulled down two toilet seat covers and sat down. I felt as if I had to go, so I pushed. Something plopped out of me and it made a splash. I was afraid to get up but I got up and looked at this large dark mass that looked like liver. I put my hand over my mouth because I knew that was my baby.

"Are you okay in there?"

I went to open my mouth, but the joint in my jawbone clicked and my mouth wouldn't move.

"Are you okay in there, miss?"

I wanted to answer, but I couldn't.

"Miss," I heard her banging on the door.

I felt my mouth loosen. "It's gone," I said. "It's gone."

"Honey, open the door," someone said, but I couldn't move. Then I heard myself say, "I think I need a sanitary pad." I was staring into the toilet bowl when I felt a hand hit my leg. "Here, are you sure you're okay in there?"

"Yes," I said. Then I flushed the toilet with my foot and watched my future disappear. I put the pad on and reached inside my shopping bag, pulled out a Raiders sweatshirt I'd bought for Richard and tied it around my waist. When I came out, all of the women were waiting for me. "Would you like us to call your husband? Where are you parked? Do you feel light-headed, dizzy?"

"No, I'm fine, really, and thank you so much for your concern. I appreciate it, but I feel okay."

I drove home in a daze and when I opened the door to my condo, I was glad I lived alone. I sat on the couch from one o'clock to four o'clock without moving. When I finally got up, it felt as if I'd only been there for five minutes.

. . .

I didn't tell Richard. I didn't tell anybody. I bled for three days before I went to see my doctor. He scolded me because I'd gotten some kind of an infection and had to be prescribed antibiotics, then he sent me to the outpatient clinic, where I had to have a D & C.

Two weeks later, I had a surprise shower and got enough gifts to fill the housewares department at Bullock's. One of my old girlfriends, Gloria, came all the way from Phoenix, and I hadn't seen her in three years. I hardly recognized her, she was as big as a house. "You don't know how lucky you are, girl," she'd said to me. "I wish I could be here for the wedding but Tarik is having his sixteenth birthday party and I am not leaving a bunch of teenagers alone in my house. Besides, I'd probably have a heart attack watching you or anybody else walk down an aisle in white. Come to think of it, I can't even remember the last time I went to a wedding."

"Me either," I said.

"I know you're gonna try to get pregnant in a hurry, right?" she asked, holding out her wrist with the watch on it.

I tried to smile. "I'm going to work on it," I said.

"Well, who knows?" Gloria said, laughing. "Maybe one day you'll be coming to my wedding. We may both be in wheelchairs, but you never know."

"I'll be there," I said.

All Richard said when he saw the gifts was, "What are we going to do with all this stuff? Where are we going to put it?"

"It depends on where we're going to live," I said, which we hadn't even talked about. My condo was big enough and so was his apartment.

"It doesn't matter to me, but I think we should wait a while before buying a house. A house is a big investment, you know. Thirty years." He gave me a quick look.

"Are you getting cold feet?" I blurted out.

"No, I'm not getting cold feet. It's just that in two weeks we're going to be man and wife, and it takes a little getting used to the idea, that's all."

"Are you having doubts about the idea of it?"

"No."

"Are you sure?"

"I'm sure," he said.

I didn't stop bleeding, so I took some vacation time to relax, and finish my dress. I worked on it day and night and was doing all the beadwork by hand. My mother was spending all her free time at my place trying to make sure everything was happening on schedule. A week before the Big Day I was trying on my gown for the hundredth time when the phone rang. I thought it might be Richard, since he hadn't called me in almost forty-eight hours, and when I finally called him and left a message, he still hadn't returned my call. My father said this was normal.

"Hello," I said.

"I think you should talk to Richard." It was his mother.

"About what?" I asked.

"He's not feeling very well," was all she said.

"What's wrong with him?"

"I don't know for sure. I think it's his stomach."

"Is he sick?"

"I don't know. Call him."

"I did call him but he hasn't returned my call."

"Keep trying," she said.

So I called him at work, but his secretary said he wasn't there. I called him at home and he wasn't there either, so I left another message and for the next three hours I was a wreck, waiting to hear from him. I knew something was wrong.

I gave myself a facial, a manicure and pedicure and watched Oprah Winfrey while I waited by the phone. It didn't

ring. My mother was downstairs hemming one of the brides-
maid's dresses. I went down to get myself a glass of wine.
"How you feeling, Marilyn Monroe?" she asked.

"What do you mean, how am I feeling? I'm feeling fine."

"All I meant was you awful lucky with no morning sick-
ness or anything, but I must say, hormones changing because
you getting awfully irritating."

"I'm sorry, Ma."

"It's okay. I had jitters too."

I went back upstairs and closed my bedroom door, then
went into my bathroom. I put the wineglass on the side of the
bathtub and decided to take a bubble bath in spite of the bleeding. I must have poured half a bottle of Secreti in. The water
was too hot but I got in anyway. Call, dammit, call. Just then
the phone rang and scared me half to death. I was hyperven-
tilating and couldn't say much except, "Hold on a minute,"
while I caught my breath.

"Marilyn?" Richard was saying. "Marilyn?" But before
I had a chance to answer he blurted out what must have been
on his mind all along. "Please don't be mad at me, but I can't
do this. I'm not ready. I wanted to do the right thing, but I'm
only twenty-nine years old. I've got my whole life ahead of me.
I'm not ready to be a father yet. I'm not ready to be anybody's
husband either, and I'm scared. Everything is happening too
fast. I know you think I'm being a coward, and you're probably right. But I've been having nightmares, Marilyn. Do you
hear me, nightmares about being imprisoned. I haven't been
able to sleep through the night. I doze off and wake up dripping wet. And my stomach. It's in knots. Believe me, Marilyn,
it's not that I don't love you because I do. It's not that I don't
care about the baby, because I do. I just can't do this right
now. I can't make this kind of commitment right now. I'm
sorry. Marilyn? Marilyn, are you still there?"

I dropped the portable phone in the bathtub and got out.

My mother heard me screaming and came tearing into the
room. "What happened?"

I was dripping wet and ripping the pearls off my dress but somehow I managed to tell her.

"He come to his senses," she said. "This happen a lot. He just got cold feet, but give him day or two. He not mean it."

Three days went by and he didn't call. My mother stayed with me and did everything she could to console me, but by that time I'd already flushed the ring down the toilet.

"I hope you don't lose baby behind this," she said.

"I've already lost the baby," I said.

"What?"

"A month ago."

Her mouth was wide open. She found the sofa with her hand and sat down. "Marilyn," she said and let out an exasperated sigh.

"I couldn't tell anybody."

"Why not tell somebody? Why not me, your mother?"

"Because I was too scared."

"Scared of what?"

"That Richard might change his mind."

"Man love you, dead baby not change his mind."

"I was going to tell him after we got married."

"I not raise you to be dishonest."

"I know."

"No man in world worth lying about something like this. How could you?"

"I don't know."

"I told you it backfire, didn't I?"

For weeks I couldn't eat or sleep. At first, all I did was think about what was wrong with me. I was too old. For him. No. He didn't care about my age. It was the gap in my teeth, or my slight overbite, from all those years I used tò suck my thumb. But he never mentioned anything about it and I was really the

only one who seemed to notice. I was flat-chested. I had cellu-
lite. My ass was square instead of round. I wasn't exciting as I
used to be in bed. No. I was still good in bed, that much I did
know. I couldn't cook. I was a terrible housekeeper. That was
it. If you couldn't cook and keep a clean house, what kind of
wife would you make?

I had to make myself stop thinking about my infinite
flaws, so I started quilting again. I was astonished at how radi-
ant the colors were that I was chosing, how unconventional and
wild the patterns were. Without even realizing it, I was fusing
Japanese and African motifs and was quite excited by the re-
sults. My mother was worried about me, even though I had
actually stopped bleeding for two whole weeks. Under the circumstances, she thought that my obsession with quilting was
not normal, so she forced me to go to the doctor. He gave me
some kind of an antidepressant, which I refused to take. I told
him I was not depressed, I was simply hurt. Besides, a pill
wasn't any antidote or consolation for heartache.

I began to patronize just about every fabric store in
downtown Los Angeles, and while I listened to the humming of
my machine, and concentrated on designs that I couldn't believe *I* was creating, it occurred to me that I wasn't suffering
from heartache at all. I actually felt this incredible sense of
relief. As if I didn't have to anticipate anything else happening
that was outside of my control. And when I did grieve, it was
always because I had lost a child, not a future husband.

I also heard my mother all day long on my phone, lying about
some tragedy that had happened and apologizing for any in-
convenience it may have caused. And I watched her, bent over
at the dining room table, writing hundreds of thank-you notes
to the people she was returning gifts to. She even signed my
name. My father wanted to kill Richard. "He was too young,
and he wasn't good enough for you anyway," he said. "This is
really a blessing in disguise."

I took a leave of absence from my job because there was no way in hell I could face those people, and the thought of looking at Richard infuriated me. I was not angry at him for not marrying me, I was angry at him for not being honest, for the way he handled it all. He even had the nerve to come over without calling. I had opened the door but wouldn't let him inside. He was nothing but a little pip-squeak. A handsome, five-foot-seven-inch pip-squeak.

"Marilyn, look, we need to talk."

"About what?"

"Us. The baby."

"There is no baby."

"What do you mean, there's no baby?"

"It died."

"You mean you got rid of it?"

"No, I lost it."

"I'm sorry, Marilyn," he said and put his head down. How touching, I thought. "This is all my fault."

"It's not your fault, Richard."

"Look. Can I come in?"

"For what?"

"I want to talk. I need to talk to you."

"About what?"

"About us."

"Us?"

"Yes, us. I don't want it to be over between us. I just need more time, that's all."

"Time for what?"

"To make sure this is what I want to do."

"Take all the time you need," I said and slammed the door in his face. He rang the buzzer again, but I just told him to get lost and leave me alone.

I went upstairs and sat at my sewing machine. I turned the light on, then picked up a piece of purple and terra-cotta cloth. I slid it under the pressure foot and dropped it. I pressed down on the pedal and watched the needle zigzag. The stitches were too loose so I tightened the tension. Richard is going to be the last in a series of mistakes I've made when it comes to picking a man. I've picked the wrong one too many times, like a bad habit that's too hard to break. I haven't had the best of luck when it comes to keeping them either, and to be honest, Richard was the one who lasted the longest.

When I got to the end of the fabric, I pulled the top and bobbin threads together and cut them on the thread cutter. Then I bent down and picked up two different pieces. They were black and purple. I always want what I can't have or what I'm not supposed to have. So what did I do? Created a pattern of choosing men that I knew would be a challenge. Richard's was his age. But the others—all of them from Alex to William—were all afraid of something: namely committing to one women. All I wanted to do was seduce them hard enough—emotionally, mentally, and physically—so they wouldn't even be aware that they were committing to anything. I just wanted them to crave me, and no one else but me. I wanted to be their healthiest addiction. But it was a lot harder to do than I thought. What I found out was that men are a hard nut to crack.

But some of them weren't. When I was in my late twenties, early thirties—before I got serious and realized I wanted a long-term relationship—I'd had at least twenty different men fall in love with me, but of course these were the ones I didn't want. They were the ones who after a few dates or one rousing night in bed, ordained themselves my "man" or were too quick to want to marry me, and even some considered me their "property." When it was clear that I was dealing with a different species of man, a hungry element, before I got in too deep, I'd tell them almost immediately that I hope they wouldn't mind my being bisexual or my being unfaithful because I was in no hurry to settle down with one man, or that I had a tendency of always falling for my man's friends. Could they tolerate that? I even went so far as to tell them that I hoped having herpes wouldn't cause a problem, that I wasn't really all that trustworthy because I was a habitual liar, and that if they wanted the whole truth they should find themselves another woman. I told them that I didn't even think I was good enough for them, and they should do themselves a favor, find a woman who's truly worthy of having such a terrific man.

I had it down to a science, but by the time I met Richard, I was tired of lying and conniving. I was sick of the games. I was whipped, really, and allowed myself to relax and be vulnerable because I knew I was getting old.

When Gloria called to see how my honeymoon went, I told her the truth about everything. She couldn't believe it. "Well, I thought I'd heard 'em all, but this one takes the cake. How you holding up?"

"I'm hanging in there."

"This is what makes you want to castrate a man."

"Not really, Gloria."

"I know. But you know what I mean. Some of them have a lot of nerve, I swear they do. But really, Marilyn, how are you feeling for real, baby?"

"I'm getting my period every other week, but I'm quilting again, which is a good sign."

"First of all, take your behind back to that doctor and find out why you're still bleeding like this. And, honey, making quilts is no consolation for a broken heart. It sounds like you could use some R & R. Why don't you come visit me for a few days?"

I looked around my room, which had piles and piles of cloth and half-sewn quilts, from where I'd changed my mind. Hundreds of different colored thread were all over the carpet, and the satin stitch I was trying out wasn't giving me the effect I thought it would. I could use a break, I thought. I could. "You know what?" I said. "I think I will."

"Good, and bring me one of those tacky quilts. I don't

have anything to snuggle up with in the winter, and contrary to popular belief, it does get cold here come December."

I liked Phoenix and Tempe, but I fell in love with Scottsdale. Not only was it beautiful but I couldn't believe how inexpensive it was to live in the entire area, which was all referred to as the Valley. I have to thank Gloria for being such a lifesaver. She took me to her beauty salon and gave me a whole new look. She chopped off my hair, and one of the guys in her shop showed me how to put on my makeup in a way that would further enhance what assets he insisted I had.

We drove to Tucson, to Canyon Ranch for what started out as a simple Spa Renewal Day. But we ended up spending three glorious days and had the works. I had an herbal wrap, where they wrapped my entire body in hot thin linen that had been steamed. Then they rolled me up in flannel blankets and put a cold wash cloth on my forehead. I sweated in the dark for a half hour. Gloria didn't do this because she said she was claustrophobic and didn't want to be wrapped up in anything where she couldn't move. I had a deep-muscle and shiatsu massage on two different days. We steamed. We Jacuzzied. We both had a mud facial, and then this thing called aromatherapy—where they put distilled essences from flowers and herbs on your face and you look like a different person when they finish. On the last day, we got this Persian Body Polish where they actually buffed our skin with crushed pearl creams, sprayed us with some kind of herbal spray, then used an electric brush to make us tingle. We had our hands and feet moisturized and put in heated gloves and booties and by the time we left, we couldn't believe we were the same women.

In Phoenix, Gloria took me to yet another resort where we listened to live music. We went to see a stupid movie and I actually laughed. Then we went on a two-day shopping spree and I charged whatever I felt like. I even bought her son a pair of eighty-dollar sneakers, and I'd only seen him twice in my life.

I felt like I'd gotten my spirit back, so when I got home,

I told my parents I'd had it with the smog, the traffic, the gangs, and L.A. in general. My mother said, "You cannot run from heartache," but I told her I wasn't running from anything. I put my condo on the market, and in less than a month, it sold for four times what I paid for it. I moved in with my mother and father, asked for a job transfer for health reasons, and when it came through, three months later, I moved to Scottsdale.

The town house I bought feels like a house. It's twice the size of the one I had and cost less than half of what I originally spent. My complex is pretty standard for Scottsdale. It has two pools and four tennis courts. It also has vaulted ceilings, wall-to-wall carpet, two fireplaces, and a garden bathtub with a Jacuzzi in it. The kitchen has an island in the center and I've got a 180-degree view of Phoenix and mountains. It also has three bedrooms. One I sleep in, one I use for sewing, and the other is for guests.

I made close to forty thousand dollars after I sold my condo, so I sent four to my parents because the money they'd put down for the wedding was nonrefundable. They really couldn't afford that kind of loss. The rest I put in an IRA and CDs until I could figure out something better to do with it.

I hated my new job. I had to accept a lower-level position and less money, which didn't bother me all that much at first. The office, however, was much smaller and full of rednecks who couldn't stand the thought of a black woman working over them. I was combing the classifieds, looking for a comparable job, but the job market in Phoenix is nothing close to what it is in L.A.

But thank God Gloria's got a big mouth. She'd been boasting to all of her clients about my quilts, had even hung the one I'd given her on the wall at the shop, and the next thing I know I'm getting so many orders I couldn't keep up with them. That's when she asked me why didn't I consider opening my own shop. That never would've occurred to me, but what did I have to lose?

She introduced me to Bernadine, a friend of hers who

was an accountant. Bernadine in turn introduced me to a good lawyer and he helped me draw up all the papers. Over the next four months, she helped me devise what turned out to be a strong marketing and advertising plan. I rented an 800-square-foot space in the same shopping center where Gloria's shop is, and opened Quiltworks, Etc.

It wasn't long before I realized I needed to get some help, so I hired two seamstresses. They took a lot of the strain off of me, and I was able to take some jewelry-making classes and even started selling small pieces in the shop. Gloria gave me this tacky T-shirt for my thirty-ninth birthday, which gave me the idea to experiment with making them. Because I go over-board in everything I do, I went out and spent a fortune on every color of metallic and acrylic fabric paint they made. I bought one hundred 100 percent cotton heavy-duty men's T-shirts and discovered other uses for sponges, plastic, spray bottles, rolling pins, lace, and even old envelopes. I was having a great time because I'd never felt this kind of excitement and gratification doing anything until now.

I'd been living here a year when I found out that Richard had married another woman who worked in our office. I wanted to hate him, but I didn't. I wanted to be angry, but I wasn't. I didn't feel anything toward him, but I sent him a quilt and a wedding card to congratulate him, just because.

To be honest, I've been so busy with my shop, I haven't even thought about men. I don't even miss having sex unless I really just *think* about it. My libido must be evaporating, be-cause when I *do* think about it, I just make quilts or jewelry or paint T-shirts and the feeling goes away. Some of my best ideas come at these moments.

Basically, I'm doing everything I can to make Marilyn feel good. And at thirty-nine years old my body needs tighten-ing, so I joined a health club and started working out three to four times a week. Once in a while, I babysit for Bernadine, and it breaks my heart when I think about the fact that I don't have a child of my own. Sometimes, Gloria and I go out to hear some music. I frequent most of the major art galleries, go to just about every football and basketball game at Arizona State, and see at *least* one movie a week.

I am rarely bored. Which is why I've decided that at this point in my life, I really don't care if I ever get married. I've learned that I don't need a man in order to survive, that a man is nothing but an intrusion, and they require too much energy. I don't think they're worth it. Besides, they have too much power, and from what I've seen, they always seem to abuse it. The one thing I *do* have is power over my own life. I like it this way, and I'm not about to give it up for something that may not last.

The one thing I do want is to have a baby. Someone I could love who would love me back with no strings attached. But at thirty-nine, I know my days are numbered. I'd be willing to do it alone, if that's the only way I can have one. But right now, my life is almost full. It's fun, it's secure, and it's safe. About the only thing I'm concerned about these days is whether or not it's time to branch out into leather.

THE LOVER

O

Andre Dubus

LEE TRAMBATH WAS a fifty-five-year-old restaurant manager, with three ex-wives and five children. He was a slender, dark-haired man with a trimmed beard that was mostly gray, and he lived and worked in a small Massachusetts town, near the sea. The children were from his first two marriages, three daughters and two sons, grown now and spread up and down the eastern seaboard from Charleston to Portland, all in places he liked to visit. None of them was married; they all had lovers. Lee was on good terms with the two mothers of his children; time had healed him, had allowed him to forget whatever he and the women had done to each other, or removed the precision of pain from his memory; and sometimes, sitting alone in his apartment or strolling on the boardwalk along the river flowing a mile or so to the ocean, he wished as a boy does: that in some way his first marriage had never ended, yet his second had occurred so the daughter and son from that one would be on the earth; and that he and the two women and five children were one family. This frequent wish was never erotic: his images were of him and the two women and five children in living rooms, dining rooms, on lawns. It was the third wife, and the women in their forties whom he dated after his divorce from her, who made him refer to his last marriage as absolutely his last.

His third wife was nearly forty when they married, she had two daughters who were aging her with their listless work in high school, slovenly lives at home, strong-willed disobedience, and unsavory boyfriends, whose tight clothing seemed only a cover to get from their cars to the house and, with the girls, back to their cars. Lee did what he could, with tender hesitance; the girls' father had moved to Houston when they were six and eight, and sent them checks on birthdays and at Christmas. Lee silently predicted pregnancies, abortions, and a few years of too much drinking and cocaine. Then after college, which even they would be able to attend and muddle through, they would work at jobs to pay for clothes, cars, and apartments; and, like most people, they would settle softly into mundane lives. For Lee, the household was often frenzied and barely tolerable, with three females crying at once, but he was forty-nine, he had spent most of his adult life with families, and he could bear it.

His wife did not hold up as well, and told him to get a vasectomy. He did not want to. Gently and reasonably he said he would not mind being sterile if it simply happened to him, if nature retired him from the ranks of fertility; but he did not want it done to him by a doctor; and, more importantly, he did not want to choose to have it done, but this was a hair he could not split for her. She was not gentle, and if her argument was reasonable, her scorn for his feelings, her crying and cursing him for not loving her, made reason hard to discern. She would not make love with him until he gave in; and he did, because he understood her fears more than he understood his resistance, and he wanted to keep peace, so when he consented he began to see her demand as a request that could not be made calmly. Who could turn away from a drowning woman because her plea for help came not as a whisper but a scream? Undressing for surgery, he felt he was giving up his life as he had known it; and afterward, when he brought his sperm to be tested, he hoped the surgeon had failed; or, rather, that his sperm remained, undaunted by scalpel, or his wife, or himself. His wife was relieved, and soon he was too, and peace returned, or they returned to it.

When it did not last, when its not lasting slowly burned to ashes all kindness and respect in the marriage, when the marriage ended and Lee Trambath was in a bachelor apartment again, and seeing his two stepdaughters there and in restaurants, and dating again, he thought of his vasectomy as a concealed deformity, something he was hiding from women. No one he dated wanted more children, but still he always felt he was dissembling, until he told them, and one and all looked into his eyes as though he had spread yellow roses between them on the bar, the dinner table, or the bed.

He had married his first two wives when they were in their twenties, and he was the first husband of both; and always, however small, the shadows of sadness and failure were cast upon him: all his love and serious intent had increased the population of divorcees by two. His union with his third wife was his first with a divorcee; and her ex-husband, or what he had done to her, or what she believed he had done to her with no provocation at all, was a fulcrum in her marriage to Lee: he could trace the extremities of her anger and sorrow to that man he had never known. Now, dating, he collided with the presence of a man, or men, he only knew because a woman was pouting or crying or yelling or throwing a kitchen utensil at him, once a pot holder, once a breadboard. The pain and bitterness, fear and distrust, of these women seemed all to be caused by one of his gender, not only husbands and lovers, but fathers and stepfathers as well. Confronted by these lives in which not one woman, including the woman herself, had ever been anything but kind, generous, and consoling, he began not only to believe it but to feel responsible for it, and he tried to atone. No one he dated ever accused him of being harsh, cruel, inattentive. They praised his patient listening, his lack of fear and cynicism in the face of love. They never accused him of anything; still they made him feel like a drugged coral snake, sleeping and beautiful, which they took the risk of wearing around their throats while the clock ticked, and the effect of the drug subsided: with the first slow movement of his flesh, they would grab him and hold him on the table and, with an oyster fork, pierce his brain.

He began to wonder what he had done to his wives. The first had never remarried, had kept his last name, and for the past seventeen years had lived on Cape Cod with one man. The second had married again, and the third was dating. What cracks had he left in their hearts? Did they love less now and settle for less in return, as they held on to parts of themselves they did not want to give and lose again? Or—and he wished this—did they love more fully because they had survived pain, so no longer feared it? This could not be true of his third wife: she would need a strong, gentle, and older man, someone like a father without the curse of incest. But perhaps the first two wives were free of him, were saved. Lee was so afraid of what he might have done to his daughters, even his stepdaughters whose lives he had entered when they were already in motion at a high and directionless speed, that he wondered about them as he did about the time and manner of his death: seldom, and with either terrible images or a silent blankness in his mind, like a window covered with shining white paint. With the women he loved after his last marriage, he started smoking again, and drinking more.

There were three of these women, separated by short intervals of pain, remorse, and despair. When he and the last one had their final quarrel—she threw the breadboard—he was nearly fifty-five, and he gave up on love, save the memory of it. Always his aim had been marriage. He had never entered what he considered to be an affair, something whose end was an understood condition of its beginning. But he had loved and wanted for the rest of his life women who took him in their arms, and even their hearts, but did not plan to keep him. He had known that about them, they had told him no lies about what they wanted, and he had persisted, keeping his faith: if he could not change their hearts, then love itself would.

As a young man, in his first marriage, he had done some erotic dabbling: one-night stands whose causes, he now knew, were alcohol, night, and vanity. This had only scratched his marriage: a little blood showed, nothing more; for his wife had also fallen from grace, and in the same way. Theirs was a confessional marriage, and the purging of one and forgiving by the other deepened their love. The marriage ended much later, when their sexual mischief was far behind them, and Lee would never understand all of its ending any more than he could explain why, on their first date in college, there was already enough love between them to engender the years it would take to have three children and let their love die. He learned how quickly love died when you weren't looking; if you weren't looking.

At the restaurant a flaxen-haired young waitress flirted with him as a matter of course. This was Doreen Brodie. She was tall, and her limbs looked stronger than his. Some nights he had an after-hours drink with her, sitting at the bar, and her blue eyes and thin red lips aroused his passion and, more tempting, swelled his loneliness till it nearly brimmed over, nearly moved his arms to hold her. He did not touch her. She was younger than his children; he was old, a marital leftover wearing a jacket and tie.

He had come to believe that only young women still trusted love, believed in it. He knew this could not be true, that it was the inductive reasoning of his bad luck, that he simply had not met resilient older women because they lived someplace else, or lived here in this little town but somehow had not crossed his path. Yet even if he met such a woman, wasn't he

the common denominator in three divorces? Perhaps he was a
sleeping snake. He slipped into masturbation and nearly always, afterward, felt he was too old for this, too, and what he
wiped from his hand onto the sheet was his dignity. But sometimes on long afternoons when he could think of nothing but
Doreen Brodie, of phoning her and asking her for a date, of
having dinner with her, of making love with her, and so falling
in love with her, he resorted to the dry and heartless caress of
his hand; then, his member spent and limp as his soul, he
focused clearly on his life again, and he did not call Doreen.

He had married friends and went to their homes for dinner, or joined them at bars, but mostly he was alone in his
apartment. So working nights, which had been an intrusion on
his marriages and an interference with his dating, became a
blessing. He started reading history or philosophy during the
day, going for long walks, and keeping a journal in spiral notebooks. He wrote every morning before breakfast: reflections on
what he read, on people at the restaurant, sketches of the town
and river and sky as he saw them on his walks. He wrote
slowly, used a large dictionary, and took pleasure in precise
nouns, verbs, and adjectives. He liked working with colors. He
wrote nothing painful or erotic; he did not want his children to
feel pity or shame when they went through his effects after his
death. For a summer and fall, a winter and part of a spring,
Lee Trambath lived like this, till an April morning when he
woke to the sound and smell of rain.

As he dressed he remembered that yesterday he had
meant to buy coffee but, drawn by sunshine and a salty breeze
from the sea, he had walked along the river, instead of to the
store. He wanted to write about rain, try to put its smell and
sound on paper. But he had no coffee, and he put on his raincoat and a felt hat and went downstairs and outside. At once
his face and throat and hands were pleasantly wet. Across the
street was the gray river. He watched rain falling on it, and
cars moving slowly, their headlights glowing. Then he walked
to the end of the block and turned left, onto the main street.

He smelled rain and the sea. The grocery store was in the next block but his stride was slowing as he approached a newsstand with a kitchen for breakfast and lunch. In front of it, he stopped. Until nearly a year ago he had come here for breakfast, read newspapers, bought paperback books. Some time after he ducked the breadboard and backed out of her kitchen, backed out of her dining and living rooms and front door, he had begun his rituals of abstinence: his journal; his breakfast at home; his study of America, hoping to find in that huge canvas perhaps one brushstroke to illuminate the mystery of his life; his walks whose purpose was for at least one hour of light to see where he lived, smell it, touch it, listen to its sounds. Standing in the cool rain he lost his eagerness to write about it, but he kept its thrill. The rain on his face was like joyful tears, given him by the clouds; he could not recall when he had last wept. Now a new excitement welled in him: that of a holiday, and he moved to the door and swung it open and went inside, looking first to his left at the counter for tobacco and boxed candy at that wall, and beyond it the shelves of magazines and racks of books, then he looked to his right at tables for two and four where people were eating, and a long counter facing a mirror. Seated at the counter were a policeman, a young couple looking at each other as they talked, a gray-haired man alone, and Doreen Brodie reading a newspaper. To her right were three empty stools. He walked between tables and sat beside her. He had never seen her in daylight, had never seen her anywhere save at the restaurant. She looked at the mirror opposite the counter, saw him there, smiled at his reflection, then turned the smile to him and said: "Well. What brings you out in the rain?"

He took off his hat and placed it on the counter and was about to say he was going to buy coffee, but he looked at Doreen's blue eyes and said: "I woke to the sound of rain. It was the first thing I smelled." From behind her a young waitress approached and he signaled with thumb and forefinger as if gripping a cup. "Some was splashing through the screen, onto the windowsill. I didn't close the window. I wanted to write about rain, but I was out of coffee." He was unbuttoning his coat, removing his arms from its sleeves. "I've been writing things. I wanted to write its smell and sound. Its feel in April." He let his coat fall to the back of his stool. The waitress brought his coffee, and he stopped talking to pay. She was a young brunette wearing glasses, probably a year out of high school and waiting, happily enough, it seemed, for something to happen. He looked at Doreen's eyes: "It would be a separate section; the rain. Coming right after something I wrote yesterday about William James. He said that fear doesn't cause running away. Running away causes fear. So if you hold your ground you'll be brave. And that sadness doesn't cause crying. Crying makes us sad. So we should act the way we want to feel. And he said if that doesn't work, nothing else will anyway." Then he blushed. "He was a philosopher. I've been reading all kinds of things."

"Does it work?"

"What?"

"Acting the way you want to feel."

"Sometimes." He looked away from her, stirred sugar and cream into his cup. Still he felt her eyes.

"What is it you want to feel?"

Beneath his heart, wings fluttered. He looked at her eyes and the wings paused like a hawk's, and glided.

"You," he said, and they rushed in his breast, and someplace beneath them he felt the cool plume of a lie. "I want to feel you."

The lie spread upward but light was in her eyes, and she was standing, was saying softly: "Let's go."

He stood and put on his coat and hat; she had a black umbrella; she left her newspaper on the counter and he followed her out the door. She opened the umbrella, held it between them, and he stepped under it. His arm touched hers; perhaps it was the first time he had ever touched her. He went with her up the street, away from the river; at the corner she stopped and faced traffic, and watched the red light. He looked at her profile. Suddenly he felt the solidity of the earth beneath his feet. Were gravity and grave rooted in the same word? In that moment, looking at her left eye and its long upturning lashes, her nose and lips, and the curve of her chin, he could have told her they must not do this, he was a waste of her time, her fertility. Then she turned to him, and her eyes amazed him; he was either lost or found, he could not know which, and he surrendered.

The traffic light changed and they crossed the street and she led him down a brick alley between brick shops, then across a courtyard. His life was repeating itself, yet it felt not repetitious but splendid, and filled with grace. He lowered his eyes to rain moving on darkened bricks. God in heaven, he thought, if there is one, bless us. As a boy he was an Episcopalian. Then, with his first wife, he became his flesh and what it earned. Only his love for his children felt more spiritual than carnal. Holding one in his arms, he felt connected with something ancient, even immortal. In the arms of his passionate wife he felt a communion he believed was the supreme earthly joy. It had ended and he had found it again with other wives and other women, and always its ending had flung him into a dark pit of finitude, whose walls seeped despair as palpable as the rain he walked in now, after too many years.

Doreen's kiss dispelled those years. She gave it to him just across the threshold of her apartment, and he marveled at the resilience of nature. So many kisses in his lifetime, yet here he was, as though kissed for the first time on a front porch in summer in Dayton, Ohio. Oh plenitude, oh spring rain, and new love. He did not see the apartment: it was objects and shadows they moved through. Her unmade bed was boxsprings and a mattress on the floor, and quickly they were in it, his hat and clothes on the carpet with hers. He did not want it to end: he made love to her with his lips, his hands, his tongue. The muscles of her arms and stomach and legs were hard, her touch and voice soft; he spoke her name, he called her sweet, he called her my lovely, he perspired, and once from his stomach came a liquid moan of hunger. Finally she rolled away from him, toward the bedside table, and opened a drawer; he heard a tearing sound, and she sat up holding a golden condom.

"I have a vasectomy."

"What a guy. I've got an IUD."

"I've mostly been married."

"You never know." He watched her hands as she placed the condom and unrolled it. Then she kneeled above him, guided him in, and said: "I had given up on you."

"So had I."

Here it was again, the hot love of a woman, and he closed his eyes and saw the ocean at night, and squid mating on its gentle swell, a documentary he watched on television one afternoon last winter; sharks swam up and ate swaths of squid, but the others kept on, just kept on. Fucking and eating, he thought. They were why he left home, to marry and work, and here he was over thirty years later, with a woman nearly as young as his first wife when passion drove them out of their parents' homes and into the world, into a small apartment that was first an enclosure for their bed and second for a kitchen to prepare food in and a table to eat it on, and third for plumbing so they could bathe, and flush body waste. All vitality radiated from the bed, enough of it to give him the drive and direction to earn money and father children; he fell in love with them, a love that was as much a component of his flesh as the flow of his blood; and in fact it could only end with that flow's ending. Now another flow was about to leave his body: the pleasure started in the muscles of his legs where masturbation never reached, and he saw the mockery of himself and his hand, and to rid his mind of this comparison he said her name. He said it again and again, naming her flesh and his delight but the truth was as loud as their quick breath. His passion spurted from him, was gone, a bit of sterile liquid in a condom, a tiny bit if it were blood. It was enough to stain a sheet, make a child. His children would smile if they knew of this, if he told them he had waked to rain but had no coffee, so—There was nothing to smile about here. He opened his eyes. Doreen's were closed.

Soon he would soften inside her, and she was racing against the ebbing of his blood. He watched her face. Long ago he had learned that in lovemaking the one giving pleasure felt the greater intimacy; beyond a certain pitch of passion, the one receiving was isolated by muscles and nerves. He could have been watching her suffer pain; he could have been watching her die. She cried out. Then she was still, her eyes open, her breath deep and slowing. Before moving away, she reached between them and pinched the condom's opening. She took it with her, hanging from her fingers as she stood and smiled at him, and left the room.

He closed his eyes and listened to rain on the window. It saddened him now, all that rain and gray. He heard her footsteps in the hall, then soft on the carpet, and her lighter twice, and blown smoke; she sat on the bed and he spread his fingers for the cigarette, then she lay beside him and placed a cool glass ashtray on his stomach. He opened his eyes and looked at hers and said: "What more could I ask?"

"You could have asked sooner."

"I was trying to do something. Learn something. Do you know I could *own* a restaurant by now, if I wanted to? I never wanted to. I have money. I'm not just solvent; I have *money*. When I die my children will be able to make down payments on houses. Big payments. I have five children. All grown, and none of them married. Nobody's in a hurry anymore. To marry."

"Nobody has to be."

"Exactly. And that's all I ever was. What are people now? Their jobs? I started behind the bar and in kitchens. Now I read all this stuff. History. Philosophy. Looking for myself, where I fit in. I must be part of it, right? I'm here. So I must be. You know where I fit? I earn and invest and spend money. You know why? Because I fell in love. When I was very young. If I hadn't I might have joined the French Foreign Legion. Then I'd know, wouldn't I? What my part was. My part was this—" He gestured with a hand toward his penis; then he touched his heart. "And this. If you look at the country today, you see families torn apart. Kids with blood splashed on them. It all started with families. Like this, you and me, naked. People made love, settled land, built towns. Now the beginning is dying and we're left with the end. I'm part of that too. Three divorces. So that's where I fit. At the beginning and the end. It was always love for me, love of a woman. I look back and I think love needs tenacity. Maybe that's what I didn't have. And where is love in all this? It's not here. You don't love me." Her eyes were gentle as she shook her head. "Probably I could love you. But what for? Reverse my vasectomy and start over? Own a restaurant? Somewhere I missed something. Something my cock can't feel. Even my heart can't feel. Something that keeps you from fucking while sharks are eating your neighbors; while one is coming for you. I broke the hearts of three wives. It's not what I set out to do. We were in bed, and there were all those fins. I ripped childhood from five children. It'll always be with them, that pain. Like joints that hurt when it rains. There's more to it, but I can't find it. It's not walking with a cane and giving cigar rings to grandchildren. You know anyone in AA?"

She nodded. Her eyes were damp, and he knew from them what his own face showed.

"You know that look they have when it's really behind them? When they've been dry for years? Like there's a part of them that nothing in the world can touch. Not pain. Not grief. Not even love. But where do I go for that? What street is it on? Where's the door?" He held the ashtray and sat up. "Where?" Looking at Doreen, he felt tears in his throat then his eyes and on his face. "I want that door," he said, then he could not speak. His stomach tightened, his body jerked forward, and his head bowed as he wept. She took the ashtray and cigarette from him and tightly held him with one arm, and with a hand she petted his cheek, pressing it against hers; she gently rocked him.

"You poor man," she said.

He knew what she felt, at the core of her tender voice and touch. He had held in his arms suffering women and children, knew that all anyone could do was hold and touch and speak, watch and listen, and wish the pain would end. Gratefully he leaned against her, moving with the push and pull of her arm. He could see nothing beyond this sorrow, could not imagine what he might say or do when it left him in Doreen's embrace.

WEEDS

O

Bobbie Ann Mason

W HEN HE GOT home from work, Sam found his wife, Alma, in the garden. The sour smell of the composter—a green barrel in a metal frame—wafted across the rhubarb bed at him. A katydid buzzed off a squash leaf, making a birdlike noise. Delightedly, Alma held up a cantaloupe for him to see. It was misshapen, something like their old living room hassock. Her fingers were stained brown from pinching lice off stock peas. Alma's hair was frizzy and she wore no makeup and she was nearly fifty, but she never seemed to mind any of these things.

"Let's go back to the back field," Sam said. "I want to show you those weeds. I've never seen anything like them on this place in my life."

"I ain't got time." She flipped a string bean into a bucket.

"The weeds are higher than I am," he said, lifting his hand above his head. "You won't believe it."

"Snakes," she said.

"Not too many," Sam joked.

"I've got to work up peaches this evening," said Alma. "I've got a whole basket full of drops."

"Excuses," he said, exasperated. "One of these days you're going to run out of excuses."

The back field belonged in the government set-aside program. This year they were paid for not growing wheat, so the field had gone berserk with weeds. Bob Benson, who was growing some corn in one of Sam's fields, had promised to mow the weeds, but he couldn't get his tractor there now without blazing a trail through the corn. Laboriously, Sam had used his small lawn tractor to carve out a path along the edge of the field. Sam's family had been farming for generations, and he had never seen a field grown up wild like that. But now small family farms were called hobby farms—meaning that the farmers had to earn their living outside the farm and didn't have time to tend all their land. Sam worked at an air-compressor plant. There was a lot of pressurized gas in the world, he thought. Sometimes he felt he would explode.

Sam fastened the garden gate with its whittled wooden pin. From the gate, he could see his parents' old house sitting forlornly in the trees, with a cluster of junky cars pulled up around it. He had rented the house to an older man and woman who seemed settled and dependable, but Sam hadn't expected the couple's kinfolks to descend on the place. Every day there were at least five cars coming and going. It was a strain on the septic system. More than once Sam had had to go out in the woods and dig out the drainpipe. He feared the overflow would kill the trees. Renters were like the weeds, he thought, troublesome and impossible to get rid of.

It was a drought year, but weeds were flourishing. Pond weed was devouring the pond, spreading several feet out from shore already. Alma's fishing line kept getting hung up in it, and the fish weren't biting well because of it. They fed on the snails that fed on the weed. He had raked out the pond weed, spending hours grabbing at the tendrils with a garden rake and tugging them toward shore. He refused to use a weed killer, but someone had suggested geese. On TV once, he had seen geese in France, weeding strawberry beds. It seemed funny at the time, but now the notion had seized him, and he planned to get a pair of geese.

Heavy-metal music roared up the driveway. It was their daughter, Lisa. Her horn blurted out a staccato greeting. She had swapped her Mustang for a red compact with broken air-conditioning. Sam suspected she stopped by to visit them as often as she did only because their house was on the route between the plant where she worked and her apartment in town. Her dutifulness had a distracted quality about it, he thought. She shut off her engine, but the music continued to blare.

"Go with me to get some geese," he said, when he and Alma met her at her car door.

The music stopped when she removed the key and got out. She had on a loud pink outfit with large pink earrings.

"Aren't geese mean?" she asked, pushing up her sunglasses.

"Yeah, but they're supposed to eat pond weed."

"That pond weed will take the place," said Alma, scrutinizing Lisa's appearance.

"You say that about everything, Mom," Lisa said, pushing the dog away from her legs.

"What do I say that about?"

"You say that about cattails. And willow trees. And wandering Jew."

"We had to get that willow tree out," said Alma. "It was causing the pond to leak."

Lisa rolled her eyes toward the sky, and Sam glanced toward the old house through the trees. A long gold Chrysler was pulling in down there. Two hulky teenage boys and a woman in a green getup slammed doors. "They're gathering in," Sam said.

"Why don't you kick them out?" Lisa asked.

"You can't fool with people like that."

"But it's your house."

He shrugged. "They know there's nothing you can do to them. They ain't got nothing, so they take advantage. Even if you brought charges against them, they'd get away with it."

Indoors, the blast of air-conditioning and the peach-strewn table faced them. The kitchen was a mess. The house was jammed with what Sam called Alma's "savings." She saved cereal boxes, smashed flat and tied in bundles with strips of selvedge; she had accumulated a gallon jug of twist ties. The basement was crowded with jars of fruits and vegetables she had canned; the freezer was full of fish she had caught from the pond. In the winter she quilted frantically, like a farmer baling hay before a storm. She wouldn't sell the quilts, nor would she use them.

Alma said, as she ran her hands under the kitchen faucet, "The peaches are falling off with this drought, and the grass-hoppers are all gone. But there's plenty of frogs, little pale ones in the garden. I think it's the shade. In the shade they can't get much color."

Sam said to Lisa, "I wouldn't have to rent out to strangers if you'd moved into your grandpa's house like I wanted you to."

"I hate that old house! I think you should set fire to it." Lisa poked at a pale, dotted peach. She said, "Besides, I have some news."

"What?" Sam and Alma said simultaneously.

"I'm moving to Florida with Grayson. He's being trans-ferred."

Alma gasped and accidentally sat down on a stack of egg cartons. They popped and cracked. "Oh, excuse me," she said, rising; her hands, still wet, stuck out in front of her, dripping like sponges.

They never knew what to expect from their daughter. She had dropped out of college, quit her best jobs, enrolled in odd workshops. She even became a Catholic for a year. She was self-conscious about her overbite. In grade school, kids teased her and called her Squirrel-face. She had had a hard time, Sam had to admit. She was married once, but her husband drank, and her divorce hurt Alma deeply. For several years Lisa worked at the telephone company, but when the Bell System fell apart she changed jobs. Families, like the telephone company, were more diversified now, she explained to Sam one spring when she moved in with a man and his three young children. That arrangement lasted the summer.

"I've always wanted to go to Florida," Lisa was saying now. "And this is my big chance."

Alma wasn't even listening, Sam noticed. She was peeling a peach, gouging out the bruises.

The woman on the telephone said she could catch a pair of geese for Sam by the time he got there. Her place was several miles farther out into the country. Lisa agreed to go with him. They had finished supper, through Alma's silence and Lisa's nervous chatter about sea and sand.

"Don't you want to go too?" Sam asked Alma. He always made a point of asking her to go somewhere, knowing she would say no, but he kept hoping she would surprise him.

"No, I've got to work on these peaches." The peaches were pockmarked by worms, but Alma insisted they were salvageable.

In the car, Lisa said, "Grayson's going to finish training down there and then they'll send him to one of their plants. They'll pay for his training and then his moving expenses to the new place where he's assigned. It could be Oklahoma, Atlanta, or Missouri. So I don't know where we'll end up."

Sam didn't dare ask if they planned to marry. That didn't seem to be the point nowadays, but he knew that for Alma it was a major point. Alma had actually believed Lisa should have helped her former husband with his drinking problem, in order to save the marriage. Lisa had said she felt lucky she got out of it alive.

Sam said, "What do you think it will do to your mother if you leave?"

"I can't go on humoring her," Lisa said impatiently. "I think you ought to get her up in a jet airplane and take her to some big city. Chicago, say. Get her into the modern age. She acts so old, it's embarrassing."

"That's not what she needs."

"Then you should take her to a shrink. All that old-timey stuff is an act. She didn't grow up with all those doilies and pickle jars! They had television, for crying out loud."

"Don't talk about your mother like that," Sam said, coming down hard. "Let me tell you one thing."

He studied a road sign and made a deft turn onto a road partially hidden by an overgrown stand of sumac. The woman on the phone had said it was the old Caldwell place. A subdivision had sprung up on the road out to that farm—new houses, large and close together, without trees, more houses under construction. It was unusual to see a subdivision so far from town. Sam hated seeing farmland eaten up this way by an impulse to live in the country that was not much more than a fashionable idea. But Alma had been serious about it. She told him long ago she married a country boy on purpose. He recalled the time he was away in Louisville at a soil seminar and she had gone out looking for wild gooseberries, locating a quart of them in several hours of searching through some scrub acreage for a stray little bush here and there. Wild gooseberries had sharp thorns growing out of the fruit, and she had painstakingly snipped each thorn off with nail scissors. Instead of simply straining the fruit for jelly, she sought the sharp flavor and texture of the berry's skin. He praised her excessively, glorifying her extraordinary effort—like that of a craftsman who could still do delicate, almost-forgotten work. Her strength held him fast, made him never doubt her.

"What were you saying, Dad?" asked Lisa.

"I wanted to say something to you." Sam was fifty-one. He felt a choking in his throat, the sadness of being so old with living, wishing he could be headed for Florida with nothing but expectations instead of experience. "I just wanted to say—if you get down there, and if you need help—I don't want you to forget where your home is. If you get down there and get stranded, and if this guy does you bad, you've always got a ticket home, understand?"

"You don't have to treat me like I'm a kid! I know how to take care of myself!" She jostled his arm affectionately. The steering wheel bobbled.

Sam let the matter drop. Whenever he tried to express something heartfelt like that, it came off being corny. He thought she understood. But he didn't trust Grayson—a man with empty eyes, a bluffing manner, and a bushy little moustache that made Sam's flesh crawl. It made him think of the dirty brushes that he once used for horse grooming. Sam was always awkward with his daughter. He and Alma always knew they should have had more than one child, but she had refused after going through the Caesarean with Lisa. Ever since, their sex life had been sporadic and strained, punctuated with bouts of heavy passion that trailed off into forgetfulness.

"Here it is," he said, coming upon the farm suddenly. The farm had a large rambling barnyard enclosed with white wood fences. It was a picturesque place, with a tree-shaded pond and well-maintained barn, the kind of place Sam would keep if he had time.

They were admiring the farm from the driveway when a woman came from the house. "I done caught them geese for you," she said.

"Out on the pond the geese look like swan boats," said Lisa.

"Where'd you see swan boats?" Sam asked.

They followed the woman, Lillian Campbell, along the pond bank to the barn. On the pond a regatta of ducks and geese sailed. In the barnyard, a group of guinea hens, white as rabbits, trundled toward a trough, where some breakthrough discovery had been made, Sam judged by their chatter.

The two geese huddled together, quivering, in a corner stall of the barn. The male was white and the female was a buff color with a multitude of related shades in layers of feathers as carefully arranged as playing cards in a game of solitaire. She was small, compact, nervous.

"How did you catch them?" Sam asked Lillian.

"You drive geese, just like you was driving cows. Nothing to it."

She shoved the female into a mesh potato sack. Sam held the bag, feeling the woman's force as she pulled the drawstring tight and knotted it. Then, using a piece of baling twine, she bound the end of the bag the way Alma used to wrap the ends of Lisa's pigtails. The goose was upside down, her neck twisted and her head flat against the straw-covered dirt flooring. The woman swished the bag as if to settle its contents and handed it to Sam to hold while she started sacking up the second goose. The male, heavy and proud, sputtered and honked as the woman bunched him into the sack. Sam was afraid Lisa was bored. He saw her stoop to catch a scampering kitten, which rolled over, battling her hand playfully.

As they emerged from the barn, a car drove up and a man disappeared into the house.

"Hardy's come in late from the mill, ready for his supper, and when he don't get it right then and there he growls," the woman said, apologizing for her hurry. She tucked Sam's twenty-dollar bill into a pocket of her stretch-knit pants—pale blue dotted with nap balls and snags, fibers probably plucked out by cat claws and splinters, the same as Alma's were. Lillian was once pretty, Sam thought. Her figure was still hard and her cheekbones glistened with color. A fantasy charged through his head—an affair with this woman, a stranger, while her husband was at the mill (the feed mill? the lumber mill?), and the complicated adventure of concealing it.

"You're a cutie-pie," Lisa said to the kitten.

"You can have it," said Lillian.

"No, I can't take it. I'm moving to Florida."

"I went to Florida last winter and I wouldn't give you anything for it. It rained the whole week and everything cost an arm and a leg."

Sam opened the hatchback and set the geese behind the back seat. They honked—fierce, threatening squawks—as they tumbled onto the floor, their toes poking through the mesh of the sacks. The male, trying to upright himself, somersaulted. As Sam drove away, the birds fluttered around, the bags turning and jerking. The geese settled soon into a quiet fear. It was getting dark. A shadow ran across the road. Sam's eyes weren't great at night. He hadn't driven at night in at least five years.

"What do geese eat?" Lisa asked him.

"They're going to eat pond weed and like it," said Sam.

The geese were thrashing again, and Lisa seemed alarmed.

"What if they get out?"

"They won't get out."

"Will they attack us?" She gripped the handle on the dashboard.

"No, don't be silly. Hold on. We're having some fun now!" An ironic line he recalled from some movie.

At a stop sign Sam said, "Isn't this exciting?" He meant the night, the adventure, the geese, the drive in the dark with his daughter. It seemed that they hadn't done anything like this together since she was a child. As soon as she became a teenager she had lost interest in anything that grew, animal or plant. And Alma had done the opposite, as if to spite Lisa's lone foray into the social world of school and church.

Sam thought he knew a shortcut through some back roads. He turned down a road he remembered from his childhood. In the dark it was lonely and twisted. They passed ramshackle houses and house trailers. In the twilight the chaos of their forms blended into the darkness, as if they were grown into the landscape—the old machinery and cars and other eyesores welded together into one large shadowy organism.

He recalled this intersection, the next curve, then the little bridge that followed. He remembered playing in that creek once, long ago, after a storm when an uprooted tree had made a bridge above a churn of angry water. He drove on, the geese murmuring and flapping, Lisa holding on to her seat and glancing furtively back at them.

Sam slowed down before a house. "That's the house where I was born."

"I never knew that!" Lisa said, surprised.

"It's been bricked over and added on to. I remember one year we had guineas. And I remember a tricycle."

The geese honked and fluttered. A bad smell drifted through the car.

Sam said, "It was so far out they didn't make it to the hospital. I was dropped just like a calf in a stall."

"That's incredible," said Lisa. "I can't imagine you here. There are so many things I don't know about you and Mom. Now that I'm going away, suddenly it seems like I haven't paid attention."

"We'll miss you," he said, choking on the words.

He eased down on the gas pedal. The tank, he noticed suddenly, said empty. They made it home, on fumes. "Goose fumes," he joked as they raced through the night, feeling free.

Alma had turned the outside light on for them, and Lisa volunteered to help Sam stow the geese in the pen where he planned to keep them until morning. She grabbed the flashlight from the glove compartment and lighted his way as he carried the geese down to the pen behind the house. Then, grunting slightly, she supported their weight against the top of the fence while he cut the strings of the sacks and let the geese down into the pen. Then she played the flashlight on the birds' confusion as they explored the dark pen. Cautiously, they murmured like children whispering behind the teacher's back. They snaked their heads in and out of the light. Lisa laughed with pleasure, a laugh that reminded Sam of Alma in her youth.

Inside the house, Alma gave them steaming peach cobbler and watched them eat it while she tended the pressure canner. Alma said, "Why do you want to leave home, Lisa?"

"You've got to take risks sometime. Hint, hint."

"Is there something the matter with you, Lisa?" said Alma. "Something you're not telling? Cancer? Are you pregnant?"

Lisa sighed. "No. No. And no. I'm just tired of this town—the way people treat people; those old biddies I have to work with; and the way people in the social set turn up their noses and look down at the people who do all the real work in this town. I never had a chance to get out till Grayson came along. Grayson's my ticket out."

"Prince Charming," said Sam dryly.

Lisa said, "I want to get away because all the women I know here are alcoholics and the men are high on themselves."

Sam let a warm peach loll on his tongue. He felt oddly relaxed at this moment. Lisa had been a cranky baby—bottle-fed because Alma's milk wasn't good and she didn't have the strength to nurse. Alma always said bottle babies were spoiled, expecting to be given presents all the time. He was still luxuriating in the warm feeling he had about the evening with his daughter. In that moment when they had released the geese, he had felt they were sharing something special for the first time since she was a small child. It was that moment when parent and child come together as people—adults—for the first time, he thought, hoping he wasn't reading too much into it.

In the morning, Sam sacked up the geese, and Alma helped him carry them down to the pond. He loved the reflections on the pond—the sky, the fluffy marshmallow clouds, the sycamore trees, the still darkness of the mowed field, the spindly patch of cattails like roasting wieners shining in the water. In the distance was a glint of metal—one of the renters' cars arriving. Sam caught Alma staring into the pond reflections as if she expected to see her future.

Sam released the female first, then the male. He had decided to name them Lillian and Hardy. Startled, the geese honked and splashed into the water. They swam in unison, swooping together. The dog, Chester, barked at them, and they lowered and extended their long necks, huffing menacingly at him.

"Eat that pond weed," Sam urged them.

Sam and his wife headed for the field of weeds. She carried a tobacco stick with her to beat back snakes.

"Where in the world did you come up with a tobacco stick?" Sam asked on their way down the fencerow. "I haven't seen one of those in years."

"The renters had it in their things. They said they didn't have any use for it." She laughed and clawed at her blouse. "Look. I found a grasshopper so I can fish on the way home." She had pinched the grasshopper and wrapped it in a little piece of brown paper and stuck it inside her brassiere. The grasshopper was still alive. "Crappie like 'em alive," she said.

They followed the path Sam had cut with his small tractor along the edge of the cornfield. By hand he had cut back blackberry briars. Chester ran ahead, rooting into the blackberry bushes, which were growing out from the fencerow into the field. Sam had spent most of his spare time cultivating—controlling weeds and pests, coaxing food plants to grow. They called that husbandry, he learned in an agriculture course he took once at night school. Following the necessities of the seasons seemed natural and clear and easy, but when it came to being a husband to a woman, he had had his worst doubts. Sometimes it seemed a passive role, like the way you had to accept a drought year. Other times marriage seemed like the most artful of crops, requiring exquisite care. The notion that marriage produced something hadn't escaped him. But on the occasions when Alma shut him out he didn't know what farming analogies applied. He once accused her in jest of using the no-till method of birth control. The joke had hurt her and he had never challenged her again on the point. Sometimes they made love and sometimes they *seemed* to be making love, when they shared some wonder she had found—those gooseberries, a bird's nest with four glistening speckled jewels inside, a new ear of corn. Sometimes that was enough. Today he thought showing her the field of weeds would be like that. He felt stirred, hoping.

The creek had dried down to a few puddles.

"Well, Lisa likes to get out and go," Alma said thoughtfully, poking her tobacco stick in the gravel. "And maybe she can learn to love that Grayson enough to marry him."

"That's pathetic reasoning," said Sam.

Something in him felt broken, cracked by Alma's irrationality. She stood before him—square-jawed, large-boned, with delicate skin like honey. They were well beyond the midlife crisis, an idea she had thought was silly, but Sam knew he had to change something before it was too late. He loved her as much as ever, but he was afraid their love had gone into something so deep and unexplained—like the creek deepening from soil erosion—that it wasn't free.

"I used to think Lisa wanted a nice house and a family and a dependable man who'd take care of her," Alma said. "But they don't want that anymore, girls don't. I don't know what they want, and I don't think they do either."

Along the creek bank dried blackberry briars crunched underfoot, and occasionally some of the briars grabbed at Sam's jeans. A squirrel darted out in front of them and disappeared. The ground was covered with hickory nuts the squirrels had cut down.

Alma said, "For a drought year, I never saw so many hickory nuts."

She flew into them, stooping to gather them, flinging aside the split green hulls and stuffing the nuts in her pockets.

"Leave them for the squirrels," he said sharply. "Can't you leave well enough alone? Do you have to save everything you find?"

He kicked at a few nuts. There were so many things he didn't know and didn't have time to know and would never understand. The drought caused some things to dry up and some to overproduce—much like Alma, whose attentions to people had dried up while her garden was bursting. He felt heavy, heavy as the groundcover of hickory nuts. He hoped what he was feeling was only another phase, but he knew that this was the first moment in his life that he knew truly how limited time was.

"There they are," he said as they faced the forest of weeds. They were stately and wild, their thickness giving off a dusty, harsh heat. Sam guided Alma down the path he had mowed.

"Ain't these the tallest weeds you ever saw?" he said. "Look at that—there's jimsonweed and saw briar and horseweed."

"Ragweed," she said, touching the yellow floss.

"Look at that. Old foxtail and white-top weed and that old vine there. I never saw anything like it."

The weeds disgusted him. On television recently, he had seen an ancient ruin—some toppled statues and crumbling walls of an old temple in the Far East somewhere—and the weeds were growing through the stones, right through the eyes of the statues.

"There's that purple-flowered weed that used to be so bad in the garden." She touched a dark green plant with pointed leaves. "Nightshade."

"Poison," he said, feeling slightly sick.

She plucked a seed pod, a green paper lantern, from the nightshade. She opened it at its seams and turned the petals down, exposing the hard green ball in the center. She opened a second one, then held the two a certain way for him to see.

"My grandmother used to do this," said Alma, smiling. "This is the boy and this is the girl." She had fashioned one of the seed pods into a girl with a skirt and the other into a boy in pants. "In the old days, these were toys," she said.

Alma had plunged ahead of him. Now she was studying another tall weed, with a thick-headed purple flower, a flower he didn't know. Miraculously, a dozen tiny hummingbirds were feeding on the purple flowers. They had unusual markings— green heads, sienna stripes circling their black bodies.

"They're not birds," Alma said, reading his thoughts, without even looking at him. "They're hawkmoths."

Sam moved closer, and the little birds turned out to have six legs and long, rolled tongues. "How did you know what they were?" he asked.

She shrugged. "I lost my grasshopper," she said, touching between her breasts. "Reckon one of these hawkmoths would do to fish with?"

"How did you know their name?" he demanded.

She walked on. "Maybe we can gather some of Bob's corn on the way back. He said for us to get some since our corn didn't make."

He followed her, his heart high, and the pond came into view. He could see a large heron on the pond bank—a tall dusky bird, maybe a great blue. As he watched, the heron stalked curiously toward the geese. The geese fled to the opposite shore, honking like visitors arriving.

THE BRIDE OF HIS

LIFE

O

Robert Love Taylor

To LEON, CORA MAE was even more beautiful
dead than alive. They had put her wedding dress on her, according to his wishes, and used a brighter shade of lipstick
than she ever put on.

Everything was already paid for. He wouldn't have had
to pay a cent out of his pocket except he wanted her buried in
the wedding dress and that cost extra. She wore a blue dress at
the viewing and her wedding dress at the funeral. Changing
her was what cost extra. Her mama wouldn't hear of paying
for that, and so he was stuck with the tab. He didn't know
where the money would come from. In the two months he'd
been married to Cora Mae she had spent every dime he earned.
He had resolved to say something to her about this.

None of his kinfolks was there. His mother had come for
the wedding and could not afford another trip in the same summer.

Truthfully, Cora Mae had not been the bride he expected. The best part was seeing her in that white dress. It had been a hot day and he was sweating something fierce in his CCC dress uniform, but she looked cool as a cucumber when she walked out of that front bedroom and into the living room. The preacher, a fat man with big pink hands, dropped the Bible, and when Leon bent down to pick it up for him, the man touched him on the shoulder and said, Bless you, boy. The hand felt hot and heavy, as if the day itself had got ahold of him.

Now, sitting on a folding chair in the front row of the Street and Draper Funeral Parlor chapel, it was even hotter. He wore his CCC uniform even though he hadn't been in the CCC since he was married. Husbands wasn't allowed in the CCC. Now he was in the WPA and they didn't give him a uniform.

The same preacher that married him and Cora Mae stood before him, just back of the open casket, his big pink hands raised up in the air. *Lord, bless us in our frailty. Lord, guide us safe through our earthly tribulation.* He had been preaching a long time. It was easy to lose track of the words.

Leon had come to Street and Draper's early that morning. At the viewing the night before, they had told him he could if he wanted to. They understood, the man said, that he might desire a last moment alone with the deceased, and it could be easily arranged. The man, who had the whitest teeth you ever saw, seemed to expect him to want to, and so Leon thanked him and said he'd certainly be much obliged.

He realized when he left that he hadn't really wanted to. What he wished was that he could go back to the CCC camp like in the olden times and forget the whole thing. In the morning he would rise to the bugle call, jump into his khakis, and go out into the broad, hot fields to club rabbits. Late in the afternoon, he would return for a game of snookers in the camp rec room, and in the evening he and Darrold Peters would take in a movie downtown, then go to the dance pavilion at Springlake or Blossom Heath. They wouldn't go to the Arcadia because that would remind him of Cora Mae.

He was only eighteen years old and believed that life had treated him unfairly. It had started out okay. Even school hadn't been so bad, when he thought about it now. Not much had been expected of him and he knew it wasn't going to last forever. When he joined the CCC and was sent to Oklahoma City, he began to think that the fun he deserved was at last headed his way. Then he met Cora Mae.

Before that, he hadn't given much thought to the opposite sex. He had some pictures on loan from his cousin Fred that he kept in the bottom of a drawer and took out once in a while to look at. These ladies didn't have much on in the way of clothes, just scanty little things strapped here and there, but they all wore shoes. The shoes had real high heels on them. The ladies had the littlest feet. He never saw a woman in Greenwood, or even in Fort Smith, with feet that little, though some of them wore high heels. His mama, a big-boned woman with a high forehead and long neck, wore black lace-up shoes that had a thick heel not more than a inch and a half high.

For the most part, he never thought of the girls in school as women. Mary Jean Hicks, who wore lipstick and painted her cheeks, looked like she was trying too hard, and Sophie Gatewood, though built like the ladies in the photographs, had a chin like a football player and buck teeth. The prettiest one, May Rose Townley, was too tall and had long skinny feet. For a while he fancied himself in love with Berta Wells. He didn't know why. It was just a feeling she gave him when he saw her. When he looked at the ladies in the photographs he began to see her face on top of their bodies. Then when he next saw her he imagined the body of one of the ladies with its tiny undergarments underneath Berta's plain, shapeless clothes. This excited him.

He had watched Berta during geography class and it made the time go faster. She smiled back at him once or twice and, whenever she said hello, pronounced his name as if it had special meaning. Then when he made his move, tried to kiss her at a Sunday school picnic on Magazine Mountain, she looked shocked. He thought she might hit him, but she only asked him what he thought he was doing. He didn't know what to say. He laughed, which just made her madder. Anyway, it hadn't been him she smiled at during geography, but Delbert Dawes, the Methodist preacher's boy, who sat right behind Leon, carving initials on his desk. Leon figured those initials must have been D. D. plus B. W. He saw the two of them sneak off into the trees during the evening hymn sing. Since his only reason for coming had been to attend to Berta and impress her with his fine singing voice, he cussed himself out and didn't sing another hymn.

None of that prepared him for Cora Mae.

Nipped in the bud, the preacher was saying about her. Taken in the honeyed blossom of youth.

He guessed that was accurate, but even though she had been only a year older than him she seemed older, not young at all. That had appealed to him at first. The ladies in the photographs were older too, women of the world. He thought it would take a woman of the world to get at him, and Cora Mae, sitting all alone at that little table in the Arcadia Ballroom, cigarette smoke swirling around her, rhinestones sparkling, rubies and diamonds too, looked every bit the woman of the world. He didn't mind telling her so.

She laughed, but it wasn't a laugh like Berta Wells's.

After that he met her every week at the Arcadia. They danced and listened to comedy routines in between. They drank beer out of long-neck brown bottles and smoked cigarettes. He had never done any of these things before meeting her, though he had drunk rotgut and smoked cornsilk. His dancing might could've been a little smoother, but even when he came down on one of her toes she never complained. He told her what it was like growing up in Greenwood, Arkansas, and even when he stretched the truth now and then to make the story more lively she never disbelieved a word.

He should have known better. A woman her age with a little infant baby. The infant hadn't been any trouble. Slept like a log. It was what the baby meant, though. It kept reminding Cora Mae of the man that was its father. She never said so, but Leon was sure it did. She wouldn't put that man out of her mind, that was the trouble. When he saw her only on Saturday nights, Leon couldn't see this, but when he was married to her, when he took her on a week-long honeymoon to Hot Springs in his home state of Arkansas, when he introduced her to his mama and papa in Greenwood and showed her the sights of Fort Smith, when he showed her the photographs he'd never returned to his cousin Fred, when he had done all these things for her and she still wouldn't say a word about her former husband, he concluded that she never stopped loving the man.

You don't look happy, he said to her. You don't ever smile anymore.

She gave him a smile then that made him shiver. She guessed she just was missing her baby girl, left behind with her mama and papa in Oklahoma City.

What can we hope to know, flawed vessels that we are. We can't even fathom the depths of our imperfections.

Once when he was much younger, nine or ten, he and some of his friends, led by an older boy named Preston Dalton, went off together after school. Preston lived up on the mountain, farther back than any of the other boys. He was a head taller than Leon—he might have been twelve or thirteen, though in the same grade as the rest of them—and was missing a front tooth. You didn't dare tease him about the missing tooth. He was known to be mean, a rough character. Also, because of his age and his backwoods home (no one had ever been there), he seemed mysterious, a walking dark secret. Leon felt privileged when Preston Dalton asked if he and Elvin Beasley and Joe Mack Givens would like to do something different after school. All had chores awaiting them at home, but they wasn't about to make excuses to Preston Dalton. Maybe they would get to see Preston's home way up on the mountain.

But Preston only led them a little ways into the woods.

The shrubs were thick and smelled faintly sweet. Pine needles made the ground soft.

Tell you what, Preston said. Let's set down right here.

They sat.

Preston talked for a while. He said school was a waste of time. He meant to quit when he turned sixteen and do something to make money. He wasn't sure what exactly, but he had some ideas. Also he meant to have him a good-looking woman. He knew what a woman liked, he said. Then he was quiet a minute. Joe Mack asked him if he'd ever had a woman. Leon wasn't sure what having a woman meant, but he understood from Preston's grin that the question was a good one.

Wouldn't you like to know, Preston said. I'll just bet you'd like to know, wouldn't you. You all want me to tell you what it's like, don't you. Sure you do. I was just like you when I was your age. It's a natural curiosity.

To Leon, Preston was never their age. Ever since he could remember, Preston had been bigger than anybody. And he always knew things—not things they learned you in school, but things you wanted to know about. Girls, for example. Women. How to catch a frog, how to skin a rabbit.

Preston's face grew serious. He sat with his legs stretched out in front of him, not crossed like the rest of them. He had been leaning back on his hands, but now he sat up straight and spread his legs wide, moving his hands to his hips, then, to Leon's astonishment, to his crotch. He was unbuttoning his pants. Next thing you knew, he had reached in and pulled out his ding-dong.

You all got you one of these too, I'll bet you, don't you, Preston said. Less you're a bunch of girls. You ain't a bunch of girls, are you? Naw, I didn't think so. How about you, Elvin. Are you a girl? No? Joe Mack? Naw, I didn't think so. Leon? No? Well, then you got one of these just like mine, don't you.

Joe Mack was the first to begin unbuttoning his pants. Leon was next. Elvin hesitated.

What's the matter, Elvin, Preston said. You leave yours at home this morning?

Elvin turned red as a beet, but he unbuttoned his pants then, like the rest of them.

Leon tried not to look at Preston's ding-dong, which, he believed, was bigger and longer even than his daddy's. Why, it looked like a fish. His own was small, and he worried that it might never grow any bigger. It seemed scarcely bigger than a worm, or your little finger. He felt better when he saw that Joe Mack's wasn't any bigger than his, and Elvin's was actually smaller.

This here is what a woman likes, Preston said.

He began to touch himself. It looked a little like he was petting that thing. It might have been a pup he held in his lap. Then it began to grow before your very eyes. Leon couldn't help looking.

You can do it too, Preston said. You got the same equipment. Just touch it real soft at first. That's the way a woman does it.

Leon looked at Joe Mack. Joe Mack looked back at him. Should they be doing this, Leon wanted to know from Joe Mack. Joe Mack looked away and began to touch himself the way Preston showed them. So Leon did the same. Elvin was doing it too.

Feels good, don't it, Preston said.

It did. It was a little like the feeling you got shinnying up the flagpole. Leon had noticed that just a little while ago, purely by accident, and hadn't told no one about it, shinnying every chance he got. It sure beat playing baseball.

Joe Mack had a pained expression on his face. He wasn't getting a bit bigger. Leon was, though. He didn't need to look, he could feel it, he could feel that nice aching. He was touching harder, squeezing it between his thumb and first two fingers, up and down, up and down. He heard Preston breathing heavily. He saw Elvin smile and close his eyes. Joe Mack was working hard but seemed to have no luck. His forehead was shiny with sweat. Birds sang. The sky appeared to turn sideways. He had to close his eyes. Lord help!

When he opened his eyes, he saw that Preston had stopped. Elvin said, Oh, shit, God damn, and then he stopped too. Preston laughed, and buttoned up his pants. Joe Mack had his eyes closed and was still going at it, that pained look on his face, as if he was gritting his teeth. At last he gave a big sigh and stopped. There might have been tears in his eyes.

Did you feel it, Preston asked.

Sure, Joe Mack said. It was swell. God damn.

Elvin just grinned and his face was red. He turned away from them to button up his pants. Joe Mack did the same. Leon had to stand, and when he did, so did the others, even Preston Dalton. They made their way quickly through the underbrush and to the road. Preston began to whistle. He had the prettiest and fanciest way of whistling you ever heard.

Blessed are they that mourn: for they shall be comforted. Blessed are the pure in heart: for they shall see God.

He had not wanted to come here this morning. It seemed to him enough that he was staying in her house, the house her other husband still paid the rent for. It never felt right, and he wished he might now and then go back to the CCC barracks. In the dark of her bedroom she reached for him as if in a hurry. It wasn't how he thought it would be. He wanted to turn the light on and look at her, but was too embarrassed to ask. Oh, she got him going all right, but afterward turned right around and went to sleep, just when he felt like having a cigarette and talking about all the things that had happened to him that week on the WPA, some of the jokes he had heard and the clever remarks he'd thought to make on different occasions. He wasn't such a dull fellow, if she'd only give him a chance to show her.

On Sundays he lay around the house—her house and that other man's—and read the funny papers in the *Sunday Oklaho-*

man while she occupied herself with the baby, which was walking real good now and quite capable of snatching the funnies right out of your hand. Sometimes her sister Johnnie came over, the two women sitting in canvas chairs out in the tiny backyard, talking a steady stream at each other while the baby banged on pots and pans.

The night before the funeral, the baby wasn't there. She had been taken to Cora Mae's mama and daddy's. Leon stayed in Cora Mae's house all by himself. He sat on the porch until it got dark, then walked around the block. Really, he didn't want to go in that house. He would've liked to go downtown and go up in that tall bank building that Darrold Peters had showed him, with the slide that dropped right down the center of it, an inside fire escape, thirty stories or more. He would climb those thirty-some-odd flights, no complaint, and then go look out the window, just as they'd done that Saturday when, later, he'd first seen Cora Mae at the Arcadia Ballroom. The view would be different at night, the air cooler. He could look as long as he wanted to, and then go find the door to the slide. That slide hadn't frightened him a bit, and it wouldn't at night either. In fact it would be just the same at night, no windows anywhere along the way, dark and cool as you go down.

He walked around the block three or four times, pausing only to look across to the few lighted windows of Mount St. Mary's (couldn't see any of the nuns), then went into the house. Cora Mae wasn't here. He would see her in the morning, he had a appointment at Street and Draper's, she would have on her wedding dress. Why did it feel like she was here then. He turned on every light in the house. Alone, he was surely alone. She had a radio, but he didn't care to turn it on.

He went to her bedroom. Supposed to be *their* bedroom, his and hers, but he never thought of it as anything but hers. The bed she'd shared with her other husband, the dressing table with its row of little jars and bottles, the mirror she had seen herself in, her jewelry box with the diamonds and rubies and rhinestones he'd so admired when he first saw her in the Arcadia Ballroom.

He lay down on the bed, rolled to her side of it, got up, opened the wardrobe. What he wanted was a memento. Tomorrow or the next day Johnnie and Mrs. Monroe would come over here and take everything away. He could just see Johnnie wearing Cora Mae's pretty black dress, her rhinestones, her little hats, her white gloves. Mrs. Monroe would take table and chair, the throw rug, the curtains. He felt that he deserved something for his trouble.

The radio came to mind, but he couldn't imagine carrying that thing around.

On her dresser she had a framed photograph of her sister, another of her mama and daddy standing in their front yard. Those wasn't any use to him.

The baby's bed looked soiled, a rubber ball in one corner, a bottle with a nipple on it in the other, some milk still in it.

He opened the wardrobe and took out the black dress, laid it on the bed. The silvery flowers around the top, just above where her breasts would be, flashed as brightly as when he'd first seen her. It made him nervous to look at it, and he put it back.

In the chest of drawers, everything lay folded and fresh and spicy smelling. He began to take out her underthings, the silky slips, the stockings. Underpants last of all.

Then he came to the envelope. It wasn't even sealed. A fat brown envelope with a bunch of photographs and some letters. Not as many photographs as it had seemed at first, maybe a dozen or so, and just two letters. A couple of the pictures was of her sister, one with a man he never saw before, the other a studio picture marked H. C. Green on back, with the date March 10, 1931. Johnnie was younger in this picture than in the one Cora Mae had on her dresser. She wore her hair shorter then and had on a pearl necklace and pearl earrings. There was a picture of her little sister Sarah Jane, unless it was Cora Mae when she was just a girl. It might have been Cora Mae, that peculiar smile, like she was about to ask you a question. There was some more of her mama and daddy, and another that he knew was Sarah Jane, in her Sunday school dress and

with a big bow in her hair. None of these was any interest to
him.

Here was one, though. Here was the one he knew he'd
find. The man with the thin moustache, the sly grin. He stood
out in the open, no building of any kind in sight, no trees or
bushes, grass growing in clumps. Squinting, the man looked
away from the camera, as if trying to see something off to his
right somewhere. He wore a double-breasted sport coat, unbuttoned, and no tie. He had his hands in his pockets. Leon looked
for a name on the back, but there wasn't anything written
there. It had to be the husband. He knew it was the husband.
She probably took it out and looked at it often.

One of the letters was dated November 7, 1924, Cromwell,
Oklahoma, and began: My Dear Darling Daughters. Something
her daddy had written when he was away on a trip. But the
other had nothing at the top except Hello Sweetheart. Leon
read this one straight through, though the handwriting was
hard to read.

*Honey, I sure am missing you. I am not so far off really, just
in Texas, but it seems like the end of the earth because you
are not anywheres near. The car runs just fine, no troubles,
just a big dust storm forced me off of the road for a spell. They
all say this country is going under fast account of the dust,
people leaving in droves. Same in W. Okla., a crying shame.
Some say it is the dust, some say the bankers. I wouldn't
know, but I see them going, I pass them on the roads all the
time, you have to wonder how far they'll get and if it will ever
be any better. You take good care of yourself I am sending you
a big hug and a kiss and hope you are thinking of me now and
then and are not too lonesome. Your loving husband Don
Temple.*

She never stopped loving him. Why else would she save
such a letter as that. Leon put her clothes back in the drawers,
just the way they was, and the envelope with the pictures too,
only he kept out the letter and the photograph of her former

husband, Don Temple. He might put them back before tomorrow or he might just keep them for a memento.

In the meantime he'd set them on the nightstand, there, the photograph propped against the base of the lamp, the unfolded letter next to it.

Then he took off his clothes and climbed into her bed.

Awake, Leon saw the man's face first thing and didn't know where he was. He looked around. Her dressing table, the rows of jars, the hairbrush and comb. Her mama and daddy's picture, just visible on the edge of the dresser, as if they peered down at him. This is how she would feel, he thought, waking, surrounded by herself. She would look at the man's picture first thing, just as he had done. Maybe she would take it in her hands, bring it close to her. Then reread the letter. Hello Sweetheart. Honey I sure am missing you.

He remembered what day it was, what he had to do. He had told the funeral man he would be there to see her. Why had he agreed to such a idea!

He dressed hurriedly. Might as well get it over with. And, after all, he didn't need any more time in this house. He'd never spend another night at this place. He gathered up the smattering of clothes that he'd kept here, a couple of shirts in the wardrobe, some undershirts and socks tucked away in the bottom drawer of her chest of drawers. His shaving gear in the bathroom. Put it all in a brown grocery sack. Should he shave? Naw, no need, such light whiskers. He just shaved yesterday. He looked sternly at himself in the mirror. The CCC dress uniform with its brass buttons, green tie, shiny lapel insignias, suited him to a T. You could easily take him for a soldier in the regular army. Hadn't Cora Mae done that very thing when he first introduced himself. He told her, eventually, that he was in the CCC. It was like the army, he explained. Only difference was in the CCC, instead of huns you fought a desperate horde of animals that the farmers couldn't kill by themselves.

He wished she hadn't asked him what the animal was.

How, she asked, could you hit a bunny rabbit over the head.

Some day he'd be in the regular army.

He went back to her bedroom where he saw that he had left the photograph and letter on the nightstand, the bed unmade. Let the bed stay messed up. Mrs. Monroe would take the sheets anyway. He folded the letter and put it in his pocket, along with the photograph.

Then he left for the funeral parlor.

And there shall be no more death, neither sorrow, nor crying, neither shall there be any more pain: for the former things have passed away.

Mr. Udell. Won't you come right in.

It was the man with the real white teeth. He wore a dark blue suit with a flower in the buttonhole. He was half a head taller than Leon, maybe close to six feet, and he leaned his head to one side when he talked. His suitcoat fit him tight and his tie was bunched up, though held in place by a silver clasp with a pearly cross on it.

This way, Mr. Udell. Or should I say Private Udell?

Mister.

Mr. Udell, she's ready. A prettier bride never breathed.

It was a small room, hardly space enough to turn around in. A gold cross hung on one wall, pictures of Jesus in gold frames on the others. In one picture Jesus, in a white robe that dragged on the ground, carried a long pole and looked down on some children that was clamoring around him for attention.

Cora Mae's coffin was pressed up against the wall. Last night they'd had her in a light blue dress with a string of pearls around her neck. The coffin lining was a dark blue, and Cora Mae's sister Johnnie had said this outfit would match it nicely. When he had recommended the wedding dress, her mama said, Over my dead body. Her daddy stepped out of the room.

Her mama was a large woman, taller than Leon and for sure heavier, but he stuck to his guns. In the end they agreed to dress her in the blue outfit for the viewing and in the wedding dress for the burial. The funeral man said it was highly unusual to dress up the deceased twice and would mean extra expense, but he could certainly arrange things however they wished.

I won't pay a cent extra, her mama said.

Send me the bill, Leon said. And be sure and put her white shoes on her. She liked them shoes.

He felt good winning the argument, but then remembered he had no money. Well, maybe they'd let him pay on the installment plan, the layaway. You couldn't squeeze blood out of a turnip.

He shivered at the sight of that wedding dress. Had it been that white on their wedding day? The hat looked like a crown, and the white veil over her face just made her red lips look redder.

Cora Mae, I got a bone to pick with you.

He was mad at her. Look here, he wanted to say to her, look here what I found hid under your clothes. This photograph—it's him, ain't it. And look here at this letter. Why was you saving this letter if you didn't love him anymore, answer me that. Who do you think is here with you now, him or me. It's me, ain't it. Me, not him. You think he cares enough about you to even show up for your funeral? Answer me that.

When *is* the funeral, Leon, she seemed to ask him.

Why, this afternoon. Three o'clock. By four o'clock you'll be in the ground, laid to rest.

And what time is it now, Leon.

Why, it's nine o'clock. Five minutes after nine in the morning.

Then he's got six hours to get here. He could be a long ways off and still get here in six hours, Leon.

He won't come. I'm the one that's here and you don't have a idea in the world where he is. He won't be here.

We'll see, won't we.

The man wasn't going to come and that was that. Who-ever heard of such a idea. This is what was true: him, Leon Udell.

He realized he had the photograph in one hand, the letter in the other.

Well, here then, he said, take them. What good are they to me.

He dropped them into the casket. No, that wouldn't do. Someone would see them at the service and take them out. He wanted her to have them, though. It seemed to him now that that was why he had brought them here, to give them to her. He wanted her to have that picture and that damn letter. That's what he had meant by taking them out of her drawer.

Here, he said. You take them then.

He tried putting them along the side, but couldn't get them pushed down far enough, and so he slid them underneath her waist, where he could work them back and they wouldn't be seen. She lay on a satiny smooth sheet and her dress was also smooth. The photograph, being stiff, slid under easier than the letter, but he got them both where they wouldn't be seen. He hoped she was happy.

She didn't look happy. Didn't look like she cared, one way or the other. She always looked that way. There was no figur-ing her out.

Sure looked pretty though, in that wedding dress. If he was to die now, in the next six months say, he wanted to be buried in his CCC uniform. He felt healthy, however.

The thing was, now that he'd given her the photograph and the letter, he didn't have no memento. He wished he'd thought to take something of hers from the house. Well, too late for that. He sure wouldn't go back to that house. Didn't she owe him something for his trouble, though. Maybe he could take her veil. Naw, he liked seeing her in that veil. The little bouquet she clasped in her hands? That wasn't of no conse-quence.

He considered the shoes. Did she have them on her? He'd told them to be sure and put them on her. It was part of what he paid for. They better be on her. He raised the hem of her gown. Yes, by God, she had them on. They was white, just like the dress, and might have been made of satin too. They had little bows on the toes, studded with sparkling jewels, and high tapering heels.

He had no use for them, no, but the point was, she owed him something. He happened to know that she had liked those shoes. She wore them sometimes for no reason at all. Ain't those your wedding shoes, he'd asked her once. I wore them at my wedding, yes, she said.

My wedding! As if he'd had nothing to do with it.

Why are you wearing them now, he had asked her.

Because I want to, she said. I like them.

Wasn't no skin off of his back!

They wasn't so easy to get off of her. He put them in the paper grocery sack, stuffing them down beneath the clean undershirts and socks he'd brought from the house. Then he pulled the gown back down over her bare toes—they hadn't even bothered to put stockings on her. Unless somebody bent down to look, they'd never know the shoes was gone. Showed that this funeral parlor was on the up and up, he guessed. Another parlor might have thought they could get away with leaving off the shoes. Of course, they hadn't put on her stockings.

He felt he had stayed long enough.

Her mother a devout pilgrim and for many many years a faithful Baptist, her father a decent, hardworking man. An older sister who mourns the loss, a younger who will long grieve, a little brother who preceded her in that ascent from this vale of sorrow and strife and who welcomes her with open arms and a glad heart.

Surely the man was nearing the end. Her sister Johnnie, sitting next to Leon, held a handkerchief to her face, dabbed at her eyes. Cora Mae lay still, didn't give a sign of having lost her shoes. Well, but didn't she have her letter and that picture. A fair trade.

He had taken the paper sack with his clothes and her shoes in it down to the Union Bus Station and put them in a five-cent locker. He would pick them up later and take them with him. He didn't know where he'd go, but he wouldn't go back to her house. He got back from the bus depot in plenty of time. Even had time before leaving to get him a hot dog. But he wasn't the first to arrive. When he walked into the chapel, he saw that a man stood over the casket. Was it *him*? Could it be that she was right and the other husband would show up, as if for pure spite. But no, this wasn't Don Temple. This fellow didn't have no little moustache. Leon stood next to him, introduced himself.

I'm the husband, he told the stranger, extending his hand.

The stranger took the hand, but didn't hardly squeeze at all. Leon's daddy had taught him to squeeze hard when he shook hands. He'd had to practice it by shaking his daddy's hand ever so often. Grip, Daddy said. Harder! Is that all you got, boy? Come on, now. And they squeezed until one of them called it quits—usually Leon, the bones in his hand about to bust, but he was getting better at it, and he liked to imagine that someday he would force the old man to his knees.

The stranger let Leon shake his hand, but volunteered no information. The fellow might be a little slow.

I said I'm the husband: Leon Udell. Didn't catch your name.

Mildren, the man said. Mildren Bagley. I'm her cousin. I rode on a train all night to get here.

Where from.

Arkansas.

Arkansas. I'll be. That's where I'm from. Whereabouts in Arkansas.

Danville.

I'm from Greenwood myself. Near Fort Smith. I was only married to her for two months and now this. A heck of a note, ain't it.

Others began to come in, and Leon thought that this cousin should step aside so as not to be mistaken for the grieving husband. Much to Leon's embarrassment, tears was falling from the cousin's eyes. Leon figured on shedding a few tears himself, for there was nothing fair about none of this, and didn't he have a right to grieve with the best of them. But just now his eyes stayed dry.

Maybe we'd best sit down now, he told the cousin, and let the others have a look.

But the man stayed, his shoulders shaking he was sobbing so.

In the lobby Leon mixed with the other mourners, offering his hand freely and gripping firmly. He didn't know these people. They were members of her mother's church, he figured, powdery smelling ladies with black lacy veils over their faces. I'm so sorry, they told him. Oh, that's all right, he said, it wasn't your fault. It wasn't no one's fault that he could see. Just a common cold, as far as you could tell, and then that coughing and the sore throat that wouldn't quit.

Nobody that fit the description of the former husband appeared.

Cora Mae's mama and daddy came in. They had the little sister Sarah Jane with them, but not the baby. He guessed they'd left it at the neighbors'. Cora Mae's mama was not crying. She looked like she always looked, almost frowning but not quite, as if she had a thing or two to say to you but it could wait. She had on a black sacklike dress, a little hat and veil like the other ladies wore, and she carried a small white box in one of her hands. Mr. Monroe, wearing a white shirt and black bowtie, and a suit that looked two sizes too big, trailed behind her a little. Sarah Jane, though only nine years old, looked almost as tall as a grown-up lady next to her daddy, who was short, even shorter than Leon. Sarah Jane waved at him, but her mama and daddy scarcely nodded their head in his direction.

He turned away from them. At the chapel door he saw that the cousin still was standing alongside Cora Mae's open casket, looking down on her with his hands clasped behind him. The chapel was filling up. Although a electric fan had been set up in the lobby, it was plenty hot. A hundred degrees in the shade, as they said.

Johnnie came in right after her parents, escorted by a man that Leon thought at first might be Don Temple. Like Don, he had one of those thin moustaches such as movie actors wear, but he was a little too short to be Don, and slightly heavier. He looked flashy for a funeral, his suit a summery bluish gray, his silky tie blue with yellow polka dots, clasped by a shiny gold bar that had a big ruby stuck in the middle of it.

Leon, Johnnie said, this is Bill Haynes.

I've heard about you, Bill Haynes said, flashing a grin, extending his hand. Pleased to meet you, though sorry about the circumstances.

It's all right, Leon said. It ain't your fault.

Behold, I show you a mystery. We shall not all sleep, but we shall all be changed.

The preacher like to never stopped. It was very hot. Leon sat by the aisle, with only Johnnie beside him. She kept her distance, but he felt the heat she gave off and smelled her sweet perfume. Next to Johnnie, her boyfriend, Bill Haynes, fidgeted with the program card. Cora Mae's parents, with Sarah Jane, sat on the other side of the aisle, behind them the tall Arkansas cousin and the old ladies from Mrs. Monroe's church.

Seeing the mourners pass one by one in front of Cora Mae's casket, Leon worried a little, but no one seemed to notice that she didn't have her shoes on. Mrs. Monroe opened the white box she'd been carrying and pulled a Bible out of it. This little Bible, black with a gold zipper to keep it shut, she set down in the casket, and Leon hoped she wouldn't see the letter and photograph he had slid beneath her.

She didn't. Or if she did, she didn't let on. She put the Bible down and walked away.

He was the very last to look, right after Cora Mae's daddy, who leaned down and kissed Cora Mae on the cheek.

See there, he thought, it's all over but the shouting and he didn't show up, did he. I'm here and he ain't. Doesn't that prove something to you, doesn't that go to show.

He had more to say, he wanted to bring up the matter of his weekly paycheck from the WPA, his hard-earned money and where it went, but the funeral man, his white teeth shining, said it had come time to go, and closed up the casket.

Was this when he was going to cry? He turned and began to walk towards Cora Mae's parents, who were almost to the door. The rest of the crowd would be waiting outside, lined up in their automobiles. He would ride in the limousine with Mr. and Mrs. Monroe, Johnnie, and Sarah Jane. They had told him that yesterday. The hearse would lead the way.

There was more. There had to be more.

He heard a rustling noise behind him, turned and saw the four pallbearers lifting the shut coffin. They were strangers. He didn't know a one of the pallbearers. He had tried to get Darrold Peters from the CCC camp to be one of them, but Darrold already had something to do today. They were men Johnnie knew from the store downtown where she worked, and a deacon from her mama's church.

What was he doing here, with all these people he didn't know and who didn't know him. It was between him and Cora Mae, and then Cora Mae wasn't no more, and here he was with all these strangers.

Wait a minute, he said to no one in particular.

Cora Mae's daddy stopped in the doorway and looked around.

Wait just a minute here, Leon said, and now he was facing the coffin again, which the four strangers had just then lifted.

You put that thing right back down, he told them. Don't you move it another inch, you hear me.

The men stopped, one of them almost losing his grip. The funeral man began to walk towards Leon. He wasn't smiling now. His shoes squeaked. The men put the coffin down.

It's all right, Mr. Udell, the funeral man said, touching Leon's elbow. I know what you're feeling, and, believe me, I understand.

It ain't all right, Leon said, and you don't understand.

Well, then, maybe you can tell me. We can't keep people waiting. What is it, Mr. Udell.

Leon saw that Cora Mae's mama had come back into the chapel. Sarah Jane too. Sarah Jane took hold of her daddy's hand. The mama stood behind them, tall and breathing deep, her black hat shining like metal. She had lifted the veil and was giving him an ugly look.

What was it he had meant to say. He remembered only that it didn't concern them. It was between him and Cora Mae. He wanted these people to know that, and to know she was his bride. He loved her. Sure, he loved her. Didn't they know that. Why, it was as plain as the nose on your face. He loved her like he loved his own life. He loved her from the first time he laid eyes on her. He would love her forever. That's what he wanted to tell them.

Maybe it was the way the funeral man begun to squeeze his arm. Maybe it was the expression on Mrs. Monroe's face, or the way that hat seemed to snatch up the light. Maybe it was the way Sarah Jane reminded him of Cora Mae. Maybe it was the way Mr. Monroe released her hand and began to move towards him. Maybe it was the thought that Cora Mae's other husband still had time to show up.

He wasn't right in his head and he knew it. Something dark was getting darker. It's a cheat, he heard himself saying. We been cheated. She ain't got her wedding shoes on. She ain't got *any* shoes on her feet. She is barefoot as the day she was born, and not a one of you was going to say a word, was you. You was going to let her go to her grave in her bare feet. Well, I'll tell you what. It makes a difference to Leon Udell. Yes, it does. It ain't a matter of money. I will pay what I owe. It is a matter of . . . it's a matter of honor, that's what. It is a matter of honor, sure as the day I was born. You can't cheat Leon Udell. No, sir!

Then he remembered. He was the one that stole the shoes. He sat down. It was hard to breathe. He needed more air than they had in this room. For a second there he imagined that the pallbearers had surrounded him, hogging the air, but they had kept to their places. It was Cora Mae's daddy that looked down on him. He had thick black eyebrows and little black eyes set back deep.

Come on, son, Mr. Monroe said. She's gone and there's nothing in the world we can do to bring her back.

Leon felt himself being assisted, gently, to his feet, and led up the aisle towards the door of the chapel. He greatly appreciated the help. He felt weak. He realized he was crying.

Outside, the hot bright air hit him hard. I stole them shoes off of her, he wanted to say to her daddy. I took them myself, and for no reason but spite and meanness. I robbed from the dead. Is there anything meaner.

He didn't say anything. In the limousine, with her daddy next to him and her mama and her sisters across from him, he was facing backwards, aimed at the line of cars behind instead of towards the hearse ahead. He might have talked to her daddy, but not with the rest of them in earshot.

Johnnie commented on the heat. She couldn't remember a worse August.

They're all bad, her mama said.

I like June best, the little sister said. In August you know summer's over and school's about to start.

Leon brushed his cheeks with his cuff, but the hot wind had already dried the tears. Maybe the women hadn't even noticed.

She sure looked pretty in that white dress, he said.

Nobody said anything after that.

The Sunnylane Cemetery was way out on the southeast edge of town. Trees were sparse and small, yet somehow old-looking, worn out. It was high, flat ground. Off in the west the two thirty-story bank buildings looked like gray stubs—Leon couldn't tell which was the one he'd jumped down the belly of.

It wasn't a crowded cemetery—plenty spacious, he'd say, as big as any in Fort Smith and Little Rock, maybe bigger. Cora Mae's grave site seemed almost in the center of it, with a neat mound of red dirt piled high to one side. The mourners had to stand in the hot sun, the dusty wind stinging their faces, while the preacher reminded them that they was all sprung up from the dust and would be returned to its bosom on a whim.

The man had not come. It was sure too late now. He would never be here. Leon felt sorry for him. If it had been him, Leon Udell, why, he would've been here. He forgave Cora Mae for loving the poor man. Looking up from the grave, he seemed to see her rising up into the tall white clouds, bride of his life, beautiful and pure in her everlasting faithless love. *God is in the midst of her,* the fat preacher said. *She shall not be moved.*

TURNPIKE

O

Jane Smiley

IN SEPTEMBER OF 1962, when I was fifteen
and the old man was about the age I am now, he took me
with him to Columbus, Ohio, to talk to a swimming pool company about buying exclusive rights to the manufacture of
their product in our region. Forget the revolutionary cleaning system, the newly designed intake valves. These swimming pools were the most beautiful the old man had ever
seen, in rounded, sensuous shapes set into sculpted, sylvan
hillsides, swept about with brick decking and filled with blue
dappled water. I think he imagined the slopes of Clinton
County and the flats of Illinois, on the other side of the Mississippi, dotted with such oases. At any rate, it didn't strike
me funny at the time, and I was going to get out of school,
and going to leave my four brothers and two sisters behind,
and so I mostly didn't care where we were going or why.

We took his red panel truck, a '55 Ford with a '57 T-bird

engine and dual Hollywood Glasspacks that made a brassy-deep, fluttering sound. No windows except in the doors, the paint job a pure, nickless lacquer. Usually the old man finished off a truck in less than a year. His clothes were always covered with lime dust, and the trowel he carried in his back pocket sooner or later ripped out the upholstery of the driver's seat. And then there were tools and equipment to be hauled from job site to job site. He was not a methodical man, in spite of the lectures on our taking care of his things (our things being his grandthings, or things-in-law, and therefore subject to equal interest on his part). But about this panel truck he was obsessive, never driving it, and demonstrating every two months that a fastidiously polished OLD finish had far more resilience and deep-down beauty than was possible with any NEW finish. "Like leather or fine wood," he often said.

We left after work Thursday. He crossed the Mississippi into Illinois, and drove through Morrison, Sterling, and Rock Falls. The coming of autumn was not in the hot, dry afternoon air, but in the old green of the cornstalks that lined the road, and their treelike thickness. The rows were so tall and the rural roads so straight and narrow that only the height of the panel truck seemed to lift us out of that tunnel toward the clear blue of the sky.

He leaned his left arm out the window, steered with his left hand. A knob like a small doorknob, white and pearly, was attached to the steering wheel just above the crossbar. He talked without ceasing, ranging over his usual themes: how lucky we were to be our family (healthy, without disfigurement, enough to eat, lots going on all the time), my progress in school (I should always listen to the teacher, speak in the friendly way to everyone, never use swear words), girls (not all girls were like my mother). It was the customary propaganda—rather comforting. Then he said, "You know, it's strange how the two of us haven't ever been alone like this before," and I suddenly saw disadvantages to this trip that I had missed. He intended either to pry infor-

mation out or drive some in. I saw that I had lost the automatic privacy of numbers, and began at once to erect an apparently polite but uniformly deflecting surface of manner. I
said, "Guess so." But he only replied, "How about some
grapes?" and offered me the bag he held between his legs.
The old man didn't have any teeth. Sometime when we were
kids, he had had all his teeth pulled. He had gotten dentures,
but he hated to wear them, and they were always turning up
in unnatural places: on the floor of the truck under some
newspapers, in the dog's bed, outdoors in the grass. He ate
with his tongue, and pretty effectively, too. I don't remember
a meal that he didn't scarf down with the rest of us. After
years of work, his tongue got so developed that it wouldn't
fit inside his dentures, anyway, so that got to be his excuse.
I watched his mouth work and stayed alert for any reference
to the great taboo subject, my size. I had been fifteen for
three months and I stood four foot eleven. We finished the
sandwiches my mother had packed, the cookies, the bananas,
the grapes. Somewhere in Indiana I dozed off.

By the time I woke up at about eight, we were nearly into
Columbus. Bright sunlight washed in through the windows in
the back doors, and the breeze pouring through the old man's
open window already smelled of heat. He had stretched me out
on the bench in the back, covered me with his coat. I sat up,
offended. The sunlight was so brilliant in the front seat that it
sparkled around his silhouette. Immediately, he said, "Let's
stop for something to eat. What are you hungry for?" This
was a question the old man had never asked me. Our family
never went to restaurants, and it was understood that we were
hungry for what we got. The table grace, which went, "For
what we are about to receive, we thank thee, oh Lord," really
meant, "Whatever we are about to receive we are lucky to
have." I said, without thinking, "I'm hungry for a grilled
cheese sandwich, potato chips, a dill pickle, and a Coke." He
took his teeth out of the glove compartment.

He didn't say a word, and neither did the waitress, except

for, "What size?" and the old man said, "Large." The old man
was not exactly himself, or was a self that I had never trusted:
permissive, interested in my wants, easygoing. His usual argu-
ing position was that the seven children, seventeen down to
eight, were lying in wait for him, ready to trick him out of his
rightful authority, and his rightful control over family time,
money, vehicles, behavior, and space. The result of his suspi-
cion was ours: we always assumed that he was lying in wait for
us to break a rule, or worse, some unspoken but revered custom
tenuously tied to the sanctity of family life as handed down
from his father (who was still alive, and whose work in the
family business was its art, building ornate and beautiful
burial vaults at the local cemetery) and developed by him.

The diner we had found was situated not far from the
center of Columbus, but in an unusual area of brick streets
and small, ornate brick buildings. We sat by the window, and
the old man looked out at the brick facades across the street
with professional curiosity. When the waitress brought our
food, he said, "Lots of nice buildings."

"Oh," said the waitress. "This is German Village. Kind
of an old-time place. Gotten sort of run down lately, though."

"They learned that brickwork in Europe, you know. And
see those stone lintels over there, carved with vines like that?"

"Mmm."

"See it? Look at it. Yeah." He grasped her elbow and
pulled her around so that she had to look where he was pointing. I shifted uncomfortably in my seat. Maybe this was why
we never went to restaurants.

"Yes, indeedy."

"Nobody can do that anymore. My dad can do that, but I
can't. See it?" Now he let go of her elbow. Remarkably, she
smiled. She said, "Yeah. I do see it. It's pretty, isn't it?" She
crossed her arms in front of her waist and gazed across the
street, then she said, "Look at that wall over there. That's a
pretty one, too. See the way those bricks stick out in that
checker pattern?"

The old man took his dentures out and laid them on the table. He must have been feeling right at home. He smiled toothlessly up at her. "Nobody bothers to do that kind of work anymore."

She said, "Let me get you a glass of water for those." We sat with the dentures on the table between us for the rest of the meal. The sunlight shone through their water glass, and cast a lozenge-shaped, shimmering shadow across my plate.

We drove toward the Ohio State campus. The old man stopped at a phone booth, then we drove around the Ohio State campus, looking innocently, as far as I then knew, for a particular building. Breakfast had lulled me. I suspected nothing. The building, possessed of one of those bland professorial names, was hard to find. It was sunny, the campus was like a city, and I fell into a meditation on the heroic size of the entrance to the football stadium. When we parked and entered a building, I was lost in my own thoughts. The old man appeared to know just where he was going. He had his teeth in, too. He strode into the office of the chairman of the physics department, and said, "Good afternoon, my name is Martin Sorensen, and my son Ethan here is intending to go to college in optometry, so he's pretty interested in science. I wonder if you could show us around the place." I was right on his heels, thinking about football and digesting my breakfast, and so, when he stepped aside, and I looked up, alarmed, I got a full view of the face of this professor, just as alarmed.

This notion, that I was planning to be an optometrist, had begun as the old man's joke about where all his money was going when the kids (me first) started needing glasses. After he had made the joke often enough, it had turned into a conviction, but so far, the only inconvenient result had been that the old man tended to linger in front of optometrists' windows trying to read the tiny price tags half-hidden on the earpieces of frames on display. No optometrists had been brought home, or even buttonholed on the street, so I had considered myself pretty safe. The chairman of the Ohio State University physics department regarded me. I didn't speak or smile. I was well aware that I looked about eleven years old. The old man continued, "I went to Iowa State, myself, but it's better to look around for the right place, that's what I think." The old man never failed to expose himself, though. He said, "Actually, I only went there for a semester, in refrigeration. It's not like I got my degree or anything." He smiled, and his utterly regular choppers looked big and square, like rows of ice cubes.

The chairman of the Ohio State physics department who, for all I know, was J. Robert Oppenheimer himself, pushed out of his high-backed leather chair and said, "Well, let's see what there is." I was not interested in science. I was interested in cars, music, and sports. We wandered from machine room to machine room, and most of what the professor had to say I didn't catch. But he loved the old man. After a brief demonstration of a laser, they stood there endlessly, each with one hand on the machine, comparing notes on what you could cut, or illuminate, or explode with a beam of light. I nodded and presented my polite, deflecting countenance. The students walking by were, for the most part, serious and sharp featured. I recognized them as older editions of kids I stayed as far away from as possible. I had noticed that in junior high school you were allowed a single liability. Mine was my short stature. An evident interest in science, or friendship with those who were interested, would have been one liability too many. And I still resented being trotted forth and spoken about. But when we came into the sunlight, and the old man rolled his shoulders and removed his teeth, it seemed to me that I was missing something. My excuse was that I didn't need to see it, but my feeling was that missing it was a sign of native stupidity and narrowness of outlook. I got more irritable, he got more expansive. He said, "I gotta call Aqua-Fun and reconfirm the appointment."

The appointment, it turned out, was inconvenient. They would have to put him off for a night, but the president would come in specially first thing the next morning, a Saturday.

Now, added to my annoyance and resentment was an obscure sense of insult. I hazarded to trade upon our recent equality in the diner, and said, "What's the deal? You had the appointment."

"I didn't ask. Let's go to the movies." I said, "Okay," but the sight of him in his nice clothes, his teeth in his shirt pocket, wrapped in a napkin, depressed me. He looked jilted and out of place. He was a man who went to work every day, who had worked for my grandfather since the age of ten, when he started writing up orders for supplies and delivering bills. I didn't want to go to the movies, but I did want to hide somewhere. Right now wasn't quick enough for me to find that comforting darkness, but carved in relief on the facade of the movie theater was a lanky football player, a kicker in a leather helmet. Of course, the old man had to admire it for a few minutes before going in.

The idea of checking the show times and waiting around for the beginning of a film was unknown in my family. You paid your money and took a seat. The movie was over when someone said, "This is where we came in" and everyone else agreed. Certainly, we just walked into this movie, which was, as I remember, *The Manchurian Candidate*.

Movies about brainwashing were favorites of mine. Everyone knew that prisoners of the Germans, and captured spies, like Francis Gary Powers, had to strive to maintain mental order so that they could hang on to their American identities. In the same way that I planned how to get my mother's car or buy cigarettes, I planned what I would do if anyone ever tried to brainwash me. In this case, a man had been programmed by Angela Lansbury to kill the designated quarry if shown a queen of hearts. I thought he should have done what I had done a few months earlier, learned the Pledge of Allegiance backward, and said it over and over to himself. Two or three times during the movie, I grew elated with the brilliance of this tactic as a prophylactic against having your brains washed, turned into a rounded lump resting in your head like bread dough in a bowl. I liked the movie, it struck me as addressing important issues, and when we came out, I had forgotten about the perilous position the old man had me in. I wanted to ask him if anyone had ever tried to brainwash him or anyone he knew, and what his techniques would be to retain his American identity. I wanted to bring out my own idea, about the Pledge of Allegiance, and be praised for it, but I didn't know where I stood. The old man's only evident response to the movie came when there was a line about Columbus— "Good old Columbus, great football town"—and he said in a loud and embarrassing voice, "Iowa's got a good team, too." Since the Buckeyes were away at Iowa that very weekend, his remark was greeted with boos and catcalls.

The father of my fantasies was the sort who demonstrated his golf grip, or suggested good lines for getting to know girls, who had a box of cuff links on his dresser. He was a man ready to dispense the technical information I desperately sought as my interests evolved. This man moved slowly, swinging his long, slacks-clad legs with an air of ironic detachment. He simultaneously took an interest in me and humored me. There would be no passion in our relationship, no worry for my continuing failure to grow on his part and no embarrassment at his being put off by the president of Aqua-Fun Pools on my part. The father of my fantasies could take care of himself, and knew the same to be true of me.

Around five-thirty, we went to Perkins Pancake House for dinner. He ordered meatloaf and I ordered blueberry pancakes. The decor was cream, orange, and lettuce green, and when we were about halfway through our meal, a woman came in the front door, eluded the hostess, and sat down next to the old man. For a long time she didn't say anything, and he kept eating. I wondered if he noticed her. She fit in with the decor, since she was wearing a boxy lime green top, with no sleeves and six big round buttons, and a narrow cream-colored skirt. Her hairdo was bouffant, and her eyelashes were unnaturally thick and black. I thought she was beautiful. When she began talking, it was as if she were resuming an earlier conversation. She said, "The ice cream melted, but Mary said it would re-freeze, since it was just melted around the sides. But you couldn't do anything for the eggs. Half of them were broken at least, and the milk smelled bad, I thought, though Mary said she would drink it." She started to hum. The waitress, who had turned in our direction, smiled and turned away again, think-ing that this woman was with us after all. The old man finished his meatloaf and drank his milk, then sat back in his chair. He looked at the woman, then said, "Can I have the waitress get you a cup of coffee?"

"Oh, I don't like coffee. Can I have a Coke?"

"I guess so." He looked perplexed, embarrassed. When he glanced over at me, it wasn't to make an alliance with me, but to see if I was watching, to wonder what I might be thinking. I looked away, and kicked my feet against the booth.

He said, "Are you with somebody?"

"Oh, no, sir. Not anymore, that's a fact."

"I think maybe you should sit somewhere else."

"I want to sit here. You look like a nice man." Her voice had a droning quality, and the words were distinct above it.

"It's better if you don't sit here. You don't know me."

"But you've got your little boy with you. That's why I picked you. See, I don't want anyone to sit down with me. A lady alone in the restaurant, people get the wrong idea."

The waitress ambled by, curious. The woman said, "Bring me a Coke, please." The waitress glanced at the old man, who shrugged slightly and shrank away from the woman, a sign to me that he was going to give in, to let her keep sitting with us. She relaxed, actually took off her high heels and let them lay gawky in the aisle between the tables. Then, rather languidly but without prurience, she puckered her lips and made a kiss at me, the way women do to babies. The old man, pondering his succotash, didn't see her, and his face looked smooth and despicably innocent to me.

I said, "Lady, you can't just sit down with strangers in a

restaurant. Why don't you go away?" My words sounded bold and straightforward to me, adult, right out of *The Manchurian Candidate.* The old man looked up and barked, "Don't act fresh. You know better than that. Apologize."

I was appalled and ashamed in a way I wouldn't have been in the family, surrounded by the others of my species, children. In the family, the line was always drawn—my parents and my grandparents on one side, children on the other—and the manner in which the two groups addressed one another was highly ritualized. A child never actually said the word "No," never spoke in anger, always used "ma'am" and "sir," never referred to my mother or grandmother as "she." Now the line was drawn again, and a stranger was included whose behavior was evidently wrong, but I was excluded. The old man glared at me. "Apologize."

"No!"

"What?"

"She—"

"Right now." He wasn't kidding.

"Sorry."

"Sorry for what?"

"I'm sorry I spoke rudely."

"That's all right, little boy." The waitress brought the Coke. The woman took the straw out and tongued it. I felt hot from my hairline to my toes, which, I was well aware, only brushed the floor, didn't rest upon it. The father of my fantasies, I thought, would have called the manager and had the woman hauled away, by force, if necessary. She began to talk again. "Don't ask me if I'm with anyone. Just don't ask me. That's all. I've got nothing to say about that, you bet your life."

"You live around here?"

"Boy oh boy."

"Have you got a car?" Now would come the ride home, a small-town courtesy that I considered unbearably tedious.

"I'll say that again." Then she gurgled down the rest of

her Coke and stood up, not looking at the old man. She walked away into another room of the restaurant. She left her shoes. I sat stiffly. He said, "You done? Let's get out of here."

We went to a hotel. It can't have been very late, but we got ready for bed anyway, since he had been driving the night before. Our appointment with Aqua-Fun was at ten. He wanted to shower and eat first, so that we could head back to Iowa as soon as we were finished at Aqua-Fun. He told me all of this as he stripped off his good clothes, laid them neatly over the back of the desk chair, because he would be wearing them again in the morning, and set his teeth in a glass of water on the bureau. I nursed my anger, undressing as emphatically as I dared. He changed into a clean pair of shorts and a clean T-shirt, and got into bed. I put on my own clean underwear, wishing that I had something else, anything else, so as not to appear to be emulating him. He said nothing about the woman, and went to sleep while I brushed my teeth. I turned out the light. Even in those days I had trouble sleeping, and so I arranged myself comfortably on my back, hands resting on my stomach, to wait and seethe. I didn't mind not sleeping then. My wakefulness seemed gloriously private and leisurely, extra hours added to the day that were mine alone. This pleasure, added to my anger, was almost palpable and raised me to a state of unadulterated knowing. With what must have been my third eye, I saw my masterful destiny laid out in a grid of well-marked, well-lit streets. None of them was located in Clinton, Iowa, or Columbus, Ohio.

A long time later, his voice sounded in the depths of the dark room. He said, "You know, when the soldiers in the Roman Army wanted to get to sleep, they would hold their hands out like this." I looked over. His two hands made a circle in front of his face. "Then they would imagine that they were looking at a mouth yawning, and pretty soon that would make them yawn, and they would go to sleep."

I didn't answer. I was too angry to try it, and maybe

fearful that it would work. But I was tempted. I slipped my hands under my buttocks and silently recited the Pledge of Allegiance backward.

The Aqua-Fun buildings were new, and in the most egregious late fifties style: concrete block, flat-roofed, landscaped with parking lots and chain link fences. The only windows were rows of translucent glass brick, and the buildings were painted Aqua-Fun Corporation colors: aquamarine, to waist level, then a narrow stripe of navy, then yellow to the roof. I could tell the old man was disappointed. Aqua-Fun brochures, which he had passed around the dinner table more than once, exhibited much better taste: muted colors, rich plantings, families actually swimming rather than leggy brunettes in bubble hairdos flaunting beachballs. The Aqua-Fun lobby was no less garishly sterile, and the old man paused in the doorway and touched his choppers, undoubtedly wondering if he should bother even to go in. But the president himself came down at the receptionist's ring, and we were committed.

The president's windowless office was another matter entirely. Next to his desk, a friendly wooden table, was a display case that exhibited ten or twelve models of Aqua-Fun pools set into plastic hillsides, and these were interesting enough, but most of the rest of the wall space, and a good deal of the center of the room, was taken up by large aquaria, lit green and teeming with fish. When we stepped into the room, the president turned out the overhead. The tanks became floating blocks of blue and the fish themselves seemed to blaze with color. For sometime, in silence, I followed the old man around the room as he drifted from tank to tank. Mr. Aqua-Fun followed me, gazing with as much intensity as if he had never seen the fish before. I did not even ask questions. This, I knew, was a sight I would never see again. Knowing the names of the fish would not help me see it again. The only thing that would do that was soundless concentration, on the golden shapes, the iridescent blue and green shapes, the red, yellow, and purple shapes, the striped and flecked shapes, the fan shapes and the bullet shapes and the pencil shapes, all of them moving. There was one place you could stand, close to the president's desk, where four or five of the tanks seemed to overlap one another, where the fish darting and lazing about seemed to weave a pattern in the blue light and the darkness. Even the old man was silenced. He asked nothing about cost, water temperature, aquarium construction. He made no suggestions. Sometimes he exhaled deeply.

After a while, they talked business, in the dark, but I concentrated on looking and remembering. I would be the one, I knew, who would be asked to spin out this scene at the dinner table, and the eloquence of my recollection would establish my worthiness to have seen it. When we left, and the president accompanied the old man to the glaring, staring parking lot, I figured negotiations had gone well enough. Alone in front of the building, the red panel truck sat on its wheels as if poised on hooves, every line curved, gleaming, ready. This time, as we drove northwestward, aslant the setting sun, the old man didn't say anything. Between us, on the front seat, sat half a bushel of apples, our dinner, ten cents a pound. Even with his teeth in the ashtray, he could eat an apple down to the strings and seeds. I sat up. Maybe because he wasn't talking, I felt alert, and all the more so as the darkness deepened. The engine spun out a sound that I imagined as a single golden filament stretching back to Columbus and then weaving around and through the town, securing it. He spoke. I said, "What?"

"We're almost to the turnpike. Don't you want to drive? Now's your chance. All you got to do on the turnpike is hold the wheel steady. It's pretty much a straight shot from here to South Bend."

It was hard to know what to say, since I didn't yet have my learner's permit and I wasn't sure whether the old man knew I had been driving every time I could get the chance for about six months, and not only the cars of my friends and their fathers, but his cars, too. The old man was smiling his toothless grin. He was always at his most guileless when he had the most up his sleeve.

I gazed at him. I had never driven the panel truck, and

not because I didn't want to, or couldn't get at it. The fact was, my feet didn't comfortably reach the pedals. "Whatcha waiting for?" he said.

"Well—" I kicked my legs.

He reached down into the foot well in front of me, and pulled some things out of a paper sack, three blocks of wood and a roll of duct tape. He taped the blocks of wood around the pedals and made sure they were secure, then he picked his coat off the floor of the truck behind him, and folded it into a neat square, which he patted into place on the driver's seat. He looked at me, then got out of the truck, and came around to my side. I scooted over. Without glancing at him, I perched myself on the coat and tested the pedals. They were fine. Tentatively, as if I wasn't quite sure what I was doing, I pushed in the clutch and turned on the ignition, then adjusted the side and rearview mirrors. I glanced at him. He was looking at me, but he didn't say anything, and so I let out the clutch, gave it some gas, and eased up onto the road. Second gear. Third. I was going about forty. My eyes were above the wheel, but my chin wasn't. He said, "I'm going in back. Here's some money for when you get to the turnpike." He put it on the dash and hoisted himself over the back of the seat. I put the truck in fourth, and gassed it up to fifty. By the time I got to the turnpike, I could hear snoring, but I didn't feel confident enough to catch a glance backward to see if he was faking it. Somehow, I was driving the prized red panel truck, the '57 T-bird engine, and yet, somehow, he had worked it so that it felt less like a celebration than a penance.

The window was down, but the sill was too high for me to comfortably rest my elbow on it, as he did. Even so, the warm, thick night breezes bathed my face in the smells of northern Indiana: river damp, cut weeds, animal manure, something fleetingly sweet, recognizable but unidentifiable. Indiana was humid: vapors seemed to waft in the headlight beams. I let my foot rest its full weight on the accelerator block. The needle of the speedometer edged up to 82, and steadied there. I imagined myself driving all night, a driving machine, rolling peace.

Northern Indiana is flat, and the first tollbooths were visible from quite a distance, a bright swath of light across the dark highway. It looked like some sort of refuge, a haven of nighttime good fellowship, but I was sure they weren't going to let me pass through the gates. Men in uniforms? Weren't they the next thing to cops? My foot wobbled on the accelerator, but I was precipitated toward the end of my sojourn in the driver's seat all the same. I imagined the toll taker noticing my hesitation from afar as I approached, interpreting it as a guilty conscience. I bit my lip and stepped a little harder on the gas, and then I was there, under the lights, and the toll taker was a woman with blond hair. She said, "Twenty-five cents," and I stood up on the clutch and the brake and reached the quarter out to her. She said "Thank you," and I said, deepening my voice, which had changed already, "You're welcome, and a good evening to you." I pulled away smoothly, and looked in the rearview mirror at her as I shifted into second. She had gone back to reading *Life* magazine. Maybe she thought I was a midget. In the back of the truck, the old man turned in his sleep, knocking something metallic to the floor.

At eleven, after two more tollbooths, where I chatted with the toll takers and made remarks like, "Doesn't seem at all like September yet, does it?" the old man woke up and asked where we were. I didn't know. He leaned his elbows on the back of the seat, and said, "Cooling off a little."

I said, "Doesn't seem at all like September yet, does it?"

"Buggy, though. Windshield is about covered. How we doing for gas?"

Glancing at the gauge and feeling sick were the products of the exact same moment. I hadn't thought about gas in hours. But my luck held. As I looked out the window in a panic, I could say, "It's getting low, but there's a station coming up, and I figured we could make it." The Cities Service sign at the top of the hill beckoned like a halo. The old man laughed, then rubbed his face in his hands and pushed his fingers through his crew cut. I knew he was refraining from complimenting me, as he would refrain from complimenting any other buddy who was taking his turn at the driving. He said, "Well, pull off, then. Maybe they've got some coffee, too."

By Thanksgiving, I had grown two inches. My joints hurt, the small of my back hurt, and my legs ached so that I fidgeted any time I had to sit still. It was hard to walk. I had a big appetite, and special cravings that came and went—I remember a hunger for lots of toast after school was succeeded by a desire for bananas. The weekend after Thanksgiving, my parents went away for a choir festival, leaving the children in the charge of Marie, a student at the local junior college. That Saturday night, I stole the panel truck and took two of my friends and four girls over the river into Illinois, where we smoked cigarettes, drank beer, and got undressed. Afterward we rode around. I didn't need the blocks on the pedals anymore. Marie's fat boyfriend, Howard, saw us on the bridge. It was about ten. He did a U-turn and pulled up behind us. I stopped. He heaved himself out of his white Chevy and came within threatening distance. "You get those girls home and then go home. Right now."

When the old man grounded me until June, he said, "I thought you were through with this kid stuff." His tone was dramatically hurt, as always. As always, it seemed to challenge me not to care, even about the new kind of betrayal I knew I had perpetrated, and I rose to the challenge. Whenever I wanted to go out, I would go to bed, wait until he was asleep, and then ease out the basement door. There was a wanton quality to everything I did that year, since every activity began with misbehavior. What I might have hesitated to try under other circumstances I was eager to do now. I kept growing taller. By June, I was a respectable five nine, and I got my driver's license. Over the summer, I wrecked the Studebaker. My course through high school as a militant underachiever, smoker, womanizer, motorhead, was set. If he had reminded me of our trip, I would have pretended not to recall it.

Even so, I have never forgotten those fish tanks, the way, if you stood in just the right spot, they formed layers of blue light, through which the iridescent fish made threads with their sleepless swimming. Two months later, I would have been too tall to see it just that way; I would have seen it as the men did, from above. Perhaps I wouldn't have described it at the dinner table when we got back with that particular eloquence that not only made the old man pleased with me and glad to have taken me along, but also made me puff up with a new sense of owning things—the sight of the fish, but also the feeling of driving the panel truck and eating out, the sight of the old man with that physics professor and with a woman not our mother, the treasure of having been unequivocally but secretly wronged, and the yawn of the soldiers of the Roman Army. I didn't know what I owned, though. Images of the old man were bright heavy objects, like billiard balls. When they came together, they knocked apart. He had never expressed his own hopes for the trip; perhaps he thought I might see something of him, something worldly that would permit him to be admirable to his son and friendly at the same time. All I saw was an embarrassing innocence that probably wasn't there, and myself, grandly wicked.

A VOICE FORETOLD*

O

John Edgar Wideman

I FOLLOW THE photographer up the stairs. He is a
white boy from another country, with a braided beard down to
his navel. I try not to hate him as we climb, one flight and then
another and another, stopping on each landing to catch a
breath where the narrow stairwell opens two directions to flats
on either side.

He smells as if he sleeps in his clothes, so I keep my distance batting up narrow steps behind him, wondering if someone loves him and how long it takes to get past the stink, if
stink still stinks after you live with it and you're part of
what's high and rotten in his clownish drawers. He clanks.
Like he's wearing armor under his baggy shirt and baggy

*The title and other italicized lines in the text are from a section called
(Prayer) in *The Gospel at Colonus*, a musical play adapted by Lee Bruer and
Bob Telson from various translations of Sophocles.

pants. The strap of his camera is beaded many bright colors—cherry red, blue, yellow, black, green. A Native American design I think, the heads of snakes or fish or birds repeated. And we are single file, Indian style. Barely room for that up these steps. One, two, three landings, where we pause and listen, count to ourselves so we don't make a mistake.

A deep sigh on each floor, a heartbeat's pause to check out halls where scarred, unnumbered doors are sealed tight. October, but summer heat's still bottled up inside the building. Old heat. Ripe heat. I remember the stifling basements of my childhood, carrying my brothers' and sisters' dirty diapers down into the cellar to soak them in tin tubs, wet wash hanging, the funky skins of dead animals I had to duck and drag my face through. Ammonia smell so strong my eyes watered. Sweat dripping as soon as I begin wringing the diapers. I hope I'll be surprised on one of these floors by the odors of good food cooking. Somebody's dinner simmering to drown out the stink. His. Mine. All the bodies that have penetrated the front door and pounded up these steps, scuffing off layers of skin that decompose and hover in the hot air.

The photographer's my guide because he's the one who first thought of coming here, questioned the little boys on the front stoop who shook their heads, each head crowned with a different hippy-dip cap, no, they didn't know what shooting he was talking about here in this building, but pointed across the street where two dudes was wasted last week.

No. No. Here. On floor number five. In this building, where it turns out one of the boys lives, but they don't know. They forget the photographer instantly, busy again with each others' eyes, gestures. One smiles, giggles. His hand flies up to cover his mouth. Then they are perfect see no, hear no, speak no evil monkeys, frozen on the steps till the weather of this strange white man passes. Among the things they don't see is me, invisible, trailing behind him.

He is killed here. They shoot Lester on floor five. You live here and know nothing?

Huh uh. They don't know nothing mister and dropped their eyes as if they're ashamed of him for asking again.

The photographer's a tall ship listing, swaying, sea-smacked, driven by crazy winds. He's my leader. A rock I want to squeeze till blood runs out. He knew about this place, about the murder here. Now, because of him, I know. Proof in his pictures. The picture book/diary I began to leaf through, then couldn't let go, needed to squeeze till the blood ran out.

He asks the boys if they want their picture taken. Without answering they draw together in a pose. For the mirror of the camera they make themselves sullen old men, dare it to come one inch closer. Before I can warn them, he's snapped, click, click, click. He thanks them, waves goodbye and bounds past them into the dark vestibule.

Should I believe what he says? That he hitchhikes north and south, east and west, crisscrossing the country without a penny in his pocket, somehow managing to eat, find places to sleep, buy film for his camera. By any and all means possible. Dependent on the goodness, the evil in his fellow men. Vagabonding, the photographer calls it. Like ancient, raggedy Oedipus with his swollen feet wandering the land, seeking sanctuary. How long has he been on the road? His funk says years. A lifetime ripening.

When a car stops for me I get in. No matter who is driver. How many in car. If they stop, I get in. Rich, poor, young, old, man, woman, black, white. All stop. With all I ride. Sometime they offer smoke, drink, food, maybe place to stay few days. I take. Sometime they ask me to do things. Some things not so nice, but I do what they ask. You know, man. Saves trouble, man. You know. Not always so nice. Maybe not what I want, but I survive. I am still here. I learn much about your country this way.

But this is not a story about him. His Ingmar Bergman accent, the black lilt, slur, lisp, and dance he mimics in his speech, his walk. That I mimic now. His *American Pictures* brought me here. I'm behind him. In his debt. I try not to hate that either. He swaggers the way he may think Buddy Bolden or Big Bill Broonzy swaggered, but he is a pirate ship with the blues, patched canvas, filthy rigging, rotten wood, a shabby thief lurking, tilting, as if this stairwell is a secret cove from which he can pounce on his prey.

Mounting the stairs, I come to a busted window that allows me a view down to the airshaft's pit where garbage is heaped. On top of the refuse a snow of newspapers bleached white as bone. Is the debris thick enough to cushion a fall from this height? From heaven?

I, too, am seeking sanctuary, a resting place, my father's house. *Pity a man's poor carcass and his ghost/For Oedipus is not the strength he was.* This building, these stairs are in East Harlem, where the streets are gold. No one wants to stay indoors in the summer. But even in the sweet heat, if you listen, you can hear winter swirling beneath the sidewalks. A woman imprisoned under asphalt wailing, scratching, refusing to die until she climbs out and faces those who've consumed her children's flesh. Her eyes say she'll survive as long as it takes, and when she emerges into the light of day, she'll ask no questions, take no prisoners.

At last we reach the apartment the photographer brought me here to see. Corinne and Lester's place, gaping open and empty now. I notice bullet holes right away. Like gigantic nails have been ripped from the plaster. No bloodstains. No other visible signs of violence. Just the palpable emptiness of a lived-in space that has been recently, suddenly vacated. Not quite as empty as it seemed at first glance. I imagine other tenants sorting through Corinne and Lester's possessions, tossing what's useless out the apartment's one window. Hear the couple's things splashing in the airshaft's maw. A few items probably salvaged, clothes mainly, perhaps Corinne's saved for her by a friend, perhaps a pocked, cherrywood bureau that once belonged to the people Lester's mother worked for, dragged across the hall, jimmied down two flights of steps, maybe rabbit ears torn from atop a shattered TV before it's heaved

where everything else is going. The apartment stripped nearly
to the bone, except as I lean closer, adjust my reading glasses
on the wings of my nose, pick through the 5 x 7 photo hun-
grily, with the rummage-sale connoisseurship, diligence, and
studied nonchalance of the mob of neighbors looting Corinne
and Lester's bullet-riddled love nest, I notice a clothes rack,
one wheel and leg missing, collapsed in the corner of a closet,
hangers adangle where they've slipped to an end of the pole,
one of those ubiquitous kitchen chairs of bent aluminum
tubing, its vinyl seat and backrest gashed, leaking grayish
stuffing. On the linoleum, scattered sheets of newspaper, mis-
cellaneous boxes, papers too tiny to read no matter how close I
get. A thick board that must have been wedged under the knob
of the front door for safety lies splintered where it landed
when the cops brammed down the door. I know that's the purpose of the board because my father uses one just like it and
half-a-dozen other contraptions to seal himself in every night.
One busted screen, a radiator, a slashed blind drooling off its
shaft somebody stood in a corner by the window then forgot to
toss. Oh abundance. Oh sad toys. When their stuff was raining
from the window the sound must have been like fire crackling
in the pit.

The photographer said they were lovers. Lester and Corinne lived here two years, working together in a kosher restaurant, partying together in the Bandbox Bar and Grill.
Everybody called them the Two Musketeers. If you saw one on
the street you were sure to see the other. They say Corinne's
grief drove her insane. Cops might as well have shot them both
the night they broke open this door still crooked in its frame. A
mistake. Wrong address. Shooting first. Too late for questions
later. Years since the shooting and the photographer continues
to make inquiries about Corinne, in the kosher restaurant, the
street, questioning, when his travels bring him back to the
scene of the crime, the grandmother he discovered after he
learned the story and took his pictures and couldn't shake the
fate of the "ghetto lovers," as he dubbed them, from his mind.

I share his hurt, his compassion, curiosity, the weight of memory he wears around his neck on a strap. Angry I needed him to find this place, this broken promise, angry to be trapped five stories up, at the threshold of the apartment where Lester and Corinne lived.

The lighting of the picture is dismal, severe and vacant as the colorless paint of interior walls and ceiling.

We remain outside, staring in. Him first, then I stand where he stood, in painted footprints, peering over his shoulder, through his skull. His shaggy mane erratically braided like the Rasta beard he wears to his waist. Neighbors sprout like a knot on a wound as soon as cops, wagon, ambulance depart. They mill about, surly, pissed-off, injured, snubbed. Is this always how love ends? They had observed only one rubber-shrouded stretcher loaded into the meat wagon. Corinne half-dressed, half-led, half-carried down. In shock, her naked legs buckling, her eyes unfocused so she stumbled rather than walked, faltering on each landing, fighting the cops who pinned her arms into theirs. Not crazy, not screaming. Her eyes dry and wild. A little scuffle, predictable after a while, on each landing, as she fought to pull away and they fought to hold her. It's as if she's forgotten something crucial, left it behind in the apartment and was remembering on each landing she must return up the stairs to get it. But the commotion lessens with each repetition. The caravan—a cop on each arm, camouflaged SWAT cops behind, uniformed officers and plain-clothes detectives in the lead, nobody had ever seen so many official people all at once, no progress so elaborate as that 3:30 A.M. parade carting poor Corinne away—doesn't hesitate, doesn't change pace or direction. Down, down. Corinne sewed up tight in their midst, in their business that left absolutely no room for hers.

Mize well have shot her, too. Poor child. For all she was worth afterwards.

That black, bowlegged man was her life. When they murdered Lester, they murdered Corinne. Could have pitched her out the window for all she cared. She was dead the second them bullets stole her man. Shame to see a nice young woman like Corinne let herself go like she did. So fast, so fast. Seemed like wasn't but a couple weeks and she's walking the streets like one them pitiful bag people.

What makes it so bad they ain't never done nothing to nobody. Happy living together up in that apartment. Make you feel good when you see them on the street. One day in the prime of life. Next day those dogs come and both them children gone. People in there like roaches cleaning out the place.

I watch Corinne's screaming fill the room. Wave after wave of bullets smack her man back down on the bed. She crouches over him, shielding him. Both hands dig under his belly, trying to turn him, rouse him. She screams one last time. It rises, circles, climbs higher, takes him, takes her spirit with it, leaves her body stretched on a rack of silent mourning. Silence heavy as heat. Strong as stink. Rioting in its invisibleness. A burst of gunfire and her man's gone. Only a bloody mess left on the bed. By the time the cops snatch her off him, her screaming's over. Her grief something quiet, private she will pick up and finger the way her neighbors inspect the things that used to belong to her and Lester.

The photographer disappears inside his camera. To take its picture. A picture of its picture taking. I am alone now, facing a vacant room. I list its contents. Itemize what's missing. How had they furnished this space? A lamp. Where? Bed. Where? A table. Where? TV. Where? In two years they must have accumulated lots of stuff. New and used. Emblems of their fabled love.

After climbing many flights, pausing on many landings, I'm tired. The air feels weighted and thin. Both. Yes. Both. The steps are hard, steep, my heart heaves, pain binds my chest, sticks in my throat. I'm afraid now, with the white boy gone, everybody gone, afraid of what I'll find if I step alone into these tiny, stale, heat-choked, ransacked, death-haunted rooms. I will find my father there. And his father before him.

Both alone at the end. At the top of many lonely stairs. Was this the resting place they'd suffered to find. Sanctuary at last. *Portents, he said, would make me sure of this.*

Have you ever heard your grandfather talk about elevators? How you ride alone in a piss-smelling box and when the door glides open you never know what will be there to greet you. Who will leap in for a joyride. What knife or gun or cruelty waits to spring on you when the door rattles open and he enters or they enter and take over the space, wild boy kings of the elevators, junkie emperors of the old folk in the senior citizens' high-rise—who must ride up and down now that gimpy limbs and frail hearts are failing them, who must push buttons and pray their worst dreams will not jump into the car when the door slides back, will not be waiting in ambush when you step out and the door seals itself behind you, delivering you to your fate. Who wants to hold their breath as the elevator passes each floor, who can resist a gasp or cringe every time the car stops at night and the door sighs open. Who wants to ride with that lung-pinching terror or the terror of exposed blind-cornered outdoor walkways many stories up with only a waist-high guardrail the drugged, crazy ones will pitch you over. My father's father spent his last days in rooms like these and his son, my father, lives solitary, two floors above a shoemaker, in rooms like the ones in this photo I scan, scoured of love.

A voice foretold/Where I shall die. Think of our great cities. Towers of silk and gold and sounding brass as they rise and shimmer in the best light at the best hour of the day for photographing giant splendor and endless allure. These cities, these treasures heaped so high we must erect transparent elevator tubes, spiraling staircases to wind our way to the top, for the best view, pearly bubbles of car, gleaming, free-floating slabs of stair and banister curling, rising. We mount intricately and with awe. Up and up till we are thin as the thin air we must breathe at the mountainous heights we've achieved. Below us the fruited plain. The amber waves. Beams of light so powerful they are visible in daytime, cross and crisscross, fingers searching the sky, tracking it for signs of life, or perhaps lost themselves, programmed to describe lazy, random arcs horizon to horizon over and over again.

Think of the Lone Ranger. The clattering hooves of his mighty white stallion descending nude, hysterical, down, down the many floors, negotiating this narrow, nasty-smelling stairwell at an impossible, bone-busting gallop. And the masked man slumped half on a landing, half on the stairs, bleeding profusely from multiple wounds, every silver bullet spent, six-shooter cool in its holster, ten-gallon Stetson still stuck on his head, boots spit shined, eyes shut behind the slits in the black cloth that camouflages his identity.

Think of endless traffic up and down the stairs, night and day, up and down, wearing out the stairs, the building, the city, the land.

Think of up and down and paths crossing and crossing roads and crossroads and traffic and what goes up must come down and heaven's gate and what goes 'round comes 'round.

Think of what is unseen till strangers come to take it away.

WHILE IT LASTS

O

Susan Minot

BUT YOU CAN'T LEAVE,'' cried Isabel when she spotted Bonnie and George getting into their coats in the bright hall. She hurried toward them, arms thrown down in outrage, knees locked. Bonnie and George smiled at her sheepishly.

"We had a lovely time," Bonnie said.

"Dinner was delicious," said George.

"You two are no fun anymore," Isabel said. "Falling in love is antisocial."

George gazed around him, trying to remember something. Being tall he seemed to regard objects near the ground as things too far away to bother with. "Did you see where I put my . . . ?"

Bonnie smiled fondly.

"You two are ridiculous," said Isabel. She lit a cigarette. "I never should have introduced you."

George wandered off into another room. He was the sort of person who never remembered peoples' names, didn't worry about being on time for a plane. Bonnie was spellbound by his lack of anxiety. Certain worries plagued her—how to get by on her teacher's salary, what was going to happen when the lease was up, how to put something fine in the world. Being near George was like being near a cloud.

Bonnie kissed Isabel on the cheek. She would be happy to stay—Isabel was a dear friend—but she was just as happy to go. She found a special satisfaction in doing what George wanted to do. Was she giving herself up? Was she turning herself too much over to him? She didn't care.

"I'm sorry Roger got here so late," Bonnie said, thinking of Isabel.

Isabel shrugged, but showed that it bothered her. Roger worked too hard. "Par for the course," she said. "You wait, it will happen to you. When the first blush wears off . . ."

Bonnie nodded sleepily, hearing the words from far away. It was hard to imagine George letting work take over. Work, like other things, seemed hardly to touch him. He rarely talked about it. He treated it as something unconnected to his real life, something apart from *him*. One of the things Bonnie had liked about George when she first met him was exactly that: he was not overly concerned with his career. It made Bonnie feel all the more important to him. He was, simply, a person. One felt he would do whatever he wanted, whenever, however he wanted to do it. Earlier in the evening while Bonnie was helping her make dinner in the kitchen, Isabel asked if Bonnie had figured out exactly what it was that George did. Bonnie began to explain but it sounded unconvincing—she didn't know anything about business anyway—and said that Isabel should just ask him herself. "I've tried," Isabel said and one eyebrow went up. "He won't tell me."

"Found it," George said and held up a knapsack. Isabel and Bonnie exchanged a look. The knapsack was torn and stained—how like George not to notice, and not to care! In the knapsack were the mysterious papers that he carted around, from office to office, doing consulting work—Bonnie as a teacher of art history knew little about it. Sometimes he borrowed empty apartments. He had ideas for projects of his own but those were in an incubation stage, nothing yet put into practice . . .

"Rushing back to their love haven," Isabel said. She caught sight of herself in the hall mirror and sucked in her cheeks, plucking at her bangs. "So tell me," she said, "how many times are you going to do it tonight?" She puffed on her cigarette, holding it up near her ear. "Come on, how many?"

Bonnie colored and smiled. She did not know how to joke this way very well. "Just once," she said, trying a flippant tone, but also careful not to gloat. Isabel and Roger had not been having the best time together lately.

George's eyes glittered. He and Isabel joked together often. He was better at not taking things seriously. "All night long, though," he said. Bonnie liked to be near this kind of banter. It made her feel—well—not so serious.

George pressed the button for the elevator.

"How can you leave me?" Isabel cried. She grabbed Bonnie's sleeve but gazed up at George. "You're abandoning me to the elections!" She glanced back over her shoulder toward a glow of candles in the darkness. Past the high candlesticks they could see Roger, tie loosened, leaning back in his chair, holding a cigar up in front of him. The man beside him was nodding, tossing a balled-up napkin into the air and catching it. A woman near them set down cups of coffee. "It could go on all night!" Isabel said with a withered look.

"Too bad," George said, pleased. He put his leather jacket on. "Work tomorrow."

"Work," Isabel said. "I bet you've been getting a lot of work done lately. What do you do—call in sick?"

"Naturally," George said. Bonnie wondered whom he would call.

"Work has sort of fallen by the wayside," Bonnie said and for a moment felt the old worry come back to her—the unread papers, the classes shoddily prepared. Before meeting

George, these things had consumed her. She glanced up at his smooth face—there was no worry on it. She felt how much energy she'd wasted, for so long, on worrying. Her expression softened again, as if drugged.

"You two are ridiculous," Isabel said again.

"And you are wonderful," said George. It was the perfect thing to say to Isabel. He kissed her good night. "Hey, great boots," he said, and she lifted her foot to be praised, "though nothing compared to the legs in them." Isabel beamed.

"I'm glad somebody notices my legs." Then she pouted. The elevator door opened, rousing her. "You can't leave me!" she cried.

"Evening, Isabel," said the elevator man.

"Oh, Mr. Buffy!" she cried. "I want to come home with them. They're in love!"

Bonnie and George stepped into the elevator and waved at Isabel. The door slid shut. "Madly in love!" they heard behind it.

Mr. Buffy spoke, his voice gruff and startling in the humming elevator. "Love is for the birds," he said.

Bonnie glanced up at George and saw that his thoughts were elsewhere—it pleased her to know what his looks meant. He was anxious to get home. With a thrill she realized it was to be with her. "Is it?" she said to the elevator man.

"I'm not saying I wasn't in love," Mr. Buffy said in a low tone. He tipped his ear in their direction, keeping his back to them, his hand on the elevator handle, doing his job. "Twenty years ago. But it doesn't last." Mr. Buffy shook his head.

Bonnie knew this but there was nothing in her heart at the moment that could possibly understand it. There was little place for worry. She held George's hand.

"Not that I don't love my wife," Mr. Buffy went on. "But things change. You'll see. Things get different." He shrugged. "That's why it's for the birds."

Bonnie noticed that Mr. Buffy wasn't wearing his usual uniform. She had a slight pang—of worry for him. He wore a cardigan instead and crimson athletic pants. He had, she figured, not planned on being on duty tonight. Bonnie assumed that something had come up with the regular night doorman and Mr. Buffy was filling in. She felt how fortunate she and George were. Except for classes, she could juggle her hours and George certainly answered to no one. No job would be reason enough to force them out of the house on a cold night. George squeezed her hand and she looked up at him. He had a boyish face; it was unlined. It was a face that had not known hardship. For one dizzy moment, Bonnie felt Mr. Buffy was more real.

The elevator reached the lobby and she and George stepped out hand in hand. Mr. Buffy followed them across the black and white floor, hands deep in his pockets, head lowered. "Isabel," he said philosophically, "she used to be in love."

Bonnie smiled. "Oh, but she is again."

"Sure, sure," said Mr. Buffy. "Every week, every month, every hour, Isabel's in love." Bonnie smiled. Mr. Buffy was right. Isabel selected her boyfriends with an eye to their attributes and inevitably they didn't measure up. This one drank too much, this one had no sense of humor, another was not interested enough in sex. That was the wonderful thing about Bonnie's love for George so far—it didn't have to do with characteristics or personality. She loved him wholeheartedly, no questions asked.

Mr. Buffy stood in front of the glass door with the iron leaf grillwork behind and held the doorknob. But he didn't turn it, he was keeping them there. "That's why it's for the birds," he said. It seemed as if no one wanted them to leave tonight. Bonnie found a sort of comfort in it. It made her feel warm. George was not responding in the same way.

"Well, we'll wait and see," he said tersely.

"But you enjoy it," said Mr. Buffy, speaking in a low voice to Bonnie who was, at least, receptive. "While you can." The door slowly opened.

The night air was cold and sharp. "We will," she said. George's hand was at the small of her back, urging her forward. She let herself be pushed by the force of the hand, sinking back against the authority of it, but there was something which made her uneasy. "'Night," she called back to Mr. Buffy.

Bonnie and George headed off on the sidewalk.

"Because . . ." they heard. It was Mr. Buffy calling after them. Bonnie turned, craning her neck over George's leather shoulder. Mr. Buffy was standing in the freezing cold in his cardigan sweater with one arm raised underneath the stark light of the awning's bulb. He had come out after them with something more to say. But Bonnie would never know what it was: George whisked her around the corner.

Everything was going so fast lately. It was like being in a wave. Normally she'd still be upstairs chatting with Isabel over coffee, taking in the rosy afterglow of dinner. She was, she had to admit, behind at work. A stack of papers she'd put on her desk had, after a couple of days, begun to look permanent, and it was harder to think about moving it. Other things that had mattered a great deal to her a month ago she could hardly recall—it was as if they had become weightless objects and were drifting about in a gravity-free air, no longer of any concern to her. Instead, substantial before her was George's untroubled face.

They stood on Madison and looked down the empty avenue at the lights sparkling way downtown. Not a cab in sight.

George pivoted. "Let's go over to Fifth," he said and strode off on long legs. It was like being in a race. Bonnie wanted to cry out, What's the rush? The other night they'd gone out to a movie with her brother and George had not wanted to get a drink afterward. They had hurried home. George had turned on the TV. Bonnie asked him if there were something he wanted to see and he said, Not really, he just wanted to let his mind wander, just wanted to stop thinking for the day. He had held his arms out to her and said, Come here, and she'd nestled in them while he changed the channel with the automatic device, not having to move. Bonnie thought of that now, of his not having to move and not wanting to think.

"What's the matter, baby?" said George, his voice sweet. "Why the dragging feet?"

His arm came back and went around her. "Nothing," she said. Though it was minor, she was aware of it being her first lie to him.

Later at home—they went back to Bonnie's tiny apartment—Bonnie asked him how was work that day and he said, Fine, with a clipped tone, meaning he did not want to talk about it. But Bonnie was irritated he'd taken her early from Isabel's.

"But what did you do?" she said. "Something interesting? Any detail will do."

George, head against a pillow, kept his eyes on his book. "It was a day at work," he said. "No big deal."

"I know." Bonnie kicked off her boots. "I was just wondering what you do. I realized I don't really know."

"Nothing interesting," he said. "Believe me. If it were interesting I'd tell you."

"But I like to know that it's not interesting," she said, trying to sound encouraging. She sat next to him.

"Well, it's boring. I had a boring day at work. I discussed some idiotic ideas with some idiots." He looked across his shoulder at her. "Satisfied?"

It was not a question he wanted to know the answer to. She shifted away from him.

"Where are you going?" he cried.

"To get ready for bed."

"Come back soon," he said, smiling. The face meant to soften her but she turned away quickly and tried to think of something else. She'd been in a lovely slow dream and she did not want it to end. But once one was aware of being in a dream it was difficult to stay asleep. The thing that kept one asleep was not thinking. She tried to block out the disturbing things but there was a voice, insistent, breaking through the dream membrane. Hurry, the voice said, Hurry.

ON THE

U.S.S. *FORTITUDE*

O

Ron Carlson

Sᴏᴍᴇ ɴɪɢʜᴛꜱ ɪᴛ ɢᴇᴛꜱ ʟᴏɴᴇʟʏ here on the
U.S.S. *Fortitude.* I wipe everything down and sweep the pas-
sageways, I polish all the brass and check the turbines, and I
stand up here on the bridge charting the course and watching
the stars appear. This is a big ship for a single-parent family,
and it's certainly better than our one small room in the Hotel
Atlantis, on West Twenty-second Street. There the door
wouldn't close and the window wouldn't open. Here the kids
have room to move around, fresh sea air, and their own F/A-18
Hornets.

I can see Dennis now on the radar screen. He's out two
hundred miles and closing, and it looks like he's with a couple
of friends. I'll be able to identify them in a moment. I worry
when Cherry doesn't come right home when it starts to get
dark. She's only twelve. She's still out tonight, and here it is
almost twenty-one hundred hours. If she's gotten vertigo or

had to eject into the South China Sea, I'll just be sick. Even though it's summer, that water is cold.

There's Dennis. I can see his wing lights blinking in the distance. There are two planes with him, and I'll wait for his flyby. No sign of Cherry. I check the radar: nothing. Dennis's two friends are modified MiGs, ugly little planes that roar by like the A train, but the boys in them smile and I wave thumbs up.

These kids, they don't have any respect for the equipment. They land so hard and in such a hurry—one, two, three. Before I can get below, they've climbed out of their jets, throwing their helmets on the deck, and are going down to Dennis's quarters. "Hold it right there!" I call. It's the same old story. "Pick up your gear, boys." Dennis brings his friends over—two nice Chinese boys, who smile and bow. "Now, I'm glad you're here," I tell them. "But we do things a certain way on the U.S.S. *Fortitude.* I don't know what they do where you come from, but we pick up our helmets and we don't leave our aircraft scattered like that on the end of the flight deck."

"Oh, Mom," Dennis groans.

"Don't 'Oh, Mom' me," I tell him. "Cherry isn't home yet, and she needs plenty of room to land. Before you go to your quarters, park these jets below. When Cherry gets here, we'll have some chow. I've got a roast on."

I watch them drag their feet over to their planes, hop in, and begin to move them over to the elevator. It's not as if I asked him to clean the engine room. He can take care of his own aircraft. As a mother, I've learned that doing the right thing sometimes means getting cursed by your kids. It's OK by me. They can love me later. Dennis is not a bad kid; he'd just rather fly than clean up.

Cherry still isn't on the screen. I'll give her fifteen minutes and then get on the horn. I can't remember who else is out here. Two weeks ago, there was a family from Newark on the U.S.S. *Tenth Amendment,* but they were headed for Perth. We talked for hours on the radio, and the skipper, a nice woman, told me how to get stubborn skid marks off the flight deck. If you're not watching, they can build up in a hurry and make a tarry mess.

I still hope to run across Beth, my neighbor from the Hotel Atlantis. She was one of the first to get a carrier, the U.S.S. *Domestic Tranquillity,* and she's somewhere in the Indian Ocean. Her four girls would just be learning to fly now. That's such a special time. We'd have so much to talk about. I could tell her how to make sure the girls always aim for the third arresting wire, so they won't hit low or overshoot into the drink. I'd tell her about how mad Dennis was the first time I hoisted him back up, dripping like a puppy, after he'd come in high and skidded off the bow. Beth and I could laugh about that—about Dennis scowling at his dear mother as I picked him up. He was wet and humiliated, but he knew I'd be there. A mother's job is to be in the rescue chopper and still get the frown.

I frowned at my mother plenty. There wasn't much time for anything else. She and Dad had a little store and I ran orders and errands, and I mean ran—time was important. I remember cutting through the park, some little bag of medicine in my hand, and watching people at play. What a thing. I'd be taking two bottles of Pepto-Bismol up to Ninety-first Street, cutting through the park, and there would be people playing tennis. I didn't have time to stop and figure it out. My mother would be waiting back at the store with a bag of crackers and cough medicine for me to run over to Murray Hill. But I looked. Tennis. Four people in short pants standing inside that fence, playing a game. Later, I read about tennis in the paper. But tennis is a hard game to read about at first, and it seemed a code, like so many things in my life back then, and what did it matter, anyway? I was dreaming, as my mother was happy to let me know.

But I made myself a little promise then, and I thought

about it as the years passed. There was something about tennis—playing inside that fence, between those lines. I think at first I liked the idea of limits. Later, when Dennis was six or so and he started going down the block by himself, I'd watch from in front of the Atlantis, a hotel without a stoop—without an entryway or a lobby, really—and I could see him weave in and out of the sidewalk traffic for a while, and then he'd be out of sight amid the parked cars and the shopping carts and the cardboard tables of jewelry for sale. Cherry would be pulling at my hand. I had to let him go, explore on his own. But the tension in my neck wouldn't release until I'd see his red suspenders coming back. His expression then would be that of a pro, a tour guide—someone who had been around this block before.

If a person could see and understand the way one thing leads to another in this life, a person could make some plans. As it was, I'd hardly even seen the stars before, and now here, in the ocean, they lie above us in sheets. I know the names of thirty constellations, and so do my children. Sometimes I think of my life in the city, and it seems like someone else's history, someone I kind of knew but didn't understand. But these are the days: a woman gets a carrier and two kids in their Hornets and the ocean night and day, and she's got her hands full. It's a life.

And now, since we've been out here, I've been playing a little tennis with the kids. Why not? We striped a beautiful court onto the deck, and we've set up stanchions and a net. I picked up some racquets three months ago in Madagascar, vintage T-2000s, which is what Jimmy Connors used. When the wind is calm we go out there and practice, and Cherry is getting quite good. I've developed a fair backhand, and I can keep the ball in play. Dennis hits it too hard, but what can you do—he's a growing boy. At some point, we'll come across Beth, on the *Tranquillity,* and maybe all of us will play tennis. With her four girls, we could have a tournament. Or maybe we'll hop over to her carrier and just visit. The kids don't know it yet, but I'm learning to fly high-performance aircraft. Sometimes when they're gone in the afternoons, I set the *Fortitude* into the wind at thirty knots and practice touch and go's. There is going to be something on Dennis's face when he sees his mother take off in a Hornet.

Cherry suddenly appears at the edge of the radar screen. A mother always wants her children somewhere on that screen. The radio crackles. "Mom. Mom. Come in, Mom." Your daughter's voice, always a sweet thing to hear. But I'm not going to pick up right away. She can't fly around all night and get her old mom just like that.

"Mom, on the *Fortitude*. Come in, Mom. This is Cherry. Over."

"Cherry, this is your mother. Over."

"Ah, don't be mad." She's out there seventy-five, a hundred miles, and she can tell I'm mad.

"Cherry, this is your mother on the *Fortitude*. You're grounded. Over."

"Ah, Mom! Come on. I can explain."

"Cherry, I know you couldn't see it getting dark from ten thousand feet, but I also know you're wearing your Swatch. You just get your tail over here right now. Don't bother flying by. Just come on in and stow your plane. The roast has been done an hour. I'm going below now to steam the broccoli."

Tomorrow, I'll have her start painting the superstructure. There's a lot of painting on a ship this size. That'll teach her to watch what time it is.

As I climb below, I catch a glimpse of her lights and stop to watch her land. It's typical Cherry. She makes a short, shallow turn, rather than circling and doing it right, and she comes in fast, slapping hard and screeching in the cable, leaving two yards of rubber on the deck. Kids.

I take a deep breath. It's dark now here on the U.S.S. *Fortitude*. The running lights glow in the sea air. The wake brims behind us. As Cherry turns to park on the elevator, I see that her starboard Sidewinder is missing. Sometimes you feel that you're wasting your breath. How many times have we gone over this? If she's old enough to fly, she's old enough to keep track of her missiles. But she's been warned, so it's OK by me. We've got plenty of paint. And, as I said, this is a big ship.

TWO STORIES

O

Bret Lott

I WAS AN ORPHAN AT AGE eleven, my mother dead of the 'flu, my father not two months before she passed on having broke his neck on a log just under the water at the bend in the Black River, the bend nearest town where the post oak lay low to the water, and where in spring the light through leaves breaks across the river so that nothing can be seen beneath. He broke his neck right then, right there, with the quick and simple dare of diving into water, and when I was a little girl of eleven with both my mother and father gone, me living suddenly with a grandmother I'd only met three times before, I used to imagine it wasn't the 'flu that killed my mother, but a broken heart at the death of her beloved.

But the truth of the matter was he'd moved into a logging shack a year before he'd broke his neck, and only showed up to our house at twilight on Saturday nights to have at my mother, then to attend church the next morning, his black hair slicked back and shiny with pomade. It was the thick and sweet smell of his hair that woke me up Sunday mornings, me staying up just as late as the two of them the night before, listening through the walls to the mystery they tended each Saturday night, the pitch and twirl of sounds I'd never known before, but knew just the same: my momma and daddy.

Sunday mornings we would go to church, where we'd sit in the pew, me between them, their only child, and after church we would file out of the sanctuary into air even hotter than inside, live oaks thick with gray moss like clumps of a dead man's hair fairly lit up with the noise of cicadas, everyone everywhere fanning themselves with bamboo and paper fans printed with the words to "Amazing Grace" on one side, Psalm 23 on the other. Daddy would shake hands with Pastor, pass time with whoever might want to, all the time his one arm round my mother's shoulder, his hair shiny, little runnels of sweat slipping down his sideburns. He acted the part of my daddy, would even on occasion hunch down and kiss me on the cheek, pat my hair, smile at me, though everyone in the entire congregation, and even those heathens not in attendance, knew they no longer lived together.

Once we were home, he would simply see us to the door, give me the pat on the head good-bye I hated even more than his showing up at sundown the night before, and kiss my momma full on the lips. Then he turned, stepped down off the porch. Without so much as a backward glance or the smallest of waves, he headed off down our dirt road, back to the logging shack not two miles away.

Momma and I watched him go each time, watched until the road took him deep into pine and cypress, the green of wild grapevines everywhere that swallowed him up. I wished each Sunday afternoon that green would never let him go, never give him up to a logging shack and whatever mystery he was during the week, my daddy gone from us for no reason I'd ever know. We watched him go, and only once we could see no more movement, no more slips of white shirt through the shield of green forest, did we go in. My momma always went in first, though it had been her he'd given his kiss to, her who'd given her whole self to him. She turned, her eyes down to the porch floor, and moved on inside. I was always the last one out on the porch, just watching that green, hoping he would not find his way out of there.

The day he broke his neck was a Tuesday, and I was already home from school, out on the porch with my tablet and thick red pencil, doing my figuring for the next day, Momma inside and quiet like every day other than Sundays and our trips into Purvis now and again. Since Daddy'd gone, those visits to town had become ordeals for her, her standing in the dry goods store and touching a bolt of gingham, a tin of baking powder, looking at them as though they were troubling bits of her own history, things she knew she needed but hated all the same. I always ended up taking her by the hand to Mr. Robineaux at the register, her giving her feeble smile to him as I placed our items on the glass counter, him never meeting our eyes but smiling all the same, as though the fact my daddy left us weren't common knowledge.

So that on that Tuesday, when I saw four men through the green of the forest, I was the one to go into the house and take her hand and lead her up from her cane rocker, the one she spent most hours of the day in, and out onto the porch. The men had cleared the trees by then, and I could see them, their hair wet, faces white, jaws set with the weight of whatever lay in the doubled-up gray wool blanket they toted, one man to a corner, the middle sagging, nearly touching ground with each step they took. They were dressed in only undershirts and blue-jeans, barefooted all of them, and I remember taking that fact in, their feet red with the dust of the road they'd walked.

I wasn't afraid, not even when Momma, behind me, whispered, "Oh," then, louder, "Oh. Oh." I heard her take one step back, then another, but there she stopped. The men were close now, off the road and onto our yard, their eyes never yet looking up to us; men I couldn't place from anywhere. I looked behind me to Momma, saw her there with a hand to her face, covering her eyes, the other hand at her throat and holding on to the collar of her dress.

I turned to the sound of the men on the porch steps, felt myself backing up too, the four of them moving toward me and struggling with the burden they bore, the wool blanket seeming heavier than anything I'd seen before. Yet they were gentle with it, eased it up and onto the porch itself and inched toward us, finally letting it down onto the wood with a grace I would never see again.

They stood back from it, four men with hands on their hips, eyes on the heap before us. Then one of them, a man with hair as black as my daddy's, hair flat and wet with strands of it long down and into his eyes, squatted, his elbows on his knees, eyes still on the blanket. He put out a hand, held it a moment above the wool, a moment that would become hours farther on in my life, but then he reached down, took hold of the blanket, and pulled it back to reveal to us my dead and naked father.

His head was bent back from us, so that what I saw first was his throat, already swelled and purple. His face was gone from me, twisted up and away, and for a moment I had no genuine idea in my head who this was, or why he had been brought here. The blanket had been pulled back far enough to bare his chest and arms and stomach and one leg, the edge of the blanket left just below his waist, so that next I saw the pencil-thin line of hair that started at his navel and traced its way beneath the gray wool, disappearing there. He had no hair anywhere else, his skin already turning the milk-white of the dead, his arms and the one leg I could see bent at the joints, him all movement and peace.

"We was swimming," the man with the black hair said, still squatting. He still held the edge of the blanket, and my eyes went to his fingers, watched for a moment as he held the material, slowly rubbed his index finger and thumb together. "We was swimming, and then he just didn't come up. He was jumping off—"

"Stop," my momma let out, her word choked and hard in the air. "Stop."

The man looked up. His fingers stopped moving, his eyes on my momma.

I looked up to her. She still had a hand to her eyes, the other at her throat, and then I moved toward the blanket, toward the body I still didn't know was my daddy. I wanted to see the face, know who it was, and as I made my way toward where I would see him, two of the men who'd carried him here moved out of my way, their hands still on their hips, still not having spoken a word.

I stood next to the man with the black hair, and looked down at my father's face. His lips had gone blue, his eyelids gray, his hair matted and snarled.

The man let go the blanket. I didn't move, not yet certain what any of this meant.

Then he put his hand to my back, held it just below my shoulder blades. The touch was near nothing, only contact.

He said, "Your daddy was a good man."

But the words didn't mean anything to me. I was thinking of Sunday mornings and the smell of pomade, and of me sitting between the two of them while Pastor gave up to God our congregation's prayers, and how my God had finally answered the prayer I'd been whispering to myself while Pastor pleaded for everyone else: I wanted him never to come back.

Here was my reward for righteous, heartfelt prayer, for asking in Jesus' name what I knew would make my momma and me better off in the long run, no matter what it was those sounds I heard from their room meant.

Which is why I reached down and picked up the edge of the blanket the man had let fall, and pulled it back over my daddy, covered him up. The four men were watching me now, waiting, I figured, for whatever might happen next.

I said, "Bring him on inside." I paused, then said, "Somebody go find Pastor, too."

We buried my daddy the next day, him lying out in the room off our kitchen just overnight, time enough for Pastor to have his hand at trying to comfort us, and time enough for my momma to dress Daddy in a bundle of fine clothes I'd never known we had.

As soon as Pastor'd made his way in the door, my momma'd looked him square in the eye, her chin higher than I'd ever seen it, and said, "Bring a coffin tomorrow at noon. Mr. Reeves can bury him out back."

Pastor only nodded, took his hat from his head, held it with both hands. For some reason I thought I could see fear in his face, as though her merely meeting his eyes were enough to destroy him, or as though she'd suddenly become someone else, a woman with standing, bearing, a voice he knew he had to listen to.

She said nothing else to him, though he stayed until after dark, reading to her from the Psalms and Ecclesiastes and the Gospels of Luke and John, first by the light from the falling sun outside the windows, then by the fire. All that time she only sat in the rocker, her chin still just as high, Pastor hunched with the work of recognizing words in a room too dark for reading.

Then he left, his Bible tucked under one arm, the hat in both hands as he backed his way to the door, me standing there and holding it open for him. When he made it to the threshold he paused, glanced down at me. He reached out a hand to me, touched my head, and I twisted away from under his palm, the move some instinct in me. I wanted no one, ever, to pat my head again.

"Jewel," he said, smiling. "You'll be fine." He looked at my momma, still in the rocker. "The two of y'all will be just fine. Given time, and the Lord willing."

My momma gave him a small nod, let her eyes fall back to the fireplace, the dying light there, and he was gone.

As soon as I heard the sound of his wagon making its way into the black green of the forest my daddy would never make his way from again, Momma stood, her chin now low on her chest, her hands limp at her sides, her eyes nearly closed. She stood before the fire a moment, then turned, and I followed her back into her room, listened in the dark while she made her way to her chest of drawers. I heard the low groan the bottom drawer made as she pulled it out, heard her move hands through whatever clothes were in there. Then came the sound of the drawer pushed closed, a small, high scream of wood on wood, and I turned, not certain where she was behind me, but knowing we were moving from there to the room off the kitchen, where the men had laid my daddy on the table.

We moved through the kitchen, this room dark, too, the only light the small bits of flickering red that made their way from the fireplace in the front room. I was leading us, heading for the room my daddy lay in. I could see nothing in there, only black, a black so black it seemed to crawl into me once I was in the room, a darkness that came in through my eyes and ears and skin, and I remember closing my eyes, holding my breath, afraid the darkness would swallow me up. My hand was in front of me, feeling the air for whatever was there, and then I touched rough wool. I stopped.

Behind me came the sound of a match strike, the sudden and awful smell of sulfur in the air, and I opened my eyes.

Momma had lit a candle she'd gotten from somewhere, before me now the heap that was my daddy, covered with the blanket. Across the gray folds and contours danced my own shadow, Momma with the candle held high behind me. My head and shoulders were huge, moved across him, bobbed and jumped with the light from the candle, and I knew I would never be that big, knew I could never move in such fanciful ways, my daddy now dead.

"You go on into the front room," Momma whispered behind me. "You leave us two alone." Then she was beside me, my shadow trailing off the blanket and, I could see out the corner of my eye, taken up by the wall. I was even bigger now.

I stood there a moment, reached to the wool again, took a piece of it in my hand and fingered it the way the man with black hair had. Then I let it drop, looked at Momma.

She had a bundle of clothes under one arm, the candle in the other. The light illuminated her profile, beyond her the black room again. She swallowed hard, her chin down, her eyes never leaving the blanket.

I couldn't recognize her. I'd never seen her before, never seen the hair pulled back and tucked above her neck, the soft curve of her nose, the pale skin of her cheeks. A lady stood next to me, one whose beauty I'd never felt nor could lay claim to, and I knew already she was on her way to dying, something inside me, maybe the Holy Spirit, maybe God Himself letting me know what was ahead, the word *orphan* suddenly too close, loud in my ear.

Missy Cook—that's all we were allowed to call her—was my mother's mother, and lived in Purvis proper, on Drayton Avenue in a big house with windows and drapes and fine china plates we actually ate off of, my momma and me. I'd only met her three times before, a tall woman with gray hair coiled up in a huge bun atop her head. She wore eyeglasses with silver rims, behind them green eyes like bits of broken glass sunk deep into her sockets, boring into us with them like red-hot pokers, an old woman aware of her powers. The last time we were out to her house was just before daddy'd left for the logging shack; the other two times I'd been too small to recognize an occasion. But I'd seen the papered walls, seen the niggers there at her beck and call, seen her furniture and'd been told to stay off of it by the woman who now wanted us to come live with her.

A little after sunset two days after those four men'd brought to us my daddy, we arrived at that house on Drayton

Avenue, and climbed down off Pastor's wagon, the three of us having sat together on the seat, behind us only Momma's rocking chair, our clothes wrapped in bedsheets.

It hadn't been Missy Cook to meet us at the door, but a frail niggerwoman, and once inside and the door closed behind us—another nigger had appeared from around the side of the house and'd started untying the rocking chair, Pastor all the while still seated up at the reins, his eyes straight ahead—Momma turned to the woman, said, "Molly, how are you?"

Molly paused a moment, as if this pleasantry might be some test, her answer either right or wrong. She tried to smile, gave a small curtsey, and said, "I fine, Miss Patricia." She swallowed, glanced up to me, said, "It nice having you back to home here. The two of you," and curtsied again.

"This is true," came a voice from behind us, and we all three turned to it. Then Molly was gone.

Missy Cook was coming down the stairs, one hand on the polished banister, the other at her chest. The frown I'd always seen her with was still there, chin held high, her deep and frightening eyes shrouded even more so by the thin light from the gas-lit chandelier above us. She had on a beige dress with a high, stiff collar that encircled her throat, and I remember touching my own throat, wondering how she might breathe. Her waist was pinched down near to nothing, and I tried to imagine, too, the corset she wore, and how that might cut out breath altogether. She seemed to float down the staircase, the hem of her dress simply dancing about her hidden feet, so that for a moment I thought maybe she *had* died, was in fact a ghost before me, choked to death by the clothing she wore.

I looked down at myself, at what I had on: a pale yellow cotton dress with a row of buttons up the front, my school shoes, no socks.

Then I looked at my mother, who wore a dress much like my own, but long enough so that her ankles didn't show, the dress waist pinched in some. I knew she wore no corset, her shape a young woman's, not the filled and forced shape of the woman who now moved off the stairs and toward us, her hands low and open in front of her, coming to take ours. My momma's chin was high, too, and I saw the muscles in her jaw begin to work, her teeth clenched, and suddenly I recognized the line in my mother's chin, and how she'd held it high two nights before, and why, perhaps, Pastor had cowered in whatever small way he had. She was Missy Cook's daughter.

Momma put out a hand first, and I followed, the three of us forming a small triangle there in her foyer.

Missy Cook hadn't yet looked at Momma, but at me, her hand warm in mine, softer than I had imagined it would be. She said, "I am deeply saddened at your daddy's passing," and I let myself believe her for an instant.

Momma said, "No you are not," and let go Missy Cook's hand, moved past her and to the staircase. She put a hand on the banister, placed one foot on the first step, and stopped. She looked up the staircase, said, "Jewel."

I was still holding Missy Cook's hand, felt her fingers going tight around mine. Her eyes had never left my face.

I pulled my eyes from hers, looked at the polished wood floor, the gleam of the chandelier there. I said, "Yes, ma'am," and she let go my hand. I walked around her and toward Momma, who held out her own hand to me, and the two of us started up the stairs.

At the landing I looked back downstairs, saw Missy Cook hadn't moved, still stood with her back to us. My momma didn't even look.

Later, after we'd gone through the boxes of new dresses stacked in the room we were to sleep in, all of them made of lace and fine linen and pearl buttons, and after we'd eaten the pork chops and cheese grits and okra and biscuits Molly'd brought up to us on that same fine china, Momma and I climbed into bed together, the two of us wearing matching white nightgowns with thin pink ribbons at the wrists and neck. Then Momma climbed back out, went to the gas key at the doorjamb.

But as she reached for it, Missy Cook opened the door, held her hand over the key. I took in a breath, Momma bringing a hand to her face as though Missy Cook might hit her.

"No one in this house," Missy Cook said, smiling at me, though nowhere in her face any bit of joy, any piece of happiness, "will touch the gas. This is my responsibility, and no one else's. Please remember this." She twisted the key, the room slowly going dark until the gas gave a small pop. She pulled the door closed behind her. She hadn't glanced at Momma, but'd only looked at me.

Momma stood in the darkness a few moments, then came back to bed. Once she was settled, I could hear nothing, the absence of sound deafening somehow after living where we had. I wanted words from my momma in the room, wanted night sounds, something familiar to help put me to sleep, and for a moment I even wished I might hear the sounds Momma and Daddy made Saturday nights, something, anything, to fill the dead air in here.

As though she'd felt what I wanted, she whispered, "This is a dangerous place. We have to be careful, or we'll be swallowed alive here."

I knew what she meant, had seen already the power in her momma, in her hands and eyes, in the warm food, the fine clothes, but some part of me, even after seeing whatever darkness lay in Missy Cook's green eyes, wanted to give over to it, to nestle down into the warm bed we were in, to get up tomorrow morning and find a meal already cooked for us, put on crisp clean dresses and live this way.

"But—" Momma started again, and there was a soft knock at the door. A crack of light pierced the room, then filled it as the door opened just wide enough to let in Molly.

She whispered, "It's just Molly, Miss Patricia, Miss Jewel. Come to get you old clothes, take care of them for you."

"In the corner," Momma said, and we both watched as

she made her way to the end of the dresser and leaned over, took the pile of clothing up in her arms.

"We see you in the morning," she whispered.

I said, "Good night," Momma silent beside me. Molly pulled the door closed, and here was the silence again, the dark. I whispered, "What were you going to say?"

But then I saw the color at the window, the faint dance of orange and red across the black glass.

Momma was out of the bed before me, made it to the window first, and as I neared her I could see her black silhouette against the growing color, my momma's hands to the window. Each finger was outlined in an orange that grew brighter even in the seconds it took me to get to the window, stand next to her, place my hands against the cool glass, too.

I looked down at the yard behind the house. A fire was burning down there, about twenty yards back into the rows of pecan trees. The nigger who'd unloaded Pastor's wagon for us stood next to it, and though he was too far away for me to see his face, I could see he had a hoe in one hand, and was leaning on it, the other hand on his hip. He was just looking into the fire, his head down.

Molly appeared beneath us, coming from inside the house and down the back steps to the yard. She was carrying something, and I knew before she was halfway to the fire that it was our clothes, the clothes she'd just gathered up in our room.

The nigger at the fire looked up, stood taller, his hoe at the ready while Molly came toward him. She stopped at the edge of the fire, her back to us, and started in to peeling off piece by piece of our clothes, tossing each garment into the fire. I watched, silent, as she peeled off what I knew was my dress, the one with the buttons up the front, though I couldn't see any of them. Molly held it up, looked at it a moment, the material illuminated, and dropped it on the fire. Thin wisps of flame shot out beneath it, then swallowed it up.

"That nigger," I said out loud.

But Momma said, "She's a good nigger. She's only doing what she's been told."

I turned to her, saw her face flicker with the movement of the fire, the color almost lost on her, and I thought I could see in her profile something of her mother. I said, "Why?"

She nodded at the fire, and I turned back to it. Molly was holding up Momma's dress now. She gave her head the smallest of shakes, turned to the nigger with the hoe, who seemed to shrug, their gestures so small I might have been imagining it all.

Molly dropped Momma's dress on the fire, this time the flames out from beneath it bigger, thicker, and the nigger reached in his hoe to the fire, stirred it up. Sparks lifted into the air, bits of light that melted before they even cleared the trees.

Momma said, "She's doing what she's been told." She paused. "You watch this, because this is for you and me. You and me are supposed to be seeing this, supposed to be standing right here and watching it all." She stopped, and Molly dropped in the last piece, one of Momma's old thin petticoats. "Somewhere in this house Missy Cook's watching this, too. There's not anybody in this house, maybe not on the whole street, who's not watching this. But it's for you and me."

Then the nigger dropped the hoe, disappeared, headed away from the fire to somewhere near the house and to our left. I glanced up at Momma. She hadn't moved, but when I turned back to the fire, I heard her swallow hard, say, "I know what Marcus has gone for."

He reappeared, this time carrying something high and over his head: Momma's cane rocker. Molly edged back from the fire as he came closer. He stopped, eased the chair down from his shoulders, and laid it on the fire. For a few moments nothing happened, the frame of the chair like some strange and twisted skeleton, but then the seat caught, and the wood of it, and the flames grew higher until the sparks it gave off drifted high and above the tops of the trees before giving up.

"This is for us," she whispered, and I didn't look at her,

afraid of what I might see, afraid the stranger I'd seen her to be only two nights before might be even farther away.

I didn't take my eyes off the fire until Marcus'd given it the last stir, then buried the ashes with the hoe, Momma next to me the whole time.

The day she died, two months and three days later, began with me sitting with a pencil and tablet in an overstuffed chair I'd had Marcus pull close to her bed. She'd taken ill two weeks before, and hadn't eaten in four days, taking in nothing more than sips of cool water Molly gave her.

The room was kept dark all day, summer beginning to rise around us in thick walls of heat. My legs kicked beneath me as I passed time writing the alphabet in my best cursive hand, and it'd seemed somehow that the room was cooler that morning than any of the last fifteen. Perhaps, I would later think, it was due to the rain that would arrive late that night, after Pastor had come to tend to the dead once again, and after he would once again try to pat my head in some gesture he figured must be comforting. Or perhaps it was due to the heat my momma gave off, the fever I could feel even from where I sat. Or maybe, just maybe it was her soul already departing even as she spoke there that morning, the cool I felt nothing physical, but the feel of my momma leaving me.

She whispered, "Your Grandpa Jacob," and my legs stopped kicking. I turned to her. I'd thought her still asleep, but her eyes were open, one hand on the pillow near her cheek, the other across her chest. Her hair, unbraided and fanned out on the pillow, was wet at the temples and hairline. She swallowed, closed her eyes and opened them again. "Your daddy's daddy."

I said, "Momma, don't talk. Don't—"

"He was a thief," she whispered.

"Don't," I said again, but she looked at me, her eyes full and small in her face.

"You listen," she said, and looked at the ceiling, brought

the hand from her chest to her forehead, let it rest there. "You need to know what stock you're from. I'm telling you." She paused, let her eyes close, and of course I wondered where this'd come from, her speaking, and wondered if it had to do with the cool in here, or the quiet, or the darkness she'd lived in these two weeks. "Your daddy's daddy was long dead before I met Joseph. But people knew about him. People knew Jacob Chandler was a thief. He was." She took slow, deep breaths, and for a moment I wondered if she was awake at all, or if she might be in some haze, maybe even talking in her sleep. But it didn't matter. She was giving me what I finally saw I wanted: some history of my own so I would know my place here, no matter how fine the dresses I wore, no matter how fine the china. Since the night of the fire I hadn't let Missy Cook look me straight in the eye, and at breakfast the next morning, during which my life's guidelines were laid out—no skipping school, no playing with the niggers, no turning down the gas by myself before going to bed—Momma and I sat silent, our eyes on the food before us. We never mentioned the fire in the backyard. Ever.

"Your daddy's momma was just a cracker, left him with Joseph when he was only two," Momma whispered. "And Jacob left your daddy with his sisters, crackers living in shanties up near Columbus. That's how your daddy was raised. I thought he would be different." She paused. "He wasn't. But it wasn't stealing he was bad about. It was me." She swallowed again, and I looked at the tablet, rubbed my finger across a row of letters, saw the smudge I made.

"Your grandpa," she went on, "was caught stealing horses, and they brought him in to Columbus, run him through court and had him up to a tree just north of town, him sitting on one of the horses he'd stolen, a rope around his neck. All this before sundown the same day. They was going to hang him. And your daddy was there, sitting on the shoulders of one of them sisters. He was there to watch his own daddy get hanged for horse stealing."

All this time I was staring at the tablet and how the printed blue lines there on the page seemed endless, lines and lines and lines, my dull scratches all over it only soiling the page, destroying those perfect and perfect lines. She was talking more clearly than I'd heard her in the last two weeks, but that was nothing I cared to think about. I only wanted to look at the paper, and to imagine this man, one I'd never heard spoken of before, perched on a horse and ready to be strung up. This man I was blood kin to.

"Then they gave the horse a swat, and the thing was gone, your grandpa hanging and swinging from the tree. The way your daddy told it, the only sound he could hear was the creak of the rope. He says he watched his own daddy's feet stepping on air, trying to find something firm to stand on. But there was nothing."

I turned to her, saw her eyes were open wide, her mouth closed. One hand was at her throat, moving slowly back and forth, her eyes focused on nothing. "And then," she whispered, "the rope broke. It snapped up near the limb, your daddy tells me, and Jacob fell to the earth. He didn't move for a while. Neither did anybody watching. But then he sat up, looked around. And he was smiling. And then they let him go, because it was God's will. The sheriff just bent over him sitting there on the ground, loosed the rope round his neck and the one round his hands, and they let him go. It was God's will."

I was looking at the tablet, and here came my momma's hand, reaching for it. Her hand was white, as white as my daddy's body'd been when they'd pulled back that wool blanket.

I let her take the tablet, watched as she brought it close to her face. Her hands had started to trembling with the effort, and I thought I could see tears in her eyes. Her mouth was only a thin line now, no color. Slowly she set the tablet down on her chest, let it lay flat there, her eyes gone to the ceiling. "It's a story," she said, "your daddy told me a hundred times. A thousand. A story he said was of a man who'd lived through death. That's why he told it." She paused. "But I wish his daddy'd been killed. I do."

She closed her eyes, and a tear squeezed out, slipped down her cheek and into her hair. "Lord forgive me," she whispered, "but I do. I wonder how Joseph'd been different if he'd seen his daddy die, and I think he might have been a good man if his father'd died before his eyes. But he didn't, and he kept this story of a man who couldn't be killed, and that's how come he turned out like he did."

Her hands were on her chest now, laced over the tablet, and I whispered, "Why'd you marry him then?"

"Love," she said right out, the word quick and soft from her. And, just as quiet, she said, "Hate." She paused. "I knew I loved him. I knew I hated my momma. Those two things are why I married him."

She shot open her eyes. She was smiling, the look on her face as strange as any I'd ever seen her give, and I thought that maybe the fever'd gone through her brain, ravaged her such that she'd gone mad. She reached the tablet over to me without looking at me, and I took it, then scooted a little deeper into my chair, away from her.

She said, "But you have to know about this family, too, and what your stock is from here. From my momma. You got to know that, too." Her eyes were still to the ceiling, as if the painted tin up there with its shapes and swirls was giving something important to her. "There's things about my family you need to know, things Missy Cook won't ever tell you." She was still smiling, and I could feel myself pushing even deeper into the chair, my hands holding on to the arms.

"This one you won't ever hear her tell, because she knows it's true. The reason we've got all this," she said, and though she made no gestures, no moves of her hands or eyes to show me what she meant by *this,* I knew she meant the house, the clothes, the food, the niggers. What else was there? "The reason we got all this," she said again, "is because she married a man from Pittsburgh, the man who was my daddy. And her daddy and this Yankee were in cahoots together, buying up land and houses and banks after the war with money Missy Cook's daddy'd been able to lay his hands on through my daddy. Don't ask me how, but that's true."

She closed her eyes, the smile grown even wider now, and took hold of the top edge of her sheet with both hands. There was joy in her now, some gleam to her white face and hands, pleasure found in telling me all this.

"But that's not the story. That's not the one I want you to keep." She swallowed hard, opened her mouth and took in hollow, quick breaths. I wanted to reach toward her, to touch her, to stroke her forehead and tell her to stop, to save herself. But I didn't, because I wanted the story.

"No," she whispered now, "no, what I want you to take is this: before the war, the town of Columbus was known as Coogan's Bluff. That's Missy Cook's maiden name, Coogan. Her daddy was who the town was named for, and that's because he owned the most niggers. He owned the most niggers in that part of the state, and he wasn't even in the Confederate forces because he owned so much land, and so many niggers." She stopped again, and suddenly she seemed to be disappearing with her whispered words, her breaths only shallow gulps, and I remember the room going even colder a moment, remember gooseflesh all up and down my legs and arms, remember holding myself in the near dark of the room, the tablet lying in my lap. My momma was still smiling, her eyes still closed, her fingers clutched and drawing taut the sheet up to her neck. "So when the Columbus, Ohio, militia march into town," she whispered even more quietly now, her words only ghosts in the room, "they liberate the niggers, they rename the place, and they burn down every last piece of property they know belongs to the man named Coogan. Missy Cook's daddy. But they can't find the man, and do you know why?" She stopped. She turned to me, and before I realized what she'd asked, she was staring at me. But she wasn't looking at me, I could see. Her eyes were on me, but passed through me, so that my momma was already gone, and I thought again of her profile in the light of a candle held above my dead daddy, and how God had planted in me the knowledge she would die even back then. This was what my momma was leaving to me, the only legacy she knew to give: stories of who I was from, however failed their lives.

I looked down, said, "Why?"

She laughed, the sound in her like dead leaves underfoot. She turned to the ceiling again, and I knew she wasn't of this world anymore.

She stopped laughing, tears drifting down her cheeks. She whispered, "I watched my daddy get slapped cross the face by Missy Cook the first time he told me this story, and I watched him laugh in her face, Missy Cook standing above him, him in his favorite chair in the parlor, her with her hand back to hit him again. But he'd only laughed, and then, because she didn't know what to do with that hand held high, palm open, she came straight to me sitting on the divan, and slapped my face. And my daddy only laughed harder at that, brushed back tears from his eyes. Missy Cook just left the room." She paused, reached up a pale hand to her face, and gently touched her cheek, the look on her face surprise, her eyebrows knotted, her mouth open. "She'd hit me right here, on this cheek, right near my eye, because I'd only listened while my daddy told me why they never found my grandpa." She paused, swallowed. "Missy Cook's daddy'd dressed as a woman, and hid out in a nigger shanty. And when those Ohio militia came through to liberate all them niggers, let them know about what Mr. Lincoln'd given them, the niggers still hid him, put him into a barrel and let him hide. Dressed as a woman and hiding in a barrel, right there in front of all them niggers he owned, every one of them laughing their nigger hearts out, I'm certain, and then when the militia's gone, and they're all freed slaves, they just brought him out of the barrel, and stayed with him the rest of their lives, them and their children and their children's children. Molly, Marcus, all the field niggers. They're all sons and daughters of the ones hid my grandpa when he was dressed as a woman and balled up in a barrel. And don't think they don't remember it, neither."

My hands were together in my lap, beneath them the tablet and my sad scrawl, evidence of my trying to make logic out of lead on paper.

She whispered, "So you take those two stories now, and you decide. Two stories of people who lived through their own deaths. You take them both, and you decide why I'd marry your daddy." She paused. "You take them both, and you decide which of the two is your own." She stopped, and I hadn't the courage to look at her, simply stared at my hands in my lap. "You choose which of the two you want to take: one who'd lived because it was the will of God, no matter how bad the life he led. Or one who saved himself, God be damned, and passed on to his daughter a shame so fierce only hate could cover it up." She gave a small laugh, the sound only thin air forced from inside her. "Or you could do the wise thing, and pass all this up. Make your own story. Maybe going out into this world with these stories like stones in your pockets won't make a bit of difference. The Lord knows it wasn't that way for me."

I swallowed, closed my eyes. I said, "And now you're going to leave me here." I held my hands even tighter, felt the grip of bone against bone.

She whispered, "It happens to all of us one day," her words so quiet I had to hold my breath to hear. "Your momma and daddy leave you at some point, and then you are on your own. Everyone ends up an orphan. Even me. I been an orphan since I was born."

I let out my breath, opened my eyes. I looked at her. Her eyes were closed, a smile on her face, her fingers holding tight the sheet.

She died late that afternoon, when I was downstairs in the kitchen, drinking cold buttermilk Molly'd poured for me. It was Marcus who'd been there when she died, him to come into the kitchen, his eyes down to the floor only because I was in the room, I knew. He said, "Miss Patricia, she passed on now." Molly gave out a quick breath, looked from me to Marcus and back to me, her eyes never really meeting mine, but falling somewhere on the middle of my chest.

That night, once Pastor was gone, my momma's body taken to the mortician's for a proper burial, I climbed into bed with the same nightgown on I'd worn our first night here, when we'd watched our old clothes burn like pine straw in the night air. The gas light above me was still on, and out of habit I sat there, smooth cool sheets around me, and waited for Missy Cook to push open the door, give me the same practised and dead smile she gave each night, then turn off the gas.

I was alone, finally. Molly'd seen me to my room, touched me with the gentlest hands I could remember. But now I was alone, sitting in my bed, waiting for the woman who'd struck my momma for no good reason but that she'd been witness to the truth of her family.

So I waited no longer, did the only thing I could. I climbed out of bed, went to the door, and reached up, slowly twisted the gas key. The room grew dark around me, the furniture there—the dresser, the bed, the armoire in which hung my and my momma's fine new clothing—all changing into huge and ugly shapes, drowning in the darkness I was giving. Then the room was black, and I heard the faint pop of the gas shutting off.

I had two stories, the hard and sure memory of them. Jacob Chandler, and a man named Coogan, late of Coogan's Bluff. They were with me, stones in my pockets, but already shiny, polished in me, reminders to take hold of my own story, make like my mother'd urged. Missy Cook couldn't have me. I wouldn't let her take into me, wouldn't give up to her and her eyes. Turning off that gas was a move just as logical, just as inevitable as pulling the wool blanket over my dead daddy barely two months before.

I climbed back into bed, drew the sheets up around me,

and settled in. I thought of pretending sleep, waiting for Missy Cook to open the door to find I'd broken the first rule she'd put on me the night we'd moved in, but there was no reason to pretend. It didn't matter what she thought or did. If she chose to beat me in my sleep, I'd awaken. If she chose to do nothing, I'd be asleep already, moving toward the day I would leave here all that much faster.

I closed my eyes, let the dark and sleep take me up.

TIGHTROPE

O

Roberta Silman

THE TELEPHONE RANG the morning after Kate
had had the dream, one that recurred with a peculiar regular-
ity over the last twenty-five years; she was young and thin and
wearing her old brown winter coat and the weather was damp
and gray with no sign of leaves on the elms yet, although she
could spot a few crocuses near the roots of the old thick trees
as she scurried from building to building in a vain effort to
avoid his angry stare and cold voice. When, at last, something
unknown forced her to enter his cluttered office where, even in
her dream, she could taste the dust, he would say, "Why
haven't you come to see me?" and she would awaken in a cold
sweat.

Why that dream? It had no basis in reality. She had
never failed to visit Professor Nossiter—at least twice a week
that last year, once in her official capacity as reader for his
literature course, and another time, usually over the weekend,

just to talk. He had never been angry at her. "Henry isn't an angry man," one of his colleagues had said when Kate first asked about him. Nor did Kate think she had any guilt. Yet the dream persisted, and its appearance usually presaged a letter from him, or a message through a third, or sometimes a fourth party.

So she wasn't surprised when, at a little before eight in the morning, the telephone rang, and it was Henry. His voice was a filament of sound and all he said, all he seemed to have the strength to say, was, "I think you can come now."

"I'll be there late this afternoon. I don't know exactly when, but sometime around six," she said.

Her first thought upon hanging up the telephone was: Let the snow hold off. Then she threw on her jacket and hurried out to the barn to tell her husband that the call she had been expecting had finally come. He nodded as briefly as if she had told him she was going to the feed store; when their eyes met, he said, "I'll drive you to the bus."

Unlike her relatives and friends, Henry Nossiter had registered no surprise when Kate had announced a few years after graduating from college that she was marrying a Virginia farmer and planning to live on the edge of the Piedmont Plateau south of Roanoke. He had lived on a tobacco farm in upstate New York when he was a boy and in adulthood he had lived his bachelor life in many places; he knew that what you needed to live you brought with you. The day she told him about her marriage she came to his office and he insisted they look up the town on the big map of the United States he kept folded in his desk; she recalled that he chuckled with delight that her town was not far from one called Rural Retreat. "That's perfect, what every writer needs," he said. Then he stood for several minutes in front of the ancient literature section of his library and finally presented her with an Aeschylus—in Greek and English. "None of the translations are that good," he admitted, something he would never do before, "and at least you will have the Greek to refer to."

He had not even been dismayed when she confessed she barely had time to read when her four children were small. Or when she aged more quickly than she might have if she had remained in New York. Kate was careless about the Virginia sun, so that her face became lined. Her hips widened with each child, and her hair was tied back simply into a thick bun that had more gray than brown in it. Still beautiful hair when she let it down, but what with the children and the chores and the poems in her head, she wore it pinned up most of the time. Only when she was pushing open the door to Henry Nossiter's office on her yearly, then less frequent, visits to New York would Kate admonish herself for her bun and her hastily daubed makeup. Yet none of that seemed to matter to him.

"Prettier each year," he would say, then make his way around his enormous desk filled with piles and piles of books and papers and bend his head and kiss her delicately on the lips. She was a tall woman and he was a few inches taller than she.

Kate's last visit was in spring; she had her youngest child, Jamie, a boy of ten, with her and after the three of them had walked slowly to the cafeteria for lunch and then back to Henry's office, Jamie had whispered, "If Mr. Nossiter is getting old, why does he walk like a little calf?"

A while later she had sent Jamie on an errand and then she turned to Henry and told him she would come and take care of him when he needed her. He had no one else who could. He was the youngest of a large family, now all dead. He lived in an apartment he'd shared with his brother and his brother's wife; it had been assumed that his sister-in-law would take care of him, but she was in a nursing home, suffering from senile dementia.

"My nieces and nephews have their own lives, and they all live out of town," he admitted. And of course there were former students, some of them famous teachers and writers. "They do beautiful eulogies," he had once told her, "but that's about all."

After Kate was finished speaking, Henry thanked her and told her *his* plan, which was to go into a home—a paragon home, he assured her, one of the lucky things about living in this city. "But I must go soon, when I'm able to walk and in my full senses, otherwise they won't take care of me when I get sick."

Kate shook her head. She couldn't see him living away from his office and his apartment. The thought of him leaving his life a day earlier than he had to was more than she could bear; more, she knew, than he could bear, so she replied very quietly, "There'll be no more talk about a home. Stay in your apartment and come here every day as you always have, and when you can't do that, call me, and I will come." As she spoke she wrote down her telephone number on a piece of file card. When she saw him place it in his wallet next to his identification, Kate knew he would do as she wished.

She had spoken that day last spring as firmly as he had told her, twenty-five years before, "You are a poet. Forget about teaching and get yourself a job that will allow you to eat and write your poems. I've been in this business for a long time and I know the real thing when I see it."

She had only stared at him, incredulous, but Henry Nossiter had not backed down. Each time a poem was published, then the chapbook, then the real book, and a second, he had been the first to receive them. And when she visited him all her work was on his desk, within reaching distance of his chair, next to the ashtray and the ever-present carton of cigarettes: Fatimas when she first knew him, then Camels, and finally Kents, when he had been told he had a spot on the lung.

Before Kate went to pack, she stood at the kitchen sink, hoarding the view of the morning sun as it veered through the deciduous hillsides of the mountain, then lit up the flat spot— what they called the "overlook"—in front of a stand of hemlocks. She had not known when she married that this exquisite valley would be hers each day, but now that she was required to leave it for who knew how long, she needed to fill her eyes to the brim with it. Whenever she went away, she sometimes longed for it so badly that her throat ached, and once she had been troubled by nightmares of great logging trucks and saws ripping through the woods.

When her husband kissed her good-bye at the bus station where she would get the bus to Washington before boarding the train to New York, he placed two hundred-dollar bills into her palm—money that he must have been saving for this emergency. Kate smiled gratefully; as usual she hadn't even thought about money. "Don't forget Jamie's recital a week from Saturday," she reminded him. "And be sure to give yourselves enough time to prepare for Alice's party." Their second child was going to be sixteen in three weeks; for a moment Kate's eyes burned at the thought that she might be gone that long, but her husband didn't blanch at her cautions. They had been over this plan of hers many times, and he had reminded her of its pitfalls: that she was not a nurse and might have to get one, that she would be terribly cooped up in the apartment, that she would miss the children. There was no need to go over it anymore.

What you must do, you must do, his eyes now told her, and quickly Kate boarded the bus.

New York was bone cold, colder than the Blue Ridge, colder than she remembered from her college and working days there, colder than anything she had ever known in New England as a child. As people left Penn Station they adjusted scarves across their noses and mouths like children playing gangster. A fist of icy air buffeted her face as she stepped out into the city, and the new buildings, "the needles," the cab driver called them, rose like knives slicing off more light, and more, to create caverns of shadow that grayed and deadened the grid of broad avenues and narrower side streets.

Now, at the end of the working day, a blanket of hatted and kerchiefed people covered the sidewalks in a closely woven swath that amazed and depressed Kate. How could they live with so little air, so little sun? How could she live without the openness of the valley for this coming stretch of time? Then Kate remembered her husband's eyes and swallowed hard and asked the cabdriver why there were so many people. "It looks like Christmas, but that was almost two months ago," she said.

At the next light he turned and stared at her. He was too old to bother with the sliding window between them. "They live here, lady. And they say it's worse in Tokyo."

She didn't answer, and he ignored her until they began to approach the address she had given him, an old apartment house on Central Park West where movie stars and news anchormen and talk show personalities now lived. "You work for one of those celebrities?" he asked with sudden interest.

"No, I'm going to visit an old teacher. He's sick." But the truth only whet the man's curiosity. As she paid he looked her up and down, and she could hear him telling his wife about a big woman in an old jacket and slacks and heavy hiking boots who had gotten out at this fancy apartment house.

Though she was earlier than she had predicted, the doorman had been alerted to her arrival, and he insisted on carrying her bulky leather suitcase through the lobby that looked like a gracious club. As Kate let herself breathe in and out more normally, she realized how frightened she was.

Henry had waited to call her as long as he possibly could, and now a very sick, hunched-over man in his pajamas and bathrobe and slippers stood before her. When they kissed, Kate noticed they were the same height for the first time. His skin was leaden and felt like wet plaster, but behind his glasses his eyes still gleamed faintly. He walked with a cane, and when they reached the living room he sank into the pillows of the sofa, as if he had returned from a long journey. On the coffee table were three items: the scrap of file card, another piece of paper with the name, address and telephone number of Henry's doctor, and an ancient ivory box Kate recognized from Henry's desk. It was filled with fifties and hundred-dollar bills.

"The doctor wants you to call," he told her, then leaned back and closed his eyes. "Being home at dusk is strange," he added. "The city is less alive than late at night." His habit for the last fifty years had been to leave his office no earlier than midnight and sleep until around nine. His first class was never before eleven when he was teaching.

"I'll call the doctor after you get back into bed," she told him. He nodded and she led him to his room, which was surprisingly neat. He had lived in this apartment for the last ten years; before that he had had his own small place farther uptown, closer to the university. "I haven't been to my office for a week," he said as she helped him into bed, "but they sent a packet of mail this afternoon. I'll go over it in the morning." Since his retirement almost a decade ago he had spent most of his waking hours attending to the mail.

When Kate helped Henry remove his robe she saw that his neck and chest were a series of depressions covered by an almost transparent layer of skin. The sight made Kate start; she had never seen him in anything but a suit or a sport coat and always a long-sleeved shirt and tie, for she rarely saw him in summer.

How will we manage? she suddenly asked herself, then pulled a chair closer to the bed so he didn't have to turn his head to see her. But when she saw the relief in his eyes that she was here, she thought: I have managed before, I will manage now. Her sudden apprehension reminded Kate of her mother's quivering voice after she had called to tell her she was settled on the farm. "But you don't know a thing about cows and horses," her mother had said.

"I will figure it out as I go along," Kate had replied cheerfully. And so she would now.

In about an hour Henry was breathing peacefully, so she went into the kitchen and called the doctor. The man told her what she knew: Henry was dying—of emphysema and lung cancer. He had refused all treatment and the only thing he would allow administered was pain medication, first by mouth, then, later, with shots. "We can get a visiting nurse for those," the doctor offered.

"No, it won't be necessary. The cows get shots all the time."

"Of course. How stupid of me to have forgotten that," the doctor said. Although they had never met, the man knew all about her. He told her he had ordered a hospital bed to be delivered tomorrow. "And whatever drugs you need, and a commode," he added. When she had dialed the doctor's number, Kate had thought she would ask him how long, but now it seemed irrelevant. And obscene.

There was a second bedroom, larger than Henry's, where Kate had thought she would sleep, but it was easier to put sheets and blankets over the couch in the living room and stretch out there. The next morning she saw that the bedrooms were too dark for either of them; a new building had gone up next door, and living in those rooms was like living in a shaft. She decided she would put the hospital bed in the living room and move the couch back into a corner near the window. That way Henry could see her whenever he wished.

On her way out to get groceries she asked the doorman if the fireplace in the living room worked. "Why, of course, madam," he replied, as if everyone in this city had a working fireplace.

"Can you get me some wood?" she asked. When he mumbled something about it being scarce, Kate put a fifty into his hand. Immediately his manner changed. "I will need enough to keep a fire going steadily," she told him, then hurried out. She moved slowly through the crowd, trying to make eye contact, hoping for a faint good morning, or even a narrow smile. But nothing until she reached the sparkling clean deli around the corner where she was greeted with, "And what can we do for you today, young lady?" Kate was so grateful she had to stop herself from buying more of the overpriced merchandise than they needed.

When she returned Henry was in the living room. His cane had slipped to the floor, but he was proud to have made it out here all alone. She had hoped the sleep last night would refresh him, yet he was still so very pale and weak. But his eyes brightened when he saw the newspaper she'd bought from the neighborhood kiosk. Then he looked around.

"The cleaning lady retired a few months ago, after the summer. I called an agency, but what they sent was awful. I'm sorry. The back rooms are even worse."

"Not to worry," she said. "We won't bother with the bedrooms anyway. We can put the hospital bed right here, in front of the fire, and I'll be comfortable on the sofa."

Henry shook his head. "The fireplace has never worked properly." Kate didn't answer and made some tea and toast, which he nibbled, then she insisted he go back to bed. She wanted to tidy the living room before the bed arrived.

By early afternoon the living room smelled of furniture polish, the bed was set up, the fireplace was seasoned and glowing steadily, and the fingers of frost that had sprouted on the insides of windows had begun to melt so that the peeling sills were wet. Kate put some old towels on them, then considered the next task: a bath. She had thought Henry might try to resist, but when she mentioned it she saw he simply didn't have the strength. He lay in her arms as placidly as Jamie had last year when he had the chicken pox. How thin he was! His bones seemed about to poke through the skin and where there were no angles the flesh fell in neat folds. But there was nothing even remotely embarrassing about it, and when she had to lift him from the tub, Kate thanked God for all the diets she hadn't been able to stick to; she would need every ounce of brawn she had for the chores that lay ahead.

When he was bathed and shaved and dressed in fresh pajamas, Henry looked better. He managed to eat some of Kate's soup, and while she was sorting the mail, he caught her eye and whispered, "Katie, remember how hard I used to work to define *Agape*?"

She stared. Of course she remembered. The first lectures each fall: *Eros, Agape, Sophia, Hubris.* Two kinds of love, wisdom, pride. And he was the only person in this world she allowed to call her Katie. But before she could answer, his eyes closed and his chin fell gently onto his chest.

After about four days Kate established what she described to her husband as a holding action. Henry wasn't getting better, but the strength didn't seem to be seeping out of him as rapidly as it had when she first arrived. So she wasn't surprised when, at breakfast of the fifth day, he said, "I think it's time for the eulogizers," and directed her to the top drawer of his desk, where she found a list of his former students. A few who worked here in New York had already called, but he had instructed her to tell them he was recovering from the flu. Now it was her job to go through the list and tell them the truth.

Kate would rather have done all the milking by herself for a week than make those telephone calls, but she forced herself to check off each name. When she finished he said, "You look exhausted. It was a replay of *The Death of Ivan Illyich,* wasn't it?"

She sat down and shrugged. "Not exactly. I think they're all going to get here."

But Henry knew. "The ones who wanted the most from me will show up last. I've seen it time and again." Then he tried to read the paper. She didn't mind it when he sat and stared into space, or slept, or tried to eat; it was when she saw him trying to read the same line over and over in the paper that Kate could feel herself wanting to cry.

The men all had the moldy look of scholars about them: some were bald with long flowing fringes of hair, others had thick moustaches and beards, all of them looked older than their photos. The women were surprisingly chic. As each one arrived Henry introduced Kate as clearly as he could, but her identity remained a secret, because if any of them had heard of her through her poems they knew her only by her maiden name. And most of them were older than she; from their manner she knew they thought she was a family retainer, for they treated her with the polite but disinterested courtesy that most intellectuals reserve for menials.

In many ways it was a relief. After the third day of visitors Kate stopped bothering to wear a skirt and stockings and decent shoes and got back into her old clothes and hiking boots. It didn't even bother her when, one evening as she was filling the compacter with garbage, she overheard, "She's a long-lost relative from the farming part of the family, I think."

"No, you're mistaken. She's a practical nurse who took care of his brother. I can swear I've seen her before. It must have been when his brother was sick."

Kate could have cleared it up by saying, Of course you saw me—with my husband and two older children at the party for his seventy-fifth birthday six years ago. Then I was a guest, like you, and my hair was done and my clothes were party clothes. But that would have embarrassed them because they all prided themselves on their marvelous memories. Still, if she had had the choice she would have preferred not to hear "Such a big gawky woman, isn't she?"

"No, just a little plain. But she's gentle with him and seems capable."

Finally, the last of them had come and gone. By then Kate had been here a little more than two weeks. Henry left his bed less and less, the baths dwindled to every other day, then every third, the pain medicine was administered more often, the doctor came and strengthened the dose. Henry's food was largely liquid, but he still had some interest in it.

The living room had become a world. Every few days more wood was delivered; often a bag of pine cones was included, and the fire became a steady presence that breathed with them. They both listened for it and for each other. Although she spoke to her family on Sundays, thoughts of her husband and children seemed to grow fainter, receding to some distant future place, just as the books which lined the walls of this room seemed to drop farther and farther from her line of vision. Henry slept more and more; when Kate had to leave the apartment for food or drugs she would leave a large sign hanging at the foot of the bed so he wouldn't be frightened if he woke and found himself alone.

At the beginning of the third week, the poems began to come: line after line rushing through the air, hovering around her head like gnats until she could write them down. Astonished by the flow of words that assailed her, Kate tried to fix each phrase, put it exactly where it belonged. Once she found herself reciting Eliot's lines: "Words strain, / Crack and sometimes break, under the burden, / Under the tension, slip, slide, perish, / Decay with imprecision, will not stay in place, / Will not stay still." But if he recognized them Henry gave no sign and only smiled when he opened his eyes and saw her sitting on the sofa, surrounded by mounting piles of paper.

"How good that you can work," he murmured when Kate looked up and smiled back. Then she continued to cover the paper with her hurried scrawl. For it seemed to her that all the poems she had been carrying in her head as she bent to the myriad tasks of her life—to her husband's and children's and animals' needs—all those poems were surfacing and were there, in the very air around her, to be had for the taking.

The doctor came again, and then again. The pantry grew bare, was filled, grew bare once more. Slowly the fist of cold outside loosened. Henry spoke very little now, saving his words only for the important things; phrases tightened to monosyllables, small clues to what he really wished to express. Sometimes

Kate understood, sometimes she didn't. But when he curled up on his side and grimaced with pain, she could reach out and put her hand on his; when he opened his eyes she was there for him to watch; when he tried to eat she would tell him about her husband, their children, that beautiful valley. Sometimes, and only if she was sure he was asleep, Kate recited her own poems aloud, testing the words upon the fragrant, piney air.

Life was suspended, she realized—yes, this is what it means when one says those words. She felt as though she and Henry were venturing very slowly across a tightrope. Yet now, neither of them was afraid. She didn't even wish this slow, arduous journey would end. She could go on like this forever, she sometimes thought.

One afternoon a gust of wind blew a pane from one of the windows. While they were waiting for a handyman to come and replace it, Henry motioned her to lift the bed into a higher, almost sitting position. The break in the routine had made him more alert than she had seen him for at least a week. As Kate cranked the bed she could see him summoning all the energy he had, more energy than she thought he still had, and her body grew rigid with fear. The doctor had warned her that this sometimes happened right before the end. But when he spoke, in a voice Kate recognized from the past, all he said was, "I didn't know when I called that it would take this long."

"There's no rush," Kate told him; then she smoothed the blankets over his legs and feet and went to the door to answer the bell.

IT'S TIME

O

Michael Martone

I REMEMBER THE TIME each year when my husband cut back the raspberry bushes. I always thought he took too much, afterward a row of whittled spikes where once a tangled mass of brambles boiled along the fence. He ripped out the dead canes altogether, brittle straws, pruned the branches down to nothing. He dug up the newly rooted tips where last year's growth had bowed over to the ground and took hold, the first long stride into the garden. Every spring, I believed they would never grow back, but in a few weeks, with the days lengthening, the stubby canes streaked with red, budded, shot up overnight.

Does it count as a first word? The other raspberry, the sound my daughter made, her tongue melting into slobber between her lips, stirring before dawn in the tiny bedroom down the hall. It was dark, and the wet blasts helped me navigate, the floors covered with her blocks and toys. Her room was pitch, the only light the daubs of radium I swiped from the factory outlining the rails and bars of her crib. At night it looked like a bridge lit up, suspended over the varnished surface of a wide, still river. The paint had dripped on the floor, formed a tiny drifting phosphorescent slick. My daughter tottered about. I could see only her shadow, her shape blotting out the dew of pulsing light behind her. She sprayed her one note greeting. When I picked her up, her tongue rasped next to my ear. I felt her whole body going into the sound, her breath dying down, her spit a mist on my cheek.

"Don't go," my husband had said. "Stay in bed. She's not crying. Ten minutes more. Let her go."

I could see he was looking at the time. I watched the luminous dial of his watch float up off the nightstand. The little wedge the hands made rotated as he fumbled to right the face. From eleven o'clock the time spun to a little past six-thirty. "She's up early," I heard him say. The little constellation spiraled back to the table.

Often there were flecks of paint in my hair. He said he could always find me in the dark. He'd kiss me through a cloud of stars. I'd shake my head and the sparks spilled down onto the pillow, sprinkling his face. My fingertips too lit up, stained where I held the brush and the tiny pot. I became distracted with my own caresses, streaks of light tracing his back, neck, hips. Flakes of light caught in the hairs on his chest and eyebrows, blinked on and off as he opened and closed his eyes. Where I kissed him I left welts of throbbing light. His lips grew brighter. It seemed like the fire should die out but it didn't, would only disappear with the dawn in the windows. We could see everything then and still hear our daughter down the hall cooing to herself, inventing a language to call me to her.

This was in Orange right after the war. They used women at the factory there to paint the clocks. Our hands were steady. We were patient, perfect for the delicate trimming, outlining the numerals with the radium, down to the marks on the sweep face, sketching hairlines on the minute hand. I had sable brushes I rolled on my tongue to hone a point sharp enough to jewel each second. The paint was sweet and thick, like a frosting laced with a fruity essence. We'd thin it with our spit. Rich and heavy like the loam in the garden. It was piecework. At the long tables we'd race through the piles of parts, my hands brushing the other hands, reaching in for the next face or stem. The room was noisy. Alvina sang to herself. Blanche reeled off recipes. Marcella clucked. We talked with our eyes crossed over our work, "She had to get married. They went to Havre de Grace by train and were back by noon the next day." We paused between each sentence or verse as we dabbed the brushes to our lips. It was as if our voices came from somewhere else. I'd look away, out the huge windows to the brilliant sky. I can still hear the buzz above the table as something separate from the people there, another kind of radiation in the room that never seemed to burn out. The stories and the songs blend into one ache.

What more is there to tell? Our bones began to break under the slightest pressure—getting out of bed, climbing stairs. Our hair rinsed out of our scalps. Our fingertips turned black and the black spread along the fingers by the first knuckle while the skin held a wet sheen. Our hands were negatives of hands. The brittle black fingernails were etched with bone white.

But this was after so many of those afternoons at the plant with its steady northern light. I remember cursing an eyelash that fluttered onto a face and smeared my work, how I damned my body for the few pennies I had lost, the several wasted minutes of work. "I'll race you, Myrna!" There were many factories in Orange, and their quitting whistles at the end of the day were all pitched differently. The white tables emptied, the heaps of silver parts, like ashes, at each place. Another shift, the night one, would collect the glowing work and ship it somewhere else to be assembled. We ran to the gates, to the streetcars waiting, to the movies that never stopped running. It was all about time, this life, and we couldn't see it.

At the trial, not one of us would speak, and the newspapers said how happy we were, considering the sentences already imposed. We sat there with our smiles painted over our lips to hide our teeth. During recess in the ladies, we powdered over the bruises again. We couldn't blot the lipstick, since our skin was so tender. Four clowns in the mirror, mouths like targets, stared back at us. We couldn't cry. It would ruin our work. In court, we listened to the evidence and covered our faces when we laughed at what was being said. I watched the clerk who recorded everything, his pencil stirring down the page. Sometimes he would be called upon to read testimony back, and I was taken by the accuracy of his words. I remembered the speeches that way. It seemed right, right down to some of the sounds he noted, pausing to insert *laughter* or *unintelligible.* I liked these moments best, when the words were the only solid things left in court. The lawyers, the witnesses, the gallery, the jury, were all poised, listening to the clerk. They might have been an audience from another time. The only thing left of us was that string of knots on paper, the one sound in the room.

My daughter loved the fresh raspberries in milk. The white milk coated the scoring between the tiny globes on each berry in the bowl. It looked like the milk drying on her tongue. The berries as they steeped turned the milk pink. She grabbed at the fruit, crushing it into her fist and then sliding the pulp into her mouth.

I haven't been able to speak since soon after the trial, and eating now, even the raspberries so ripe they liquified when I picked them, is painful. The berries have seeds that shouldn't hurt the way they do. I can't explain this to my husband, who sits reading the newspaper on the other side of the table, his fingers smudged with ink. I make the same sounds now the baby made, little whines and grunts. He's already used to it. I feel I am being whittled away like the nub of the pencil I write this with then sharpen with the paring knife. Why do people lick the lead point? Perhaps it is just a gesture of thought, a habit, hoping that the sound of a voice will rub off.

I'm not afraid. I know this now. It happened this morning when I was picking the berries. The bees were in the late blossoms on the canes above me. The canes trembled, about ready to bow over. Sweat scalded the skin of my arms and neck. The berries hung in clusters everywhere among the thorns and sharp leaves. I have no feeling left in the tips of my fingers, and as I watched my black hand close on each berry, the fruit seemed to leap from the stem into the numb folds of my palm. So little had held the berry in place, a shriveled ball and socket. The berry, a dusty matte red that soaked up the light, bled a little, a pool in my palm. I thought about sucking the raspberry into my mouth, straining it through what was left of my teeth. I thought of my daughter. Instead, I reached out for another berry and then another, dumped them into the pint baskets squashed and ruptured, and rushed them into the house. I found a pencil and a piece of paper to write this down. Each word fell on the page, a burning tongue.

TWENTY

O

Helen Eisenbach

For Sally

Y<small>OU'RE A LOATHSOME</small> creature!" shouted
Mr. Ferlinghetti at his newly ex-pregnant wife. Later
the nurses agreed that his contorted, purple face had
been even more horrible than his words, though his wife,
reclining comfortably in her hospital bed, seemed to find
them both oddly satisfying. "You will call her Regina, for
my mother."

"Just what you deserve," said Louise, "a perfect baby.
You can't find a thing wrong with her."

"There's no point in discussing the success of your little
scheme," said her husband. "I'm going home. I'm not coming
here again."

"Good," said Louise Ferlinghetti. "Toot doesn't much
care for you anyway."

. . .

By the time Toot and her mother returned home, Mr. Ferlinghetti had stored the mountain of toys in the hall closet and the house looked more or less as it had nine months earlier. When Mrs. Ferlinghetti went to hang up her coat, a catcher's mitt landed squarely on the top of her head, but she chose not to mention the incident to her husband. "I'm glad you're back," said Anthony Ferlinghetti. "I'm damned tired of eating out of cans."

"You poor man," said Louise. "I'll ask my mother to send you some of her recipes."

When Toot was seven, she was given a little brother. Her parents explained that this was her reward for being such a well-behaved child, but privately she suspected it had more to do with Manuel, her mother's prize pupil, whom Toot loved deeply. Sometimes when Manuel was finished with his lesson and her mother left the room, he would pull her over to his lap and place her fingers on the piano keys, covering them with his own to guide her. When she told him she would rather lie on the couch with him like her mother did, he would hug her so tightly she could feel his body shake with laughter.

"What's going on here?" Louise would demand, coming in from the kitchen with steaming hot coffee and bending to ruffle their hair, first her daughter's and then Manuel's. Toot's hair was flaming red. Manuel (who was dark in every element of his being) would murmur into her ear that she was going to grow into a stunning woman some day, sighing as if the burden of waiting until then was almost too great to bear. Eventually he would lift her off his lap to join her mother on the couch, and Toot would go to the nursery to stare at her brother.

Until the age of twenty Rafael Ferlinghetti's best friend was his sister. When he was very young she would come into his room late at night and sit at the foot of his bed, talking in a low voice. "You are going to do great things," she would whisper. "I expect the world of you." Her mother had told Toot this when she was a baby, but as chances of Louise doing as much for the child who caused her husband such unalloyed satisfaction seemed slim, Toot felt compelled to take the job upon herself.

"Your father is an odious little man," Louise had told her young daughter. "Thank God you have nothing of him in you. You are going to be an extraordinary person; I felt it the first time you looked at me. Your father's furious that there's nothing wrong with you he can blame me for. It makes him sick you're turning out so well."

Rafael used all the toys his father had bought for what had turned out to be Toot, but his favorites were the ones she had worn almost beyond salvation. He and his sister would throw the ragged ball back and forth summer evenings, taking turns using the one catcher's mitt. When Toot gave him a brand-new glove one day, his face fell at the thought of giving up his beloved old one, so she kept the gift herself.

"What's *emission,* Toot?" he asked her, screwing up his body to throw the ball.

"It's when an object gives something off. Something escapes, like heat."

"What's *gonads?*"

"Look it up," said Toot Regina Ferlinghetti to her brother.

While Rafael inherited his mother's musical gifts, it turned out that Toot possessed her father's sharp, analytic mind. In high school she invented several computer languages, but she was chiefly known for her willingness to take a dare, no matter how dangerous. She was also a wonderful dancer. Whenever Rafael heard the scratchy portable record player going he would run into her room; she and her friends never minded dancing with him. Toot's friends all had long hair and pretty legs and he loved to watch them laugh with his sister.

One day when Rafael was twelve, he came into the living room to find his sister crying. How could Toot be unhappy? The world possessed a cruelty he had never before dreamed existed. He went over to her and buried his face in her lap.

"Don't ever fall in love with a woman," Toot said, sounding more angry than sad. "She'll break your heart."

Rafael studied her blotched face with grave eyes and nodded.

"I mean it," warned his sister, starting to cry again.

Rafael patted Toot's brilliant red hair consolingly. "Okay," he said.

When Rafael was eighteen, he decided to move in with Jonathan Edwards, his piano teacher. Louise Ferlinghetti was unenthusiastic.

"He only wants one thing," she said. "Far be it from me to meddle, but I thought you were smarter than that."

"He's been married, for God's sake," Rafael said, "he's got a *daughter* my age."

"Since when does that mean anything?"

"Christ, Mama, he just wants to get me ready for the fall competition. He means to make me famous."

"I'm sure he does, dear," sighed his mother, turning back to her student compositions, "but for what?"

Jonathan Edwards had clear blue eyes, cheekbones that seemed to have been sliced out of glass like contemporary sculpture, and a way of magically transforming the most ordinary events; studying with him was like living with the promise of a miracle around every corner. Soon Rafael grew so obsessed with practicing that Jonathan had to force him to go outside at regular intervals. Not even crisp sunny days or the smell of popcorn outside movie theaters could distract Rafael from the memory of Jonathan's clear voice turning passages of music into portals to another world. How could Jonathan sweep him out the door when there were mysteries to be experienced, savored?

One afternoon when Rafael thought he was alone, he was surprised to come upon his teacher, eyes closed, in the bathtub. Rafael had thought he was at a conference on the island; yet after two particularly intensive days with Rafael, here he was, fast asleep, submerged in water. Rafael stood over him, oddly transfixed; here was his teacher naked, looking like a boy not much older than Rafael, his forearms draped over the sides of the tub. Rafael studied the lines of his chest, the curve of his hip and thigh; he could not have said how long he stood there. Finally he cleared his throat, reaching to shake Jonathan by the shoulder. The other man came groggily awake, blinking.

"Aren't you supposed to be somewhere?" Rafael turned and smiled into the mirror, combing fingers through his hair.

"Oh, Jesus!" Jonathan plunged from the water like an animal surprised by gunshots. "What time is it? Why didn't you wake me?"

Once Jonathan had reached behind him for a towel and left the bathroom, Rafael was able to speak in a normal voice. "I just realized you were still here a minute ago." He could hear Jonathan frantically plundering his closet.

"It's not your fault." Jonathan was hardly listening, slamming drawers and briefcases. "Have a good evening," he called moments later from the stairs. The last thing Rafael heard was his teacher's last-minute "Practice!" as he slammed the front door behind him.

The remainder of the evening Rafael found himself unable to concentrate on his playing. The house seemed filled with echoes; the recurring image of Jonathan lying in the bathtub, face serene, body glistening, the muscles quiet just beneath the surface of the skin, haunted him. (His face grew hot thinking about it.) He made his fingers go over the most difficult passages again and again, but it was no use; at last he bolted from the piano, going to Jonathan's liquor cabinet. Pouring himself something red, he swallowed deeply, enjoying the burning sensation in his throat. He refilled his glass, feeling a sudden, perverse longing for a cheap cigar.

"Did you?" murmured Toot as the woman in her arms launched into a heartfelt explanation of how she'd felt Toot was fated to be at her side throughout eternity the minute she'd lain eyes on her. This conversation (like several others before it with completely different yet eerily similar partners) took place in the interval between the first puff of the other woman's postcoital cigarette and the chaste final kiss at her front door.

"I feel we've moved on to a much more intensely personal plane," her companion was saying as Toot made her escape to the bathroom.

Already? thought Toot, heart sinking. "Don't you think we should get to know each other a little better first?"

"I know you," the woman said with chilling assurance.

Toot had heard this particular tone before; at the very least it spelled the end of a life unhampered by hidden meanings, the death of any simple enjoyment she might be allowed to feel in another person's company. "Probably not as well as you should," she pointed out, coming back to sit for a moment. Just once she would like to forgo the early precipice to instant coupledom. "You and I may not actually be as compatible as you think." The proprietary warmth with which her companion was weaving her hand through Toot's hair indicated that her words were falling on deaf ears. "I know you have to get back to your thesis, even though this"—she extricated herself—"was lovely." A hand reached out for her, but she moved toward the bathroom (this time for an indefinite period, perhaps years). "I'll just run you a shower."

When at last Toot closed the door behind her guest and

turned to absorb the silence of her apartment, the relief that flooded her was so strong it rivaled any pleasure she had felt in years.

For several nights Rafael stayed up very late, listening to the sounds of Jonathan getting ready for bed. When was this going to stop? he wondered. If anything, it seemed to be getting worse. When he closed his eyes he saw visions he couldn't explain; he seemed powerless to control them.

One evening he sprang out of bed and went downstairs, seating himself at the piano. The house seemed to be warning him not to shatter its solemn hush. He paced the living room, running fingers through his hair.

"Rafael?" came a faint call from upstairs. He started, frozen where he stood. "Is something wrong?"

"No," he called back. "I can't sleep."

"Come talk to me."

He climbed the stairs, the blood pounding in his ears, and went into the darkened bedroom, hovering by the door.

"Sit by me."

He obeyed, swallowing; his mouth was dry.

"Are you worried about the competition?"

The concern in his teacher's voice slowed his pulse. He shook his head, then realized Jonathan couldn't see him and croaked out a "no."

"It's only natural to be nervous," soothed Jonathan. Now Rafael could make out the glint of a bare chest out of the covers; he bit his lip, looking away. What he wanted, more than anything, was to rest his cheek against that hot skin, to feel the beating of Jonathan's heart against his face. "But Rafael, you're going to be wonderful! You'll make us all proud." At this Rafael flung himself off the bed. "Stop," came Jonathan's command, and Rafael halted, color flooding his cheeks. "Come back here and tell me what's bothering you."

Rafael collapsed on the bed, not allowing his eyes to explore the outline of the body under the covers (the specifics of which he could describe in merciless detail). "I can't tell you." His voice came out so low he wasn't sure Jonathan had heard.

"Of course you can, now hush. Just say it."

"I—" Rafael peered intently into Jonathan's face; if only he could transmit his feelings to Jonathan's brain without having to give words to them.

"Oh, is that all?" sighed Jonathan, regarding him calmly. Rafael's heart battered his chest as his friend lifted up the covers, smiling. "Come on, then," said Jonathan, "get in."

It turned out Toot was able to push all thoughts of sex from her mind for an entire month. This isn't so bad, she told herself: really, all it took was self-control. When several months had passed without incident she decided that perhaps a solitary existence was just the thing for her after all.

Half a year later, she caught herself seriously contemplating the charms of one of her bracingly manic ex-lovers. It was clearly time to seek outside help.

Sometimes after they made love Jonathan would get up and sit naked at the piano, playing for Rafael as he lay in bed smoking expensive cigarettes and feeling deliciously self-indulgent. "Will I ever be as good as you are?" Rafael would ask.

"At the piano? Dear boy, you're already a disgrace to me here. It's most disheartening."

"Still, you're not so bad," Rafael conceded, "I can stand listening to you."

"Brat," Jonathan would answer fondly, turning to do something about the complacent grin on his pupil's face.

The day after Rafael took first place in the competition, Jonathan's ex-wife called.

"I've got to pick up Amy," Jonathan said, hanging up and turning to Rafael, his face pale. "Her mother's going to Guam."

"Great! I've been wanting to meet Amy."

"Are you insane? You can't stay here. My little girl is coming to live with her dear papa for the entire summer."

It turned out Amy had no intention of living with her inhibiting, overauthoritative father. "Very nice of you, Dads," Amy said, "but I don't want to be saddled with you any more than you want to be saddled with me. I'll stay the night, of course, but tomorrow I find my own place."

"Amy, this is Rafael," Jonathan said. "My prize pupil."

Amy studied Rafael's glossy black hair and creamy skin and shook his hand. "You look very nice in my father's shirt," she said. "You should wear all his clothing."

Amy was out the entire next day. When she came back, exhausted, she announced that she had found a place to live. "I'm going to crash here tonight," she apologized to Rafael. "I just can't face sleeping on bare wood floors."

"That's fine," Rafael said, giving her a glass of wine. He was immensely cheered at the prospect of company, as Jonathan was out with old friends for what promised to be a marathon evening. It occurred to him that Amy had wavy blond hair and a smile which, though nothing like her father's, was equally devastating. As she stretched out on the chair next to him, the faded jeans seemed to transform her crossed legs into living sculpture. As his eyes repeatedly moved over the large sweater that barely concealed the outline of her breasts, he had to admit he was in the clutches of an enormous crush.

Jonathan Edwards, laden with drink and remorse, returned to his apartment at four A.M. When he climbed into bed, an apol-

ogy on his lips, the rude discovery that his bed was empty
jolted him one step toward sobriety. He lay awake for the rest
of the night (roughly two hours) worried that the boy might be
seriously injured and not merely displeased with him. Sleep
came at daybreak, forestalling his decision to call the police
and the morgue.

The next afternoon, when he finally arose, the apartment
was hushed. He knocked on the door to the spare bedroom in
case his daughter had come back and spent the night. When he
heard her grunt he went in and sat on her bed. "If you sleep
any later it'll be tomorrow, honey," he said, patting her shoulder.

"Mm," she said. He noticed dark hairs on her pillow but
decided this was information with no significance.

"You really should get up," he said.

Amy sat up and kissed her father. "Okay, Pops," she
said. She smiled, reminding him that someone who looked like
his ex-wife could still be beautiful. "You're the Dad." She got
out of bed and put on her clothes, unembarrassed to be dressing in front of him. She was nineteen, Rafael's age; Jonathan
wondered how many men had seen her naked. She had a beautiful, fresh young body. He wondered if Rafael had found it
beautiful. He wondered where Rafael was.

"Well, gotta run, old man," said his daughter. "Time to
buy all sorts of apartmenty things. You're coming for dinner,
of course." She left the apartment, her long hair flying behind
her like a banner.

Rafael walked for hours. He was nineteen, almost twenty. It
was time to face facts. Not only had he just slept with a girl he
had known for less than twenty-four hours, he had slept with
his lover's daughter. Plus he had enjoyed it tremendously. He
was either a terrible pervert or a badly misused innocent (he
was unable to decide which). When it began to grow dark, he
gave up, going home. As soon as he saw Jonathan, he burst
into tears.

"Amy's invited us for dinner," Jonathan said, putting his arms around Rafael. "At her new apartment."

"Jonathan," Rafael sobbed. The misused innocent theory was out of the question, he saw immediately.

"Don't, sweetie," said Jonathan.

"I can't help it. I feel so awful."

"She's a lovely young woman. *I* like her."

"You don't think I'm vile? You don't hate me?"

"If she weren't my daughter I'd shoot her head off," Jonathan said. "Now go get dressed for dinner."

Some time passed, but Rafael was unable to sort out the jumble of his emotions. He decided to go to New York to visit his sister, Toot, who (unbeknownst to him) had just escaped an entanglement with a humorless linguist and was living a wild bachelor life avoiding anyone remotely connected with Columbia University.

"You're gorgeous," she said by way of greeting, when she opened her door to find him standing there.

"I'm so glad you're here. I couldn't call, I wouldn't have known what to do if you weren't home. You look wonderful."

They kissed. "I consider it an insult that you're taller than I am," Toot mentioned, noting that Rafael looked remarkably like Manuel. "What's wrong?"

"Sit down," Rafael said. Toot put up some coffee and then sat down, patting the couch next to her. "Well," he said, taking a breath. "I don't know if Mama told you I moved out—"

"That was a few years ago, wasn't it?" (He nodded.) "How's the living situation worked out?"

"I slept with Jonathan's daughter last month." Rafael remembered, then brushed aside, her warning to him that day long ago. "We haven't been the same since. I mean, the sex is still good, but it's changed somehow. I don't feel I deserve his love anymore."

Toot studied his face for several minutes. "Mama didn't tell me anything about this," she said finally.

"She knew what would happen before I moved in. I hadn't any idea and she already knew."

There was more to the story, clearly. "Is his daughter living with you now?"

"Oh no, no; she just came to visit and I met her. She's wonderful." Rafael closed his eyes and stretched out next to her. "You'd love her. I've never laughed so much in bed."

"You mean Jonathan can't supply you with the raptures of adolescence?"

"Fuck that," Rafael said. "I love him. I hardly know her. She's fun."

"Is he making you feel guilty?"

"That's just it. I don't understand why he didn't throw me out on the spot. He acts as if it's no big thing that I slept with his daughter—his *daughter*! He acts as if it has nothing to do with us."

"He could be right," said his sister. "Jonathan is not a stupid man."

"I don't want to talk about this anymore," Rafael said. "Is your piano tuned?"

After two weeks a woman showed up at Toot's door. She had green eyes and a beautiful smile. Toot wondered if she was perhaps the young Faye Dunaway.

"Hi," the woman said, "you don't know me."

"True," said Toot.

"I'm looking for your brother. Is he here?"

"He's at the ballet," Toot said, "but you can come in and wait for him if you want. It'll be a few hours. Do you want something to eat?"

"That would be great," the other woman said. "You're Toot? I'm Amy."

"I thought you might be," said Toot.

. . .

The next afternoon Rafael showed up, his face flushed with pleasure. "Fantastic birthday gift," he said, kissing his sister on the cheek and stealing a gulp of her coffee.

"Did you find someone who truly appreciated *la danse*?" Toot asked.

Rafael cast his eyes downward. "I should have called." Abruptly he beamed, unable to contain his pleasure. "I came across the most beautiful boy," he confessed, "and I couldn't seem to help but—"

"Look, I'm glad you enjoyed yourself," his sister interrupted, "but I have to tell you something. You'd better sit down."

That moment Rafael heard the sound of the shower being turned off in his sister's bathroom. "Why didn't you tell me you had someone here?" He rose to his feet as quickly as he'd gotten off them. "I'll come back later when you're—"

"No—Rafael—" That very instant Rafael turned to see Amy walking from the bathroom to his sister's bedroom. A moment later she came into the living room wrapped in a towel.

"Well," she said. "Hi."

"Fuck," was all Rafael could think to say. He lunged for the kitchen, closing the door.

"Rafael, come out here," Toot called. "We have to talk to you."

"She didn't do anything," Amy said. She could feel Rafael standing just on the other side of the door. "It was all my fault. I just fell head over heels for her." She glanced at Toot, paling. "I'm so sorry."

"Don't worry about it," said Toot.

"I'll try not to let it happen again."

"Let's not go to extremes." Toot smiled. "We could at least give it a few dozen more times."

"Fabulous," said a voice behind the door.

"Look, Rafael, I've come to take you home." Amy turned

back to him. "My father's going crazy without you. You've got to decide whether you love him or not."

"Of course I do. Anyway, it's none of your business." Rafael rested his cheek against the door. "What about us?" he asked more quietly.

"I told Dad it was just the caprice of youth."

"It wasn't just sex."

"I didn't think so either, until now." She looked at Toot and grew red-faced. She couldn't believe how utterly and enthusiastically she had ravished a complete stranger—a *female* stranger. She couldn't believe how much she wanted to do it again that very minute. "Rafael, I've fallen in love with your sister!"

Toot was uncertain how to respond to this information. All signs indicated this was a good time to flee, but she felt an uncharacteristic urge not to stray very far. Her best option seemed to be a shower.

"You do everything fast, don't you?" Rafael said, coming out of the kitchen after his sister had left the room.

"Some things, it's true," said Amy, "but this is different. What am I going to do? She may not even like me, really."

"How inconvenient for you," said Rafael.

"Don't be an ass, you don't love me. You love my father, and so do I. Now get home to him."

"Shut up," Rafael said, furious. "Go away." He went to pack his things. "I wish you every happiness. Good-bye."

"This is no way to treat your daughter-in-law," Amy said, "or your potential sister-in-law. No matter how each of us"—she paused, as if to remind him of his own actions the previous evening—"has strayed. Now sit down and wait for your sister to come out of the shower."

"All right, but then I've really got to go," Rafael said. He wanted to be home before it got dark. This trip had been no help at all. He sat, staring at his hands, and wondered if the perfect thing to say to his sister under the circumstances would occur to him before she opened the bathroom door.

THE WRECKER

O

Norman Lavers

Fᴇʙʀᴜᴀʀʏ 2, 1843, aboard the steamer *Venture,* en route New York City.

In pursuance of my series of interviews with "Famous Men in America" for the *New-York Tribune,* I was sent (all my expenses kindly paid!) to an island on the Florida "keys," to spend several days with Emile Nain.

The Panama-bound steamer I took from New York coasted the entire length of Florida, inside the Gulf Stream, and close in to the edges of the banks of coral. I sat on the bow, with my legs dangling over the guards, and watched by the hour the delightful flying fish skittering along ahead of us, the dolphins playing in our bow wake, the purple nautili floating on the water, with their tentacles trailing many feet below them in the clear water. The minute poisonous stings in these tentacles, wrapping about the hapless swimmer, are reputed to cause an excruciatingly painful death. How many things in nature, I reflected—the delicate-hued nautilus, the lithe tiger, the vibrantly colored coral snake—are in equal parts beautiful and deadly. Man is the same, of course. The aspiring creator of the great cathedrals, of transcendent works of art, is the self-same intelligence that built the cruelest machines of war.

This melancholy, if hackneyed, reflection occurred to me as we noted the huts of the wreckers and their trim, ducklike crafts, lying in the offings. Their living was made at the expense of the misery of the mariners who shipwrecked on the dangerous reefs, or foundered in the stupendous storms, of this treacherous coast. Perhaps it is my own lack of charity, but I could not imagine them wishing us well, since every ship passing them unscathed was, in a manner of speaking, money out of their pockets.

At ten o'clock that night, the steamer hove-to and flashed signals to landwards. A small cutter that had been waiting for us appeared immediately at our side, a sailor scrambled up the rope ladder, displaying an immense girth of tattooed bicep, took my bag and hooked it in an instant to a special sling rigged on his back. Although I was unencumbered, I crawled with much less agility down the ladder after him, to the decks of his small boat, its steam engine chugging and clanking noisily. The sailor, who introduced himself as Kroll, obviously took great pride in his organization of the equipment, and in his handling of the boat, in which he had great dexterity. He was about five feet tall, and every least operation caused his muscles to ripple or swell. He was so swift and efficient in his movements that I did not at first notice he was completely missing his left hand, severed at the wrist in, no doubt, some long-past accident. What actually drew my attention to it were the number of clever dodges, amounting finally to a high art, he used to compensate for his damaged member. The sling on his back with which he had managed my bag while hauling himself down the ladder one-handedly, was only the first example. In moments we were making through a series of channels in the numerous mangrove islands.

We reached the private harbor of Mr. Taylor, at whose home the famous painter was residing while he painted the fauna of the region, and who (Mr. Taylor) had graciously invited me to be his guest as well. There were two trim clean-rigged schooners lying at anchor, ships, with their great breadth of beam and light draught, built for speed and seaworthiness in the most dangerous seas. Clearly, Mr. Taylor was himself a wrecker. I was happy to have discovered this before making some unseasonable comment. However, I wondered how could a man with the sensitivity and civilization of M. Nain submit to live with one of these vultures?

The large three-story house of woodframe construction appeared very handsome in the moonlight. I hadn't exactly expected tents, but I was not prepared for such opulence on this remote edge of civilization. Mr. Taylor himself met me at the door.

"Ah, excellent," he said, extending his hand. "I've waited supper for you. Come in, come in."

He was a handsome ramrod straight gentleman of about fifty, clean shaven, lightly but athletically built, slightly gray at the temples, with alert penetrating eyes.

"I am extremely honored to have you here," he was good enough to say. "I have read all your travel books, and I don't know if I admire your style or your intrepidity the more. With you, and M. Nain, whom I consider the first painter of nature in the world, in the house at the same time, I feel I have, for this too brief period, brought the culture of the civilized part of the world to my lonely and primitive outpost."

He led me through a large handsome library, richly paneled. We paused before a dramatic painting of curlews, at once recognizable as the work of his illustrious houseguest.

"To be perfectly candid, sir," I said, "I had expected your 'outpost' to be a good bit more 'primitive' than I am in fact finding it. The furnishings are closer to what I would expect to find in a fine house in Paris or London. You must have gone to great effort to get them out here."

"In fact they have all come to me." He paused a moment to let me work out the implication of what he had said. Then, "I should tell you frankly, and at once, that I am a wrecker. Since my calling is much maligned by people who do not understand it, I always try to say something about it to my guests quickly, before they make, as all do otherwise, some disparaging remark. It saves embarrassment all round, I find."

My lame smile did not quite conceal my own guilty conscience, and I thought I saw his eyes twinkle briefly. In fact he had quite won me over, and I was prepared, now, to hear that the true case of wrecking was not so heinous as I had misguidedly suspected.

We went into the dining room, where Mr. Taylor's daughter Laura was waiting for us at the table. I guessed her to be thirteen or fourteen—though I was later told she was nineteen. Her face, with its fine bones and delicate proportions, was like an exquisite work of art in blue-veined porcelain, and can never have been touched by the savage subtropical sun. Her large eyes were as clear and confiding as those of some young animal yet to learn the treachery of the world, and might have betokened simple-mindedness, except that in her case they indicated a vestal purity of one unfitted for commerce with the real world. Her body seemed as frail as a nestling's. She greeted me with a tiny birdlike sound, and looked back down at her lap.

"Laura has been in the highest anticipation of meeting you," Mr. Taylor said, "as she has formed a very favorable impression of your writing." I glanced over, trying not to reflect my surprise, and thinking with horror of some rather rough passages I had allowed into print. "I have shewn her those of your works I thought suitable," Mr. Taylor said, with his quick tact. "She was attending a convent school in New Orleans, but when I learned that M. Nain would be spending half a year in the Floridas, and had consented to make this house his headquarters, I at once called her back home. I felt

not only could she polish her French through her daily inter-
course with M. Nain, but also receive tuition from him in
flower painting, at which she appears to have some aptitude.
M. Nain, by the bye, is already sleeping. But it has been arranged that you will join him on a collecting trip tomorrow.
Kroll—that is the man who brought you in—will awaken you
at four. I apologize for the early hour, but M. Nain wishes to
take full advantage of the daylight."

"I'm looking forward to it," I said.

We had sat down at a massive, very handsomely carved
mahogany table with a dazzling damask tablecloth, heavy silver
cutlery, and fine China dishes. The negro butler filled our gob-
lets with amber wine and served us a fresh salat of langoustine,
followed by delicious clams served uncooked in the half-shell,
and then a fine light dish of fish sautéed in a delicate sauce.

"Thank you, Robert," Mr. Taylor said, when we had been
served. Then, when he had left the room, "Robert was trained
in French cuisine, and I think he is a genius in his calling. We
are very fortunate that he agrees to stay out in this remote
place. He is, as are all our few servants, a salaried free-man.
We keep no slaves here. We are not ranting Methodists, but we
do not believe one human being should own another."

I of course applauded this enlightened view, and became
the more anxious to hear about Mr. Taylor's profession, of
which I was now thoroughly convinced I had formed an incor-
rect opinion through my superficial knowledge.

Miss Taylor excused herself in a tiny voice, and retired.
Mr. Taylor and I repaired to an upstairs deck, completely
screened against insects, where we were served a compote of
tropical fruits, and then drank brandy and smoked excellent
Cuban cigars.

"Though you are too polite to ask me," my host began,
"you would be an unusual person if you were not somewhat
curious about my profession. What you have heard, and indeed
logic would tell you this, is that we are little better than—I
believe the usual expression is 'vultures,' putting out lights to

lure unwary mariners onto reefs, and then drowning or murdering any survivors. The truth is somewhat less sensational,
though indeed it is a calling taking great skill and steady
nerves. As to luring the unwary, there is no need. The coast is
so treacherous with reefs and storms that large numbers of
ships are lost every season. This is so whether we are here or
not, and what we salvage is what would otherwise simply be
lost. As to murdering the unfortunate crews, this is so far contrary to the real case, that in fact, we are the distressed mari-
ner's best, and indeed only, friend. Since it is our calling, we
patrol the dangerous parts of the coast during every storm
with our seaworthy craft and skilled crews. If a ship is in trouble, we are instantly on the spot to save the crews, and if possible the ships themselves. I suspect for every crew lost on this
coast, the wreckers rescue ten crews. You will be the most surprised to hear that we work very hard to save the ships as well,
though it obviously is money out of our pockets to do so. Well,
it is, indeed, but our own code of honor is very strong, and I
speak for every wrecker, from the crudest and least educated.
Whatever the motley of culture and language, the poverty of
background, I have never met a wrecker who was not an intrin-
sic gentleman, and neither will you."

My journey down on the steamer had been so restful and
pleasant, my conversation with Mr. Taylor so relaxed and delightful, that, though I did not go to sleep till nearly midnight,
I felt quite refreshed and eager for the day's adventure when
Kroll knocked my door at four.

Kroll, speaking a manner of Arcadian, or as they say it,
"Cayjun" French, swiftly introduced me to the great man, but
we barely muttered our *enchantées* in the rush of leaving without breakfast. I am afraid my first shadowy glimpse of him in
the darkness was not very prepossessing. I made out a large
hulking heavyset figure, waddling absurdly, and constantly
hawking and spitting. But I supposed very early morning is
not a fair time to form one's first impression of someone.
Without ceremony, M. Nain gave me a large heavy wooden

box, presumably of painting paraphernalia, shouldered another himself, and Kroll, with a heavy tea chest perched on one shoulder, his other, handless arm akimbo, led us to the pier, where we disburthened ourselves into a pinnace. Kroll quickly had the sails up and managing expertly with the, to my senses, dead calm, soon had us moving with a hiss of water out of the harbor, where we picked up a gusty little wind, and soon were shooting along. I noticed that he had rigged up a sort of clamp like a mountaineer would use in rappelling to help him feed out or take up tension on his lines with one hand. It occurred to me that his life might be less interesting to him if he were whole. We traveled briskly for about two hours through channels and islands of mangrove. M. Nain, a large dark mass in the bow, was snoring noisily.

At sunup we made fast to the mangroves, waded ashore through surprisingly cold water and sat on a shell beach, while Kroll, with his somewhat ostentatious efficiency, hustled about frying eggs and bacon, and brewing us up some delicious coffee.

M. Nain, who had as yet disdained to exchange more than a word with me, now sat a little apart from us, completely absorbed in picking his nose, looking at his finger, then rubbing his thumb and forefinger rapidly together. At such times as these the interviewer who has had his expensive way paid to a distant and remote place feels a very special form of loneliness and despair.

Kroll, no doubt used to the taciturnity of his charge, quite ignored him, but chatted away with me. He said he knew every inch of the land and water for miles around, and could instantly find any kind of bird or fish or mammal or plant he was asked for. This day we were heading for a cormorant colony to take some of these creatures in different plumages for a painting M. Nain was beginning.

We set out again after eating, and in a short time reached an area of overhanging mangroves in which we could see by the hundreds the nests of the cormorants. We pulled up right un-

derneath the nests, sending black clouds of panicked birds flying, with a great squawking and dropping of excrement, which
we guarded ourselves from as well as we could.

"Wait a few minutes, now," Kroll said, smiling confi-
dently. M. Nain looked back at us from the bow, and smirked.

We waited quietly for about five minutes, and then the
wheeling birds, one after the other, came back and began to
settle. Soon they had all returned, seeming to forget our presence. Kroll gave a signal, and he and M. Nain cut loose with
their arsenal, firing one gun till it was exhausted, then picking
up the next. Birds splashed into the water all about us. Frag-
ments of nests, young birds, and dripping egg yolk showered
us. When the adults had all flown out of gunshot again, we
quickly picked up the fallen and wounded. Kroll then raised
himself into the overarching branches with one powerful arm,
and using his knees to clamp himself in position, shinnied up
the mangroves with a saw in his belt, and sawed off a limb containing two nests, in one of which was a clutch of white eggs, in
the other two scrawny young birds. He placed the eggs and
nestlings carefully in the pockets of his baggy pantaloons, and
lowered the nest to us on a line, before scrambling back down
to the boat himself.

The formerly saturnine M. Nain smiled happily, showing
his strong white teeth. His skin was oiled with sweat, his clothing splashed with gore and black powder stains. He now chat-
tered volubly while he made numerous notations in his
notebook about the colors of the bill and eyes and feet of his
victims, and made rapid tiny sketches. He told me how invalu-
able Kroll was, with his extensive knowledge of the wild pro-
ductions of the area, of how many birds and mammals they had
killed in a very short time. I asked him how promising he felt
young Miss Taylor's painting was, and he set down a crippled
bird whose neck he had just wrung to give a a loud smacking
kiss to his gory and powder-blackened fingertips: "Mag-
nifique!" he said; "that she was filled with virginal promise;
that she learned more from observing one of his strokes than

his usual pupil learned in a month; that he thought she would soon be more partner than pupil." He paused, and we both regarded the bird at his feet, whose head spun back around as its wrung neck unwound.

Then Kroll was sculling after a frantically swimming bird with a broken wing. Each time it came up from its despairing dives, M. Nain smacked it again with the end of an oar. The great painter giggled with glee.

Whatever reservations I may have formed of M. Nain as a man, these were progressively softened by my respect for him as a craftsman. When we got back to Mr. Taylor's house and carried our booty up to a roofed-over fish shed above the dock, and Kroll and M. Nain spread the birds out in a series, I realized that their slaughter had not been the casual and indiscriminate thing I had imagined, but that they had in fact fired with perfect deliberation and accuracy, for the series included birds of each plumage and age type, every bird a prime specimen. While Kroll knocked together a small cage for the young birds we had brought back, and seined out a bucket of minnows to feed them with, M. Nain with a small pocket knife began skinning the dead adult birds with astonishing speed and delicacy, carefully wiping off any stains with bits of moistened cotton wool batting, then sprinkling cornmeal on the skins to soak up grease. The whole time he spoke to me unceasingly, about what he was doing, his plans, his difficulties with his publishers, the problems he constantly had raising money, the incompetency of his competitors, the stupidity and lack of taste and judgment of the French for overlooking him, the astuteness of the Americans for buying his books. I filled notebooks with his conversation, hoping that, as always, when I at length got home and read my notes from one end to the other, the pattern would appear, the story I was seeking. But in truth I would have preferred him to remain mute, so that I could have watched with full attention his thick, beringed fingers, which moved with such easy dexterity. With sticks he built a sort of inner skeleton, about which he wound the cotton wool, until he had before my eyes created exactly the shapes of the muscles, the viscera, the breast cage, so that when he took the skins, like gloves turned inside out, and carefully reversed them back onto his dummies—voila!—there once again was the cormorant as it had been, but now preserved forever from corruption, and to preserve it further from the beetles and moths that would turn feathers and skin to dust, he made sure he was upwind so he would not inhale any crystals, then sprinkled it thoroughly with powdered arsenic. The birds were now wrapped around with yarn to hold them in position while they dried, some with wings folded, some with wings extended as in flight, or some with wings half open, as though just settling. Necks were curved in various positions, as in life. The legs and broad webbed feet were placed in attitudes as standing, or swimming.

And now a minor miracle indeed: the birds that had, in life, been scraggy, skinny, reptilian, hideous, now in such perfect *imitations* of life, had become to my eyes quite beautiful.

Not ceasing a moment his monologue—mainly of his financial woes—he covered a paper with paintings of feet, bills, eyes with astonishing depth in them, that seemed to be set in moveable sockets in the paper itself. He did this not from the actual birds, all those parts having altered already in color, but from his detailed notes and his memory, which he said would itself shortly fade if he did not paint them now.

The day was without a breath, as hot and steamy as any jungle, all of us perspiring copiously when we made the least physical effort. I was completely washed out, but M. Nain, seemingly impervious to the effects of the heat, continued working at great speed. When he had prepared all the skins, we carried them into the large room he was using as studio, and he began suspending them from the ceiling by wires, as one might a puppet, in various lifelike positions, as flying, landing, standing and arching their neck to observe an incoming bird, &c. I was most curious to see the actual painting begin, but in fact it was now late afternoon, and the light began to fail, and M. Nain told me he only worked by natural daylight.

I went outside then, and to my surprise, the sky that had been clear was now entirely occluded. White clouds like scales, extended from horizon to horizon, and from the east black clouds towered. Kroll, I noticed, had dragged our morning's boat high up on the beach, and was making all loose things secure. The schooners had been carried out to the middle of their small harbor, and were strongly anchored a good distance apart from one another. Kroll looked smugly satisfied. "We'll have some work tomorrow," he said. "Will you come?" "Will I ever!"

The gale broke exactly at sundown. We were completely prepared for it. All the windows were strongly shuttered, so we could see little besides the bright flash of lightning showing through the chinks, followed on the instant by the stupendous crack of thunder, and as the vast winds and sheets of rain, no doubt driven horizontally, smashed into the windward side of the house, we felt the wood frame "shaken to its foundations," that worn expression taking on for me literal signification.

I was excited and exhilarated and began the evening—we played desultorily at cards—talking animatedly. But I quickly saw my host and the illustrious painter had each withdrawn somewhat within himself, both, it was clear, absorbed in what would be their very different work on the morrow. We all turned in early, though I stayed awake for some time, writing up my notes and listening to the storm, which at first had alarmed me, but as soon as I realized how sturdily the house could ride it out, I relaxed, and enjoyed its very fury.

Kroll woke me before light. We left M. Nain snoring in his room and went outside. The air was deliciously cool, a steady but not too heavy wind blowing. The seas continued to roar where they struck the beach. The saturated ground resembled the aftermath of an artillery barrage, trees uprooted and downed, limbs and loose foliage lying about, smashed remnants of boxes and barrels strewed the beach. Kroll rowed us—a rope ingeniously looped to his wrist to hold the left side oar—directly out to where one of the schooners was leaping at its anchor, and, following his direction, I waited till the schooner was in a wave trough just as the rowboat rode up high, and stepped out directly upon the deck. The ship was manned by a crew of as wild-appearing vagabundos as I have witnessed. Where they had come from, I knew not. Immediately sail was unfurled, and we headed out of the harbor, Kroll at the wheel. I went into the little galley and found Mr. Taylor tense with excitement. He was himself cooking up a breakfast for us of bacon and eggs and black coffee. Whatever other weaknesses I may have, I have never in my life felt the least twinge of nausea from rough seas, so I did not need to worry about humiliating myself in that way, and ate heartily.

We worked our way south along the coast toward some notorious reefs near the sea lanes. Flotsam was everywhere. As the sun rose we saw that the ships of other wreckers were all about us, moving with the sinister grace of roving carnivores, pausing to examine each cask or box, as I had yesterday watched a large garfish swimming actively to hold himself stationary in the tide rip, and then touching with his long toothed snout each bit of material that floated past him, to test it for edibility. Our crew was absolutely silent, eyes craned to water. Barrels and bits of stove-in wood grew suddenly more abundant in the water, and also the other wreckers' boats came closer and closer together, as we neared a scene of disaster. One of our men shouted, and we hove-to on the spot, and a long hook was put down to turn over the floating corpse of a youth of about nineteen, with black hair and trimmed beard. "It's a French sailor," someone said. "It must have been a French ship on the way to New Orleans." The body was released, to wash on in its own time to watery dissolution. While I had been snugly and safely falling asleep, I reflected grimly, this poor devil had had a few violent and bitter moments of despair before strangling on his final breath.

We continued on to where the water was completely covered, over a wide area, with a heaving raft of boxes, barrels, beams, and other debris, and to one side of it we saw the crushed and sodden hulk, like a smashed rib cage, hanging low in the water, keel upward. Now we had men out in the small boat making lines fast to objects, while those aboard winched them onto the deck. All the wreckers about us were frantically involved in the same, to me, morbid and depressing business. I spotted another dark blue shirt-back lying just at the surface, arms and legs loosely trailing from it. The bacon and eggs rose in my craw, and I had just time to turn over the downwind railing when my breakfast came up in a momentary orange blur and sprinkled into the water.

We were out till dark cruising. Last thing, we heard report of another wreck, to the north, and immediately plans were made to head there the following morning. This worked out happily for me, for otherwise we would have anchored where we were, and continued cruising south the next two or three days. But this way it was just as easy for us to go back to the house and spend the night there, and continue on northward the following day. I had had enough of wrecking, however, and elected to stay behind at the house the next day, to continue my interview with M. Nain.

The following morning I arose early and went walking about on the compound. It was quiet and empty. The ships were gone, having left well before light, and the harbor was deserted. The sky was clear, and very little breeze, and the sea almost back to normal. I felt completely alone in this abandoned corner of the world, but in fact must have been under scrutiny, for a servant came out to me to bring me a large and delicious cup of hot chocolate with a cinnamon stick in it. I went back to the library and wrote in my notebook until about ten, when my breakfast was brought in to me. I had seen no sign of M. Nain or of Miss Taylor, and assumed they were both still sleeping. But after I had eaten it occurred to me to wander over to the studio and see what progress had been made on the cormorant painting.

I looked through the glass doors and they were both in there. She was standing at her easel wearing a light morning coat over which she had tied a thin smock. She looked, as before, fragile and rather defenseless. He stood behind her, overlooking her work, obviously giving her tuition. For some reason I paused, and did not continue walking in, as I had intended. At that moment he stepped up tightly behind her, so that the front of his body must have just touched the material of the back of her clothing, and reached his right hand around to guide her right hand, and, to steady her and himself, just touched her on the left side with the flat of his left hand. From my angle it looked as though the fingers of that hand might just have been in contact with the base of her bosom on that side. I fancied she flushed, and her breathing became difficult. His large torso hulked over her and seemed to surround her tiny form with his insistent intimacy. Her eyes were wide, and, I thought, confused. I turned and withdrew before they chanced to look up and see me.

Surely it was my imagination, but it had seemed so intimate—more than that—I had a vision of his thick round fingers, and the speed and skill with which they had gone inside the plumage of the birds, after making the smallest imaginable incision—

What should I do? There was no going back in there for the present. The confusion on my face would be patent, and what if I met confusion on theirs? What was now my moral position in this household? Should I take M. Nain aside and say something—but what? By what presumption? Should I say something to Mr. Taylor? But what might the consequence be? And what did I know really? Obviously wisdom counseled silence. I might be wrong, &c. &c. It's not my affair, &c. &c.

Yet there remained in my imagining the image of a naive and defenseless young animal, its parent not present to defend it.

A stroke of fortune conveniently extricated me from facing the dilemma, at least right then. A small boat appeared in the harbor from a passing steamer. It brought a message from my editor. I was to go in the boat back out to the waiting steamer and continue with it on in to New Orleans, where a celebrated opera singer had been murdered in a love triangle, and his wife was on trial for her life. I was to cover the event, which my newspaper clearly hoped would be sensational enough to sell many thousands of copies. Normally I would have groaned, but at just this moment I gladly packed my tiny kit, with a final stroke of cowardice leaving a note for M. Nain—who was three rooms away—and another for Mr. Taylor when he should return, advising them that I was called away for perhaps two or three weeks.

The trial was as vulgar and overwrought as I had anticipated, and I was able to send off the kind of dispatches so dear to my editor's heart. So far as he was concerned, I had now justified my expensive trip, and my interview with M. Nain was simply a kind of bonus that could go on a back page sometime. But in all fairness there was something else, something not my editor, but my best readers would notice. I carry with me a certain guilt about my craft, invasive as it can be, intruding so often on others' misery. But in New Orleans I somehow got the chance to speak privately with all the leading figures; there was something in me they responded to, and they opened up, and I saw that for all the literally operatic trappings, a human story was unfolding, touched, at moments, by tragedy in the formal sense. I managed, in my writing, to capture some of that truth of human beings acting in extremis. That modicum of truth, which rose directly and necessarily out of the trash, somehow justified it for me, justified my prying and so often meretricious trade.

I had put completely out of my mind, out of my conscience, what I had seen in the studio of the wrecker's house. At the moment the return steamer's boat dropped me onto the beach before Mr. Taylor's house, and I climbed up from the dock, it came flooding back. I speculated, however, that the crisis had past, and was beyond anything I could do.

I had sent word ahead of my arrival, and both Mr. Taylor and M. Nain greeted me on the verandah. It was getting along in the evening and quite dark out, but the house was brightly and festively lit. They were together, chatting amiably. Miss Taylor was not present. I must come at once to the studio to see what had been accomplished, they said almost together. There was a lightness and levity I had not before seen in either gentleman. M. Nain, fresh shaved and brushed, and dressed in simple elegance, was youthful and quite remarkably handsome.

"First this, behold," said Mr. Taylor, when we arrived. M. Nain was smiling proudly behind him.

The painting was gorgeous. The black snaky fish-smelling birds, so brutally slaughtered weeks before, had been transformed. Metallic iridescence glinted on their lustrous plumage. The sinuous motions of neck, breast, partially opened wings tied all into a balanced and unified composition, that yet seemed to continue its twisting motion before our gaze. Eyes seemed to turn slightly in their deep-set sockets, and to catch different glints of light. One bird swam, and its feet could be seen beneath the surface. The others stood upon or climbed a gnarled and broken bit of mangrove. Epiphytes and lichens clung to the wood. "Mademoiselle Laura painted the vegetation," M. Nain told me. "She is no longer my pupil. She is a full partner."

I attempted to betray no emotion, but a pang went through me at his words. At what cost to her innocence was her achievement, I wondered.

"There is another addition to my house, in its own way as magnificent," said my host, and led my eyes to another corner of the room, where, while a place was decided to locate it permanently, stood a vast sideboard, four rows of drawers, a flat surface, then a mirror. It was made of some black wood, as smooth and sinewed as the skin of a muscular negro.

"It's very fine," I said.

"Let me shew you," he said. He partially opened one of the drawers—it was an immense drawer almost five feet wide. Then holding it at one extreme side with one finger, he pulled and it opened straight and smooth, coming forward almost of its own volition. With the slightest touch, still on that far corner, he easily closed it.

"This is workmanship such as cannot yet be found in the New World," Mr. Taylor said, with a connoisseur's satisfaction.

I nodded, and mumbled something that I hope sounded appropriate, but at just that moment, all unbidden, the image came to me of the drowned French sailor, arms and legs flowing with the tide.

To cover the pause in our conversation, I said, "Where is Mademoiselle Laura?"

Mr. Taylor nettled his brow for just a moment. "I had hoped she might stay up to greet you, but I believe she has retired to her room." I turned to look at M. Nain, who met my eye for an instant, then shrugged and turned his back.

I pleaded weariness from my travels, and went to my room. I had indeed notes sufficient for my interview, and needed only to check with M. Nain on a few facts, confirm a few dates, which I could do in several minutes in the morning. The Panama steamer was passing tomorrow about noon on its return voyage to New York, and I had already arranged for it to pick me up. I usually dislike returning from my journeys to the workaday life in my office at the newspaper, but this time my relief was profound. The painting, I had to admit, had affected me strongly. It had raised by several degrees my appreciation of what it was possible for a painting to be. And though I have no knowledge in furniture, I had been made to see an artist's hand in mere wood. But there remained a sour aftertaste. The cost, I kept thinking.

In the morning, I breakfasted alone in my room, then descended to the studio, where I met M. Nain. I very quickly asked my few questions, made my final notes, and packed away my papers. Just at that moment we heard a sound in the hall outside. We went to the door and opened it, and saw Laura approach, walking on her father's arm.

"I hope you had a pleasant and useful journey," she said in a clear voice. "I am pleased to see you back." Then she smiled. "I'm going in to see the painting." We all reentered the studio.

"It has the touch of a master on every part of it," I said, "including the brilliantly painted vegetation."

She stood separate from her father now, and turned to regard me. I would scarcely have known her. She seemed to have gained an inch in stature. She wore a modest décolletage, and her breasts were full and expressive. On the other hand, I thought the skin of her face had coarsened, and her eyes had narrowed and lost their transparency. Yet as I watched she seemed to unfold and unfurl like a flower or like a bird coming into its full plumage before taking flight.

THE FACTS OF AIR

O

Antonya Nelson

SHE HAD LEFT A pretty-enough life behind her, and because she could not yet be certain she had taken the correct step, Regina probed each new day the way one might old fruit, only too ready to find rot. She had been in her new home two days when she lost one of her cats in a sandstorm. Regina had not lived in Tucson long enough to understand that the storm was unusual, troublesome not only to a newcomer but to old-timers as well, people who took for granted benign, happy weather. Nor did she know that, for the duration of her time there, she would not experience another like it. For the year that followed, Regina anticipated sandstorms the way she had used to blizzards or tornadoes in Ohio, battening down against the luminous sky and the facts of air.

The second cat, sister to the missing one and a homebody by nature, stuck close to Regina's heels, howling plaintively, as if recounting her side of the story. It was a late afternoon in

September and the sun burned, though barely, on the wavering line of the horizon. The door slammed behind Regina and sand stung her skin like bits of broken glass. She tried to shield her eyes, face a friendly direction, but the wind and grit were omnipresent, erupting from nonspecific sources.

Giving up the search, Regina sat defeated in her new dining room, gathering her wits. Sand flicked at the aluminum-cased windows. Door frames rattled and wind sent the loose lawn furniture sailing from the front porch into the gravel driveway. She had rented this home—"home" because its owners had not yet taken their belongings and so a family personality remained—from a divorcing couple. One of them was, apparently, a gynecologist; on the concrete porch, arranged as a kind of centerpiece among the transient plastic chairs and chaise longue, was an inert stainless-steel examination table, complete with stirrups. Though the house had once obviously been custom-designed for these absent people and all its parts therefore desirable, half-empty it spoke of carelessness and waste, mutinous betrayal. Looking around at the ornately carved dining room chairs, Regina believed the family had tried to purchase a solidity, a comfort, they could not summon from one another. She felt not sorry for them but superior.

The wind seized the house like a birth contraction. Above Regina on the roof, a clatter followed; soon a piece of grill-work covering the swamp cooler toppled down onto the withered backyard, blown bowleggedly on its corners across the dead grass until it fell into the contaminated swimming pool and slowly sank. Regina clutched her arms as if they, too, were in danger of disengaging.

She could not imagine that her cat would survive—her mere nine pounds would be nothing in this wind—and decided to go ahead and cry about it. The cats had been the largest constant in her life for the last eight years. They pre- and post-dated her marriage; they reminded her of the good parts of single life. Most recently, they'd allowed themselves to be contained like luggage and hauled across the country, unpacked on the other end in the land of galing debris and dirt. Regina was thirty-two years old and by choice alone; it was not too much, she told herself resolutely and with no small part self-pity, to need her pets. She watched this unfamiliar city become further obscured in the churning air and thought nostalgically of Ohio, where storms originated in clouds and fell toward the earth, adhering to the basic laws of gravity and weather; life on the desert, it seemed, would be upside down.

Overnight the wind died and the dust rearranged itself over the cactus land. Lux, the missing cat, came home, her coat heavy and dull with grit, her eyes weary and resentful. She was not the same animal she'd been. Regina offered her a guilty smorgasbord of foods, everything a cat could want, cream and lox and rank canned beef and quivering raw liver and diced cantaloupe, Lux's old favorite, but the animal would not eat, turning her gray nose up at it all. She did not seem to recognize her sister, though she didn't attack her, as she might a truly strange cat, but snubbed her, as if her experience out in the storm had elevated her to a plane of suffering the uninitiated would not appreciate. Regina thought of her friends who'd given birth; Regina would understand, they claimed, when she had a child of her own.

Regina's husband had ferreted out her phone number, and for a few weeks, his were the only calls she received. She continued to answer the phone because the odds kept building that it would have to be somebody else on the other end.

"Lux has a fever," she told him. She'd been testing the black pads of the cat's feet every few hours. When her paws felt abnormally warm, the two of them would head for the Emergency Vet clinic a few miles down the road. Regina's rented house was on the high desert outside of Tucson; she had believed the open-aired sanctuary of a western city's outskirts would be just what she required after her separation. She and Lux became such frequent late-night visitors at the clinic that the vet quit charging her for anything more than the medication; still, the bills ran up. Regina would hold Lux's front end while the vet bunched the gray fur at the back of the cat's neck and gave her an injection. Then the two women, the vet and Regina, would dunk Lux in a stainless-steel sink of cold water. Soaking wet and shivering, the animal had the slick, grotesque look of a newborn creature, and Regina felt a frightening aversion to her.

"They have this disease here," she told Tom over the telephone, "called Valley Fever. It's from fungus in the air. Everyone gets it, but only some people get it bad. This man walks up and down Speedway talking to himself and scratching his back until it's bloody. Valley Fever went to his brain."

" 'Speedway'?"

Regina paused, vindicated all over again in having left her husband. "See, Tom? Is it possible for you to ever really get the point? I tell you stuff about this horrible disease, this poor bastard, and you say 'Speedway.' "

"I'm just saying, 'Speedway'? Like a racetrack?"

"Anyway, there's Valley Fever in the air, getting sucked down in everybody's lungs. Speedway's just a street."

"So what *is* the point, Reg? You chose to go there."

She sighed, not sure herself. "Why did you call me?"

"You don't know what you're doing," he said in exasperation. "You're like a sleepwalker, about to step off a cliff."

Regina pictured then his laborer's raccoon-eyed tan, the soft white skin his sunglasses protected, the way his brown hair seemed permanently indented by the cap he wore, the way he whistled through his widely spaced teeth when he enjoyed himself, the way his slim hips never quite held his pants. At a distance, these things endeared him to Regina; in person, she had found them insufferable, just the presence of him, his long arm not even on her, but near her in the mornings. He was messy, indulgent, forgetful. His breath smelled of aluminum cans, he liked to make love in the middle of the night when Regina could barely rouse herself. It was no better in the middle of the day when he was seized with an urge to grab and squeeze and knead and push at her until she could barely breathe. He liked to mold. Though by the climb's end, their sex satisfied her, the journey up was stifling and mechanically arduous; he was heavy, his thinness an illusion. She had imagined nothing more pleasing than waking, fully rested, floating among the linens of a large cloudlike bed by herself. The thought that she might not need anyone again—that weight— seemed clean and freeing.

"I want to keep you," Tom said. "I love you."

"That won't get us anywhere," Regina said. "You can't just love me, unqualified like that, it's ridiculous. I don't believe you."

"Well, I do."

"The news at this end is: Lux doesn't have Valley Fever."

"Neither do I," he said, gathering steam. "I don't have cancer or worms or leprosy, either. I own my own teeth. If you fly home right now, leave your stuff, fuck the Toyota, I ask no questions. That's a good deal."

His anger, more than his affection, inspired conciliation in Regina. "I know it's a good deal," she said quietly.

"No, you don't," Tom said, and then hung up. He had, in the past, ripped the phone from their kitchen wall. Regina, model of restraint, had clapped dispassionately from the doorway, refusing to join in, to ignite. He was flammable; she was not.

She now looked out her window into the gaseous glare of Tucson and felt dishonest, still, despite having left behind the marriage she believed to be the crux of her unhappiness.

Regina's move to Tucson had not been entirely random; she'd been promised a job at her uncle's law office. Her family, who had not very much confidence in her, assumed it was Tom who'd initiated the breakup and Regina who needed solicitous consolation. Her uncle's wife, Nanette, made sure to include

Regina in dinner parties and introduced her to every divorced man she knew. Nanette was an energetic twenty years younger than Regina's uncle and was his second wife. He was her third husband; the two of them believed in getting right back on that marriage horse.

It was Nanette who brought Matthew to Regina's partitioned cubicle one lunchtime and presented her as, "Our separated friend," winking broadly behind the stranger's back.

He did not smile, and when Nanette had gone, he said to Regina, "This feels like a pity date to me."

"Oh?" she said, rankling.

"I mean, you don't know me, I don't know you. To be frank, I don't even like your aunt, no offense." He hadn't moved from standing at the doorway, hands balled in his suit pants pockets.

"Stepaunt. Half-aunt, by marriage."

"My name's Matthew Lewellen. I'm only a clerk, anyway, down the hall. I'd be just as happy if we called this quits. Just say it was a pleasure meeting you."

"Certainly," Regina said. "Nanette can be—"

"Pushy," Matthew said. "I worked here when she was going after your uncle. Used to call half-dozen times a day and accuse me of losing the messages. Aggressive, huh? Her perseverance paid off, though, didn't it? Squeaky wheel gets the grease?"

Regina smiled politely; his tone might have been unkind, and his questions were surely rhetorical. His physique and attention span seemed poorly matched to office work and he kept shrugging as if to slip from the confines of his business suit. He reminded Regina of Tom.

"Let's just say hi to each other in the halls, huh?"

Regina agreed.

Lux's case confounded Dr. Dierst, the emergency clinic vet. She was a pretty and athletic-looking woman, suntanned and well muscled, a tawny-eyed blonde whose hair hung down her back in a weighty braid, hair so long it had passed attractive and moved onto freakish. A copper-colored mole like a little penny rested just above the left side of her upper lip, giving her face a quirky sunniness that had nothing to do with her personality, which, Regina came to understand, was without humor. Regina's jokes and asides drew only quizzical, analytical looks from Dr. Dierst, as if she were diagnosing not the cat's problem but the owner's.

Dr. Dierst had eleven cats of her own at home, none of which she allowed outside her trailer. They were all female, all spayed, she told Regina, all slightly overweight. In the looming night, Regina, frightened by Lux's lethargy and hot paws, drove toward the dark strip mall and its single light, the red neon word *Emergency,* feeling that if she could just arrive there, simply unload her anguish onto the capable unsmiling Dr. Dierst, everything would be okay, or, at least, off her own shoulders. In this black hour she appreciated Dr. Dierst's solemn professional concern, her lack of irony, that steady unmoved mole.

However, when Lux's temperature had been successfully lowered, when the cat sat complaining in her aerated traveling box, her gray coat dry and lovely once more, when the bugs could be heard hurling themselves stupidly against the glass of the waiting room window, Regina thought her own panic— speeding down the country road, fishtailing around corners— and the doctor's somber approach to Lux's (or any other animal's) health overdramatic. This emergency, after all, was not about people. It was in this sneering mood that she would think of Tom, the way they goaded each other to depths of cynicism and black humor.

"Here," Dr. Dierst said after the fifth late-night visit, handing Regina a rectal thermometer and jar of petroleum jelly. Regina wanted to scoff in embarrassment; such provocative equipment. "Normal is a hundred and one, a hundred and two. Bring her in when it tops a hundred and four. Otherwise, sponge her."

During the next few weeks, Lux's temperature pushed the mercury to the end of the thermometer. Regina would hold the cat's tail up and watch the silver edge past 104, 105. Lux slept next to Regina in bed, a curled ball of heat on the sheets that Regina reached for in her sleep. She woke several times a night to touch the animal's dry nose leather or paw pads, at least once a week driving to the clinic for a shot. Sometimes she lay in her dark bedroom, listening for the cat's small breathing, terrified that she would wake one night to silence. She would jolt from dreams, read the time on her digital clock and be ashamed she had not wakened sooner, had not verified Lux's living more recently. With no other human in the house, without Tom to tell her she was going overboard, her priorities had rearranged themselves and lost context, a state she could be aware of and still not remedy. Her hand covered the cat's rib cage, which rose and fell irregularly, as if Lux were sighing instead of breathing, and Regina felt she might not be able to bear the cat's dying.

The other cat, well but neglected, began misbehaving. She used her litter box less and less, preferring to dig and deposit in the plants or sink or even, once, on top of a door. She knocked over the bathroom trash and shredded tissue, spread tampons and Q-Tips and wadded Kleenex across the floors. Regina came home from work to find the trail, cursing the cat as she cleaned. She allowed neither animal to go outdoors, following Dr. Dierst's example, and though Lux didn't seem to resent being locked in, her sister rampaged through the house. When Regina located the bad cat, she smacked her and banished her to the basement, throwing her down the carpeted stairs in anger, as if punishing the animal's heartiness. The cat landed at the bottom hissing and spitting, her eyes, in the basement gloom, glowing up at Regina demonically.

Regina shut the door and found solace in the sick Lux, who was always where she'd been left, asleep on Regina's bed. Lux still purred, still met Regina's petting hand with the upward nudging of her head and back, *more, more.* She could be coaxed into eating now and then, drinking water, licking ice cubes. The animal seemed to have fallen into a dreamy trance, as if preoccupied or sedated.

This was Regina's new life, centered almost exclusively around the care of her cat. Tom continued calling to hear her voice. She'd surprised him when she quit their marriage; she'd done it before worse had actually become worst. Though he would begin their conversations amiably enough, he always came around to asking why she'd left, what in him had merited abandonment.

"Just for future reference," he would try to joke. "What was my big mistake?"

"It wasn't you," Regina insisted. "You deserve better."

"Please," Tom said. "Please spare me that kind of patronizing *bull*shit."

"We are exactly the kind of people who bring out the worst in each other," Regina said. "You turned me into a shrew, and I made you act like an asshole."

"Oh, fuck you, Regina."

"See what I mean?"

"How can you be so cold? I never knew anybody as cold as you." Of all the insults ready at Tom's disposal, this one struck hardest.

To him, she began to underplay the severity or frequency of Lux's fevers. How good an idea could Regina's leaving seem if, as a result, one cat was dying and the other was defecating on the tops of doors? Also, he would be the first to tell her she was no longer behaving within the acceptable boundaries of concern for an animal. She'd spent over five hundred dollars, a month's rent. It was important that Tom think she could make it without him. Besides, he was a dog person; he liked an animal you could knock around. He'd always told Regina she spoiled the cats and she told him he was jealous. He kicked them off the bed and threw things at them when they walked on the counters or tables. Cats, he said, didn't know their names or places, unlike dogs, who actually cared what their owners thought of them. Regina told him he wanted a pet who could properly grovel. But he'd grown to tolerate the cats, teaching them to spar with him, little paws darting at his fists. He refused to call them in the falsetto "kitty-kitty" Regina used, so he developed a whistle and, by means of positive reinforcement, trained them to respond to it. In the six years they'd all lived together, Regina thought he'd come to find their idiosynchrasies charming, one cat's love of expensive chocolate (she would not touch Hershey's), the other's habit of sleeping beneath the bathroom throw rug.

"Put her down," he recommended concerning Lux. "You'll spend beaucoup bucks, otherwise. You never did know when to say enough."

"Oh, really? And not so long ago I was 'cold.' "

"Cold to me, sister; a sucker for those cats."

Regina and Tom had no children, and she often thought that was their problem, that the ordinary transfer of affection from husband to offspring had not occurred. But the predictability of such a solution annoyed her. She had entered love as one enters a party, intoxicated by possibility. What magical thing might happen? What did the evening hold? But parties wore on too long and rarely proved to transcend the given boundaries—the ice cubes melted and the food grew crusty, inevitable victims of exposure. Dresses rumpled and neckties wilted. The revelers became sleepy and fussy and drunk. And then the evening would end, as had her marriage, with the anticlimactic knowledge of the tedious cogwork behind the magic, the effort of joviality, the dirty clothes and day-old newspapers jammed into closets. Their marriage counselor (Tom's desperate, uncharacteristic idea) based all her advice on the premise that marriage, like any fine and enduring art, required work. But that was exactly Regina's point: who wants to work? She had persisted in believing that love should not be a job.

She lied and said she missed the seasons. Here, she told Tom, it was either hot or hotter. Instead of trees, great loopy saguaros ambled across the landscape like gunslingers. And then there were the prickly pear, cholla, organ-pipe: thickhided, antagonistic vegetation. The competition for water was stiff. Every day, she told him, driving to and from work she crossed a bridge over what they called a river, a huge dry wash. This wash had provided acres of loose topsoil and sand for the storm that had left Lux ill. Tom launched into an enthusiastic account of a Midwest fall that was meant to make her nostalgic, things he could take pleasure in only by parading them for Regina's envy. The turning leaves, the clarified air, the noise of migrating birds.

"Sounds great," she said flatly. She could have told him she lived where the birds were migrating to. She could have said it was almost November and she was still wearing shorts, that her legs were still tan. A window was open to the warm night air, thick with the oily smells of creosote and mesquite. Owls and mourning doves vied like melancholy wind instruments. In the distance she could see the endless chain of taillights feeding into the city, she could see the gravel quarry, could make out the faint metronomic beep of dump trucks in reverse. True, there were few trees, but so much the better; in their absence, Regina had developed a fondness for the curmudgenous silhouettes of the cactus. She envied their self-containment, the skeptic distance between them and other life.

Over lunch one day, in the middle of a conversation with the other office secretary, Regina panicked with intuition: Lux was no longer breathing, dead this very second because Regina had not been there to prevent it. She'd called her house earlier and spoken into her answering machine, reassuring words meant to calm the cat should she be listening. Ridiculous, Regina told herself as she drove the whole way home on her lunch hour. There would be no time to eat, just enough to feel foolish at discovering the cat to be neither better nor worse than this morning, to get in the car and return to work. Still, try as she might, Regina could not back her dread into the corner. She tried to delude herself into believing that the cat, as repository for so much of her attention, could not simply die. Regina realized she had never worried about Tom this way, had never, even when anxious to be with him, feared for his life.

At home the bed was empty. Regina, heart pounding, began searching in places the cat could not be, inside drawers, behind blinds, finally relenting and looking under the dresser. The cat lay panting in the shadows. When Regina dragged her out, encouraged by the animal's struggle, she saw that Lux's feet were swollen like tiny baseball mitts. Beneath the fur a smooth tautness, the skin shiny and heavily bloated like sated ticks. Her fever was high, but Regina was too alarmed to investigate the number. She raced off to the clinic, rocks popping loudly under the truck's oil pan.

Because she had only come to the clinic in the night, she was not accustomed to seeing other people waiting. Regina had begun to stake a certain claim to the office, the way one might to a particular restaurant booth or library nook, one's private public place. She resented other patients' occupying the scooped plastic seats, their pets on their laps or at their feet like sacrificial offerings. The receptionist smiled in a huge false manner. Her white medical jacket hung stained and unbuttoned, obviously of inadequate size to cover her.

"Did you have an appointment?"

Regina expected to say her own and Lux's names and be instantly ushered in: oh, yes, *that* cat. But no recognition lit this woman's face. "Without an appointment," she said smugly, "you'll have to wait for at least an hour."

Regina, indignant, nearly told her it was this cat and her puzzling illness that'd paid the clinic's rent the last few weeks, waived fees notwithstanding. Instead, she sat in the last available scooped chair with the box at her feet. When the man across from her, older and holding a small terrier, leaned over to look inside the box, she took grim pleasure in his astonished expression.

"She was stung?" he asked. "It was wasps?"

Regina told him the whole story, elaborating as much as she had pared down for Tom, emphasizing now what she had wanted with her husband to make subordinate. The man, a lover of all animals, offered his appointment time to her. His dog, he said with relief, merely needed booster shots.

"Count your blessings," Regina advised him.

The daytime vet was a nocturnal-looking young man with small, twitching facial features. His favorite animals, he told her, were cows. There was a patient beast for you. Obviously, he lacked any bedside manner with cats. Lux scrambled and hissed and scratched him as he lifted and probed with his little long-nailed hands. But he diagnosed her disease in less than five minutes.

"Allergic to herself?" Regina repeated, trying to understand.

"It's the immune system," he said in his adenoidal voice, his eyebrows and nostrils flittering. "Lux's is defective, basically. Because she's weak, other stuff is gonna hit her hard. She doesn't have defenses, basically." He ran his tongue over his upper lip and sparse whiskers. "We'll put her on steroids. It's not so uncommon a disease in cats. People have it, too. I bet she's a runt."

Regina nodded, thinking of her other cat, the healthy firstborn, terrorizing the house in her undeserved incarceration. "If this is so common, why didn't Dr. Dierst find it?"

"Beats me," he said. "You realize we have to charge emergency rates on this, right?"

Lux was not contagious; her disease, built uniquely and inextricably in, endangered only herself. After her feet returned to normal size, her mouth became scabbed. Little bits flaked off from her gums, which bled, then healed. Regina had been told to expect this. Every day she had to fight to get a steroid down the animal's throat; every day she wished it were the other cat who had to take a pill because she was, as a rule, more passive, happy, though who knew lately? Still, the steroids worked. Since Dr. Dierst had been unreliable concerning Lux's disease, Regina decided to forgo other advice the woman had given and let the cats outside again.

" 'Auto-immune deficiency'?" Tom said. "AIDS?"

"AIDS is *acquired,*" Regina began, "Lux was born with this—"

But Tom wasn't listening. "Somebody been buttfucking your cat, Reg?"

It had been made clear to him in the past few months that Regina wasn't coming back. When she didn't respond, Tom began clicking the dial tone, yelling, "Hello, hello? Anybody there?"

"I guess crassness is one of the new stages of grief," Regina said. "I guess I should have expected it." But Tom had already hung up on her.

She was glad the cat was healthy, but in place of the all-consuming worry a restlessness settled in her. She missed the way caring for Lux had preempted the other tediums of living, the preening and mating, the looking for love. As a way of remedying this, she turned to the neglected house and yard.

The divorcing family had allowed realtors to handle the upkeep and renting of their old home, discarding it wholly, the way a hermit crab does a shell. The fruit trees in the backyard had nearly died; in Arizona a mere two weeks without water could be fatal. Regina chose one of the four bedrooms and began filling it with the family's forsaken belongings, games, clothing, wildlife books, medical degrees (it was the husband who had the MD). Once started, Regina moved the majority of the house into this room, opening the door and tossing inside a lampshade or set of drapes. It intrigued her how much was superfluous, ornamentation to the basics of living.

In the backyard was a small swimming pool, filled with dead leaves and muck, its water as viscous as a natural pond's. Textured slip-proof paper curled from the diving board. The pump did not work properly and sent a stream of muddy water

into the pool instead of out. After simplifying the rooms of the
house, Regina began spending her free hours skimming the
swimming pool and soaking the sparse trees. She remembered
the real estate agent naming them for her, minneola, tangelo,
lemon, grapefruit, some munificent hybrid called Fruit Basket
Surprise, which was supposed to produce all the citrus, limes
right next to tangerines. Regina would flip on the underwater
pool lights at night and admire the gradually clearing depths.
Without leaves and seeds and mud, it was a larger body of
shining water. Though the weather would not permit swimming for months, the sight of shimmering blue water, the
sound of it running from the house's pipes and into the
ground, soothed Regina. She sat on the sun-warmed concrete
steps outside her back door and listened to the saturation.

Since she could claim to know only a handful of people in all of
Tucson, Regina was delighted to see Dr. Dierst at the benefit
auction. Local artists had donated their work to be sold; pro-
ceeds went to the homeless. Regina had gone because it was
Christmas and because, when Nanette had called to invite her
to the office holiday bash, Regina had felt the prideful necessity
of having other plans. For the auction, she spent an inordinate
amount of time selecting an outfit, standing before her closet
trying to remember what fashion was all about.

The benefit was being held in a downtown hotel lobby
where, on other occasions, the homeless flopped. Regina, nervous, a stranger still to the city, wandered about drinking the
free wine as a way of occupying her hands. Dr. Dierst stood at
the top of a stairway, studying a painting of two men and a
cat. The men, emaciated, purple, and gaunt in heavy acrylics,
held hands and looked at the cat, who sat in a windowsill in the
absorbed posture of the hunter, eyeing a bird outside, oblivious
to the two men. Regina had made her way up the stairs, jock-
eying around the plastic champagne glasses, until she stood beside Dr. Dierst, who also seemed to have come by herself. She

looked at the painting and tried to see why it would captivate the humorless Dr. Dierst so thoroughly.

Regina said, "I didn't recognize you without your white jacket."

Dr. Dierst peered into her face as if into a two-way mirror before finally saying, "How's Lux?"

Regina, fortified by champagne, made lame jokes about Lux's burgeoning steroid bulk, the way she terrorized the neighborhood cats and disqualified herself from the feline Olympics. Her antics, as always with Dr. Dierst, fell on deaf ears. The copper mole never shifted. At some point Regina realized she was assuming a friendship, a familiarity and concern where there were none. Dr. Dierst must have had hundreds of patients; the overfriendly type was probably an occupational hazard. She kept flicking her eyes toward the bottom of the stairs.

"So how are *your* cats?" Regina asked.

"Excuse me," Dr. Dierst said. "I see a friend I have to talk to."

"Oh. Sorry to have kept you. I just wanted to say hello." Regina watched her move down the stairs, looking for the alleged friend, but lost sight of the blond braid before seeing where it went. She turned her attention to the painting Dr. Dierst had been studying. She recognized in the men's absorption in the cat her own, past, unhealthy obsession with Lux. Thankfully, that time was gone. She decided to have more to drink.

Later, after she'd bravely horned in on a few conversations and not only committed to memory the art up for auction but grown to loathe it, she found herself standing next to Dr. Dierst again. Again, they were both alone.

"Did you find your *friend*?" Regina said, the word sodden with sarcasm. She didn't care. She didn't plan to see this woman after tonight. Her cat was well and she had begun to miss Tom and the city she knew, Columbus, its damp brick avenues and terrariumlike gardens and monstrous fecund homes seeming the safest, most desirable places in the world. Over the course of the evening Regina had come to view Tucson as sinister; she'd stepped outside for a moment to clear her head and witnessed a man's jump from a slow-moving car. He'd fallen into the street, rolling, cursing without emotion at the departing vehicle, then simply sat on the curb and began patting his pockets for cigarettes. The event, plus her drunkenness, had made her feel wrongly placed here, unsuited to the dry, ragged edges of the west.

"Want to come meet my cats?" Dr. Dierst repeated in her serious voice, brown eyes narrowed defensively. "I mean, you seem so interested in my cats . . ."

Regina focused on the face before her and felt the world flip-flop. Dr. Dierst, though beautiful, was shy! The ejected man on the curb was a sad case, his plight the very example of what this auction concerned. "Yes!" Regina said eagerly, her earlier aspersions concerning Tucson instantly renounced. "Yes, I could use some coffee maybe."

Regina tailgated Dr. Dierst (could she possibly call her Laura?) to her trailer. The woman's Bronco seemed too large for her, her head poking up over the driver's seat like a child's. The park was an older one, and Regina realized there were more trees clustered here than she'd seen since she left Ohio. Tricycles, lawnmowers, hanging laundry. Why had she thought this city so unlike her native one? The two vehicles rolled over speed bumps. Until she saw the Christmas lights lining Dr. Dierst's trailer windows, Regina had not felt the holiday season upon her.

She followed Dr. Dierst up the aluminum stairs and through the front door, chattering about Christmas depression. The trailer smelled of litter box and wobbled like a docked boat as they entered. Regina had the feeling someone else was there, in a back room, some dark, napping sensibility just out of sight. The compact kitchen was illuminated by the multicolored Christmas tree lights hung over the sink.

"Oh, don't turn on any others!" Regina exclaimed, as Dr. Dierst made a move toward a switch. "They're so festive."

Dr. Dierst whistled and cats came running.

"That's just how my husband used to call my cats!"

The sound of them thudding from chairbacks and windowsills could be felt in the floor; they were the presence Regina had sensed. She shut her eyes for a moment to test the depth of her inebriation and went into a spin; it was more serious than she'd expected. Around her feet swirled a luxurious sea of cats. She heard purring. Their odor was overpowering.

"The last time I was in a trailer," Regina said, opening her eyes and trying to collect herself, "the whole group of us were at one end, probably twelve people, Tom's family. The thing tipped like a teeter-totter."

"Huh," Dr. Dierst said drily. She was pouring food into a large saucepan on the floor, squatting to see it in the dark. Her taillike braid fell into the concircular attitude of a sleeping snake on the floor.

"It seems like more than eleven cats," Regina said cheerily, hearing her voice clatter in the room like a loose ball bearing. It was the last bright thing she could summon in herself; she grew more languid by the moment, drowning in the evening's liquor, in the warm feelings she suddenly had for Tucson.

Dr. Dierst put the cat food away and sat at the kitchen table on a bench, doing nothing further. One leg tucked compactly beneath the other, braid beside her. Where was the promised coffee? And why didn't she now turn on a light? Regina wondered for a second if the woman weren't sinister, too. Cats who couldn't get a place at the food pan walked on the plastic checkerboard tablecloth, on the back of the bench, around Regina's feet. Their animal presence, the way they passed through the room like velvet, made her think of a jungle, of humidity, or of having a dream of being a cat herself. Their vision was limited like this, was it not? Strictly nearsighted? She seemed to recall a photograph of blades of grass meant to resemble what cats might see. She could not tell whether she should trust them, whether she should want to rub against them, to be rid of her sociable clothing, to feel the wet and dry parts of their noses exploring her, inquisitive and discreet.

Dr. Dierst said, "Sit down."

Regina obeyed, grateful for instruction, falling gracelessly next to her on the bench.

"My husband always said I was a sloppy drunk," Regina confided, though what Tom had said was that she was a slutty drunk. "Were you ever married?"

"No."

"I'm separated," Regina said. "Like an earthworm."

Dr. Dierst gave her a minor gratifying smile. Her mole rose, fell.

Regina asked her if she'd ever lived with anybody.

"Just my father. He died a couple of years ago. This was his trailer."

"It's nice. I like it. Like a boat."

"We got along until I was twenty-five or so. Then he couldn't handle it when I discovered I was a lesbian."

"Oh." Regina felt a small flame of dreadful sobriety light in her suddenly.

Dr. Dierst was still talking. "I couldn't ever tell him to his face about being gay, he just wasn't that kind of person—and I wasn't either, really—so I sent him a letter, even though we lived together, and told him the truth as best I could. He never said a word about it. Not one word. I wondered if he even got it, but I knew he had. That kind of letter doesn't get lost in the mail. After he died, I found my letter in his things, in a sealed envelope that said For Laura Only on the outside. He'd saved it, except he'd cut out every word that had to do with lesbianism, just literally cut them out."

Regina said, "That's terrible."

Dr. Dierst shrugged. "He loved me. I loved him."

Regina wanted to object: it was not love. But she felt unqualified to make such a proclamation. The trailer and its odd lights and smells now depressed her. She thought she understood why Dr. Dierst surrounded herself with cats and their satisfiable and simple needs—and their neediness. But it was stifling hot; these animals had been intended to prowl outdoors, to hunt, to mate, things Dr. Dierst denied them and then claimed to be in their own best interests.

Dr. Dierst, without looking at her, laid a hand on Regina's knee, and though Regina realized when it happened she had known it would, the moist palm still seemed surprisingly heavy and far too human.

"Do you feel a little electric surge?" Dr. Dierst asked quietly.

Regina felt nothing, really, except a lack of energy and thorough confusion. She laid her own hand over Dr. Dierst's by way of cowardly answer.

"I'd like to love you," Dr. Dierst murmured, turning her face toward Regina's.

Regina pulled back. "I'm drunk," she explained, though she'd sobered considerably since coming into the trailer. She'd been misunderstood. "I have to go," she said, or meant to say but only managed to mumble as she fumbled for the small door handle, turning a window knob by mistake. She stepped on one of the cats, whose screech seemed to make physical the anguish in the room. Regina didn't stop, despite having no idea where she was going, none, directions gone from her mind. All she knew was that she had to get out.

Tom waited for two months before calling Regina, a piece of restraint she both appreciated and found nerve-racking. In this time Regina had made the effort of getting the attention of Matthew Lewellen. She needed a point of reference; he would have to do. The episode with Laura Dierst had upset her more than it should have, more than a similar pass from a man would have, she knew. She was disappointed in her narrow-minded reaction and kept playing the evening over, trying to convince herself that if she could do it again she would make love with the woman.

She and Matthew met at a pizza restaurant in the middle of town. For the first half of the evening they interrupted each other and for the last half said nothing. Pizza suddenly seemed to Regina the food of children, disturbingly messy. Matthew appeared to understand she had not invited him for himself and spent his time glaring at her.

"It's been real," he said sardonically when they parted.

When she came home she found Tom's voice on her answering machine. He rambled to the end of seven separate interludes of tape, by turns angry and hateful and tearful. Listening, Regina was only curious as to what he would say next. His feelings, like his body and home, were not accessible to her, a realization that disturbed her more than the actual words Tom spoke. But she came to attention during the eighth message, when he said, "By the time you get this, I'll be out of your hair forever and you'll be glad." The tape rolled, oceanic as sonar, then there was the single beep that meant the end of messages received.

Regina's eyes widened. She tapped the buttons and listened to Tom's phone ring ten times before hanging up, then hit 0. The operator acted as if this kind of emergency had so much precedence there was a standard modus operandi.

Regina waited for an hour, staring at the phone, hugging her cats. As soon as she'd hung up from talking with the Columbus police, she'd gathered Lux and her sister to her, locking the doors and pulling the shades, taking shelter.

When someone finally called her back it was Special Officer Sharon Hoagland, a deep-voiced older woman who said Tom was fine, intoxicated, lonely, only interested in scaring Regina. It was apparent from her tone that Tom had told Officer Hoagland everything and that she, too, held Regina responsible. There was the same distant, accusing noise of sonar on the line.

"What time is it out there?" Sharon Hoagland asked.

Regina, caught off guard by the question, blinked once before looking at her watch. "Midnight," she said. "A little after."

"Well, it's past two in the morning here. It's always later in this part of the country, know what I mean?"

"I guess," Regina said, though it felt plenty late to her in her own time zone.

By way of signing off, Sharon Hoagland suggested coolly that Regina need not worry, that Tom had promised her he would never call again.

Regina looked around her empty, clean house and decided to drive for a while. She took the highway toward the mountains and into the Saguaro National Monument. She drove for hours, circling side roads and trying to lose herself, listening to the radio and smoking cigarettes, feeling the statuesque cacti all around her like accomplices. She got gas in Ajo. She circled Tucson as if to contain it. When she saw signs, she considered on-ramps to I-10 eastbound. In two days, she could be with Tom, she could drive up to their small house and surprise him, have sex with him, lie in his arms. Make him happy.

But she could not claim to love him. She sat at a railroad crossing near South Tucson, the only witness to a long lumbering freight train. She could not claim to love anyone. The obligatory emotion she held toward her parents was tempered by the fact of life they'd given her. What good was it? What design? She felt the lack of something vital in herself, some code or human gene she missed. The coldness Tom had accused her of made her quiver; she felt now she had denied his accusation based solely on the temperature of her skin, as if he had been speaking literally.

Regina drove home by way of the vet clinic. It had become four in the morning. In Columbus, for Tom, the sun was rising and last night was washed away. Regina saw the glowing EMERGENCY sign and thought of Dr. Dierst inside. She pulled into the parking lot and glided to a halt. Without the cat, there could not even be the pretense of an emergency. She tried to be tough with herself, discern what it was she wanted, precisely. She was thirty-two years old and not sure she'd ever loved anyone. What would she have to learn in order to love Dr. Dierst? What steps did one take toward warmth?

The clinic and parking lot were lighted but no one seemed about. Regina waited, rolling down a window. She watched the bugs and listened to the neon hum of the red EMERGENCY. After perhaps thirty minutes, Dr. Dierst came from the back room and stood at the front desk. She stared unblinking at Regina, her life a dead earnest endeavor. She was not wearing her white coat, and Regina felt she was looking inside a dollhouse. Suddenly a cat jumped up on the counter next to Dr. Dierst and rubbed against her. A cat from home, Regina thought, for company.

Dr. Dierst simply held her hand up and the animal took her pleasure, rubbing, nudging, sliding. Regina thought painfully of Lux, shamed by the memory of throwing both cats out the back door before she drove off, hardening herself, willfully ignoring the threat of coyotes.

She and Dr. Dierst stared at each other through the glass. Regina thought this could not be happening, yet it was. Depending on how long they could do it, any outcome seemed possible. If one of them smiled they might be friends. If Dr. Dierst motioned Regina inside, Regina could go. If Regina drove away she could never come back. What did she want? She could not manufacture love where there was none, but the question was sapping her, pulling her inside out, making her crazy; nothing had been solved by leaving Tom, nothing. There was no new life; you turned an hourglass upside down and simply rearranged the sand.

Dr. Dierst looked down to follow the cat's departure off the desk, the fleeting black streak, and Regina saw the serious eyes, the vertebra of braid, the mouth that had no laugh lines forming around it. The hand, held now in empty air, that could have stroked Regina. She remembered the image of the cut-up confessional letter and took this opportunity to start the engine. She pulled away, watching the hood of the small truck overtake the curb, the highway. She felt at one with the machinery as she flew into curves, accelerated without pause all the way.

Just before the turnoff to her dirt road, Regina noticed a glinting reflection in her headlights in the scrub at the side of the road. She was exhausted and drove another mile or two—

rocks again banging underneath—before feeling duty bound to double back. She then had to drive slowly by the brush a few times before the glint caught her eye again. She parked and got out, leaving her headlights on.

Morning was filling the sky fast, a cold and clear sun rising behind the Catalina mountains. Hidden in the palo verde trees and scrub was the wreckage of a burned car, an old wreck, nothing left in it but springs and glass shards, small pieces of charred cushion, melted plastic dashboard, and radio buttons that had once spelled Buick. Its skeleton showed a large sedan. The license plate was intact and had the symbol of a wheelchair before its assortment of numbers. She looked for signs of a person, bones or clothes, but there was nothing.

Regina sat on a nearby rock and tried to blame sleeplessness for her feelings. She believed she could drive her own car off the road and kill herself, though not for love, like Tom, but for its absence. She believed she might have reached the end—most certainly the bottom. In the past, hope had come to her in the form of a new home, a new landscape, but what was here? The sun rose, its light hitting her as it would have in Columbus, two hours earlier. She felt void of desirable qualities, charity or love or patience or tolerance. She enjoyed the disaster she'd found here. She felt sure she would come home to discover her cats eaten by coyotes. She would deserve it.

When she tried to locate the wrecked car a few days later, she couldn't. She drove back and forth until she grew impatient and decided she was succumbing to melodrama.

This would mark the end of looking for signs, good or bad, the end of testing each day like bath water.

Naked in bed one night during the following summer, almost a year since her move to the desert, Regina opened her legs in a dream, or not quite a dream, but the halfway point wherein one makes a request, selects the numbers and waits for the song to play. It was so palpably hot—frustration made concrete by the weather. Earlier in the evening she'd seduced Matthew Lewellen and brought him home, but found that in this heat she could not bear his body in her bed; she had become so adept at throwing off human contact that when they were finished she discovered it was easy to ask him to leave.

Later in the summer, during the monsoon season, there would be a flood in the dry wash; the reason for its empty width and depth would finally become clear. Regina and the cats would be isolated in the desert house and helicopters would come in the night to shine lights and broadcast instructions, as in a war. The road and bridges would wash out, and live frogs, dropped from the clouds, would suddenly appear in the swimming pool. One cat would eat a frog and throw it up for the next few days in sickeningly identifiable pieces, and Regina would not take her to the vet. The water and electricity and gas would all go off and Regina would have to eat peculiar, cold canned goods and talk on the (mercifully) functioning phone. The desert, she would come to realize, is not a place for either high winds or saturating rains, a place that tolerates no extreme other than heat, its element. She would want to call Tom and beg him to forgive her. But gone so long from him, and so far, she would have no memory of her own old phone number and would have to look it up.

But for now, six weeks before these facts, she lay feverish in bed, only beginning to fathom the desperation that would drive her to need, and then be denied, her husband, hoping tonight simply to dream of something erotic that might displace, however temporarily, loneliness. The rehabilitated cat slept on top of the sheet and, between her legs, through the thin cotton, Regina felt her own moisture flow toward the animal. Clean me, she thought, remembering a sea of cats. She wished to dream about that small rough tongue, its natural pinkness, the nubby raised texture of it, navigating whiskers, the flicking alert hunter's tail. She wanted release. She wanted to be clean. Very gently right there, she thought, right there.

HARM'S REACH

O

Scott Russell Sanders

No matter how tired he was from his daylong wrestling with the city's broken-down equipment, Gordon Milk never could go to bed until all four of his children had come safely home from their evening prowls. Who knew what might happen to them out in the darkness? His sons might fall prey to other men's daughters, his daughters to other men's sons. A gang in matching T-shirts might jump them, and so might a thief, a druggie, a weirdo. Flower pots could hurtle down at them from a window ledge. Rats grinning with rabies could rush from sewers and bite their ankles. On the freeway a drunk in a jalopy or a nodding trucker might swerve across the median strip and clobber them. A rioting mob could swallow them, an apartment building could burst into flame as they passed, a tornado could snatch them into the sky.

"Fat lot of good your worrying will do," his wife, Mabel, would remind him, with an exasperation only slightly dulled by twenty-odd years of marriage.

"You get your beauty sleep, pigeon," Gordon would reply. "I'll be along in a bit."

Then he would stay up rehearsing dangers long after Mabel had gone down grumbling to their musty bedroom in the basement. He puttered in the garage, oiling his wrenches, or he pored over garden catalogues at the kitchen table, or he stretched out on his astro-lounger in the living room and skimmed the newspaper, glancing every now and again at the television, where painted faces opened and closed their mouths like tropical fish. All the while he kept one ear cocked for the rattle of the front door.

Ordinarily, he was not a worrying sort of man. His buddies at the city maintenance yard liked to pull jobs with him, because no matter how fast things were falling apart, Gordon's hands never shook, his head never came unscrewed. His mastery of tools and the calm in his big ugly puss took the urgency out of broken sewer mains and burst boilers and runaway trucks. "No sweat," he would say, rolling up his sleeves. By day's end those sleeves and the rest of his shirt and every stitch of clothing he had on were soggy with sweat, but it was the sweat of overheated muscles, not of nerves.

Little in this chancy world had caused Gordon Milk to worry until the night when Mabel delivered their first baby, a mewling girl whose scalp bristled with the black hair of a panther. Gordon put his ear to the baby's lips, to convince himself that she was breathing, and what he heard was a tiny accordion playing the song "Don't Let Anything Hurt Me." That daughter was now a senior in college, her panther hair cut lopsided and her face left unpainted so as to discourage romance, and still the boys trailed after her with incandescent eyes. During the twenty-one years since her birth, Gordon had winced every time he imagined any of his children suffering harm.

All one summer, the child who made him lose the most sleep was Bruce, their eighteen-year-old, who was saving up for college by working the evening shift at a pizza place. "I make dough to make dough," Bruce liked to say. Finished at eleven, he usually came slouching in before twelve, which was bad enough, since Gordon's alarm would go off at five. Then the boy started coming in later and later, well past midnight, past one, past two. Waiting up for him, Gordon imagined enough disasters to supply the evening news for a year.

"Overtime," was all Bruce would say when he finally arrived.

Gordon was so relieved to see the boy come home in one piece that he did not push him for an explanation. Besides, reading the symptoms of chapped lips and bloodshot eyes, he guessed what had been keeping the boy out so late. This hunch also came as a relief, for Bruce at eighteen was half a dozen years behind Gordon's own pace in succumbing to a frenzy for girls.

Then one morning when Bruce wandered in at three, Gordon woke from a doze in the astro-lounger, beat away the newspaper which had collapsed over his face, and before he could stop himself he grumbled, "If you get her in trouble I'll break your skull."

"Her who?" said Bruce. "What trouble?"

Coming fully awake, Gordon felt he should soften his words. "I'm not saying don't enjoy yourself. It's only natural, a boy your age. But just remember where kissing leads to."

Tall, fair-haired, green-eyed, too handsome ever to be mistaken for a son of the dark and dumpy Gordon Milk, Bruce was also shy. For years he had built up a science of girls in his head, and his theoretical knowledge was astoundingly detailed, but his practical knowledge of how one actually behaved with them, especially when it came to the infinite gradations of love beyond kissing, was far more limited than his knowledge of subatomic physics.

"I haven't been hanging around with a girl, Dad."

"Don't tell me you got those chapped lips from a *boy*?"

"No boy, either."

"Then what the hell *have* you been doing after work?"

Bruce rolled his eyes. "You wouldn't understand." For

about five years now this had been his devout conviction, that Gordon, immune to poetry and passion, a battered old workhorse with a tenth-grade education, a leftover from some earlier stage in evolution, could not read even the headlines of the future. "It wouldn't make any sense to you, Dad."

"Try me."

Bruce ran his tongue over his lips, which was how they had become raw to begin with, and said, "I was hacking."

The word made Gordon think of butchers, muggers, clumsy carpenters. "Hacking what?"

"You know, working on a computer. The manager lets me use his micro after Pizza Pizazz closes."

Gordon, able to run or fix any machine that possessed a motor and gears, considered himself too old to fathom computers, those electronic mazes. "You keeping the books for him? Doing inventory or something?"

"No, I'm not keeping the books," Bruce replied indulgently. "I'm just fiddling. Writing programs, making up worlds, trying stuff."

"Messing around."

"If you want to call it that." Bruce went sulking away to bed, flinging back over his shoulder: "I said you wouldn't understand."

But to Gordon, the pleasure of messing around with machines—customizing cars, rigging up windmills, rebuilding player pianos—made perfect sense, even if he didn't know beans about computers. Remembering how the passion for tinkering had first gripped him as a boy, when he built a short-wave radio out of scrap from an electric razor, a toaster, and a sewing machine, Gordon could not very well say no a few days later when Bruce asked to use part of his college savings to buy a make-your-own computer kit.

"Everybody I know already has a system," Bruce pointed out.

"Everybody you know comes from a family with more money than we've got and fewer mouths to feed," Gordon replied.

"It would prepare me for life in the twenty-first century."

"I'm still worrying about next week."

"Just think," the boy persisted, "if I had my own system, I wouldn't have to stay out so late. And you wouldn't have to fall asleep in your chair, worrying about me."

That clinched the argument.

When the kit arrived, Gordon offered to help put it together, figuring he could at least read the instructions aloud while Bruce plugged in the mysterious chips and transistors. Bruce said thanks but no thanks. Lugging the boxes, he disappeared into the attic bedroom he shared with his ten-year-old brother, Danny. Within seconds, Danny emerged, banished from the site of creation, his fists full of baseball cards. "Big Boo's got a bug up his kazoo," he announced.

"Watch your mouth," said Gordon.

For the next three days, while sounds of whistling filled the attic, Danny was exiled to the screen porch, and Bruce himself only staggered from the room once every few hours to raid the kitchen, his bloodshot eyes fixed on some inner diagram, his lips cracked from nervous licking. He forgot his job at the pizza place. When the manager called, Mabel told him the boy had come down with a fever, which was true after a fashion. Talking with him during his food excursions was pointless, a fact that did not keep Gordon from asking how the assembly was coming along nor keep Mabel from scolding him to get more rest. Bruce mumbled indecipherable answers, his mouth full of bagels slathered with peanut butter or cookies layered with salami and banana.

On the fourth day, the manager of Pizza Pizazz called to say that Bruce was fired.

"You didn't pay him enough anyway, you skinflint," Mabel shot back over the phone.

Early on the fifth day, at an hour when only drunks and lovers and ambulances haunted the streets, Bruce let out a triumphant yell that woke the girls on the second floor, the grandparents on the ground floor, Danny on the porch, and Mabel and Gordon in the basement. In pajamas and robes and fuzzy slippers, the Milk family rushed to see what was up, and they found Bruce tickling the keys of the finished computer, his eyes hypnotized by the black screen over which pictures and words played in eerie green light.

"Now we're cooking with gas," he murmured.

Those were among the last words anyone heard him speak, until a week later, when the hum of not one but two voices filtered through his perpetually closed door. To the astonishment of Gordon and Mabel, who were listening from the attic stairway, the second of those voices sounded like a girl's.

"Do you believe it," Mabel whispered, "our shy Bruce in there with a brazen hussy!"

"How did he sneak her past us?" Gordon whispered back.

"I just hope he remembers where kissing leads to."

"It's only natural."

"Natural my foot," Mabel hissed. "It's these modern girls. It's this world we live in. Sex everywhere you look."

Gordon cleared his throat, making a noise reminiscent of a diesel starting on a cold morning, then rapped on the door. The two voices never paused, Bruce murmuring baritone and the girl lilting soprano. Cautiously Gordon opened the door a crack and peeked inside, afraid of what he might see. There sat Bruce at the computer, speaking into a microphone and staring at the screen, where a girl's face glimmered, her skin the color of butterscotch pudding, her blond hair in rapturous curls that threw off sparks, her lips a glossy pink. The motion of those lips and the sultry voice purring from the speaker were not quite synchronized, as in a foreign movie with English poorly dubbed.

At the moment when Gordon and Mabel crept into the room, the girl was saying, "ruffled parasols, although sunbonnets or palm branches also will do."

"And if it rains?" said Bruce.

"Umbrellas," purred the girl on the screen. "Slickers and galoshes, depending on the force and duration, and then rowboats, submarines, arks."

"And for snow?"

"Long underwear, wool socks, boots, down-filled coats. All manner of fires. Hot chocolate. Desire."

"For boredom?"

"Books and flowers and the night sky."

"For the blues?"

"Pretzels and yo-yos."

"For heartache?"

"Love."

Mabel did not like the drift of this, nor did she like the mummy hollows in her son's cheeks. "Brucie? Sweetheart?"

"Hey, buddy," Gordon said. "Hey, big guy. Aren't you going to introduce us?" It required the full weight of his hand on the boy's shoulder to break into this entranced dialogue.

At last Bruce looked around at him with crimson eyes and said, "Huh?"

"Who's your friend here?" said Gordon, waving at the girl on the screen.

"Where'd you meet her?" Mabel put in.

"Is she talking to her own machine somewhere, and hooking up with you like over the telephone?"

"Is it long-distance?" Mabel demanded. "And who's paying?"

After much prodding, Bruce explained that the girl whose face they saw and voice they heard was a phantom, his own creation, an image generator coupled with a voice synthesizer. He threw out a good many other terms that whizzed right by Gordon and Mabel—resident memory, terminal errors, motherboard, ram-drives, spoolers, incremental loops, bits and bytes—all the while licking his lips from excitement. They understood for sure only that the girl's name was Daisy.

"She's like a ventriloquist's dummy?" Gordon suggested.

"Not at all," said Bruce. "The program is self-revising, pulling data from info dumps, changing parameters, growing up. It's so complicated I never know what Daisy's going to say."

"You quit a good job to sit up all night yakking with a machine?" said Mabel.

"She understands me."

Mabel lifted her palms toward the ceiling in a plea for reason. "She understands you, but you don't understand her?"

This contradiction did not puzzle Gordon, for whom females had always seemed opaque, while he felt himself to be transparent before their shrewd eyes. He checked out the girl on the screen, the hair like a storm in yellow seas, the eyes the color of grass, the pudding skin. Nothing at all like Mabel's, it was not a face he would have chosen, but he could see that for Bruce it was the shining image of love.

"You'll ruin your health," said Mabel. "You'll strain your eyes."

Instead of answering, Bruce dove back into his conversation with the phantom girl.

Daisy's voice became as familiar in the house as the gurgle of plumbing and the wheeze of the furnace. She laughed, she sighed, she lectured, she moaned. For hours at a time she never spoke louder than a whisper, then suddenly she hollered, she broke into tears or song. The two sisters found this murmurous dialogue to be an embarrassment, Danny thought it was just plain dumb, and the grandparents considered it one more proof that the younger generation had gone haywire. In their basement bedroom, Gordon and Mabel could hear the sugary tones seeping down through the heating ducts.

This continued for weeks, weeks of sandbag sleep for Gordon, who did not have to worry about what Bruce might be doing outside in the treacherous dark. Mabel, however, fretted enough for both of them.

"What if he decides to marry her?" she protested one night.

"It's only make-believe," said Gordon.

"Could he get some kind of disease from that machine? A virus or something?"

"I don't see how."

"Why doesn't he find a real girl?"

Surprised by his own lucidity, Gordon answered, "Because the real ones terrify him."

The family woke up one Saturday to the noise of a quarrel banging down from the attic. For an hour or so the entire house throbbed with shouts. Bruce would holler, then Daisy, then both at once. Gordon wanted to go referee, but Mabel said, "No, let them fight it out."

By midmorning the attic was silent, and then at noon to everyone's amazement Bruce came downstairs for lunch. Wearing fresh jeans and T-shirt, shaved for the first time in a long while, his golden hair curving in wet rows from the comb, his sleepless eyes glazed with bewilderment, he announced that he had broken up with Daisy.

From their seats around the table, the other Milks all stared at him, none more intently than Gordon, who saw that the young face had been scratched by the fingernails of grief.

"I'm glad to hear that," said Mabel.

"Now maybe I can move back into my room," said Danny.

"Love is a prison anyhow," said Jeanne, the oldest child, the one with panther hair cut lopsided to discourage boys.

"She was getting too serious," Bruce explained. "So I called it quits."

"What did you do, erase her?" Gordon asked.

Bruce frowned at his grilled-cheese sandwich. "I couldn't go that far."

During the afternoon, while everyone else was out, Gordon and Bruce cleaned the carburetor on the lawnmower, the first time they had worked together in ages. Elated by this, Gordon suggested that when the mower was finished they should play a game of catch. Neither one could remember where the baseball gloves were, so Bruce went inside to look.

"Try Bluebeard's trunk in the attic," Gordon called after him.

Half an hour passed, and Bruce did not return. Gordon stuck his head in the kitchen, but before he could yell "Hey, buddy!" he was silenced by the watery sound of sobs leaking down from the attic. He kicked off his workboots and crept upstairs as quietly as his gorilla feet would allow. The sobbing voice was so broken, he could not decide whether it belonged to Daisy or to Bruce.

The door to the attic bedroom stood open. Gordon, his arms oily to the elbow, his big hands curled, gazed helplessly in at his son, who sat before the dark screen of the computer, head thrown back, wailing. The baseball gloves lay forgotten in his lap. Such pain under my own roof, thought Gordon. There were no tools for this aching, no walls to keep it out. Although strong afternoon sunlight poured in through the gable window, in Gordon's eyes the attic seemed to grow dark, and his weeping son seemed to waver like a candle flame caught in a midnight wind.

SAME OLD

BIG MAGIC

O

Patricia Henley

Hᴇ ᴋᴇᴘᴛ ᴛʜᴇ ᴍᴀᴘs. They'd had a cardboard Kahlúa box of maps, forest service maps, topo maps, road maps, some of them from the early sixties when his parents had taken him and his brothers on road trips in the summers. She had to admit they were mostly his maps, though she'd grown to love them, their gift of anticipation, their memory of blind stabs at settling down, of wilderness euphoria. After thirteen years the Kahlúa box was soft as dish towels along the corners.

"That's my favorite boulder in the Cascades," she told her sister. They were both on the wagon, drinking cranberry tea and talking early marriages. "We camped under it in February one year and walked up into the mountains and hugged trees." Her sister said, "You were stoned, right?" "Yeah," she said, smiling and shaking her head yes and flipping the photo album page. "And we lived to tell the tale."

Hitchhiking can make you hate each other—or forge a link between you that can't be broken. They had taken two major trips by thumb: one from Oregon to Arizona in the middle of winter and one from Lumby, British Columbia, to Seattle, also in the winter. During these trips, life went on. They made love in the A-frame North Face mountain tent; she complained about how cramped she was on top. She sometimes cried at night, missing her sisters. They fed fragile, hopeful campfires, drinking brandy and talking, weaving the toughest cloth of their fears and desires, finding out what they believed in. They fought over whether to eat in a restaurant or cook over a camp fire. They never had any money to speak of, but there was a stamina to their love. They prided themselves on having endured. Seventeen below, Nevada, camping in an arroyo among cages of snowy sagebrush. That's love of a different color, her girlfriends said. Hard-core. They did it to see Monument Valley in the winter, rime like crystal sugar everywhere. They did it because they thought they were both born to the road.

Once they had a cabin with a big black Monarch cookstove. This was in the beginning. Lightning pinwheeled into their bedroom and he leaped from the bed and found a book of poems and read her a poem in the storm. They carried water from the creek and shared a zinc tub of steaming bath water. She scrubbed his back with a loofah. They made love in the parsnip patch in broad daylight. At night there were always the stars and he knew them by name. At a garage sale, they bought a cast-iron skillet and an Oriental rug. From second-hand Modern Library hardbacks, they read stories aloud to each other. There were always pileated woodpeckers, red whips of willows, evening sunlight only a gold band above the mountain; there were always animal tracks, lichened stones, creeks, applewood, fir, wild plums; there were always, always the stars, and his arm around her as he named them: *Orion, Cygnus, Sirius.* He smelled like Balkan Sobranie tobacco and wool Woolrich shirts, and his arms were archetypal arms, arms of the woodsman who'd saved her from the wolf within.

The day they moved away from the cabin they stood on the porch and cried in each other's arms. That was the first loss they'd ever shared, shocked at its sweetness.

In town, the first town, the elementary school blazed white as sand in the winter sun. He was a student at the college and she taught at the elementary school. Kites tattered from the cottonwoods beside the playground. Their wantonness required practice. "Talk to me," she said. "You have to have a bit of the ham, the rake, in you to do this. Coax me. Be sly. You know how easy I am." Beyond the shutters an evening snowstorm muffled streets; all the cars had forgotten how to travel; they moved as though forced awry by enchantment, into berms and woodpiles. "The words," she said, "can be about how much you know I'll like it." "How does it feel for you to come?" he said. "It's like stealing something." "Stealing home," he said. She was a marauder, slip of a woman in the flying night, stealing whatever she could, fingers tender and blind, grafting bliss to truancy, crazed absence of self. It was something like an old blues song: that bad, winsome, visceral. She knew how it worked. They found them—the very words—and they became his charm and code, his mojo, sweet-bone totem, the rib and thorn in their fenny winter bed.

They each had private dreams and these were difficult to realize together. The first time she talked about moving away, she cried into a brakeman's bandanna until her eyes were puffy. Finally he said, "Maybe it's a good idea. Maybe I need to be on my own, too." She said no. She said she'd figure out some other way to make her dreams come true. That was in the second year and they had eleven more years to go.

For a long time they took turns moving for each other; the one who followed always felt cheated.

Even now, when she peruses certain maps, she imagines all the places they slept outdoors together. Beside rivers, with that rushing, that glassy, green blooming of the waves: Clark Fork, Gallatin, Yellowstone, Lochsa, Columbia, Methow, Okanogan, Entiat, Wenatchee, Skagit, Rogue, Klamath, Williamson, Santiam, Umpqua, Bella Coola, Fraser, Thompson, Quesnel, Chilcotin. Too numerous to mention were the creeks and lakes. And the mountains they ranged: the Cascades, the Rainbows, the Monashees, the Purcells, the Selkirks, the Tobacco Roots, the Madison Range, the Big Belts. Field mice; blackened pots; wood-smoked sleeping bags zipping together; their breath visible in the mornings; aspens shimmering; cutthroat winds. They were caught in the bite of the mother's moon tooth.

At Shi-Shi Beach near Neah Bay, they slept together outdoors for the last time. To the Indians, Shi-Shi meant *big magic*. The unrestrained Pacific dumped rain on them four days running. Deer cavorted in the surf. They visited a man in a nearby cabin and drank mescal and traded life stories and waited out the weather. He was drunk enough to eat the worm. She has a crescent-shaped scar—petite petroglyph—on the back of her right hand, from falling into a rocky, rain-swollen creek on the walk out. She thinks it's a scar that won't fade and that pleases her, to have the mark of Shi-Shi.

.   .   .

Before that particular July, for several years, they practiced moving away from each other. They were getting used to the idea. First there were separate pleasure trips. Then they began going away to work, a month here, two months there, a summer. Finally she took a job in another state, 1700 miles away. They thought they could manage; they were good at reunions.

They broke the rules like pottery, with that little regret. Their letters of break-up crossed in the mail, one of many blessings that befell them over the years. When next they met—after the divorce was final—they were rife with happy grief, a blessing in itself, they realized. He lived in a small wooden house beside a gang of Macintosh trees. The apples were nearly ripe. The whole tiny house smelled of fresh pocket bread; he baked bread so often, the muslin curtains gave off the odor of yeast and sugar. They cried, made love, slept. They had left an open bottle of Polish vodka on the kitchen table. Once, in the middle of the night, she went out to the screened-in porch. An inverted yellow kayak glowed under the clothesline. She couldn't deny feeling free, a kind of joy in the soles of her feet. The night had grown frost on the dull grass; smudge pots tilted under the trees. Stars stirred above them like fading fires, trying to focus through mottled clouds. This is how she thought of the stars: blurry, a little drunk, still there.

THE TWO MOST

BEAUTIFUL WOMEN

O

Jonathan Baumbach

I STAYED SINGLE for several years after the collapse of my fifth marriage, not looking for trouble, or not looking for the same trouble I had had five times over in the past. What I was looking for (in fact, I was hardly looking at all), was something new, something qualitatively different from any of my previous adventures in the relationship trade. What I imagined myself to want was a woman without the self-doubts and insecurities that had caused most of my other marriages to come to grief.

This was my reasoning. A beautiful woman, given the values of the culture, would have less to prove than someone marginally attractive or someone, as in the case of my fifth wife, so vastly overweight as to seem socially unacceptable. The more beautiful, I thought, the less reason to be vulnerable. At the same time, I was wary of the dangers of narcissism. I wanted a woman so thoroughly beautiful, so secure in her sense of it, that the impression her beauty made on others had ceased to interest her.

An ideal is never easy to find, but the pursuit of it has its own obsessive interest. During this period, between my fifth and sixth wife, I dated only women who were (in my eyes) surpassingly beautiful.

In my quest for the right woman, the perfect one, I met with a series of disappointments. I was a producer in Hollywood at the time, with a string of small successes in low-budget horror films and so I had access to some (all, I sometimes thought) of the most beautiful women in the English-speaking world. I did not use my position to woo these women.

I'd like to describe the nature of my disappointments—some of them. We're talking about a period of seven years here. Between the ages of twenty-one and thirty-eight, I had been married five times. The longest period between marriages had been eighteen months, and that was after the breakup of my first. When I married for the first time, I assumed in my fading innocence it was forever.

So this was a period in which I was (while in pursuit of an elusive ideal) learning to be alone. I made it a point not to have a woman sleep over—at least not the same woman, I was on a quest—more than four nights a week. I studied privacy as if it were advanced calculus.

The disappointments were small, but continual. Beautiful women, I kept discovering, the ones that crossed my path, had no more self-confidence than more ordinary women. Take Sarah Hubb.

Sarah Hubb was not an actress or a model but a writer and film editor, and the most interesting beautiful woman I had met in Hollywood up to that point.

She was prematurely white haired.

She was not really what I was looking for, not at all (never) what I had in mind.

I fell in love with her on second or third sight, fell in love with the idea of her as opposed to my idea of something else.

She didn't like me at first, not much, not for the longest time. That was a liability. It wasn't that exactly either, the not liking. It was that she didn't take me seriously, didn't believe when I said I loved her that I never lied about matters of the heart.

Why didn't she believe me?

"You talked of love to too many other women," she said. "Words overused lose their meaning."

Yes. Yes. Yes. Still, I thought it had to do with feelings about herself, her prematurely white hair, her small breasts. I never believed it had to do with me.

The more I protested my love to her the cooler she became to me. We had the same conversation, variations on it, on several occasions. She suggested that we end our affair (and why did she need my consent?) and I presented arguments for continuing things as they were.

And each time she relented, agreed to continue, as if continuing were a matter of no choice, an aspect of defeat.

She had a history of falling in love with storm troopers, wife beaters, emotional torturers, marginal sociopaths. She was attracted to men, she said, who had no doubts.

One day at a party on the yacht of a man who was considered the hottest of the new breed of producer-directors I saw the most beautiful woman in the world standing between my host and his current wife. Her beauty, the intensity of it, scared me. I couldn't look at her and I couldn't look away.

I kept track of her, knew at almost every moment where she was, who she was talking to or standing next to, without going up to her or seeking an introduction. My opportunity would come. It was a smallish party in a small space. If I didn't move, she would eventually find her way to me.

I was prepared to be disappointed when we finally met.

Her name was Nadia and she spoke English with one of those accents that American actors used to use when playing immigrants or characters in foreign countries. She was almost as charming as she was beautiful.

"What do you do?" I asked her.

"I don't do," she said. "I merely am." She laughed at the pretentiousness of her remark, mocked herself.

"Are you an actress?"

"I'm a guest," she said. "A guest, from where I come, is also actress."

That was the extent of our conversation during our first encounter. I omit something. "I'd like to fuck you," I said to her. It was what I said to attractive women that year. I was into direct expression of feeling.

It took a moment for her to react. She raised her eyebrows in a mild display of outrage and walked away. Perhaps it was the wrong thing to say to her.

The only thing to do was to apologize and I waited a suitable time—twenty minutes exactly—before going after her. She was talking to Lucretia Oldwyn, the wife of the man who owned the yacht, and I approached on the pretense of paying respects to my hostess.

That done (Lucretia presented her cheek to be kissed as if it were the pope's ring), there was the inevitable introduction. I held out my hand to Nadia, waited for her to say we had already met, which she didn't. She shook my hand as if we were meeting for the first time.

When Lucretia moved on, Nadia said to me, "You're persistent, aren't you, Mr. Cole?"

Her beauty overwhelmed me, deprived me of speech. I searched her astonishing face for a flaw. "I want to apologize for my crudeness," I mumbled.

"It's forgotten," she said, turning away and then returning to stare at my face as I had hers. She had more poise than almost anyone I had ever met, woman or man. Yet there was something vulnerable about her too, something invisibly and mysteriously vulnerable, which made me admire her all the more.

I thought of saying, You're the most beautiful woman I've ever seen, but I didn't. I didn't want to emphasize what I thought of as her advantage. Instead I said, "I like the way you look."

She half smiled at my ungenerous compliment. "You intrigue me," she said with her intriguing though undefined accent.

I gave her my card. "You ever take a screen test, Nadia? I'd like to put you in front of the camera."

She fingered my card, studied it, then turned it over as if a more interesting message might be hidden on the reverse side, then handed it back. "I'm afraid not for me," she said, reproducing her charming smile as if she were on camera.

And why didn't I believe her? She assumed the worst, I imagined, had every reason to assume the worst. And I compounded the misunderstanding by denying what on the surface of things seemed undeniable. "My offer of a screen test was not a bribe to get you to sleep with me," I said. "That's not my style."

She waved off my objection as if to say it's unnecessary to defend yourself to me who is not interested enough to make such judgments about you. A moment or so later, she found her excuse to move away.

Later, much later, I saw a screen test she had taken for the man who had given the party on his yacht and I was surprised at how lifeless she seemed. The camera frightened her and she hid from it by denying herself.

At about that same time, or perhaps a week or so earlier, I saw her in her first film, in which she played a courtesan (of sorts) in ancient Egypt with one eyebrow raised and her odd French-Roumanian accent and no other conviction whatsoever. I was her lover at the time and escorted her to the screening. She had no idea how bad she was, couldn't understand the audience's mocking laughter at her most serious moments. To console her, I said I would put her in a movie in which her great charm and luminous beauty would shine through whatever role she played. I gave her my word, something I don't do lightly, that I would make a star of her. It was then that I arranged to see her impossible screen test.

She was a stunningly beautiful woman for whom the camera had no love. It turned her to stone with a glance. Her disastrous test seemed a prophecy of the zombielike performance she gave in her first film.

I recognized that the problem was more daunting than I had imagined, but never for a moment (perhaps I had some unexpressed doubts) did I believe I would fail on my promise to her. It was a time in my life when I refused to acknowledge the impossible. How difficult could it be to make Nadia as goddesslike on screen as she was in person? All I wanted was an illusion that stood up to the real.

I haven't mentioned how we got together, how I took her away from H. K. Oldwyn. I haven't mentioned it because there's really little to say that does me credit. I wore her down, I pursued her as if she were the most important thing in my life. And at some point Oldwyn tired of her—I suspect his wife insisted he break it off—and sent Nadia away. The chronology has its gray areas. Perhaps she had already become my lover before H. K. Oldwyn was disposed to give her up.

It's possible that Lucretia found out her husband was sleeping with Nadia and demanded that H. K. choose between them. That was what Sarah Hubb told me, though how she knew I had no idea.

When I told Sarah Hubb that I intended to marry Nadia, she said she would marry me herself to save me from such a disastrous alliance. That's when she told me about Lucretia Oldwyn forcing her husband to throw Nadia out.

In Nadia's version, she had been the one to break with Oldwyn. "The man had what you would call unacceptable needs," she said. "All I want was to be his good friend. What he want I am shy even to tell you. What he want was humiliating to me."

Obsessed with fulfilling my promise to Nadia, I spent six months staring at her with a movie camera, put her through the ordeal of at least a half-dozen screen tests, using different cameramen and different equipment before even concerning myself with a script. She had astonishing purple eyes, but in one of the tests in which the background was a similar velvety purple, it looked as if you could see right through her head.

When Nadia moved out of H. K. Oldwyn's guesthouse, she moved—it was to be a temporary arrangement—into mine. As a matter of fact, I had no guesthouse or had only a guesthouse. I offered what I had to offer, a room in my house, which turned out to be the one I slept in. That wasn't my intention: to have her move in with me, to have her move into my bed.

I had wooed her so relentlessly she assumed, or appeared to assume, that I would do anything for her. "I'm going to have to move in with you for a while," she said. "I hope that's not inconvenient."

"My pleasure," I said. "My house is yours for as long as you want to stay."

"I knew you want me to live with you," she said. "You've been after me to be with you since we met. Now you get your way, okay?" It was her stance to take nothing from anyone, even of course when the evidence said otherwise. She made a point of retaining the illusion of her independence.

Even though she was the most beautiful woman I had ever seen, I began by invisible degrees to tire of Nadia, though I didn't allow myself to assimilate that knowledge until she had gone. (As sexy as she was, she tended to efface herself in love-making as she did before the eye of the camera.) Tire is perhaps the wrong word for what I felt. Or that it was myself I tired of and not Nadia. Nadia was never less than advertised. She wasn't unintelligent or without imagination or without traces of a sense of humor. She merely, in some essential way, wasn't there much of the time. And I never tired of looking at her astonishing face.

For a stunningly beautiful woman, she had no vanity. It irritated her to be stared at and since I couldn't not look (she was my obsession), I had to observe her on the sly, a voyeur, in a sense, in my own house. Perhaps her most interesting quality was the unexpectedness of her charmingly eccentric European accent.

So I developed this movie project for Nadia about a goddess who comes down to earth to find out what it's like to love a mortal. Not a new idea but recooked with a few new spices. Our story.

A week into shooting the picture, which was called *Heaven on Earth,* she complained to me (in bed) that she couldn't work with the director, a benign tyrant with a gifted eye, a man I had chosen for the elegance of his frames. He didn't know how to talk to people, she purred in my ear; he shouted too much; he insulted her intelligence.

I said I would take care of it, though did nothing (I never liked being manipulated), assuming the problem would take care of itself. The situation worsened. Nadia reiterated her demands with greater and greater passion. The man was a brute, she said, a thug, a gangster of cruelty, he could not be tolerated a moment longer. If he continued as director, she would have no choice but to leave the film.

I said I would talk to the director, whom I knew to be a reasonable man, no more autocratic than the general run, but Nadia insisted the problem between them was beyond reconciliation.

As chance would have it, the next day I got a note from

the director asking for a meeting. His complaint, it turned out, was similar to Nadia's, though from an opposing standpoint. The woman was impossible, he said, was untalented, did not take direction. He could not work with her. So of course I had to replace him. What else was there to do?

The problems didn't end. The second director, who was a cut less distinguished than the first, who had a reputation as a woman's director, got along with Nadia from the word go, managed her by making love to her, handled her by handling her. Of course I didn't know that at the time. The dailies I saw were banal but serviceable. Nadia, however, looked beautiful—almost as beautiful as she did in real life—and that for the time being seemed sufficient. I brought in another writer, a novelist with two screen credits and a drinking problem, to enliven the script.

We saw so little of each other—I had to be on location in Mexico for a while with another project—our relationship seemed to move in reverse. We grew estranged before we had arrived at intimacy. Sometimes she looked at me when I came through the door of my own house after a few days' absence as if I were a potentially dangerous intruder.

"I didn't expect you back so soon," she said on one occasion when I arrived unexpectedly. Something in her voice made me want to open all the closets or look under the bed.

I looked for flaws in her beauty, sought disillusionment. Only in certain light was such scrutiny rewarded.

I had won the most beautiful woman in the world and I didn't know what to do with her now that I had her. Though we talked of a future together, we shared no intimacy beyond our willed sexual games. She might have been Miss Mars (what a title for a film!) for all I understood of her. Something, some part of her—her soul, for God's sake—was always held back. Was that the attraction? Her elegant opacity? I loved her the way a camera loves certain faces. On my internalized movie screen, Nadia was the defining image of female beauty.

We didn't hold conversations so much as report our adventures to each other while apart. Her stories were almost always unconvincing and rarely if ever interesting in themselves. They nevertheless had the considerable charm of ingenuous lies told unaffectedly by a beautiful woman. Sometimes I watched her tell the stories rather than listen to the words. Her flawless face was her undeniable authority.

After a while even our sex life began to run downhill. Her lack of pleasure in our various sexual games undermined my own. She seemed to have zero sense of herself beyond physical image. She loved to be admired but not stared at, afraid that staring would uncover some aspect of herself she needed to keep secret.

When she announced in bed that she had decided to get her own place, I said, "Why don't you marry me instead?" That had been on my mind for a while, the idea of asking her to marry me.

She seemed less surprised to receive the offer than I had felt in hearing myself make it. "I didn't know people like us got married in this time," she said. That was the only answer she gave me.

The picture I was producing with her (and for her), *Heaven on Earth,* despite my having to replace the director and the male lead, was near wrap-up. Virtually all of the principal shooting had been completed.

I had the fantasy that after the movie was released (and our respective careers advanced) we would wrap up our life together by getting married. The film, in a certain sense—allow me this—would be our wedding gift to each other. If I wasn't in love with Nadia, not wholly, not irreversibly, I nevertheless doted on the movie of us together I carried around in my head.

Sarah Hubb was the cutter on *Heaven on Earth* and that, of course—I see this now in retrospect—had to be asking for trouble. I didn't know then that Sarah Hubb cared enough for me to be jealous of Nadia. The movie opened and closed in the same week and was the source of amusement to a number of reviewers, who were inspired to new heights of wit by its mischances. Nadia, who was the main source of the critics' malicious fun, was not amused herself. "I don't think I'm so bad," she said to me. "Do you think I'm so bad as they say?"

What could I tell her? That I would sooner put my arm in the path of a chainsaw than watch *Heaven on Earth* a second time? That it had taken a major act of will to survive its hour and fifty-minute duration the first time? "They missed the point," I said.

"They did," she said, "didn't they? I was supposed to be to laugh at. The real joke is on them, though the picture was not at all perfect."

"It had its faults," I agreed.

She was in her room packing her steamer trunk. I watched her without saying anything. In this town, when you failed, people treated you as if you had some communicable disease.

"I think I go to Paris for a while," she said. "When I get back if you still want, if we both still want, maybe we tie the knot. Yes?"

A car came to the door to take her to the airport—I offered to drive her myself but she wouldn't have it—and we shook hands to say good-bye, as if we had never been lovers at all.

And so the most beautiful woman in the world left me, never, I suspected, to return. She was wearing a short black raincoat and a purple miniskirt, which is how I would remember her, when she climbed into the backseat of the limousine. She waved from the car as if she was dismissing a servant, and as I turned my head away, she disappeared into the future.

That was not the end of her in my life, only the presumed end.

Three months later I received a letter from Nadia (postmarked Roumania), announcing that she was returning to the States in ten days. That wasn't the whole message. She was ready, she wrote, "to be the loving wife you had been all your life in looking for."

The letter could not have arrived at a more unpropitious moment. Sarah Hubb had just moved in with me and we were talking—I was talking—about our getting married. I had assumed that Nadia was out of the picture. Sarah was saying "I'd have to be crazy to marry you" more often now, so I had to believe, whether rightly or not, that her resistance to the prospect was diminishing.

When I showed Sarah Nadia's letter, she said (we had been talking about something else, about who had played the male lead in the movie *Dark Corridor*), "If I were you, I'd call my lawyer." Then she said, moving her hand through her white hair, "If you really want to marry this Roumanian gold digger, I'll pack my bags and take off. This lady has no plans to make trouble for you."

"And you think the other lady has?"

"I think the other lady wants to marry you. She says so, doesn't she? She says you proposed to her and she's accepting. You did propose to her, didn't you?"

"That was a long time ago," I said. "A proposal doesn't mean forever."

"Talk to your lawyer," said Sarah Hubb, who came from a family of lawyers and knew how dangerous they could be to the unwary.

I didn't talk to a lawyer, not then, procrastinated on what to do about Nadia, ended up writing her a letter (which said very little) to an address that I had no certainty would reach her. My intention was to delay her return until I was clear as to what I wanted.

Two weeks later—it seemed like the next day—Nadia and her steamer trunk arrived on my doorstep. It was past midnight, perhaps several hours past. Sarah Hubb had already gone to bed for the night and I was watching a movie on videotape. I tended to fall asleep more readily in front of the television set than almost anywhere else. So her arrival—I wasn't quite sure where I was as I got up to answer the door—had the aspect of a dream or a dream within a dream.

"It was no good to leave," were her first words, her accent heavier than I remembered it.

"Did you get my letter?" I asked.

She looked ruefully at me. "You never write," she said. "You never write a word."

"I sent a letter to you," I said, "telling you that I had not expected you to return and that I was living with someone else."

My beautiful guest looked heavenward, which in this case was at a light fixture in my vestibule. "Yes," she whispered. "The letter was sent nowhere and to nowhere it arrive safely."

"I sent it to the address you left me," I said.

Her eyes filled with tears—the first time I had seen her cry not on screen, not in performance. "All my money is spent in getting here. You need to let me stay. Nothing else I ask for, nothing."

How could I refuse such a request? I said I would stake her to a hotel room for two weeks, would drive her to one as soon as I fixed us both a cup of coffee.

Nadia stayed around for a while, finding new excuses each day not to leave, playing havoc with my life. After three days of her unwanted presence, she no longer seemed the most beautiful woman I had ever seen. I began to discover flaws in her face I had never even imagined before. Her astonishing purple eyes were too close together, were getting closer as the days passed. Her flaws mocked my initial judgment of her. I could no longer look at her (though there were moments, I confess, when it was as it was) with unequivocal pleasure.

It was not that Sarah Hubb was any more impatient than I was with Nadia's uninvited presence. It was just that she didn't trust that I preferred her to Nadia, and the more I insisted on it, the less she wanted to believe me.

I had to do something to keep her, so I did what I had done so many times before, I proposed marriage, proposed that we marry as soon as possible. I had married once before in California so I knew something about the licensing laws.

"Yes, of course," Sarah said. "Yes. But not while that woman's living with us."

"She's promised to leave in a few days," I said. "The only way to get her to leave against her will is to call the police and I don't want to do that. If we got married, Sarah, it would speed her along."

"I don't want to talk about it," she said, turning her beautiful face away. "The subject depresses me."

There was no warning or announcement in advance. One afternoon at about two o'clock, a taxi appeared at my door and Nadia boarded without a word and was gone.

The day after that, Sarah and I got our licenses and two days after that—perhaps it was even the next day—we got married at the house of friends. That was how I got married for the sixth time after vowing to myself never to get married again.

We had a six-day honeymoon in Paris, which I will talk about later, then returned to my house to live and to resume our respective work.

We had a surprise in store for us, the one that Sarah had anticipated.

How I found out is less important than what it was. I was being sued by Nadia (and her high-priced lawyer) for breach of promise, palimony, and something called "sexual malfeasance." I didn't take it seriously, thought I could clear it up directly with Nadia without having to deal with her killer lawyer.

The problem was, I had no way of reaching Nadia, no forwarding address, no names of friends who might know where she was. I checked her former room, checked to see if anything telling had been left behind.

It was three-ten in the morning and I had been unable to sleep—the business, you see, had upset me—so I went into her room. I went through the drawers of her dresser, I looked under her bed, I looked in her bed. She had been thorough or perhaps had never unpacked. The only thing she had left behind were a stack of publicity photos, five-by-sevens. They were machine signed, Love always, Nadia.

Eventually, I found her, ran her down. Though I'm thought of as an outsider in this town, there are people around willing to do me a favor. She was living in a small Malibu hotel, her rent (I learned this later) paid for by the married lawyer who had taken her case. I went to see her, bribed my way past the desk clerk and went directly to her room unannounced.

At first she wouldn't let me in, said she hated me. When she opened the door, when she finally opened the door, it was a shock to see her. "Don't look," she said. "I'm not myself." Her hair was scraggly, unwashed, her face swollen out of shape. She was virtually unrecognizable.

"What the hell happend to you?"

"I have fucking allergic reaction. Don't look at me. I want to say you are the most selfish man I ever know."

"Is that why your lawyer is suing me?"

"Yes. Not at all. You should leave. I'm not to talk to you."

"Your lawyer told you not to talk to me. That's it, isn't it? He's afraid if you talk to me you'll change your mind."

"Please to leave." She pointed to the door, an unconvincing actress even in real life.

"Are you on something, Nadia? What's wrong with you?" She was stumbling and I held on to her.

"What's wrong with you?" she said, mimicking me. Then she began to scream. I tightened my hold on her and eventually—the screaming went on for a long time, it was a tantrum she was having—she fell into silence, as if all the noise in her head leaked out.

"You were the most beautiful woman I ever saw," I said. "The most beautiful."

"You liar," she said under her breath.

"The most beautiful woman anyone ever saw."

She pushed me away and I released her and she went around the unmade bed and sat with her back to me. "You shouldn't say that. You have no right to say such things to me. I don't listen." She put her hands over her ears.

"Why do you think you have a right to my money? Whose idea is it?"

"What?"

I repeated the question in a considerably louder voice, and I got the same unacknowledgment, the same—"What?"

I moved toward her. "Talk to me, Nadia," I said.

"I'm your wife," she said. "I give you my best years. You use me up."

"Is that what your lawyer told you to say? Nadia, you only lived with me for eight months."

"I'll tell you something," she whispered, as if someone who mattered might overhear. "I really hate you. Really. Really. Really."

This was the most deeply felt thing she had said to me in all the time I knew her. I felt obliged to acknowledge what I sensed was going on. That's why I did what I did. It may have been the only thing I could do. The pushing her against the wall, that was for love, for what she had meant to me, for what had never been said. The responsibility is mine. I fucked her against the wall. It felt to me like an obligation, a concluding gesture. Then I went home to my wife, to Sarah Hubb.

She knew where I had been and knew what I had done, which is to say I confessed the worst. And she didn't forgive me, would not forgive me, not ever.

I had made the wrong choice twice.

And as she pulled away from me, drew further into herself—women have that secret place—she seemed unbearably beautiful.

I made periodic efforts to erase the damage, apologized, refused to apologize, insisted that I had done nothing wrong, pleaded for her to relent and forgive me. In the short run, each of my strategies, whichever, had some positive effect. "It's over," Sarah would insist, or "It's forgiven." Or: "I don't blame you, Jack." But nothing changed.

We lived together like strangers in a death camp for another six months. Much of that time I spent trying to ingratiate myself to Sarah Hubb. Someone had to keep the marriage going and I was the only one to whom it seemed to matter. Whenever she admired something or seemed to—a necklace, a painting, a movie camera—I contrived to make her a gift of it. She received my gifts with embarrassed indifference.

I whispered to her in bed one night, "I chose to marry you."

She sighed in her half-sleep, as if my voice were an intrusion on some better dream.

I continued to pursue her favor, worked at it relentlessly, determined to keep this marriage from failing. I thought of this, my sixth marriage, as my last shot.

How did it seem to her, this persistent ineffectual wooing, this unencouraged pursuit? I imagined the worst: contempt and a kind of horror.

I thought about what was going on between us, how foolish it must have seemed, and I thought, Well, why don't I try something else. The thing is, I couldn't think of anything else to try.

I said to her over dinner, "If you don't want to live with me, why don't you move out?"

"I'll move out if you want me to," she said.

I didn't understand her response. "If you're going to be my enemy, I'd like you to move out," I said.

She looked at me, her eyes narrowed, a last reading of the text. "Okay," she said.

We were polite to each other for the rest of the meal, as if we both regretted what we had allowed ourselves to say.

Whatever had been decided seemed irreversible. Shortly after dinner, Sarah went into our bedroom to pack. I knew what she was doing, and I didn't want her to go, but I made no effort to dissuade her. I made no effort because I assumed that nothing I might say would change her mind.

Someone rang the bell just as she completed packing and I was the one to answer the door. I called to her, "Sarah, it's for you."

"Just a minute," she called back.

The friend who had come for her—I knew him slightly, he was someone she worked with—waited for her in the doorway. "She'll be a minute," I said.

He waited for her by looking the other way, staring off into some unpopulated distance. Her delay seemed interminable.

When she arrived she kept her head averted, said nothing, not even good-bye, and it was only after she was gone that I realized—her face seemed remade—that she had been trying to disguise that she had been crying.

It meant nothing, her tears meant nothing. I closed the door, though I don't remember closing it, and I walked through the house, visiting in turn each of its twelve rooms. Sarah Hubb was in none of them. I had the sense that I was missing something obvious, that Sarah's apparent absence was a manifestation of my forgetfulness. I had misplaced my wife, who was five foot six and weighed 118 pounds, in this oversized house. There was loneliness in every room.

It was not that I didn't understand what had happened with Sarah Hubb. What I didn't understand was something else, how it had happened, how I had let it happen. I had no language to know what it was that I didn't know.

I saw her at work from time to time—she was editing a film I was connected with—and for a week or so we avoided each other, and then we began to fall into our old banter, the way it was when we were first friends.

We pretended, or seemed to pretend, that this is the way it had always been, that nothing had intervened—not living together, not marriage, not betrayal and disaffection.

For no reason, or some reason—there is always some reason—I found myself thinking about my honeymoon with Sarah Hubb, focusing on one incident in particular.

We had been shy with each other in Paris, inexplicably distant and diffident. A certain wariness had developed between us without recognizable cause. Leaving a restaurant after dinner, we got into a mild argument about whether we ought to walk back to our hotel or take the metro. I urged walking. Sarah Hubb pretended not to care, acquiesced to my insistence. We walked a block or two in silence, then she said in an uncharacteristically harsh voice: "You don't love me. You shouldn't have married me."

I said something like, "What do you mean? Of course I love you."

Her remark was not repeated. She leaned toward me and we kissed. She swayed when I held her, seemed by turns frail or fierce, some twig in the wind or the wind itself. We were in the middle of the street, several blocks from our hotel, cleaving to the same space.

"Let's find a cab," I think I said.

Her grip became tighter. "Five minutes," she pleaded.

I didn't understand what she wanted. People stared at us as if we were some form of street theater. "It's silly to do this in the street," I said or tried to say. Her mouth seemed to swallow my words, steal them before they were spoken.

Her abandon in this public place, which was uncharacteristic (Sarah tended to be shy in public), fueled a kind of anxiety. A cab was coming and I signaled to it, but it went by without acknowledgment.

"I don't want to be anywhere else," she whispered. "Do you?"

The question was asked as if it had only one answer. I said, "What I want is to be alone with you, only that."

It was a damp night and seemed to be getting wetter, a serious storm in imminent promise. That was my recollection. It may have been that I confused the weather with my feelings.

Eventually, we disentangled and I found a taxi and we went back to our hotel room.

We took off our clothes in a rush of activity, but didn't touch for the longest time, stood naked a foot or two apart looking at each other in exquisite anticipation. Sarah seemed to be shivering from the cold, though our room was if anything hotter than ideal. I was in a fever, my face burning. I didn't want to begin, even to move toward the prospect of beginning, because to begin meant ultimately to end. The idea of ending, you have to understand, was unbearable to me. Finally I held out my hand to her, which she ignored at first, then held on to loosely with two hands as if it were a damaged bird, something inordinately fragile. So much tremulousness and hesitation over doing something we had done a hundred times before. What was that about? We met under the covers, entering the bed from opposing sides.

There was a shocking intensity of feeling between us that night, an intensity that threatened to make anticlimax of the next day or the next week or the next twenty years. It left us nowhere to go. "My life," she whispered to me. "You're wonderful," I think I said in return. That may have been all that was said. They were insufficient acknowledgments of what had passed. Not lies, but impassioned evasions.

In the morning, I was burned out and frightened. Whatever it was that possessed me that night, I knew I had to avoid its recurrence to survive. So I turned off, sought calmer air. Later, when I became aware that that intensity of feeling was gone forever from my life, I secretly mourned its loss while pretending to be unconcerned. What else could I do, what else could I possibly do?

My sense is that that night in Paris represented the high and low points of our marriage, love and heartbreak, which were the same, love and love's loss. The rest was terminal disappointment.

I let myself believe—I never wholly believed otherwise—that Sarah Hubb never loved me. Never. Everything else between us was read in light of that assumption. She didn't love me, never loved me. Her gestures to the contrary didn't mean what they seemed.

So I lost her. If I ever wished to undo anything, I might have wished unwritten that last scene with Sarah Hubb the night she left (the day I asked her to leave) forever. Yet I suspect even if I had not asked her to leave, even if I had found the words to make possible reconciliation, the outcome would have been more or less the same. We were not getting along. Eventually, if not then, a month later or a year or five years down the road, we would have found our way apart. It's my rule of thumb not to look back. I rarely have regrets or admit to having them.

BROKEN GLASS

O

Melanie Thernstrom

T HE MAN SLEEPING next to Gretel under the
frayed red-and-white-backed comforter is pretty. He has dark
brown eyes and black curly hair and light brown skin, which
smells slightly of sweat in a way that is somehow innocent and
makes her think that he had been working hard at something
simple, like tilling fields. He is pretty now, and must have been
prettier as a child. He sleeps with his back toward her in the
bed on the floor—she imagines his mother washing it in a big
enamel tub with curling claws. There were five children in his
family; his mother must have given a lot of baths, come evening. They were Catholic, and moved often. He had a happy
childhood. She asked him about it, and he replied, surprised, he
didn't have many happy memories, but he thought he remembered the feeling of having been happy. She wished she had
pressed him. He must remember something—a tree house, a
rabbit—she almost wanted to wake him up to make him tell her

some happy specifics. His mother, he told her, is as nice as could be. Gretel nods; she can picture that: *as nice as could be.* And he has some older sisters, too, two or three. One of them is named Cassandra. She recites these things, the store, the little sum of things she knows about him, greedily, while he sleeps. She runs out within minutes; she puts her hands on his back, meaning: *she has no more.* He awakens; she moves into his arms to stop from seeing whether he is cross—to try to fool him out of it. His glance falls down on her stomach. She looks down and catches a glimpse of her skin, which strikes her suddenly as suspiciously white, and she looks away, a familiar distaste.

"You had an appendectomy," he says, tracing the faint blue braid of stitchings. She remembers suddenly Christmas-time, London, and being taken to the hospital in a shiny London taxicab. Her mother and brother had been at a Shakespeare play in Stratford that night, and they left before it was over, and even though it was too late to catch the last train, they sat in the station all night, just to be urgent, and her little brother cried. Her mother told her this later, about her little brother, to show he is sweet. When she awoke in the morning there was an enormous bouquet of red-petaled tulips, and a doctor with blue eyes who called her princess. Open your eyes, Princess; you're all well now. And there were other things too: the shade of the walls and sheets, pale pink, eggshell almost—she could remember, if she wanted, precisely the shade, and how it was raining when she stepped out onto the street, and how white rain makes her skin feel, but it saddens her that she has access to the memory only through his fingers. She wonders, as always, when she will remember herself through herself—if she will remember. In her mind, it has something to do with being a woman that makes it this way—*incompleteness,* a magazine article would call it, a women's psychology article in a women's magazine. She would scan it contemptuously and think how she hates psychological clichés. *Women need men to return them to childhood.*

She looks at him again; he looks complete. She can see him

quite clearly in the late blue night. It seems to her, too, that
that is why he is so pretty, although she could be making that
up, in light of the article. There is a copy of *Grimm's Fairy
Tales* by his bed, in the top of the wooden bookshelf. On the
lower shelf are some dried autumn leaves—maple leaves she
thinks, large and five-fingered, like rust-colored hands, or
things to write on. She reaches for the book and opens its
cover. Inscribed in loopy childhood letters with slate-gray pencil is his name. It strikes her as almost unbelievably beautiful;
she looks away, ashamed, so he won't see how beautiful it is to
her. Read something, he tells her, and she looks to see if he
really wants her to, and then reads aloud the story of the little
tailor. He reads some too, his hands over hers on the thickened
page. Good things happen to the little tailor. On the wall is a
quilt his grandmother made; she looks at its squares of blue
and white and pictures his grandmother stitching at them with
invisible threads, thinking of him, and wondering whether to
put in a third color—green perhaps, or chartreuse—or whether
to keep it as it is.

She had met him first at a costume party; his face had
been powdered white in imitation of a clown. Tonight, he had
brought her to the apartment on his motorcycle; it had been
damp, a quarter breath of rain dusting her cheeks and tangling
in her hair. She kept trying to hold her skirts in her hands, but
the material was too thick to keep gathered together, and she
was afraid it would entwine in the wheel, and catch. He had
given her his helmet, and when they had pulled up next to a car
at a red light an old woman in it had said, actually shouted
through the open window: *"You should marry that man, he has
given you his helmet."* He had smiled, and she had leaned forward and put her hands in his pockets. The leather felt soft as
worn cashmere, copper colored, and her skirts fell down, a sudden damp on her knees.

They had talked about marriage once. They were sitting
on stools at the counter of an Irish bar drinking cognac and
watching couples folk dance on the floor. The women wore wide

skirts that turned into pleated circles as they twirled. She was trying to persuade him to dance with her. He didn't want to, but he said he was sure she could get someone else if she wanted, and she pouted a little and said no. She wanted him. And then the conversation turned to marriage, and she said she always thought that people who lived together must get along unusually well because otherwise why would they choose to live together when they weren't getting credit for being married? But, of course, she wanted to marry, she said, to be married, and he smiled and said that if he ever did marry it was likely to be for taxes or some such reason, and involve simply a trip to the justice of the peace. She heard the word simple, and had the sudden thought that whoever he married would really really like him, and would feel none of the secret nausea she always tasted when she envisioned herself in too many layers of pointed white lace, being congratulated by her parents' friends. She asked him once again if he would dance with her, and he said, gently, no.

There are three rooms in his apartment; each of them is filled with things. She outlines them as she lies next to him in bed. The kitchen has an unusually large number of reds in it. On the red chipped counter is half a tomato cut open like a flower, its petals small and seedy. The cover of a cookbook is also red, and the plastic handle on his shiny silver scissors. She wonders dimly if she will cut herself with them, or her fingers. The teapot on the stove is black and fat-bottomed; a kettle, she thinks, a black iron kettle that sings on the stove tears and sad tales: *careful, careful, he will break your heart.* He had made tea when they first came in, and warmed for her a heel of bread. She was startled that he had made bread. She asked him about it a couple of times to be certain. He asked her if she wanted some dried pea soup, and she had said yes, and he told her that she ate a lot. She was always cold and hungry. The tea was strange and spiced; he gave her a piece of hollow gourd the size of her little finger. Some tribe somewhere she had never heard of drank their tea in this way—Argentina, perhaps, or the Amazon. She couldn't figure out how to drink from it, though, so he held it up, his fingers on her lips, as if telling her to hush, and the gourd was quiet and cold as driftwood, or the stem of a lute. And she tasted tea, sweet and spiced.

He played Brazilian music while she ate; she had never heard Brazilian music before. Thinking she was still cold, he closed the window, and the glass chipped in a single jagged piece, like a figure in a stained-glass window. Damn, he said, and, suddenly resourceful, she picked it up and told him she could put it together again. Its sharpness was lovely in her palm; how lucky, she thought, that it fell out whole. And, although she never fixed things, she knelt on the ledge and put it back in, taping with clear tape around each of the edges, and pressing down with her nails until the tape stuck and stayed, invisible as a halo. He looked at her, surprised, and said that it fit. She wondered if he would keep it that way, or if he would replace it after she had gone.

On the walls around the room were posters in reds and purples with block letters stamped threateningly across. *Viva la Revolucion. La revolucion.* Half a salad spinner lay on the counter, its base filled with curly green lettuce, but the top piece missing. He was too poor to buy the other half, he said, and when she looked worried, he laughed at her. He had bought it for pennies at a garage sale. Underneath the window hung a papier-mâché rooster. It was glazed and shiny, with black eyes and orange feathers. It had been made in Mexico by autistic Mexican schoolchildren. For some reason, of all the things that he had, it was this in particular she imagined she would recall; she knew no autistic children, she knew practically no children anymore, and, standing there in the kitchen, she felt a sudden certain conviction that she would never in this life possess such an object. No orange rooster would ever call to her beneath her windowsill. This, she decided, was the difference between them. He is poor and pretty and reads things in Spanish at the kitchen table, while she was none of these things, and knew no other living languages. While she spent years in school doing well at a language now only a paradigm for other languages, others were learning tongues that were spoken, in which food and wine could be ordered, and eaten. She tried not to dwell on this, to see Ecclesiastical Latin as a personal prophecy. She could read inscriptions on medieval churches; she was confident she could parse them and identify all the cases. *Imiatio Christi: bonum vita imiatio christi.* He had first learned Spanish by going to a village with *A Hundred Years of Solitude* and a dictionary. He had no money, though, and he ate green peas until he felt like the hero in a French novel in which the hero eats only green peas and eventually goes mad. And she thought again, with wonder, how really differently they have lived.

She had never seen him study, of course, but she could imagine it so clearly—bent over the lamp, yellow at night—that she thinks that she has. He is studying Latin America and writing particularly about some peasant uprising or revolution in Mexico. She wants to ask which one, when it happened and whether they won, but she is afraid that there was only one, and she ought to know what it was by now. When she asked, spellbound, whether his family was Mexican, he smiled and said no, and when she asked why his skin was so brown, he replied he didn't know, but they say people come to look like the things they think about. She thought about this a lot: what it means she looks like, or will come to look like. She wonders if he likes women who are dark.

Her apartment, on the other hand, is ugly and empty. It has nothing at all in it—not even food. When she comes home she always opens the refrigerator to make sure there is no food, and there never is any food. There is food in the cabinet, though, which is the place she looks second. It's not the kind of food she likes. Dry raisin bran, soft graham crackers, tomato paste, a decaffeinated kind of lemony tea, and one promising item: a small flask of vanilla, which is always cheeringly full because she has nothing in which to use vanilla. Her kitchen is not ill-equipped, of course, and there is nothing which says that she can't, for instance, go shopping and make pumpkin bread. She likes to make bread—one of her happiest summers, the summer she turned seventeen, she spent baking bread and having bread and tea with her favorite friend, Steven, while her father asked if she ought not to have a job, and pointed out that other people's children considered themselves too old not to work.

Perhaps the reason Gretel couldn't do anything in the apartment is because it was never really hers. It was her Iranian roommate's apartment, and on the day that she met him, he and her mother had had a long discussion about Iranian politics, which is something her mother was interested in and knowledgeable about, while she sat politely on the couch and listened. He told her father later that he thought she was pretty, and her father smiled and it was decided that it would be a good place for her to live. The apartment was square and new, white-walled and formica-countered, with a heavy sliding glass door through which she could see sheets of blank snow eight out of twelve months. She stopped looking after the first two. She had imagined the apartment would feel modern, but it turned out only sterile. Everywhere there were fake Iranian decorations. She thought they were the ugliest things she had ever seen. They couldn't be fake, he truly was Iranian and had come over to study electrical engineering only the year before, but she felt positive they were—the ghastly doll mannequins, the pictures of women dancing in contorted positions with shells glued to their exposed flesh—she hated them so nauseatingly she was unable even to dust the walls. An entire year went by without her having dusted once. She would never make bread in that apartment.

It was not an inexpensive apartment, though, and, besides, she was not poor; she could move to another and redecorate, anytime she wished, anywhere she wanted. She recalled the things in his rooms again as if it were that simple: *collect some ideas and redecorate.* Borrow, beg, steal, or buy. She was not good with money: she alternately had none at all—not even sandwich money—or was unbelievably careless, as if emptying all her change into a fountain just for good luck, because she imagined perpetually that she was in need of luck—or some peculiar approximation thereof—*rich but not rich*. At this moment, though, she had money, and was being careless. Redecorate.

Poor, modest, pretty: the lovely fairy-tale three. The people in tales who marry for love in spite of their parents' wishes marry people who have these three qualities. And *kind*—she had forgotten about kindness; there must, in fact, be four qualities. The Princess marries the Student, the Nobleman takes in the Waif. *And keeps her*—does he keep her? Does she grow up; does she metamorphose? She wished she remembered, and wonders whether it always ends the same, or whether it depends on the particular Waif-girl, and the particular way in which she is a Waif. She would like to know on what it depends. My God, though, is it really necessary that they be one or the other? doesn't she know any stories where the people are equals? She thinks about this for a while, trying to think whether she does.

Of the four qualities, it seems to her, she has the best claim for modesty—although self-hatred, the magazine article would remind her, *self-hatred is not humility.* Low self-esteem, poor body image, inadequate perception of boundaries—*no sense of self,* the magazine would say. *Selfishness,* she thinks suddenly, *is having no self to have a sense of, to give away or not give away, to keep or to share.* No, that is going too far, that would not be in the magazine. A need to regress to childhood: childhood regressional longings and tendencies—the belief that beautiful things belong to someone else. The rooster, clumsy and orange. Has she nothing to give?

He is asleep already, or half asleep, his breathing soft. She listens, breath by breath; she also is almost asleep. The blankets drape over his waist, while she curls with the quilt up to her chin as close to him as she can, to stay within the enclosure of his warmth. She remembered her mother telling her that people in poor countries sleep with their animals in order to keep warm. She had liked that idea so much she had asked if she could have an animal, and her mother had said naturally not. His chest is bare; it might have been his bare-chestedness that first made her think of tilled fields and animals and warm-earthed places. She wants to put her hands on it. She is wearing his sweater under the covers; she can never go to sleep until she is completely warm, and she is almost never completely warm. She moves closer, trying to settle a little further into sleep. The wool is rough on her skin; he bought it, he told her, from a Peruvian peasant woman. She can feel the stitching; she herself has several white wool sweaters, but they are not like this—a speckled egg color, unevenly stitched and temptingly wide knit. She imagines putting her fingers between the stitches, like poking at the llamas in the llama cage at the zoo. "It suits you," he had said, glancing at her briefly, and she was as pleased as if he had told her she was gorgeous. Morning moves a little closer; light changes in the room. She doesn't want to fall asleep; when she awakens the night will be over. It will be time to go; the story finished. It's time to go now; the story's all but writ. The Princess came to the Scholar's cottage, and saw his things, his papier-mâché rooster, *and realized the poverty of her own inner life.* There was plenty of imagination, but no materials in it.

A woman came in, the story composes in the bleak light, and because it was cold out, or because he felt sorry for her, the man let her stay the night. He didn't know that she was going to look at his things, though—appraising, one by one, as if she were trying to steal them, or to trick him out of something precious—solitude perhaps, or completeness. A story, a symbol, a memory, an image. And did she get them; did she pocket them; and could she then take them home with her? Can you take things for yourself when they are taken from someone else?

"Gretel," he says suddenly, the name surprising, as if she were hearing it for the first time. He reaches over, just at that moment, and puts a hand on her stomach, twining the other in her hair. She holds still, thinking he will take them away in a moment, but he doesn't. She rests her head on his chest, nuzzling, until her cheek curves into his shoulder blade. Holding both his hands, she is still putting the last lines together as she falls asleep: *You left first thing in the dawn. You imagined for a long time afterward you would see him again, would meet him accidentally on the streets or be told of him, although you did not know by whom, but it was just that: imagining. It was a singular story. It happened once. You met a man one dreary day, and he brought you home, and invited you up, and because you were bold and frightened but thought you were lucky, as girls in fairy tales are always lucky, you followed him up the dimly lighted stairs and opened the door into the rooms where he lived. He gave you something to eat and drink, and you saw how he had written his name in his childhood* Grimm's Fairy Tales *book. When you awoke the next day, and went out onto the streets—happy, you awoke happy—you imagined you would be able to go back another time. But you couldn't; you couldn't find your way. Perhaps the doorway with the stairs had disappeared, or perhaps there was another reason, a reason you would never know. And although it didn't have to be this way because it was a modern story (and you could, for instance, have telephoned him—you had the number—or sent a postcard now and then, or any number of other things; he might have been perfectly willing, happy even, to keep in touch) you never did. But whatever you had come to steal, or be given, or simply to look at, had been looked at. And you always remembered it.* Always, exactly, just like that: the shade of orange, burnt, glazed, the way she feels when she feels about herself, and standing there waiting, the damp London rain shivering, falling, catching on the white face of childhood as she awakens—a glass washed clean through which are seen, warped and bright, possibilities of home.

NIGHT

O

David Huddle

Help me with this, baby girl," my father told
me. He was turning on all the lights in our living room. This
was the year we lived in Seattle, the year I started becoming
aware of how much he drank. I must have been around eleven.
We had a rambling house with a huge window that looked out
over Puget Sound, a window that was almost the whole wall of
our living room. I remember feeling good about the lights I
could see coming on down there around the bay, but feeling
anxious about my father wanting so many lights on in the
house.

He and I were at home alone. He and my mom had had a
fight a couple of days before this evening, and she'd flown back
to New York for a week or so. My brother, Randy, and my
father had had a fight earlier that afternoon. Randy had
stormed out of the house, with my father screaming at him to
come back that very minute and Randy screaming back at him.

When my brother was thirteen and fourteen, he and my father fought like that pretty often. This was a Saturday, I think; they mostly fought on weekends.

I'd hung around the living room, sort of keeping an eye on my father, because I'd learned that he didn't like being surprised by any of us coming upon him unexpectedly, especially if he was in the pantry pouring a drink or in the kitchen getting ice. He didn't even like it if you were just sitting in the living room, looking at a magazine or listening to a record, and he walked in on you without already knowing you were there.

I'd kept meaning to tell Randy about this trick I had of keeping Dad in sight, or keeping him aware that I was around, because that way I didn't surprise him and set him off. Lots of times he'd walk in on Randy, who'd have a glass of milk and a plate of cookies or a sandwich and his school stuff strewn all around the sofa and coffee table; then my father would start yelling at him for being a slob and a deadbeat, and they'd be into it again.

This was also around the time that I caught on to how I could use my tennis training to sidetrack him from drinking so much and picking on Randy and my mom. If I could get him out on the court with me—we had an old-fashioned red clay court at that house and this Japanese gardener who kept it in perfect condition—if I could get my father out there with me, and get him moving enough to work up a sweat, then he usually drank a lot less and didn't pick on us nearly as much.

But this particular morning, he and I had had only about an hour's workout before he had to go downtown to have lunch with some people from his company, and when he came home that afternoon, he went straight to the pantry. Then he ran into Randy in the living room and started yelling at him, Randy stormed out, and I spent the rest of the afternoon sort of softly stalking my father around the house, now and then saying, "How you doing, Dad?" or "Do you want anything from the kitchen, Dad?"

My father had gotten quiet about half an hour before he

turned on the lights, but that wasn't unusual. I could tell from his facial expression that he knew I was around and that he wasn't angry at me. He had been standing at the windows, looking one way and then another. Then he began switching on every lamp in the living room, and I knew something strange was happening. "Now go turn on the lights in your bedroom, baby girl," he told me. I suddenly understood that he was afraid of something.

I had probably seen more than most eleven-year-old girls had. Our parents had taken my brother and me with them on trips to Europe, the Philippines, Hong Kong, Japan, and Australia, and we'd lived in London, New York, Houston, and now Seattle. I'd seen my father angry and happy and even depressed, but I hadn't ever seen him afraid of anything or anybody. I did as he'd instructed me, turned on the lights in my bedroom, even the lamp on my dresser that almost never got turned on. When I came back to the living room, I could hear him moving through the rest of the house, turning on lights, I supposed. Momentarily he came back in with me and asked if the drapes were open in my room. I told him I thought they were.

"I think they're afraid of light," he told me. "At least that's what I'm counting on."

"Who, Dad?" I asked him. Usually he didn't like being questioned, and so I made my voice sound friendly and interested, as if we were having a little conversation about a football team he'd read about in the newspaper.

He was on his way to the pantry to get a fresh drink, but he made a gesture back toward the living room window and said, "Go look for yourself."

I moved to the big window and stood there for a long time, looking out one way and then another, as I'd seen my father do. At first I'd been curious to see what might be out there. I imagined animals of some sort—maybe wolves or coyotes I thought, since this was the West—and then I imagined gangsters. But I saw nothing except the terraces of our front yard, lights of the neighbors' houses, and then the usual pretty lights around the bay far in the distance. I really did look hard out there until I knew for certain that I wasn't going to see whatever it was my father was seeing.

When I turned back to the living room, he was staring at me, and I knew he had been staring at my back while I stood there. He had brought a bottle of Canadian Club in from the pantry and set it on the floor beside his chair. He was sweating, and he had loosened his tie. My father is the only man I know who wears a coat and tie to relax in. He worked for an import-export company that was known for its executives wearing good clothes; my father took pride in being the one who set the standards for everyone else in the company. Every year after Christmas he bought half a dozen new suits and at least that many sports jackets and trouser sets. He had literally hundreds of ties. For me to see him that night sitting there in his shirt-sleeves with his tie loose was the same as for somebody else to see her father stripped down to his underwear.

"Put on some music, baby girl," he told me. I must have given him a questioning look because then he spoke to me impatiently—as if I should have known this all along—"They're afraid of music."

Music seemed like a good idea to me. I started to put on Peter, Paul & Mary, because that was my favorite record in his and my mom's collection—it had belonged to her in college, I think—but he saw which one I'd picked and told me, "Not that one."

"What would you like to hear, Dad?" Again, I was careful to keep my voice normal and friendly, not to upset him. When he didn't answer right away, I turned to look at him. He had his eyes on the window. I waited awhile and then said very softly, "Dad?"

He jerked his head around toward me and shouted at me, "You'd better get a record on that stereo right away, or you're going to have a lot of trouble come and visit you."

That about trouble coming to visit was something he said

both when he was kidding and when he really meant it. I'd learned to know which it was by the tone of his voice. This time he definitely meant it. The *1812* Overture seemed to me the best choice because that was what he listened to sometimes after he and my mom had had a fight. Maybe for that reason, I'd gotten so I hated it, especially the really loud parts, where my father always stood up and waved his arms and pointed like he was the conductor of the orchestra. When I put it on and came back to the sofa to sit down, my father nodded at me, picked up the bottle of Canadian Club, and poured himself another drink from it. He sipped, nodded, and told me, "I think we've got a chance, baby girl."

When that side of the record finished playing, he looked at me, nodding toward the stereo. I got up to change it, then started to slip off to my bedroom—mostly because it was that last part of The *1812* Overture that I hated the most. "Where you going, baby girl?" my father asked.

"To put my pajamas on," I told him, which was a smart thing for me to say. He wouldn't have liked it if I'd just said "To my room." I remember thinking I'd gotten pretty smart about the way I could deal with him.

"Hurry on back," he said. "I'll worry about you if you're gone too long."

He'd made his voice sound sweet, but I knew that he was lying to me, that it was himself he was worried about, that he didn't want to be by himself. That was a first, too. I'd gotten used to thinking of my father as temperamental and unfair and a bully lots of times. But those seemed his due as a father and as a man who had a high-pressure job and made a lot of money. So far as I knew—though, being only eleven, what could I really know about him?—he hadn't lied to me before. He'd made me do lots of things I didn't want to do, he'd even slapped me a few times, but I'd never been aware of his trying to get me to do something by lying to me.

"I will, Dad," I said, and even as I spoke those words, my father seemed to be shrinking in my mind. You know how

when you're little, your parents seem huge to you, and maybe
with my father I'd hung on too long to that way of thinking
about him. Actually, he was a pretty normal-sized man, five
eleven and 165 or 175 pounds, and so maybe what was happening as I thought about it in my room, changing into my pajamas and bathrobe was just that I was starting to see him for
what he was, a regular person. But I remember feeling sad
about him and worried. The whole house seemed weird because
of having all the lights on, which made even my own room seem
like not my room.

I took a chance and tried to stay in there until the record
was over, but pretty soon, my father knocked on the door and
called out, "Hurry it up, Angela." So I went out right away.
He didn't use my name unless he was mad or just about to get
that way. He had gone to stand at the window again, and I was
glad he was doing that instead of conducting the music. I sat
on the sofa, trying to think my brother back into the house.
Because I'd read some article somewhere about "The Powers
of the Mind," I was always trying to think something into happening. It didn't work for getting Randy back home that
night; he'd gone to stay with one of his friends from school.
But at least it did give me something to do while I sat up with
my dad.

When the music ended, my father looked at me and gave
that little movement of his head that meant he wanted me to
put on another record. I started to ask him what he wanted to
hear next, but I changed my mind. Somehow I liked it better
without having to hear him say anything and without my having to say anything to him. So I just started with the first
record on the left-hand side of his and my mom's collection and
figured if he kept on making me play records for him, I'd go
through them that way, so as not to have to think about which
one to play next.

That was the longest night of my life. My father woke me
up a couple of times to go and turn the record over or put on
another one. But now that I think back over it, I doubt that it
was all that late when my father finally passed out—maybe, at

the outside latest, it was midnight. But at the time it seemed like he and I had fallen through the bottom of the night and it wouldn't ever get to be morning again.

What finally happened was that I became aware of a long stretch of silence and snapped open my eyes. My father was slumped over in his chair, asleep with his mouth open. For a moment I thought about trying to move him into the bedroom, but then I realized that with him asleep, I was finally free to do whatever I wanted to do. I got up and turned off the stereo and went all through the house turning off lights and closing drapes. I took my father's glass into the kitchen and rinsed it out, and I put what was left of his bottle of Canadian Club back in the pantry. I wrote my brother a note and taped it to the outside of the back door where I knew he would come if he came back at all that night; I told him to come tap on my window, and I'd let him in the house. I checked to see that all the doors were locked, and I took a last look at my father. I could tell that he wasn't dead or sick or anything, he was just very soundly asleep. Again, I was tempted to try to move him to the sofa, or just to loosen his tie a little more, but I really didn't want to touch him. I could just imagine waking him up and his saying, "Put on another record, baby girl."

I'd already been to my room to turn off the ceiling light and the light on the dresser, and I'd even straightened up my bed and put my clothes away. I didn't usually do things like that, because we'd always had a maid who took care of my room on weekdays. But it was Saturday, and I knew I wanted my room to be exactly right when I finally was able to go to bed that night. First I went to the bathroom, then I walked slowly into my room, where I'd left the bedside light on, the last light that was on in the whole house. I remember thinking to myself as I took off my bathrobe and carefully hung it on its hook inside the closet door, "I've been a good girl tonight." Pulling down my covers and swinging my body up into bed and turning off the light, I was thinking, "Nobody knows it, but tonight I've been the best girl anybody could be."

My sheets were that cool temperature that makes you curl

up and shiver and think about how warm you're soon going to be and how sweet it will feel to fall asleep. All of a sudden I was thinking about my mom, about how not so many years earlier she'd helped me learn how to read; she'd been so excited when I started being able to sound out the words in a book, and when we finished reading one of those books, like *Frog and Toad,* we'd both be excited, and she'd give me a big hug, and I'd feel like the smartest kid anywhere.

All through that night with my father, I'd avoided thinking about my mom, the way you're afraid to let anybody see the one thing you care about the most in the world because their seeing it might spoil it for you. I must have thought my dad would somehow ruin the way I thought about my mom if I thought about her when I was out there with him. But when I was there in my room, curled up in my bed, I could think about her all I wanted to, all the way into sleep. I thought about my mom's clothes. I knew them almost as well as she did, and though I hadn't told her, I had my own favorites among her underwear and slips and dresses and blouses and sweaters. I thought about her getting dressed to go out to a party. I thought about her putting on a new silk blouse she'd gotten for Christmas from my grandparents. I loved my mom so much that night, and she wasn't even in the same house with me.

EASY

O

Jilla Youngblood Smith

M OTHER TALKS A lot these days about power. Le-
gitimate power. "The person with real power," Mother says,
"is the person with the wallet or the gun."

Although Mother doesn't own a gun, she does have the
wallet, and she is raising me and my little sister, Beckett.

"Single-holstered," I tell her.

My only guess as to why Mother is so rankled about
power is that power is like European travel or Tiffany glass.
It's something she's never had.

Dad would have argued this point. He said Mother's
weakness was her power. "The helpless have always had others
do their bidding," he said. "Don't you know that, boy?"

Who knows what kind of power Dad has found on the
corporate shores of New Jersey. "Incredibly happy now," he
wrote to Beckett and me. "Incredibly so."

Heaven help me if Mother should ever think I thought so,

but she does not have that quiet, self-assured posture that Dad had, who made us believe that even if the rest of the world were struck by nuclear catastrophe, his little family would be perfectly all right. Dad had all the answers, and even when Mother pointed out that they were fantasy, or that he was nothing but a dream maker, there was something wonderful about climbing into Dad's lap and listening to all those lies. I figure if you're going to be deceived in this life, there is no better time than when you're a kid. All that stuff about Santa Claus and a forgiving God seems necessary. Then you're properly suited up for the game of life. You can peel away your protection gradually as you get stronger. You can blame God, or Santa Claus for your lack of power until you can find it for yourself.

Mother is a secretary at the community college during the day, and the evening receptionist for Dr. Murray, a psychologist, whom she affectionately calls Dr. M, on the west side of town. It was Dr. M who got Mother to thinking about self-esteem and power. Mother's biggest complaint is that Beckett and I, after three years of Mother's hard work and devotion, do not truly respect her as head of the house.

A few evenings ago Mother stood at my bedroom door with her arms stretched against the jambs.

"Just where do you think you're going?" she asked me. I was pulling on my Calvins and splashing on the Paco Rabanne.

"Where you going, Easy?" Beckett repeated after Mother, bouncing on the edge of my bed. (My friends call me Easy because I am, or let them think I am.)

"Out," I said, clucking my tongue and winking evasively at Mother's scowl.

"With whom?" said Mother.

I gave her the dead-eye look of exasperation, because she knows I rarely go out with anyone but Walt. Walter Schultz. He's my best friend.

"Ohhh," Mother groaned. "Birds of a feather."

"Puh-lease, Mother," I said. "Don't start."

"What about your studies?"

"Finis, ma chère," I said.

"And just look at this room. It smells to high heaven, Carter."

"You'll find the fish heads under the bed," I said.

"Yech," said Beckett. "You're a sicko!"

I picked Beckett up and tossed her on the bed, and she squealed as she bounced backward.

"Do it again, Ease. Do it again," she pleaded.

"No later than midnight, Carter," Mother said as I attempted to pass her in the doorway. "And earlier if possible. I have to talk to you."

This is what I dread: Mother's talks. The long analytical breakdown of where we've been, where we are, and where we're headed. Mother never comes up with any answers, of course, but it's something to mull over. Mulling is something Dr. M has taught her to do.

"Got'cha!" I said, more eager now to escape her stiffly planted arms. I kissed Mother's plump cheek to soften my departure, and I could not help but notice how old she looked.

Walter's mother is trim and athletic, and she allows us to call her Trace, short for Tracey. It's always a good time at their house, usually a keg of beer on the weekends and a house full of people. Mother wouldn't think of serving me a beer, even if she knew it was the last thing I'd ever get to drink.

Walter pulled into our driveway in his modified Isuzu with giant tires and honked his horn. Mother pulled the curtain aside and motioned to him that we'd heard him. We all three looked down from the window as Walter got out of the truck and walked onto the lawn, brushing lint from his trousers. He looked slicker than ice in his designer clothes, his shades, and his loafers without socks.

"He *looks* more interesting than he really is," Mother said. "I just don't understand it, this fake feeling of well-being that's sweeping this country. You boys have no real sense of yourselves."

"You can't have it until you have it," I said.

It's difficult to tell your mother you have more power than she does. It's just something you know. You can't tell her you are merely hanging out in the safety zone until your time comes. It's also difficult to tell her that what you admire about your best friend is his ability to lie to himself, and that you admire your own ability to see that he's doing it. Walter tells himself he's perfect, even when he's scared to death and screwing things up. But Mother would rather me get to the truth of things. Reality, she calls it. But the truth is never a beginning, as I see it. It's always at the end of something, something to look back on. The truth is dead stuff, I want to tell her. It will be lying at my feet soon enough.

Walter and I went into Georgetown and walked up and down M Street until we got the feel of the city. Then we went to Winston's, our favorite bar, where the beautiful women stand wall to wall, like posies just waiting to be plucked. Being underage, there are always the momentary jitters about whether our phony IDs will be accepted. Once that's accomplished we can comfortably carry out our method of operation.

Walter and I stand back away from the crowd. We rarely order a drink, at least not at first, proving that we are not just eager punks dying to tie one on. We pretend we are uninterested in the females, which is another thing that makes us appear older. Then all that's left to do is wait for the girls to ask us to dance.

Walter checks out the other guys who are obviously not in from the burbs as we are, and sometimes he makes fun of the way their ears stick out, or he cuts on their dyed hair, or their punk clothes. He nearly gives it away that we are not who we seem to be.

Winston's was slow that night, so we left, neither of us having enough money to get drunk, or even fantasize about taking a girl somewhere, for fear she would expect us to pay. We rode around Georgetown for a while, and talked to some guys from Texas at a traffic light, and then we went home.

When we turned down my street I saw that the second floor of my house was screaming with bright lights, and I remembered the promise to Mother that we would have a talk.

"Schultz," I said. "I think I'm good for another few hours. Let's cruise."

"Sorry, Ease," he said. "Trace has a house full, and we're packing the truck tonight for the beach. Or I'd ask you over."

"You want to stay over here then?" I asked.

"No, thanks," Walt said.

"She'll be in bed," I said.

Walter pulled into our driveway. He leaned back into the seat, his tanned arms stretched taut against the steering wheel.

"Face it, Ease. She hates me. But it's not her fault, right? Trace says she's just a warped idea of the sixties trying to cram herself into our generation."

"She worries," I said.

"Yeah, about all the wrong things," he said.

"Maybe," I said. "She thinks we're destined to be yuppies, that we'll fit in anywhere as long as we're well paid and fed."

"All right by me," said Walt.

When I climbed the stairs Mother was calling to Beckett to turn out her light and settle down.

"Hi, Easy!" Beckett called, leaning down on the side of her bed in order to see my face. "Did you get any tonight?"

"What on earth!?" Mother called from her room. She appeared in the hallway, her nightgown buttoned to her throat. "Where did she hear such a thing?" Mother went for Beckett, and Beckett covered her head with a pillow.

"She doesn't know what it means," I said.

"You want to bet?" Mother challenged, and pulled Beckett's face up to hers. "What is it Carter *gets,* Beckett? Do you know?"

"NO!" said Beckett impishly, her face squinched where Mother's hands held it. "I just know he always gets something when he goes out with Walter. I don't know what they get."

"Is that where you heard it?" Mother asked. "From Walter?"

"Yeah," Beckett said. "Walter always says it. 'Getting any?' he says."

Mother slumped to the floor at Beckett's bedside, and put her face into her hands.

"Is she going to cry now?" Beckett whined.

I put my finger to my lips to shush Beckett. "Let's turn in, Mother," I said.

Dr. M is heavily bearded, and it would be kind to say he is heavily built, but he is fat. His right leg is stiff at the knee, and he walks with a cane, exaggerating his limp, it seems, on one occasion more than another. This may be my imagination, about the exaggeration of the limp, since I saw him in public only once. He was unaware at the time of who I was.

There are *some* infirmed people who evoke pity. I find myself eager to smile at them or say a few friendly things to prove to them their condition is unimportant. But Dr. M is of such a personality that it made me angry when he slowed me down at the revolving door. It annoyed me that such a grouch deserved a special parking place.

We were standing side by side in Drug Fair. I was paying for my copy of *GQ*, had already put my money on the counter, when Dr. M nearly pushed me aside with his snake-carved cane and demanded attention from the clerk. He asked her the price of her best cigars and told her to wrap him a dozen.

"Yes, Dr. Murray," the girl cooed and smiled, which is how I learned it was him. The girl was a cute little babe I had seen around, but she didn't acknowledge me. She was under the doctor's spell, and continued to smile at him only, as if he were Edward G. Robinson (because that's who he looks like). Dr. Murray didn't return her smile, *or* thank her, and what a show he made of his departure, stopping once to check his balance as the girl rushed to unlock a special side door and let him out.

When Mother announced she was inviting Dr. M for dinner, "He's been so good to me" is how she put it, I was happy I had not told her I had met him, or that I had seen all of him I ever wanted to see. I preferred it that Mother was unaware of my prior knowledge. Prior knowledge is, Walter says, one of the greatest disadvantages in this life. "It's better to walk into things dumb," he says. "Then there's less at stake."

Guests at our house are a rare event. Mother avoids it because she has little time now, holding two jobs, to entertain properly. My rowdy crew would ruin the furniture, Mother says, furniture that isn't even paid for yet, so any happy notion of a party like the parties at Walt's house is out of the question.

On the day Dr. M was coming to dinner, Mother double-waxed the foyer and hung new curtains. When she put an extra leaf in the dining room table, I knew we'd be spreading it on thick.

Dr. M arrived late, throwing his polyester sport coat across a chair, and dragging the metal tip of his cane across Mother's newly waxed floor, the screech of it sending chills down my spine.

Beckett was crouched in the landing of the stairway, eavesdropping, while Mother showed Dr. M to the sun room just off the living room. Mother was nervous, throwing her arms around in animated gestures, and pressing down the sides of her hair, which had been overmoussed by the hairdresser.

I stopped in the stairs where Beckett sat. "Listen, Princess," I said. "Don't be falling all over yourself for this dude. Just play it cool."

"Don't you like him?" she asked, her green eyes turned up at me.

"You got it," I said.

"Well!" Beckett announced. "Mother said I could sing a medley for him if I wanted."

"Don't you dare, Beckett! Just say you don't feel like it now. Say you changed your mind."

Beckett stood up. "Say you mind your own business, Ease. I *never* get to sing!"

"Join the school chorus then, Pumpkin, but don't be singing to this asshole."

Beckett marched on down the stairs, swinging her arms with determination.

"Oh, Beckett," Mother said. "Come meet my nice boss. Where's Carter?"

"In the stairway, *listening,*" she said. "Easy says you're an asshole."

I was entering the room when I heard my little Judas betray me. Dr. M bristled, as if he were shocked, maybe hurt a little, his wide eyes closing down to a squint.

"Carter!" Mother said, breathing heavily. It's an unfeminine thing; Mother breathes like a horse when she gets upset.

I pinched the back of Beckett's neck. "Tell the truth now, Princess," I said, increasing my grip until she hugged her head to her shoulder.

"I did tell the truth," said Beckett.

"If you don't mind," Dr. M said. "I think I'll sit." He flopped into the chair next to the window, his leg straight out in front of him.

"WELL!" said Mother. "It's clear that neither of you are prepared to behave. You may have dinner in your rooms."

"Nonsense," said Dr. M. "It's only language, Patricia. Two syllables, *ass* and *hole.* No hard feelings. Right, Carter?"

I nodded, but I felt like punching out his lights for the way he'd just put me away with the tools of his trade.

During dinner Beckett and I were seen and not heard. It was far more punishing to sit there and listen to Dr. M educate Mother on her shortcomings, and ours, than to spend the evening in my room. The old bastard probably knew that. He talked until the candles burned themselves out, and Beckett's head was nodding.

"So, you see, Pat," he concluded. "We evade our problems by calling them everything else but what they are. Sometimes we can't see them for what they are. It's natural to be self-protective."

"Speaking of protection," I said. "I think I'll put my little sister to bed."

"Oh, of course," Mother said distractedly, her mind still clogged by the fascinating Dr. M. "Thank you, Carter. I'll be up later to tuck her in."

From Beckett's room I heard Mother clearing the table, and the drone of the doctor's voice continued. His cane scratched against the floor as he followed Mother from the dining room to the kitchen and back.

"I don't like him either, Ease," Beckett said sleepily, crawling into her bed.

When Mother and Dr. M returned to the living room with their coffee, I crept down to Beckett's hiding place in the stairway.

Dr. M sat back on the sofa out of my view, his cigar smoke signaling through the room, but Mother was fully visible to me, turned sideways on the sofa facing him, her back straight, her coffee in her lap. I sat motionless in the dark, and listened to their hushed voices grow friendlier and more familiar.

"It's not going to be pleasant, you know," Mother said. "Carter's just at that age. He knows everything, and yet, he knows nothing. Surely you understand this better than anyone."

"Yes," he said, and I saw the doctor's thick hand reach out and touch my mother's cheek.

"Beckett will be much easier," Mother said. "She's pliable."

"They'll be fine," he said. "Just give Carter some time. As it is, you and I see each other every day. We're not in any rush."

Mother sat her cup down on the coffee table and leaned toward him out of my sight. Then they rose and entered the sun room, which was now in total darkness.

Walter didn't answer his phone, so I pulled on my jacket and decided to walk to his house and wait for him there. On my way out I listened momentarily from the foyer to hear again the hushed conversation of Mother and Dr. M.

As I walked across our lawn, the shadows of the street-lights drew soft patterns on the grass. Mother had heard me leave, and appeared seemingly out of nowhere from the back of the house, her face flushed and pretty.

"Just where do you think you're going?" she said, her hands planted firmly on her hips.

"Out," I said.

"No later than midnight, Carter. And earlier if possible. There's something I have to tell you."

"Got'cha," I said.

Mother went back inside. She locked the screen door, and pulled the wooden door closed.

Love, Walter says, is a cover for violence. "I read that somewhere," he said. "But it sounds right, doesn't it? In the end it's all just a matter of who controls who."

PERFECTION

O

David Long

SHE WAITED WHERE she could see the highway, where she could see the lights coming.

Did you have the motor running?

She had on the black Fido Dido shirt and a blue jean jacket. It was chilly—it was October, after all—but she ran the engine for only a minute or two and shut it off, the radio with it. Inexplicably, the radio was making her jumpy.

Why parked there, not down in the high school lot? Wouldn't that be customary?

I told you, the bus was going to drop him off there.

The boy, Storm?

Yes. Storm.

She sat watching the yellow blinker, sagging on its cable, rolling with the wind. Across the street was the Varner Bar, sheeted in red-brick tar paper. Around the corner, a grocery nobody went to and the post office and half a street of sad-fronted houses. Behind her the moon was coasting past the grain tanks.

I'm not clear on why you were meeting Storm there.

Does that have to be part of this? I just was, OK?

So the bus with the Varner players was coming back from Co-bolt and you were waiting there and you were alone?

Uh-huh.

She watched the traffic. Once in a while somebody made a U and stuffed a letter in the box, but mainly it was cars and pickups sailing straight through, slowing from seventy-five to maybe sixty for the light. A few people came in and out of the bar. Hardly anybody she recognized.

Shelley, when did you first see Mr. Poe?

She was thinking ten more cars, then it will be the bus. Then ten more. Of course, because the game had gone into overtime, which she couldn't know yet. She was invisible, a dark car sitting in the dark, with a girl inside singing invisibly and thinking nothing will spoil this perfect perfect night.

Her father had won a trip to Oahu—he and her step-mother, Janet, had flown from Great Falls on Wednesday. Her father sold crop insurance, set up IRAs, juggled debt for the ranchers. What he'd won, actually, was a seat at a company seminar, a write-off. He packed along his golf clubs, Janet took a load of clingy evening wear that showed how long-waisted she was, like pulled taffy. I'd just as soon you didn't stay here alone, he said. That's so ludicrous, she said. Then Janet was all hurt. I wished I knew what makes you treat your father like you do, etc., etc. This isn't a slam against you, honey, her father said. I asked your aunt to stay over, that's all. Common sense, OK? Shelley contemplated a hard sulk, but abruptly changed her mind. Marta was her mother's sister and it would not be a disaster. Marta would come every night but Friday. Friday, Shelley would take the car to the game in Cobolt and afterward she and Stace would stay at Mary Jo's. Except not actually. That was the one element that bothered her, deceiving Marta. But it was minor. It fluttered away when you weighed it against Storm.

So. But she didn't go to the game. She went straight from school home and sat in the tub, swirling with oil, the blaster blasting, then changed the sheets, installing the blue ones, which would make Storm's smooth dark body look even smoother and darker. She put about fifteen candles on the table by the bed. She'd been sleeping with Storm since early summer. Well, not sleeping. Maybe she'd dozed a little with his arm going numb under her, but this was the whole expanse of night, and in her own bed, where he belonged, *finally.* When she woke Saturday he'd be there, and weird as that would be, it was also the point, wasn't it? So she'd put him on the bus and said, Keep your mind on the game, now, huh? and squashed her breast against his arm, making his face flush as it smiled. The first time would last as long as a milkshake, but the next would be a thing of perfection, long-drawn-out and lush. After that she thought she would like to do it in the shower. The hot water lasted approximately fourteen minutes if nobody'd been using it. Then she went and wrote a fake 800 number on a pad tilted against the clock radio so Storm could see it. When he asked, she'd laugh, That? That's the *Guinness Book*!

Finally the bus ground to a stop and the door sighed open and there is Storm carrying his duffle. He seems tired, his back slightly off-line, the bag clunky, dragging. He looks up, searching for her, but he's on automatic pilot. When he slides in beside her she sees blood crusted in the corner of his mouth. It's nothing, he says, but half his front tooth is gone, snapped off on the diagonal, leaving a sharp edge. Instinctively, she kisses it, not hard enough to hurt. I blew it, he says. Actually, his kick from the twenty-two sent them into overtime in the first place. He was lifted off his feet, his helmet slapped and butted, and for that moment felt completely aligned, and without thinking of her specifically knew himself to be endowed with a sweet safe reserve of time just ahead. But then after a fumble in the OT he set up from the eighteen, a chip shot, and shanked it right, where it landed out in the shadows of the running track, chased after by grade school boys. And two plays later, with a Cobolt running back en route to the far goal line, a toe cleat shot through his mask and the tooth was gone, swallowed in a knot of blood and mucus. So he says, I blew it, and means, obscurely, more than the kick. It's as if he's betrayed not the team but the gift of weightlessness.

She listens, touching him, but her thoughts are already torn.

Did you get out of the car and go over to Mr. Poe?

I didn't, no.

You had no idea how badly he was hurt, then?

I knew he was hurt.

But you didn't do anything.

I, no—

She broke herself of counting cars and watched the window of the Varner Bar, where a Silver Bullet sign was blinking slightly faster than the yellow light over the intersection. They'd synchronize for a second, then spike off. For the hell of it, she clicked on the car flashers, then caught herself. *Jesus, Shelley, chill.* She rolled the window down halfway, felt the cold air on her ear. She was looking straight at the front of the bar when the door opened, the inner door, then the thin screen door. A man was tossed outside. There was a strip of sidewalk, a few lengths of freestanding cement curb, once yellow, and enough room between there and the highway for a truck to park, but the space was vacant, allowing her to see.

Describe what you mean when you say "tossed."

He wasn't totally lifted in the air. I mean his feet were on the ground, dragging, but he wasn't in control. The man who threw him out was pretty big—he had on a plaid shirt and I think a baseball hat. The man, Mr. Poe, I think he hit on the back of his head.

So you wouldn't say he fell down.

I'd say the man in the plaid shirt kind of threw him and he landed on his head, back here. She touched her hair, where it was bristled at the base of her skull. That night her hair had still been long, remnant of a shoddy summer perm.

And that's how he hit the curbing?

No. It was out on the tar part, where it was kind of sandy.

He didn't hit on the curbing?

No. Uh-uh.

All right. Now when was the first time you saw Mr. Andrus?

OK, just after Mr. Poe went down, he tried to get up. He got up on his knees, his back sort of arched like a cat's, then he tried to get up the rest of the way, one of his arms was swinging out to the side, kind of pushing at the air. He looked completely out of it. He was about two-thirds up onto his feet when the door opened again. Wayne came straight out, like he was starting to sprint, and he hit Mr. Poe in the face, straight on. Here. She touched herself again, her hand covering her nose and mouth and chin.

I heard it inside the car.

She stopped talking. How do you make them hear?

It was like he'd been hit with the end of a fence post or a brick or something. But he didn't even see it. He was completely uncovered—just exposed. *Then everything went out of him, before he even hit the ground again.*

What did Mr. Andrus do?

Went back inside. Then he came out again and he kind of just looked over his shoulder at the ground where the man was and went around the corner and over by the post office and got in his truck and drove off.

Which way?

Into town.

Then what?

Nothing. I watched him and he didn't move and nobody else came out. Right after that the team bus came.

Did the boy—Storm—did he see Mr. Andrus?

I just said, Storm got there after Mr. Andrus drove off.

Did he see Mr. Poe?

She said, Look, and Storm looked and said, Some drunk. She told him about it, but Storm didn't want to look. I think he's dead, she said. Storm said, He's too drunk to be dead. As if that meant something.

Do you know Mr. Andrus?

Enough to recognize him, sure.

How is that?

He took my sister out for a while, Karen. Do we need to talk about that?

What I'm getting at, Shelley, you're absolutely certain it was Mr. Andrus you saw?

Uh-huh.

No doubts of any kind?

No, sir.

Plus she recognized the truck. A turquoise door on a red pickup.

After graduation Karen cashiered a year for the Stedje's, then shocked everybody by enlisting in the navy—all but Shelley, who saw what her sister was really up to: testing whether she could live in Varner the rest of her life. She had this double edge. She could do what she wanted, go on larks. It didn't matter, she'd be gone soon, no history sticking to her. But she had a hard vigilance, too, because any act, any attachment might be the one thing that locked her in, nailed her down. She went out with some of the older boys, Wayne being one of them, tall and slick-cheeked, but wasn't his face smirky, restless? Nothing I'd trust this flesh with, Karen said, which Shelley remembered because she'd felt herself flinch at the word *flesh* used like that: soft white meat put in someone else's hands. God, you're easy to shock, Karen said. No, I'm not, Shelley tried to say. Anyway, the Karen and Wayne business came to nothing, one trip to the steak place in Cobolt and a few aimless excursions in his truck with the swimming pool-colored door. But Wayne and her father seemed to hit it off. Wayne came over a few Saturdays that summer and helped him salvage bricks from the old Varner Implement building. So before the night outside the Varner Bar, this was her last picture of Wayne: the two of them standing in the hot sun at the

end of the flatbed trailer, bricks and hammers in their hands,
her father sweating through his shirt, giving Wayne a lesson
in how to knock off the mortar without busting the old bricks.
They are still out there, the bricks, if anyone's curious, on pal-
lets behind the garage.

She wanted to be in the mood still. Storm had showered, but
even so he smelled like Icy Hot. She lit the candles. He was
acting shy suddenly, perched on the edge of the bed, palms together between his knees—he looked like he was sitting in a
waiting room. She was telling herself, I'm in control of this, I
can make this work. She took her shirt off. Storm was extremely fond of her breasts. She'd managed to log a few hours
on the sun porch the second week of September, dry hot Indian
summer weather. Her nipples were like mahogany, a little wide
but perfectly round, as if they'd been drawn with a compass.
There was a little wispy hair, which she didn't know what to do
about, but it was at least blond, unlike Karen's. Storm stroked
her with the backs of his fingers, lifted her breast, let the
weight settle in his hand, brought his mouth down. I don't believe you, he said, and that was part of the scenario, pleasing
him inordinately, making him just short of speechless with
pleasure. Baby, she said. But he said, Don't call me that, OK,
Shell? It makes me feel funny. What can I call you? I want to
call you something. I don't know, he said.

Then he said, Is there anything to drink, and it turned
out there was a bottle of Early Times in the cupboard, also a
bottle of Gordon's gin, but the gin was still sealed, so Storm
drank the other, mixed with Diet Pepsi. Shelley had a little
dope (wadded into the toe of one of her ancient confirmation
shoes) but the last time she'd smoked, it had given her the
spins, making her think something was wrong with it. And
Storm wasn't into it, anyway. He wouldn't chastise, he'd say,
Go ahead if you want to. But all in all, she thought, no, not
tonight.

Storm lay back and took it easy, letting her ride. She stole a look at herself in the dresser mirror, saw the points of her elbows shining as she tried to muss her hair, but something was too comical about it to be exciting. She did not, literally, think of the Poe boy again until she slid down and tried to kiss Storm a moment later. The upper lip had swollen hard and shiny. The tooth was killing him. She looked down at him and saw the fist ramming into that other face and revulsion splashed through her.

I'm sorry, Storm was saying. She could tell he couldn't concentrate. He was hard as pipe but couldn't come. She said, Baby, then, Oh sorry, Storm, and they went a little while longer before Storm got up and they went into the bathroom and he took about six Advils. Pretty soon he was asleep. Even asleep a crease ran between his eyebrows. She watched a trapezoid of mirror light waver across the ceiling. There was a clammy sheen on Storm's skin. Nestling, shifting—she couldn't find any way to lie against him comfortably.

In her dream she and Karen were straddling the peak of a barn roof, their heels digging into the shakes. It was before dawn, dewy, the wind just kicking up. Karen had a clipboard with sheets of green paper—a list apparently, under the words Secret Shame. In her other hand was a huge aluminum flashlight, the kind that takes about ten batteries. She was pointing at houses, reading from the list. *Mrs. Stedje is a luna moth,* she said, flicking her tongue, as if this was a juicy revelation. Then the shakes under Shelley broke loose, like avocado leaves, and she was sliding down the roof on her back, head first. *Dreams are moronic,* she wakes thinking, sorting it out. They're reading *The Secret Sharer* in Honors English; it's Janet who's fixated on moths, who's scared they'll breed in her clothes closet and ravage everything; Karen is long gone, on the other side of the world. Only the two fattest candles are still going—there's an alluvium of stinky red wax stuck to her contacts case. It's beginning to be light out. Storm is gone. She hopes, briefly, that he is merely in the bathroom, but when she pads in there she finds no one. There's a faint smell of vomit, but also Ajax. The sink and the floor are shiny, still slightly wet.

The next night Marta came, bringing Cracker Jack and a video, a mystery with a couple of raunchy sex scenes—she figured Marta chose it to declare which side of the fence she was on. There was an apartment, silver blue light from a TV shining on a man's buttocks. *Oooh, moon over Manhattan,* Marta giggled. Shelley laughed, the first time in twenty-four hours. Marta rolled her eyes. She was still young, in her thirties, had a nice little figure, Shelley's mother always said. She and Janet didn't get along well. They kept up the decorum, but Marta considered Janet drab and worry-raddled, believing Shelley's father jumped too soon, spellbound by desperation.

I'm dying, Marta said, hitting the pause. Shelley's father was a no-smoke-in-this-house zealot. Shelley slipped on her jacket and went out on the back steps with her aunt. Last night's wind had all but gone, and there was a smell in the air, not woodstoves yet, more like wet bark or mushrooms, obliterated a moment later by Marta's lighter.

Used to call these fags, she said. Weird world, huh? So how was it at Mary Jo's?

Storm broke his front tooth, she said, skirting the lie.

Bummer, Marta said. He had such a sweet smile. But he'll get it fixed, won't he?

Shelley nodded. She hugged the jacket around herself and looked around at the sagging skyline. When she looked back at Marta, she saw Marta knew.

Everything OK? Marta said.

Not especially, she said. She was shaking.

Marta dipped onto one knee and stabbed her cigarette into the geranium pot. We don't have to stand out here like fools, she said, putting her hand on Shelley, leading her back inside.

But she couldn't get warm. All the blood had gone into

her chest and face, leaving her limbs suddenly achy with cold.
Her jaw couldn't stop chattering. Her heart stuttered. Something's wrong with me, she started to say, I'm having some
kind of—

Here, sit, Marta said, touching her, trying to ease her
down into the kitchen chair.

But everything was firing at once. No, I can't, I—

Marta's fingers clamped on her, Marta's smell, her hair
poured over her. *Shelley!* Breathe out now, honey. All the way,
c'mon.

I—

Shh. It's OK, it goes away. Breathe now.

Monday, Tuesday, Wednesday. A fine misting rain falling. She
walked to school with her books in a plastic bag. The sky was
about six feet overhead, the color of concrete blocks. Storm had
an aluminum tooth. Nothing had changed between them, except
something had. She sat in class, hearing pages turn, hearing
the juices in people's stomachs. *At this breathless pause at the
threshold of a long passage we seemed to be measuring our fitness for
a long and arduous enterprise,* she read.

Shelley? Shelley?

She looked up sharply. Nobody was looking at her, nobody calling.

The morning evaporated. She skipped lunch. Later, she
walked to the practice field, stood out of sight under the
bleachers, watching Storm kick ball after ball. Devoid of game,
his foot made an enormous hollow smack. He hit ten straight,
then missed one, missed again, and another. He stood with his
hands on his knees, breathing hard, staring at the cleat-shredded grass.

This is what sifted down to her regarding Richard Poe. He was
a slitty-eyed pudgy boy of twenty-three, an afternoon drinker,
a pain in the ass. His father was dead. He'd moved into Varner

his senior year and lived with his mother. No one called him anything but Richard. He hassled people to arm wrestle, but he had tiny wrists and never won. When he was semisober, which was most of the time, he was an avid conspiricist, a quoter of facts and figures from obscure pamphlets. Outright drunk, he got in people's faces, shoved a little, took offense.

But never exactly hurt anybody.

After she and Storm drove away that night, a couple left the Varner Bar and found Poe still there, knees drawn up to his chest. The bartender (the man in the plaid shirt) called for the EMTs. They found a fluttery pulse. They cleared his mouth, crowded over him with an oxygen unit. It was not until ten to twelve that the ambulance took him. An hour later he was on the Life Flight to St. Vincent's in Great Falls, where he died about six o'clock.

She waited for something to happen.

In Thursday's paper: *Richard Mark Poe, born in Dickinson, North Dakota, on March 6, 1967 . . . preceded in death,* etc. etc. *Cremation under the direction of Barber and Barber.* Nothing about a service.

Nothing anywhere about Wayne Andrus.

She told Janet she had to get stockings and drove to the Safeway, but kept going, cutting over to Wyoming, following it out of city limits. She passed the slough, leeched alkali and busted-open cattails, then the wire gates of the cement company. Directly across was a small house with pressed board siding, pale blue. One old cottonwood towered over it. A branch had come down and lay across the roof, the dead leaves bristling in the wind. The mailbox said *A. Poe.* A. for Alvina. Shelley sat in the car, studying the house, running the heater. There was one light burning, back in the kitchen. A few minutes later, it went out.

She looked down at her Swatch. Five to eight.

Five to eight and the house was pitch dark.

So where are the stockings? Janet asked when she walked in.

All out of nude, she said.

Janet glowered at her.

You can go down and look if you don't believe me, Shelley said. You can just drive down there and fucking look for yourself.

You're aware that your story conflicts with what other people have told us?

I guess, I don't know. It's what happened.

Now don't misunderstand me, Shelley, I have to ask this. Is there any other reason to be telling us this? You don't have anything against Mr. Andrus, or the family—?

I told you. I don't know him well enough to have anything against him.

Have you discussed this with anyone?

No.

Not your folks, not Storm?

No.

Three items: The airline had lost her father's golf clubs— that was first. He slammed down the kitchen phone for the half-dozenth time. "Those incompetent sons of bitches." His face was crackling. Second: Lisa, his secretary, had quit, apparently, simply walked out at lunchtime that Friday he was in Hawaii, never locked up or anything. In her absence, the Mr. Coffee had shorted out, filling the back room with a strident chemical smoke—if the man in the Automobile Club office next door hadn't smelled it through the washroom vent, the whole place would've gone up. Her father spent the rest of the week in the living room, with folders sprawled across three green-topped card tables. His sunburn was peeling. *Tell me why any of this surprises me,* he said. And third: Though they both acted glad to see her (they'd bought her a rayon blouse with red and green macaws), told her Oahu was a stunner, etc., etc., some grudge, some *seed,* had embedded itself between her father and Janet, and Janet was of course too insecure to take that on, and started in on Shelley instead.

I'm not blind, she said. I can tell something's up with you. I don't expect you to like me, Shelley. But I hate when things go on behind my back.

That must be an awful feeling, Shelley said, not biting, not biting.

Was there any real question about *discussing this with anyone*? Not really.

Another weekend. Saturday was a day game at home. She trooped into the seniors' section with Stace and Mary Jo. The sky was broken now, the light cold and white. Afterward, pizza. Storm was high with the win, twisting in the booth, looking everywhere at once, the black hair falling in his face.

Out by the cars, she asked him, Could we just drive?

There's a party at Koski's, he said.

Maybe you should go to it.

You don't want to go?

I told you what I wanted, she said.

Storm looked at the other cars starting to pull away into traffic.

I'm freezing, she said.

He opened his jacket and tried to close it around both of them but there wasn't enough of it.

Go to Koski's, she said.

You make things impossible, Storm said. He backed away from her. I didn't mean that like it sounded, he said.

She put her fingers through his belt loops and drew against him again.

The one thing she hadn't told: After Wayne recoiled from the hit, his arm drawn back but the fist still intact, as if his hand would be forever that one thing, he didn't just turn and go into the bar the way she said, but looked around to see what kind of audience he might have. His eyes scanned the empty highway, then froze briefly on the old Impala, which he knew he knew. Did her hair show in the window, that ugly falling-down perm?

His chest heaved. Then she saw his chin lift, saw the moon had drawn his attention, had captivated him.

All this gesture meant to her, at the time, was that he was distracted from her, from running over and grinning down into the car. Now it made a picture she couldn't shake from her mind, a man standing with the moon on his face, another man curled at his feet. It made no difference to the moon what it looked at, she thought.

I'm bothered by why you waited so long to tell us—you know what I'm saying, Shelley? Is there some particular reason?

There's a reason for everything. No, she didn't say that.

It took her three more nights, scattered over a week, before she got out of the car. The wind was ragging at her hair. The bell made a single flat *plonk* and she had to hit it over and over.

Mrs. Poe's face suddenly filled the square glass.

Shelley realized she knew her. She was one of the cafeteria women. Her face, ordinarily, was filmy red from the steam trays, and her hair stuffed in a net. She was the one who sometimes touched people on the wrist and said, Don't take it if you're not going to eat it.

She thought, *Now what am I supposed to do?* But the woman opened the door, made way for her, arms folded, incapable of surprise.

The house smelled like vinegar. A wall heater glowed in the front room. Under each window stood a TV table full of African violets. Against the wall was an electric piano on spindly legs, a few sheets of music slumped on the rack.

The woman pointed and Shelley sat.

Mrs. Poe stayed on her feet. She was wearing sweat clothes with padded shoulders, a barrel-chested woman, the hair unpinned now, falling straight, ash blond with heavy bangs.

That's all of them, she told Shelley. Her husband. Her daughter, Rochelle. Richard.

From the kitchen came the clicking of a dog's nails, the rattle of a chain on a metal dish.

Richard found his sister, Mrs. Poe said. She was dead in her crib. This was when we were still living down in Dickinson and his father was working for Peavey's. It was a little room with yellow shades—we had to move Richard out of it after Rochelle was born because it was the only quiet place. It was a nice room for a girl, but Richard still liked it and I sometimes let him sit in there while his sister had her nap. I was hanging up clothes in back. There was always a wind. He came tearing outside, running so hard his arms were going like windmills. I watched him head down behind the elevators—a pack of cats lived down there, feeding off the mice. They were wild, mangy things, and I'd forbidden him to go anywhere near there. What on earth! I thought. What in heaven's name? Then, you see, I forgot all about him. It was dark before we sent somebody down there to find him.

Shelley's face was frozen, stricken. Mrs. Poe was standing over her saying, It's all right. You can hear this, nothing's a secret anymore, and kept on, tugging gently at the flesh of her cheek.

Richard had a counselor in school who said a thing like that would mark him, but I don't know. I don't know what it did to him. He might have been the way he was anyway. Who's to say? You can find a reason for anything, reasons are nothing, reasons are common as flies.

Shelley felt a drop of cold sweat slide down under her armpit.

Tell me the reason for falling down against a curb, Mrs. Poe said. She had pulled a Kleenex from the sleeve of the sweat suit, held it for a moment like a wilted blossom.

She drove slowly past Storm's, looking at the configuration of lights. It was a plain stucco house, battened down for the night. She kept going, went up Commerce, Varner's three-block main drag, and nosed the car up to the pay phone.

She leaned in behind the glass. Can you get out? she said.

A catch in his voice, a hand smothering the receiver.

Storm, I need to see you.

Give me a few minutes, he said.

No, it's got to be right now. Hurry. I mean it.

She sat in the car waiting for him. The moon had gone from quarter to nothing and back again. It dodged through broken clouds, hammering the edges silver. She half expected to see Wayne Andrus's truck cruise by now, as if this was all a movie. She dug a mint out of her jacket pocket. A highway patrol cut through the Town Pump and spun off without looking at her. After that, except for the whanging of a tin sign, it was quiet.

She was parked where she could see Storm come.

She'd watch how he came toward her, how his face behaved at the sight of hers. What is it that couldn't wait, he'd say, sliding in, a little breathless, his hands cold and dry. I just need you, she would tell him. Well, I'm here, he'd say. No, don't say it like that, she'd say. I've got to have more than that, Storm. Then it would be up to him to say whatever he had to say. It would have to be good and strong, it would need to carry all the weight in the world.

P O E M S

O

Tess Gallagher

N O R T H W E S T B Y N O R T H W E S T

Our stones are subtle here, a lavender that is
almost gray, a covert green
a step shy of its blue.
For eating, as with loneliness, we prefer
the bowl to the plate,
for its heaping up, its shapeliness of offering
what it half encloses. Just
when it seems the day has gone to sleep, gulls sob or
the eagle drops suddenly
from its black chambers. The silks of drowsy weddings
sham the horizon and ecstacy
is a slow mirage we drift towards, voyaging in
some eternal orient whose seasons
ache, serenely inhabit, but disdain

to yield. The *she* who rules here leans
her swanlike neck across the void, and rewards
our perpetual suspension
with an ongoing tomb—"If," she says, "you
existed." Requiring pleasure to revolve
outside its answer.

GLIMPSE INSIDE AN ARROW
AFTER FLIGHT

Two arrows glanced off each other
flying in the same direction, both
still falling, though I have charge of the memory
that one struck the ground—as if memory
could retrieve it. But once on earth
we have the privilege of staying—for only then
are we able to outdistance
every living need
in something like a death. To seem
unpresent in our most ongoing
presence. How else could it happen
that I will never live long enough
to reach the other side
of this memory without you?

Name shouted down a well, name
of someone known and loved, name I say
in perfect faith I won't be answered—keep
your silence. If you spoke back
these things we have yet to mean
would have finished, would have
left us behind
as the past of a word in air.

WAKE

Three nights you lay in our house.
Three nights in the chill of the body.
Did I want to prove how surely
I'd been left behind? In the room's great dark
I climbed up beside you onto our high bed, bed
we'd loved in and slept in, married
and unmarried.

There was a halo of cold around you
as if the body's messages carry farther
in death, my own warmth taking on the silver-white
of a voice calling across unbroken snow just to hear
itself calling. We were dead
a little while together then, serene
and afloat on the strange broad canopy
of the abandoned world.

FAN-SHAPED VALENTINE

What was blue is lavender now, as wishfulness
can accordion the paleness from a morning
in a furl of heartbeats—what those
gulls may feel, flying through a rain-
bow seen to be raining. Our twin
silences thicken us with shafts
of pouring light. Good always
to keep slatted sandalwood to
arc below the eyes in a
flush of air, the more
to bare an arched
wrist, the naked
back of
hand.

MOON CROSSING BRIDGE

If I stand a long time by the river
when the moon is high
don't mistake my attention
for the merely aesthetic, though
that saves in daylight.
Only what we once called worship
has feet light enough to carry
the living on that span of brightness.
And who's to say I didn't cross
just because I used the bridge in its witnessing,
to let the water stay the water
and the incongruities of the moon to chart
that joining I was certain of.

AT THE-PLACE-OF-SADNESS

I take a photo of the stone Buddha
gazing from its eternal moment over
the eroded bodies of hundreds of child-sized
Buddhas. Shoulder to shoulder
they say something about death
not to be offered
another way. The name given
this sacred place has changed my face.
The spirits of those with no relatives
to mourn them, an entity driving tears
inward so the face wears only the gust, the implosion
of grief.

Through the starred red of maple leaves: a man
half-visible in white shirt and black tie
held on a level with the stone Buddha—the one

in its living stillness, the other more-than-living
so he takes a step toward me
when I press the shutter
and glance up
like one of the dead
given the task of proving, with two identical stones
the difference between
a spirit and a body.

SO BEAUTIFUL

When I read
    the poems
I'd written for him
      aloud
someone said later, "You
         looked so
beautiful." His greeting
          took me by surprise,
the moment after an echo
    which cannot be said to die.

CONTRIBUTORS

JONATHAN BAUMBACH directs the MFA writing program at Brooklyn College. His novels include *Reruns, Babble, Chez Charlotte and Emily,* and the recently published *Separate Hours.* He has had three stories included in the O. Henry Prize Stories.

ROBERT BOSWELL is the author of two novels, *Crooked Hearts* and *The Geography of Desire,* and a collection of short stories, *Dancing in the Movies.* He has received fellowships from the NEA and the Guggenheim Foundation. He teaches creative writing at New Mexico State University in Las Cruces and in the Warren Wilson MFA Program.

RON CARLSON is the author of two novels and a book of short stories, *The News of the World.* He is on the writing faculty at Arizona State University.

ANDRE DUBUS is a former Marine Corps captain, member of the Iowa Writers Workshop, college teacher, and Guggenheim Fellow. He lives in Haverhill, Massachusetts. In 1988 he became a McArthur Fellow. Dubus is the author of seven books of fiction, including *Finding a Girl in America, Adultery and Other Choices,* and *The Times Are Never So Bad.* His collection, *Selected Stories,* was published by Vintage Books in 1989.

HELEN EISENBACH, a former book editor, is a novelist and screenwriter. Raised in Maryland, she attended the Peabody Conservatory and was graduated from Oberlin College. Her works include the novel *Loonglow,* published in 1988. She lives in New York City.

TESS GALLAGHER is a poet living in Washington State. Her work has been published in *The Atlantic Monthly, The New Yorker,* and *Zyz-*

ziva. Her books include *Moon Crossing Bridge, Portable Kisses, Amplitude: New and Selected Poems, The Lover of Horses,* and *A Concert of Tenses.* She recently wrote the introduction to a book of photography, *Carver Country,* about her late husband, Raymond Carver.

PATRICIA HENLEY teaches at Purdue University. Her work has appeared most recently in *Ploughshares* and *Best American Short Stories, 1990.* Her first book of stories, *Friday Night at Silver Star* (1986), received the Montana First Book Award. Her second collection, *The Secret of Cartwheels,* is forthcoming.

DAVID HUDDLE teaches at the University of Vermont and the Bread Loaf School of English. He has a collection of short stories, entitled *Intimates,* a book of poetry, *The Nature of Yearning,* and a collection of essays, *The Writing Habit,* all to be released in 1992.

NORMAN LAVERS teaches at Arkansas State University. He has held Iowa Writers Workshop and two NEA writing fellowships and his stories have recently won O. Henry, Editors' Choice, and Hohenberg awards. He has published a novel, *The Northwest Passage.*

DAVID LONG has two books of stories in print, *Home Fires* and *The Flood of '64.* Stories from a forthcoming collection have been published in *The New Yorker* and *Story.* He lives and writes in Kalispell, Montana.

BRET LOTT is the author of the novels *The Man Who Owned Vermont* and *A Stranger's House* and the story collection *A Dream of Old Leaves.* "Two Stories" is an excerpt from his new novel, *Jewel.* He lives in Mt. Pleasant, South Carolina, and teaches at the College of Charleston.

MICHAEL MARTONE is the author of three books of short stories, *Alive and Dead in Indiana, Safety Patrol,* and *Fort Wayne is Seventh on Hitler's List.* He is the editor of two books, *A Place of Sense: Essays in Search of the Midwest,* which was published in 1988, and *Townships: Pieces of the Midwest,* which will be published in 1992. He currently teaches at Harvard.

BOBBIE ANN MASON is a native of Mayfield, Kentucky, who now lives in Pennsylvania. She has received a Guggenheim Fellowship and other grants. Her book *Shiloh and Other Stories* won the Ernest Hemingway Award for First Fiction. Her other books include *In Country* and *Spence & Lila.*

TERRY MCMILLAN is the author of two novels, *Mama* and *Disappearing Acts,* as well as the editor of *Breaking Ice,* an anthology of contemporary African-American fiction. She lives in Tucson, Arizona.

SUSAN MINOT grew up in Manchester, Massachusetts. She is the author of *Monkeys,* which she began writing at Columbia University's writing program, and *Lust and Other Stories.* Her work has appeared in *The New Yorker, The Atlantic Monthly, The Paris Review,* and *Grand Street,* and has been included in the O. Henry anthologies and the Pushcart Prizes. She lives in New York City.

ANTONYA NELSON teaches at New Mexico State University in Las Cruces. Her first collection of stories, *The Expendables,* won the Flannery O'Connor Award for Short Fiction. A second collection, titled *In The Land of Men,* is forthcoming.

SCOTT RUSSELL SANDERS grew up on the back roads of Ohio. He studied literature at Cambridge University as a Marshall Scholar, and he now teaches at Indiana University. His dozen books include collections of stories and essays, as well as novels. The most recent of these books are *The Paradise of Bombs, In Limestone Country,* and *Secrets of the Universe.*

ROBERTA SILMAN is the author of *Beginning the World Again, The Dream Dredger, Boundaries, Blood Relations,* and *Somebody Else's Child.* A recipient of fellowships from the Guggenheim Foundation and the NEA, she has published stories in numerous magazines, including *The Atlantic Monthly, The New Yorker, McCall's,* and *Redbook.* She lives in Ardsley, New York.

JANE SMILEY was born in Los Angeles and now lives in Iowa, where she teaches. Her most recent novel is *A Thousand Acres.* She is the author of six other works of fiction, including *Duplicate Keys, The*

Greenlanders, and *The Age of Grief,* which was nominated for a National Book Critics Circle Award. *Ordinary Love and Good Will,* a volume containing two novellas, was also nominated for a National Book Critics Circle Award.

JILLA YOUNGBLOOD SMITH is a poet and writer of fiction. Her chapbook of poems, *Redbud,* was published in 1987 and her stories have appeared in *Sou'wester* and *Special Report: Fiction.* She lives in Washington, D.C.

ROBERT LOVE TAYLOR won the Oklahoma Book Award for his recent novel *The Lost Sister.* He is also the author of *Loving Belle Starr* and *Fiddle and Bow.* His stories have appeared in *Shenandoah, Hudson Review,* and other magazines, as well as in *The Best American Short Stories* and O. Henry anthologies. He grew up in Oklahoma and now teaches at Bucknell University.

MELANIE THERNSTROM is the author of *The Dead Girl.* She has taught writing at Cornell University and has a collection of linked short stories, *The Possibility of Home,* forthcoming.

JOHN EDGAR WIDEMAN attended the universities of Pennsylvania and Iowa, was a Rhodes Scholar at Oxford, and is now professor of English at the University of Massachusetts–Amherst. His published works include *Sent For You Yesterday, Damballah, Brothers and Keepers, Fever,* and *Philadelphia Fire.* He is a PEN/Faulkner award recipient.

· · ·

For additional information about
Share Our Strength, write or call:

Share Our Strength
1511 K Street N.W.
Washington, D.C. 20005
202-393-2925

· · ·